FAR BENEATH THE WICKED WOODS

THE WICKED WOODS CHRONICLES BOOK THREE

L.V. RUSSELL

Cover Design by Lydia Russell
Interior Formatting by Nicole Scarano

CONTENTS

PROLOGUE

LAPHANIEL

The bellows and jeers silenced at the lift of a gloved hand. The shadows halted too, pausing before creeping back around the contorted glass thrones. Candles within their holders of bone flickered and died out.

The room waited.

I waited.

Piercing blue eyes met mine, cold and amused. A slow smile lifted the edge of her mouth, teeth still clamped around the smouldering end of a cigarette. Black mist dripped from her body in a parody of clothing, her hair pinned away from her face, leaving all of her cruelty on show. Her glee.

The grinning madman at her side held the silence: It would be his signal they waited for, though it had been Niven who had demanded the punishment.

My wife's sister, Queen of the Unseelie.

The gloved hand came down and I braced myself. A crack sounded, then another and another and another, each lash giving me just enough time to draw breath.

In my head I counted them, like I counted the passing days by etching marks into the stone wall of the cell where they held me, each stroke a reminder that no one had come for me. Each lash a reminder that no one had come.

One.

Two.

Three.

Four.

Five.

Six.

Pain blazed over my back, my body straining against my bindings with every blow. I forced myself to keep my eyes on Niven. She grinned back, teeth bared.

Seven.

Eight.

Nine.

Ten.

Eleven.

Twelve.

The thirteenth forced a cry from my lips, biting deeper than the others. Wet dripped onto the black marble, pooling in streaks at my feet.

Fourteen.

Fifteen.

The bays and shrieks grew wild, drowning out the crack of the whip. Unseelie braved the wrath of their king to creep closer, tongues lapping at spilled blood, claws unsheathed, teeth glinting.

Sixteen.

Seventeen.

Eighteen.

I caught sight of the Spider skulking in the shadows. Opaque black eyes stared back at me, all eight shining with the feral light. Her teeth flashed, mouth stretched wide to reveal the length of her fangs. Over the cacophony of rabid fey, I could hear her hissing.

Nineteen.

Twenty.

Twenty-one.

She took a step forward, pausing when I shook my head, a tiny movement that sent a shock of agony through my shoulders. The room wavered, and when I looked up again, Charlotte was gone.

Twenty-two...

Twenty-eight...

Thirty-six...

I lost count. Just as I lost count of the etches upon the wall as I desperately clung to the passing of time. It all stopped making sense after the first few markings, the days and days and days all passing in a fog I couldn't keep track of.

I will come for you,

I will bring you home.

Another crack forced my head back up. Niven still watched, but the smile was gone. I kept her gaze and bit through my lip, refusing to make a sound for her.

CHAPTER ONE

TEYA

*F*rost covered the grass in glistening crystal droplets and melted from the stripped branches of the soft winter sun. The gardens were quiet and still, the lakes all frozen mirrors to the heavy white sky. Snow would come soon.

"Are there any gaps within the borders?" I turned away from the high arched window to focus upon the maps and papers spread out before me. I knew the answer already, but couldn't keep the thread of hope from my voice. I was met with pity.

"None, Majesty," Luca said, a Seelie knight new to the royal council. His long, furred ears twitched while he spoke, his tufted tail swaying back and forth nervously. "But we will keep looking."

"What of your spies?" I pressed. "What are they telling you?"

"That the Unseelie labyrinth is impenetrable, Majesty," Luca replied, glancing around him, looking for support. "There is no way in without the king knowing."

"Oonagh?"

The silver-haired faerie shook her head, eyes the colour of crystal meeting mine. "We have nothing to trade, Teya. Nothing Phabian wants."

"He would want my sister back," I said, addressing all seven fey that stood around the ancient table, the wood marked and worn by the passing of time. Leaves and acorns were etched around its edges, gilded gold. They wrapped around the table legs, vines carved out before taking root deep into the smooth stone floor.

"We cannot get close enough to her," Guelder said, her voice deep and slow. The faerie stood far taller than me, her skin rough like the bark of a tree. Leaves the colour of autumn grew down from her head, rustling past her shoulders. Her eyes were black and edged in amber, warm and kind. "There are rumours surrounding her, how the shadows dance for her…"

"I don't care for rumours," I said, my voice holding steady, although the flames fluttered in the chandelier above us. A distant rumble of thunder betrayed my apparent calm, a winter storm echoing my frustration. They followed me everywhere, the storms, slowly becoming a part of me.

I had become the Queen of Seelie by chance and circumstance. I had come to Faerie looking for my sister, but I found love instead. The Seelie crown was never meant to be mine…it was never meant for a mortal girl.

Faeries are capricious creatures, easily spurred, and so the crown of Seelie was cursed and ended up in my hands, where it would stay until my death before passing back to its rightful owner…all because I went and fell in love with one of the capricious creatures.

It was Laphaniel's Glamour that pulsed through my veins, that made the thunder roar and the clouds erupt. His gift to me, the only part of him I could be close to.

All because I made a bargain, signing a contract I didn't understand. With the help of the Unseelie, I kept my crown safe from the hands of Luthien, the rightful Queen of Seelie.

They took my husband as payment.

"Phabian will not give Laphaniel up, Teya." Nefina's quiet voice filled the room, her sharp blue eyes regarding us all coldly. "Do not believe for a moment he would trade."

I straightened; the boning of my corset pinched my ribcage. "Do you have anything to offer besides criticism?"

"At the moment, no," Nefina said, refusing to drop her gaze. She bore little resemblance to her brother, so fair in contrast to Laphaniel's ink-coloured hair, willowy where Laphaniel was lean and solid... though when I looked at her, all I could see was him. Her eyes narrowed. "But I will call you out on these ridiculous plans of yours."

"How dare you."

Nefina curled her lip. "You are too lost in grief to think straight, Teya. These ideas are madness—"

"I am bringing him home!" I cried, sending a wave of Glamour and rage across the vast table, whipping up maps and quills, sending bottles of ink sprawling across the aged wood.

"The Unseelie will send you his head in a box!" Nefina screamed back, her golden hair wild around her lovely face, breaking free from its braid. She reached across the mess for me, the sleeves of her sheer gown soaking up the spilled ink. "You know this, you saw him."

The candles flickered out, leaving the room in near darkness. No one dared to ignite them again. Nefina tightened her grip on my fingers; my next words cracked as they slipped over my lips.

"It has been almost two years."

I had offered up everything I had to Phabian for the safe return of my husband, but it had all been refused, laughed at, dismissed. My fey had called for war, to descend upon the Unseelie and tear it to pieces, vengeance for their lost king.

It had been the wise words of my counsel that had stopped a slaughter. Oonagh had stood beside me, unwavering, a voice of reason. Even Nefina had declined the call for bloodshed. If we went to war, even if we by some miracle won, there would be no doubt we would lose Laphaniel. The contract made that strikingly clear.

Reason, however, did not dull the thrum in my veins, a budding storm with nowhere to go.

That first midwinter, an invitation arrived in the sharp beak of an inky raven that turned to dust and bone the moment I took the paper from its mouth. It was a clear enough warning when even the messenger brought with it nothing but death. The words were the same as the message pinned to my door the night Laphaniel was taken: that I had midwinter to spend with my husband, three days a year for the rest of forever, and that I should be grateful.

"No one is giving up," Oonagh said from the other side of the table. "But we must do this right. We need time to—"

"Laphaniel doesn't have time," I said, watching the spilled ink soak into the crumpled maps upon the table, erasing the Unseelie lands in one swift pool of black. Oh, if only it were that easy. "The longer this takes, the more he suffers, and I don't know what will be left even if we get him back."

Nefina flinched.

"When," Oonagh corrected. I stared at her, at the hope still shining around her in a halo of light.

I said nothing in return, lighting the candles around us with barely a thought. It came so naturally now, Laphaniel's Glamour, golden threads of enchantment rising at my every whim. Oonagh opened her mouth to say something more, and I bristled, my anger redirected at the sound of the grand doors crashing open.

"Apologies for the lateness, Your Majesty."

I whirled. "Where the hell have you been?"

Gabriel slid into a graceful bow, stumbling slightly at the rush of fury I sent his way. He was filthy, hair matted around the horns that peeked through the curls, his usual smirk wiped from his handsome face.

"I need your agreement to travel to the outer borders of Faerie," he began, breath catching. "I'll require six knights…"

"What for?" Oonagh demanded, folding her arms across her chest. She eyed Gabriel's dishevelled state with unhindered disgust.

"I found something…"

"I'm not in the mood for dramatics, Gabriel." I snapped at my captain…Laphaniel's captain. "You've been gone for weeks, without a word."

"I couldn't say—"

"I could have you tried for treason," I said.

The colour drained from his face, and he lowered his eyes. The other faeries exchanged uneasy glances…unsure…wary.

Of me.

The night Laphaniel was taken, I had set fire to our bedroom and watched it burn while a storm tore apart the sky outside.

"There are rumours," Gabriel began, halting as I stepped closer to him.

"Don't come here speaking of rumours, of empty hopes, because I've had my fill of them." The ache in my chest was constant, a pain I hadn't felt since Laphaniel had taken his last breath in my arms at Niven's hand.

Saving my sister was a regret I would carry as long as I lived.

"Teya, please," Gabriel continued, his hands folding over the top of one of the many ornate chairs surrounding the table. "I truly believe this may be worth looking into."

I snatched up a goblet of wine and took a long swallow. "Go on."

"There is a witch—"

"You had better be joking."

Gabriel took a breath, glancing around to the others, no doubt looking for some sort of encouragement. He found none—they all glared at him in stony silence.

"There is a coven of witches to the far north," he said quickly. "Their High Witch is said to have untold powers. She can break any curse, any oath…any bargain."

I took another step forward, skirts swirling around my feet and sweeping up the debris I had flung to the floor. "Then why did no one seek her out before? Why didn't she break the curse holding a mortal queen to Seelie?"

Gabriel lifted his chin, meeting my furious gaze with his own, his amber eyes alight. "Because she didn't want to."

I took a slow breath. "And you decided to go to these witches behind my back?"

"No, I met with one of the coven near the Broken Wood. I didn't know if we would get an audience, if their High Witch would even agree to see you. I didn't wish to give you false hope."

"And how do you know of this coven?"

Gabriel's face lit up, the wicked smirk stretching over his lips reminding me of the devilish faerie who had swept me off my feet at a ball so long ago. "They are a fine group of witches, Your Majesty."

I rolled my eyes, my temper simmering down, leaving me deflated. "Will they see me?"

"Yes."

"When?"

Gabriel's smile faltered. "The first full moon after midwinter."

Another midwinter.

I wanted him home.

My fingers curled around the star at my neck, my heart twisting at the hope it symbolised. The fragments of Laphaniel's pendant lay within a wooden box I kept at my desk, shattered into so many pieces they would never fit back together.

Charlotte had gifted him that necklace to keep the nightmares away, and it had been wonderous to watch him sleep without fear, to not be woken every night as he screamed himself awake.

The shards of carved wood had been sent with the first invitation.

"If I may, Your Majesty," another council member spoke up. Black armour grew from her skin like scales, all gleaming an iridescent beetle black. Her oil-spill eyes were unblinking as she turned to me, her rows of tiny needle-sharp teeth jutting over her lip. "But we must also address the unrest upon the northern borders, within your own court."

I sighed, weary. "Any suggestions, Jacobina? I thought these had been dealt with."

Jacobina winced, black gossamer wings lowering so they drooped over the marble. She held her chin up, though, orb-like eyes not quite meeting mine. "We dispatched knights to deal with it, Your Majesty. We believed it was sorted, it had quietened down."

"But?"

"There is unrest again."

I had been told it would happen, that although Luthien had been defeated and sent far away into exile, there would always be some Seelie that would refuse to accept me.

"Oonagh?"

The faerie didn't look my way, but with one swift move pulled the ink-stained map of the Unseelie Court from the table and replaced it with one of our own lands. She jabbed a long finger down near the mountain ranges to the east.

"They are close to the borders, close to the wilds that stretch on endlessly. They believe they are untouchable by you, Teya, that if you dared to banish them, they would simply vanish into the unknown."

"Should we be worried?" I asked, wondering how much of my court conspired against me.

"Not yet," Gabriel replied as he leaned over the map. "But you need to set an example, Your Majesty, and quickly."

"You just said banishment won't deter them."

"The Seelie hang their traitors, Teya," Oonagh said, her soft voice carrying across the silence of the vast room. She stood straight, the white of her gown so sheer she looked like a living ghost. "And traitors they are."

Images of swaying fey invaded my mind, lifeless corpses strung up in Luthien's mansion because they had chosen to side with me... chosen to side with Laphaniel. I would never forget their faces, or the way Luthien had thrown back her head and laughed as she made them dance for her.

"Give a warning first," I said, dread coiling around my spine at the thought of executing my fey.

"They have been warned," Nefina cut in. "More than once."

I met her fierce stare, the unyielding pride within the icy blue. It would take a lot to break Laphaniel's sister, and I had witnessed her at her lowest. Nefina possessed a steeliness I admired, a determination to drag herself out of the shadows that still plagued her. Her relentless efforts in bringing her brother home nearly outpaced my own.

"A final warning," I said, allowing just enough Glamour to spark through my words to convey I was in no mood to be argued with. My council remained silent. Nefina dipped her head in rare acceptance.

"I'll ready my knights," Gabriel began, but I shook my head.

"I want a word with you." I gestured for the others to leave us, and they bowed before they left. Luca and Guelder gave Gabriel pitying looks; Jacobina bared her teeth, which could have been a grin or a warning—I never really knew with her. Oonagh kissed me upon the cheek as she swept by, her lips cold.

"I feel I am in for a scolding," Gabriel said, a smirk at his lips. The collar of his forest green tunic was smeared in what looked like blood, the fancy cuffs ripped, revealing old bruising to his golden skin.

I poured another goblet of wine; I didn't offer one to him. "Don't ever leave unannounced again, are we clear?"

"Worried about me?"

I bristled. "You're not to leave this castle without my direct say so. You want to go outside the gates, you come to me and you ask me."

The smirk faded, a scowl forming in its place. "You're grounding me?"

"Yes."

He blinked, surprised. "I did what I thought best, why raise your hopes just to dash them down again?"

"That's not your call to make, Gabriel!" I snapped, making him take a wise step back. "We didn't know where you were...I didn't know where you were...who you were with."

His eyes closed as he shook his head, curls slipping over his brow. "You thought I had joined the rebels?"

"Why wouldn't I? So many already have." Petty words. Petty and cruel.

"I have shown you nothing but loyalty from the very beginning," he hissed back, amber eyes flashing. "I was by your side the first midwinter, Teya."

Hurt shadowed over his tanned face, and I took a moment to really take in his unusually ragged appearance, the mud on his clothing, his face, his horns. More blood stained his trousers, one leg torn so I could see the skin beneath.

"Go get yourself cleaned up," I ordered. "Before you make yourself sick."

"By your command, my Queen," he replied, giving me a mocking bow. It would have really pissed me off if he hadn't stumbled while he did it. He gripped the edge of the table, knocking over my wine.

"What attacked you?" I demanded, helping him into a chair, ignoring his protests. With a glittering wave of Glamour, I summoned my healers.

"I was overly curious with a witch's serpent and it took a dislike to me. She failed to mention the venom."

"I'm sure you'll live."

Gabriel tipped his head back. "Such concern."

I pressed the back of my hand against his cheek. It was warm, feverish. "Don't add to the things I have to worry about."

He had the good sense to look sheepish. "That was never my intention."

Two plumes of emerald smoke formed before us, swirling into the wavering forms of Mara and Odette, the court healers. Their large pink eyes blinked rapidly, their ethereal forms moving into what could be deemed a curtsy. They fussed over Gabriel with flittering fingers, pulling up his trouser leg to reveal a spiderweb of mottled black veins.

"You are an idiot," I fumed. "A part of me hopes you lose that leg as a lesson."

He winced. "I thought it would be okay. It was a judgment call and I got it wrong."

"Laphaniel did the same once and it nearly killed him." I turned to Mara. "Can you fix it?"

"Yes, Majesty," she said in a voice like smoke. "A few days off his feet and he shall be well again."

"See to it that he rests," I replied before pointing a finger at Gabriel. "I'm still pissed at you."

"We can always send him to sleep, Majesty." Mara said, the words beautifully calm.

Gabriel looked up in horror. "No!"

"Don't you 'no' me, Gabriel," I snapped, temper flaring as his wound dredged up old memories. Nights spent sitting by Laphaniel's side while he fought the fever gripping him, the smell of stale sweat and bile and bad blood. The stillness and the quiet. The strange comfort of the Spider that watched over him with me. "Do as you are told, or I will knock you out myself."

"Can you walk, knight?" Odette asked, her voice as melodious as her sister's.

"Yes."

They helped him to his feet, taking some of his weight as he limped. He hissed through gritted teeth, unable to keep up the act of pretending he wasn't in pain.

"Gabriel?"

He turned, arching an eyebrow.

"Thank you."

"We want him home too, Little Red. Trust us."

I gave a nod and watched while both healers helped him from the room, their incorporeal forms far stronger than they appeared.

Trust seemed to be a word easily thrown around, one I was expected to accept without question. I was to trust we would find a way to bring Laphaniel back, when time was rushing past and we were no closer. Trust that the rebels would be dealt with, when in truth their numbers were increasing. I was to trust my court with unwavering faith…simply because they asked me to.

I swiped the bottle of dark red wine from the table before settling into one of the matching chairs surrounding the table. Without bothering with a goblet, I lifted the wine to my lips and drank until the desolate emptiness inside me had numbed.

The rich faerie wine dulled the anger I did my best to suppress, an anger that surged through my veins and had burned my chambers to the ground, snuffing out everything from the plump cushions to the enormous bed I had meant to share with Laphaniel. The flames had licked at my feet, daring to slip higher, and would have taken me too if

Nefina hadn't forced them back...forced me to see the sense and reason I had been blind to.

I had to get him back. Even if it meant playing Phabian's games. I would bow to the Unseelie King...to my sister if I had to. I didn't need my pride—I had done without it before. I was bringing Laphaniel home, then I would rip the Unseelie to pieces and scatter their ashes to the wind.

CHAPTER TWO

NIVEN

The Unseelie Queen took in the madness with a grin upon her face and drank in the chaos like the wine she readily consumed. Niven tilted her head, cascades of black hair falling across her shoulders with the lazy movement. She lived for the dances, the freedom of it all, the way she could be swept up with the writhing fey and for a night…forget and be forgotten.

The Unseelie knew how to throw a party. While the moon gleamed fat and white against the strange twilight sky, the monsters lost themselves within a frenzied waltz of clashing teeth and wailing screams. Bodies were near bare, scraps of silks clinging to naked flesh, shining with sweat and fresh blood.

Wine flowed faster than water, darker than blood, rich and heady and without end. Goblets of it lay upturned upon the tabletops, dribbling scarlet down the ruined cloths. Music bellowed around the cavernous throne room, a beating of drums that awoke every desire to dance. To give in. Such dances were little more than a feral joining of bodies, and Niven craved it.

"Are you drunk, my love?" Great shadows splayed out against the far wall, huge wings stretching and coiling, moving with the red-haired man seated on the throne beside hers. The Unseelie King surveyed his fey with a look of detached boredom, reclining back against the knotted glass of his chair, spikes entwined with its twin.

"Not nearly enough," she answered, tipping the contents of her goblet down her throat, raising it to be refilled. "I'm working on it."

"Indeed." Phabian didn't turn his head, and Niven noted how it no longer bothered her.

She drank deep before rising from her throne, her gown moving around her as if made from midnight itself. She turned and dropped into a low curtsy.

"Dance with me."

A nod, and those shadows folded away. A relief, a respite.

Niven's feet moved to the pounding of drums, the sorrowful cry of the harp, the crushing lyrics slipping from fanged mouths. The tempo increased, the howls and shrieks of the Unseelie joining the orchestra in a guttering song of anguish and madness.

Within her chest, her heart raced hummingbird fast, awakening as the others moved around her, almost daring to touch her.

But not quite.

Outside, the storm they stirred up threw itself against the windows, hurling sheets of rain down upon the glass while the sky erupted in earnest. A celebration. An approval.

The Unseelie were strong again. Niven could feel it thrum through her blood, smell it upon the Glamour spiking around the room. She saw it within the dark gaze of her lover.

Madness shone within the deep copper of his eyes, she knew that. A hunger newly awakened as the shadows obeyed his every whim.

Insatiable.

The bruises she hid so well beneath swirling mist confirmed that. Niven vowed not to fear him, a part of her doubted she could feel afraid. Not after spending a decade forgotten in a castle of misery. A smile bloomed at her lips, showing teeth.

She did not forgive easily.

Cold hands reached up her skirts, lifting the barely corporeal fabric until the chill of the air teased her skin. Fingers moved up her thighs, slow and soft, trailing higher and higher until her gasp broke free from her lips.

"Come with me."

An order.

"I'm enjoying the party." Her words were as much a caress as his hands were. "I'm not going anywhere."

The Unseelie King lifted a brow, the only visible show of his displeasure, but beneath her gown his fingers tightened, digging into her skin. Niven pushed back, her own hand finding his, a pointed nail slicing into his palm. Blood bloomed at her fingertips.

"You push your luck."

"I've yet to run out of it though," Niven purred, bringing her finger to her mouth, tasting the manic shadows that flowed through the Unseelie Kings veins. Tainting it. "Dance with me now, my love, and take me to bed when I'm too drunk to care."

She spun as if the music were for her alone, untiring while the night descended into a riot of bared teeth and bloodshed. Red soaked the soles of her silk slippers, though it was not her blood that stained the marble. She didn't care whose it was, as long as their mangled remains were gone by breakfast.

It was a poor Unseelie party indeed if no one died.

She stopped when the music faded, sweat-soaked hair lying slick across her flushed face. Her breaths panted through her lips, the taste of wine still so strong upon her tongue. She wanted more.

Silence fell upon the writhing mass of fey, stilling them as they turned to her. Then, as one, the Unseelie dropped to their knees, heads bowed low. Niven took them all in, turning slowly, her eyes falling upon the bowed heads and spread wings, the blood spread against faces like warpaint. She circled them, hand outstretched to swirl her own shadows to race around the obsidian walls, almost invisible against the black.

They were hers.

A family of blood and madness.

Home.

"Come to bed with me." Niven held out a hand to Phabian and kept his gaze as he glared at her. With a lift of her shoulder, she began to walk away, not needing him to voice his refusal.

She wouldn't give him the satisfaction of asking twice.

NIVEN WANDERED the labyrinth corridors of the castle, leaving a trail of red footprints behind her. Candles burned within alcoves dug out of the black walls, dancing off the carved stone monsters that watched as she passed. Candle stubs dripped from giant skulls, wax pooling from gaping mouths, the flames bright behind empty eye sockets.

There was a pulsing inside her, a need that hadn't been sated with the frenzied dancing. She wouldn't beg Phabian, wouldn't lower herself to insinuate that she needed him. He would come to her, of course, later in the night after he swallowed more liquor and most likely killed someone. She could wait. The sex was always better when he was angry.

But anger bubbled within her, the need for a release transforming into something ugly and cruel. It nudged deep in her mind, a bitter hatred she couldn't quell, and no longer felt a need to.

She was at the battered wooden door before she even realised where she was going, her feet following the steep steps down and down and down, way beneath the earth. The biting chill found its way through the layers of magic she wore, like it had teeth. She did not knock.

"Next time, you must come to the party," she began, curling a lip at the damp, foul little room. "Think of the fun you would have."

"I imagine our ideas of fun are vastly different, Niven," came the reply, a low voice in the darkness.

With a wave of her hand, the single pathetic candle ignited, illuminating the faerie resting on a pallet of dirty straw.

No…no longer quite faerie. Niven had no idea what he was. Laphaniel had willingly given up his Glamour, the very essence that made him fey…for love. Niven sneered, scorning the idea of such a sacrifice.

"You didn't touch your supper." Niven scooped the bowl up, bringing it to her nose before inhaling deeply. Stifling a cough, she dropped it at Laphaniel's feet. "My, that's potent. No one is going for subtlety tonight, are they? Perhaps they hoped you were hungry enough to eat it anyway."

He shifted on the straw, stretching long legs out in front of him. "I have no desire to spend the night with my head in a bucket."

She grinned. "Again."

"What is it you want?"

Niven rested a shoulder against the wall, feeling the cold slip into her bones. "I'm bored."

"Do I entertain you that much?" he asked, head cocked. "That you would rather be down here with me than in that madman's bed?"

"Careful!"

"No, you be careful," he hissed, rising to his feet. "He will grow bored of me eventually, you all will, and he will find a new plaything. Who do you think that will be?"

"Do you think you'll die down here?" Niven asked, fingernails raking over the ice lingering in the crevices of the walls.

"I know I will never see the Seelie castle again: you'll never allow it."

Niven flashed teeth. "I won't."

Laphaniel dared take a step closer, one hand against the wall. Niven wrinkled her nose at the sight of him. Filthy clothes hung from his body, dirt and dark blood streaked over his face, hair matted with it. Bruises snaked down beneath the collar of his shirt, new colouring painting over the old.

"Your shadows are growing stronger," he breathed, voice as soft as a caress.

She lifted a brow. "And?"

"Despite your thirst for mayhem, Niven," he began, voice still so very soft. She wondered if he had ever seduced her sister with that voice. "You are still human; you by rights shouldn't be able to control them at all."

"Your point?"

He closed the gap, and at one point she may have stepped back. With a tilt of her head, she met his gaze, marvelling at the power shift.

"Faerie itself has taken a liking to you. I always thought the Unseelie would either tear you apart, or you would end up ruling them."

"That almost sounds like a compliment," she said, eyes flicking to the claw marks on his right shoulder, the bite marks on his neck.

Laphaniel's lips split into a wicked smile that rivalled her own. "If I have noticed, you can bet that Phabian has too. I would be careful where you step, Niven, else you will find yourself on one of his pyres."

"I know what I'm doing."

"No, you don't," he said, watching the shadows that swirled around the room, teasing the lonely candlelight. "I just hope you're ready when it all goes to hell."

She grabbed at his neck, fingers digging in. "You are a pathetic creature," she hissed. "A soulless nothing—oh I know all about that, there are those in my court that can sense such things. You are an empty husk and you will rot away here because I want you to. You will die here, and there will be nothing left of you to reach Teya in whatever afterlife she is destined for—"

Niven recoiled as he spat at her, then regained her composure to wipe at her cheek, fighting the desire to smack him. She had gotten the reaction she wanted.

"You hateful cunt." Vehemence dripped from his words. With a satisfied smile, she turned, calling her shadows back to her sides. She ignored the words that echoed her own fears and, without another word, she guttered out the candlelight.

THE SLEEPING QUARTERS Niven shared with Phabian stretched over six rooms. Fat sofas spread out over the sitting room, claw-footed tables nestled beside them, overspilling with ripe fruit that filled the room with a sickly perfume. Two long windows overlooked the gardens, shrouded in darkness and mist, the frigid breeze lifting the heavy velvet curtains across the polished floor. The walls were carved from the same obsidian as the rest of the castle, cold and unforgiving. Nothing adorned the walls, no tapestries, no paintings, no life.

She stood at the window, goblet in hand, and watched a few faeries stalk the grounds, likely in search of something to torment. She wished them luck. Splashes of wine spilt upon the barely-there fabric of her gown as she swirled her goblet. Laphaniel's warning sounded in her head, as she too marvelled at the ease in which she could call upon the darkness and feel the Glamour pulsing from her fey. She didn't question it, took it instead for payment of the childhood stolen away from her.

Oh, how she remembered that night, how the trees themselves had danced and the wind sang through the wild oaks. She remembered how Laphaniel's hands had been cold but Luthien's were warm. Nothing else would ever compare to it, no matter how many faerie balls she attended... They never held the same thrall as her first one carried. It overwhelmed her and she had allowed it.

"You look pensive, my love." Phabian strode past her upon entering their chambers, barely giving her a glance before pouring a large glass of blood-red wine. "Visiting those dark and dank cells will do that to a woman."

"My heart is not some fragile bird," she answered, and held out her goblet for him to refill. "I simply like to know he suffers for what he did to me."

"And does he suffer enough?"

Niven brought the wine to her lips, savouring the taste of black fruit. "Not nearly."

The Unseelie King turned and drained his wine in a single swallow. He caught her by the wrist, forcing her close, red-stained lips pressing against her mouth in a kiss that stole all other thoughts away.

She kissed him back, breathing in the scent of wine, the touch of darkness that engulfed him. His shadows wrapped around her like a cape.

"I know your heart, my love," he breathed, taking her lip sharply between his teeth. "It is a wicked thing. You are wicked and you are mine."

She didn't answer, not to agree or contradict, instead she led him to the enormous bed that dominated their sleeping space. Great carved dragons held up the canopy, a veil of gossamer that swept over the floor in a pool of starlight.

With her eyes on him, she trailed a hand over her body, dispelling the shadows masquerading as her gown. She stood naked at the edge of the bed, tall and proud. Unashamed. With slow, deliberating movements, she pulled the clips from her hair, allowing it all to tumble over her shoulders and breasts in waves of shining midnight.

From the bed, Phabian looked on, desire painting his eyes black. His breath caught and he swallowed, hard, and Niven drank in the power it gave her like the wine.

"Do you love me?" she asked, tilting her head up as the candlelight danced. Glamour flickered bright and erratic, a wondrous joining of magic that stirred up the darkness around them in a private waltz.

"Do you care?" The words were a breath, ending in a delicious gasp as she straddled him. Her hands roamed over his stomach, muscled and hard, to the edge of his trousers. Niven grinned down at him as he arched his hips.

"No."

The little word was a whisper against his skin, her lips brushing against the hollow of his throat, enticing a moan that awoke every aching nerve within her. She moved her lips to his in a kiss filled with lust and hunger, her tongue seeking his, hands raking through the russet strands of his hair, tugging hard enough to force a snarl from his throat.

The rest of the Unseelie King's clothing vanished in a swirl of black, leaving only tanned skin behind. With a low moan, he flipped

Niven onto her back, huge ghostly wings spreading wide against the back wall. The candlelight snuffed out one by one until there was nothing but a velvet black and the joining of tangled bodies.

CHAPTER THREE

TEYA

*P*apers lay scattered over my desk, mountains of work for me to sift through, so endless and tiresome. Small squabbles needing to be dealt with, laws enforced, duties to be carried out despite my heart no longer being in any of it. I fiddled with the quill in my hand, spilling droplets of ink onto a letter to some faerie lord far away from the castle. I signed my name, sealed the parchment with melted ruby wax, and placed it on top of a teetering pile of ruby-waxed letters.

Oonagh liked to keep me busy, barely giving me a moment to relax or think. No matter how much paperwork she dumped at my desk, the countless meetings, gatherings, and visits she had me parading around, there were always moments when I had too much time.

Those moments, rare as they were, allowed the memories to seep in, the longing that threatened to buckle my knees. It left too much time to think about the first midwinter I had spent with Laphaniel...

The first midwinter had brought with it a cruel and unforgiving snowfall, stripping the trees with the sheer force of the wind. The lakes and rivers froze over; the waterfalls turned to sheets of ice that burst into lethal shards upon hitting the surface. Life vanished elsewhere, or simply curled up and died.

Within the Seelie castle, the great fires were stacked with enormous tree trunks, topped with pinecones that spread a wonderful, sweet scent around the hollow rooms. It was not enough to dispel the tight hand of winter, and frost still formed over the windows no matter how high the fires burned. We all took to wearing heavy furs inside, hoods up, our hands stuffed inside thick gloves that made it impossible to hold anything.

It would take seven days to travel to the outskirts of the Unseelie, so I left Oonagh in charge back home and took Gabriel with me to cross the merciless landscape. I would be granted three days with Laphaniel.

Three.

Unseelie knights waited at the border for us, none of their faces familiar beneath the hooded cloaks they wore. We exchanged no words, no pleasantries, as they led us through the barren and brittle woodland beneath the strange twilight sky. They rode upon monstrous black horses, with two curling horns protruding from waves of ebony mane, yellow eyes turning to my own chestnut mare, hungry.

Gabriel tensed beside me, his white horse snorting out plumes of fog, clearly distressed. I knew it went against every instinct of his to follow blindly into the Unseelie lands.

"I can go on alone from here," I said, speaking low.

Gabriel clicked the reins, forcing his horse onwards. "With due respect, your Majesty, you do say some ridiculous things."

The Unseelie castle loomed, black and formidable, dark walls gleaming like ink against the eerie sky. A labyrinth of nightmares, it sprawled endlessly, shifting constantly so once you were lost, there was no hope of finding a way out.

Pikes stood along the entrance like grotesque fence posts, heads in various stages of decay shoved down upon them. Wings were nailed to the walls, horns mounted upon crude plaques, and then there were the pyres.

Unlit — for now.

I could smell the scent of burning flesh, hear the echoes of the screams — and the laughter of the king who revelled in it all.

"Welcome, Queen of Seelie," the Unseelie King greeted as we entered his cavernous throne room. A host of his fey watched from the shadows, manic delight dancing upon their sneering faces. "I trust you had a pleasant journey?"

I wondered if I could tear off his head from where he stood. A lazy smile lifted his lips as if sensing my thoughts; the shadows around him stirred. There was no sign of my sister.

"We ran into a little difficulty, Your Majesty." The words were like ash upon my tongue as I sank into a low curtsy, the red silks of my gown spilling upon the marble. Gabriel dropped to his knee beside me, and I could taste his revulsion.

The Unseelie King, dressed in shadow and fear, peered down at me from his throne. "I hear you have trouble in your little court?"

I met his eye as I stood, attempting to see anything human behind his gaze. "As do you, I believe."

"Ah, yes." He grinned, his shadows stretching high overhead, dousing the candlelight. "You must have seen my wall of traitors, Teya? A beautiful sight to behold, do you not think?"

Mad. He was absolutely mad.

"You'll have no fey left if you slaughter them all."

The Unseelie King leant forward, phantom wings spreading out against the wall behind him. His fey flashed their teeth, revelling in the dark Glamour radiating from him. "Do not worry for me, Queen of Seelie."

"Where is my husband?"

His eyes flared at my demand. Then a wicked, nightmarish grin split over his mouth. Shadows skittered over the marble like demons, surging into his fey. They cawed in sick delight, whooping and snarling, a tangle of blackness and teeth.

"Where is he?" I called over the cacophony of screams.

Silence fell with a slow lift of the Unseelie King's hand. His voice was soft when he spoke, haunting. "In his room, of course. Perhaps I am not the monster you believe me to be."

With a sharp click of his fingers, a twisted wraith of a girl appeared at my side, stringy black hair falling in knotted clumps past her waist. She grabbed at my hand, her skin cold and wet. Without a word, she began to drag me from the room, but not before the Unseelie King's voice rang out behind me.

"But then again, perhaps I am."

I tore after the girl as she led me down pitch-black corridors, her footsteps leaving puddles of water behind her. I followed down winding stairs that reeked of rot and dampness. Down and down and down. My heart became brittle—I had still hoped for more.

Handprints smeared down the smooth walls, bloody trails pooling over the stone. I jerked on the slippery hand holding onto mine.

"Whose blood is this?"

The girl stared at me, too-large eyes unblinking, head slowly tilting. "It is old."

I shivered at her voice, at the tang of saltwater on her breath. "It's not Laphaniel's blood?"

"No."

"Is he hurt?"

She turned her head to look further down into the darkness before returning her gaze to me. "Right now?"

My stomach lurched at her implication. "Just take me to him."

She held out her hand again, slick fingers curling tight. "You are Teya?"

"I am."

Her words were cold against my cheek. "He screams your name."

She disappeared in a veil of mist, leaving behind a pool of brackish water that trickled down the worn stone steps. The echo of her words remained, leaving me winded as if she had struck me.

I was left standing before an ancient wooden door and had only lifted my hand towards the handle when the lock flicked and it swung open. A cell, that was all that greeted me, a cold and dank cell buried so far beneath the ground.

"Laphaniel?"

He looked up from the bundle of old straw, eyes flitting from me to the open door. I ran to him, and he flinched.

"It's me." I took a careful step, desperate to have him in my arms. "For three days over midwinter, did they not tell you I was coming?"

Of course they hadn't.

"You're really here?" His voice sounded raw, like he hadn't used it in a while…or like he had worn it out.

"I really am." I couldn't bear the distance any longer and closed the gap between us, drawing him close. He gripped me hard, fingers pinching, but I didn't care. I didn't dare loosen his hold on me.

"I'm going to bring you home," I breathed against him, taking in the new scent that coated over the wonderful spice that had been wholly him.

My hands traced over his face, lingering on the discolouration of his jaw, his neck. I traced down his shoulders, beneath the ruined shirt he wore. My fingers stilled, and he tensed.

"I'm going to kill them all," I hissed, lifting the cloth to reveal the twisted scars that reached across his back, the knotted skin still black and raw in places. "They can't do this to you."

"They already have." Laphaniel grabbed me as I stood, fingers leaving marks on the red silk. "You can't just storm up there and confront him, it will end with both our heads on sticks."

"He had you whipped!"

"I know!" Laphaniel snarled back, pushing himself to his feet. "I was there."

"I can't just sit by and let them do that to you—"

"Then fix it," he blurted, raking a hand through filthy hair. "Fix this!"

I took a breath, fighting the Glamour pressing against my fingertips that was raring to call down a storm. We stared at each other; the new distance obvious, a void stretched out by blame and fear. I would have done anything to close it.

I paced the tiny room, my elaborate gown feeling grotesque against the dirty space. There was no window, no natural light. A crumbling wall separated off a corner of the cell housing a toilet and cracked basin. I noted the absence of a blanket, a pillow, of any comfort.

"Have you seen Niven?"

"Not much." He picked at the threads on his shirt, the feeble light from the few candles catching his wedding band. "But then, I don't get called for dinner often." Laphaniel's words came out bitter, cold. I opened my mouth to speak, but he cut me off. "I'm sorry."

I shook my head. "You shouldn't be the one apologising, if I had—"

"This isn't your fault," he said as he reached for me.

I slipped into his embrace, a hand running over the slender points of his ears, a reminder that he wasn't truly human...a reminder of what he had given up for me. "One day you're going to stop saying that. My decisions led us here. I signed that contract."

"I played my part," he answered, his mouth soft against my lips. "You don't get to carry that burden alone."

The soft thump of his heartbeat was so familiar that I could pick it out against an army of beating hearts, hear its song as it played only for me.

"I will find a way," I said, savouring the scent of him, still him, beneath the tang of fear, anger, and pain. "No one has forgotten you."

"I don't think there's a way out, Teya."

"Don't say that."

Laphaniel touched his forehead to mine, words soft. "What Phabian can do with his shadows is something of nightmares. The Unseelie are afraid of him: he kills them for sport, hunts them down with his hounds. I can hear them from here. You've seen the pyres, I take it, the pieces nailed to the walls? Not all those fey were traitors."

"Is Niven afraid of him?" I could barely imagine my sister afraid of anything anymore.

"If she is, she hides it well."

I forced him to look at me. "Don't give up hope."

He smiled, a tired lift of his lips, but some of the shadows lightened from his face. "It's all I have left."

We kissed long and slow like we had all the time in the world.

Laphaniel's hands moved to the stays on my dress, loosening them with skilled fingers. He froze at the sound of knocking, head snapping to the doorway.

Another knock rapped against the wood, louder and harder.

"What do you want?" I called out, tasting the sharpness of Laphaniel's fear.

"I bring gifts to the Queen of Seelie and her Consort," came the reply, a rasping whisper. "A banquet. One of three in honour of your visit, courtesy of the King himself."

The footsteps faded away, replaced by thick shadows that enveloped the room, snaking over the stone floor to leave tables of food in its wake. Velvets and furs materialised from the inky black, cushions slipped from the smoke to replace the mouldering straw. Candles rose from the alcoves to drip wax down the damp walls, banishing some of the darkness away.

I saw it for what it was: a show of power, not kindness.

Steaming dishes filled the cell with a delicious aroma, while glass decanters bubbled with pale amber wine. Fruit lay glistening with golden sugar upon silver platters, surrounded by rich chocolates and oozing honey cakes.

"Don't!" Laphaniel gripped my wrist, pulling me away from the food. He didn't look at the feast surrounding him, but I heard his stomach rumbling. It was a hollow sound.

"When did you last eat something?" I demanded, my anger not directed at him. "Tell me."

"This morning?"

"Are you asking me?"

"The days bleed together, Teya," he said through gritted teeth. "So, I don't know."

I walked over to one of the tables, the smell from the food mouth-watering and decadent. I popped a fat grape in my mouth, tasting nothing but sweetness. I drank the wine next before plucking a strip of dripping venison from the plate. It melted against my tongue.

"It's not poisoned," I said, piling up a plate with a bit of everything when he still didn't move. "Phabian is demonstrating what he can do, reminding me of my place here. If I cause no trouble, we get this. Three days of this. Please eat something."

Laphaniel accepted the goblet of pale wine I offered and swallowed it down without a word. I poured myself a glass before refilling his. I nodded to the food, and he sat and picked at it. The wine, he drank without protest.

With the food mostly untouched and the wine almost gone, I dragged the bundle of furs into the middle of the room and made a makeshift bed, bringing over the last bottle of wine before settling down into the cosy warmth.

We passed the bottle back and forth until the edges of the world blurred and everything seemed a little less bleak. Laphaniel pulled me closer, his mouth on mine, tasting of over-sweet apples.

I deepened the kiss, hungry for him, needing him. We fell against the furs and, among the glistening dishes of untouched food, to the sound of water dripping down the walls.

He responded with a hunger of his own, hands coming up to tear at the stays of my dress, finding his way past the layers of silk. Fingers brushed over the curve of my breast, down over my hip. Teeth grazed my lip, one hand curled tight in my hair. Our breaths gasped together, wordless. Frantic.

I yanked at his shirt, needing to remove any barrier between us. I grazed over the welts of his back, and he pulled back with a snarl.

"Don't!"

He dragged my hand away, keeping it locked in his. He didn't bother removing the rest of my ripped gown before lifting me against him. We fit together perfectly, we always had done, but there was no softness to it. It was quick and rough and cold. A release and nothing else.

We lay in silence after, not quite touching. Laphaniel stared up at the ceiling, eyes far away as if he could see the sky way beyond the layers and layers of stone.

"What is it like?" he said after a while. "Being Queen?"

"Hard," I admitted. "I try to make it look like I know what I'm doing, but I don't. I think they all know that."

His hand slipped into mine. "I'm sorry I can't be there with you."

"I will bring you home."

Laphaniel nodded, looking exhausted. I swept a gentle wave of Glamour over him, making it heavy and tempting and irresistible. He closed his eyes with a soft sigh.

"You don't have to do that," he murmured.

"We can talk later, I'll still be here." I pulled him closer and he didn't protest. "I can't do much right now, but I can help you get some rest."

"Charlotte does the same," he breathed, words sleepy. "Creeps in when she can. When she comes, I always dream of you."

Laphaniel curled himself tight against me, legs drawn up, arms coming up around his head. Gone was the wonderful abandonment in which he usually slept, with arms and legs sprawled out as if someone had simply dumped him in bed.

It was a small comfort to know the Spider checked in on him. Charlotte had shown us a kindness seldom found in faeries, taking a curious liking to us when she saved Laphaniel's life deep in her underground lair.

To know he wasn't utterly alone was a gift, something to hold onto. Hope within a hopeless place.

A harsh knock at the door dragged me back to the present, the memory of that midwinter lingering like a black mist. Three days was not enough, would never be enough. It had nearly destroyed me to leave him, to prise his fingers from mine before I was led away.

"Yes?"

Nefina stepped into the room, her gown of starlight trailing behind her in waves of gossamer. Her hair was pinned up away from her face, leaving the sharpness of her cheekbones on show. Her eyes were ablaze.

"The knights have returned from the borders."

I stiffened at her tone, the quill I held pausing mid-air. Ink spilled down onto the parchment, ruining my work further. "Go on."

"Three didn't come home."

My heart stilled. I stood, trying to collect my thoughts, to not let my feelings show on my face, like I had been taught. "Who?"

Nefina kept her chin high, though tears glittered in the corners of her eyes. I wouldn't see them fall—she would make sure of that.

"Aofie, and Bracken…and Sage," Nefina replied, voice holding steady. I wanted to reach out to her, comfort her, but she froze when I moved, closing herself off. She would never allow me to pity her: her pride denied that.

Sage had ignited something in Nefina. He had brought to life a passion and freedom I had never seen in her before. He was tinder to her wildness, leaving her completely uncaged, and it has suited her beautifully.

Nefina was quick to love as she was quick to hate, and she had allowed herself to be consumed by Sage. He had become her shadow, and she, his.

"I think perhaps it is easier when they are dead," Nefina began, sweeping a long finger over her cheek to catch a teardrop, eyeing it with distaste. "There is no hope of them coming home, they are simply gone, leaving you to live around the void where they once were. The limbo you exist in is torment."

Exist. The word bit at me like it had teeth.

"I want them all hanged," she continued, eyes flashing. "Every one of them."

Anger surged through me at the loss of my fey, at those I had come to think of as friends. At the loss Nefina was left to bear. "They will be. I am done with mercy."

CHAPTER FOUR

TEYA

The frigid morning brought the threat of rain, the sky overhead crowded with bloated black clouds that barred any sunlight attempting to filter through. What little light escaped those clouds lingered over the dead leaves underfoot, catching the shards of frost that clung to the brittle edges.

Mounds of disturbed earth stood stark against the white; bright winter blooms lay atop the dirt, bound with a ribbon that snapped in the wind.

I stood upon a raised platform, the looming shadow of the castle behind me. Oonagh stood at my left, Gabriel to my right. Nefina stood a little way from us, staring dead-eyed into the gathered crowd. Her pale hair was loose around her shoulders, tendrils whipping across her unforgiving face. She glanced at me, giving me a slight nod, a dip of her chin and nothing more.

"Are you ready?" Oonagh's calm, steady voice broke through the chaos in my mind but did little to settle the churning in my stomach.

"I don't think I'll ever be ready," I answered truthfully as I gazed across the faeries that had gathered. "But I understand what needs to be done."

The heavy cloak around my shoulders was stifling, the emerald green perfectly matching the deep hue of the gown I wore. I wanted to remove it, to tear away the circlet of bronze leaves that had been woven into my hair. I felt like a puppet. A doll to be dressed up and paraded around. A child playing dress up.

Bile crept up the back of my throat as I stared out at the other platform, so very different from mine.

"If you pardon them now, you will look weak," Oonagh whispered, her cool fingers sliding through mine. "This was never going to be easy for you. You were never meant to do this alone."

I squeezed her hand before releasing it. "I'm not alone, Oonagh."

The sea of faeries below me dropped to their knees when I stepped forward, a sight that still took my breath away. Wings glimmered in the shards of sunlight that pierced the clouds, along with bared teeth and the flash of claws.

Glamour flooded the air, thick with anger and sadness. It wasn't aimed at me, but at the six faeries standing upon the raised dais with ropes around their necks. The wave of emotion pushed against my Glamour, fuelling the rage lingering just below the surface, an anger I struggled to contain, an anger that would erupt at the slightest grievance.

Already it had its teeth in me, pounding through my veins with the need to destroy something…anything. Anyone.

I had no idea how Laphaniel had ever controlled it.

"This is not what I wanted," I called out, my voice carrying out across the crowd with a confidence I didn't feel. "I gave fair warning, more than any of you truly deserve."

With a steadying breath, my gaze fixed upon the six faeries. Thunder rumbled across the clouds, awakening the storm slumbering inside me.

"You fight against me, your kin, and your friends. You slaughtered your own—for what end?"

"We will not bow to a human girl!" one of the captives bellowed, straining against the rope that bound her. Thunder boomed over the indigo sky, a fork of lightning ripping through the cloud to strike the ground just shy of the hanging platform.

"I am no longer a human girl."

A nasty sneer spread over the faerie's lips, twisting her lovely face into a mask of hate. "No, you are a parasite."

I bristled at the word, at the sullying of the gift Laphaniel had given me. With a flex of my fingers, I sought out her pulse in a sea of beating hearts. I found it with ease, thudding quick against her delicate breast. I squeezed and her eyes widened. At my side, Oonagh came closer, but I held my other hand up, warning her away.

"Your name?" I demanded, still holding her life between my fingertips.

She spat on the ground, then gasped as I tightened my grip. The other five faeries remained silent, looking down. A dampness spread down the leg of one of them. His hands trembled.

"Your name?" I called again, and she flashed her teeth, little points behind full lips.

"Go to hell, human whore."

With a sharp twist, her heart turned to dust, her body sagged against the rope and swayed.

"I won't offer you mercy," I said to the others, fighting against the blackness threatening at the corners of my vision. I couldn't faint. A sudden sharp pain shot through my arm, and I gave Gabriel a thankful glance, knowing his pinch would bruise. He nodded back, face grave. "I offered mercy and you didn't want it. I won't have war amongst my court."

The platform dropped at my signal. The ropes went taught, and there was nothing but silence.

I barely made it back to my rooms before I fell to my knees, clutching the toilet bowl. I retched until there was nothing left. Someone sat beside me, drawing my hair away from my face, while their hands rubbed gentle circles over my back.

At first, I thought it was Oonagh, until I leant back and Nefina shoved a glass of cold water into my hand. I took a sip and instantly brought it back up again. Nefina handed me a handkerchief, not quite masking the look of disgust on her face. I wiped at my mouth and sagged back against the wall.

"You did well today."

I glared up at her. "That is an awful thing to say."

She shrugged, arranging the folds of her glittering gown around her. It clung to her lithe frame, thin as a cobweb. "The rebels may think twice against opposing you now."

"I crushed someone's heart with my bare hands."

Nefina smiled at the memory. "Did you enjoy it?"

With a groan, I leant forward to spit into the bowl. "No."

"Then you are still the girl Laphaniel fell in love with," Nefina said, grabbing a damp washcloth from the sink. She ran it over my skin, oddly gentle. "If it is any comfort to you, Teya, I don't believe you will ever come to enjoy torment."

I nodded, indeed finding comfort in her words, the soft lilt of her voice. "Nefina?"

The room swayed.

"Yes?"

I fumbled for her hand. "I think I'm going to pass out…"

"I assumed you would," she said, then guided my head into her lap, unconcerned about soiling her gown. "I won't be going anywhere."

I woke in my own bed to the sound of hushed voices. A fire roared in the grate, and all the candles were lit. Light flickered over the walls of the circular room, bouncing off the tapestries and paintings I had hung everywhere to bring some life to the space. Some warmth. My bed was small compared to what had been designed for us, modest. There were no silk panels, no posts carved with dancing animals. It was a place to sleep and nothing more.

"Oh, good, you're awake." Oonagh crouched over me and tapped my cheek. "Go bathe, you reek."

"You reek, Your Majesty," I muttered, swatting her hand away. She caught it with quick fingers, leaning down to brush a kiss to my forehead.

"We're here, Teya," she said, her voice unbearably gentle. "Remember that."

It was an echo of Nefina's words, a reminder that I was not alone. I grasped her hand and clung to it like a lifeline.

CHAPTER FIVE

LAPHANIEL

Filthy water dribbled over the walls to pool in a stagnant puddle. The rivulet made a slow descent over the flagstones to the pile of straw that made up my bed, rotting it. The stalks were blackened, never quite dry. There was the constant sound of dripping.

"Count to three."

I shifted at the tightening of claws around my arm, bracing myself. "You're just going to snap it back on two."

The Spider gave a wry smile. "Humour me."

I counted slowly with my eyes closed. I made it to three and nothing happened. "What are you waiting for? AH!"

My yelp echoed, along with the sound of bone clunking together. I sucked in a shuddering breath and held it as white-hot pain blazed up my shoulder.

"I would so hate for you to think I had become predictable," Charlotte said, long fingers pressing against my arm, testing it.

The words I wanted to spit at her caught in my throat, hissing past my gritted teeth as senseless noise. Claws folded over my hand.

I waited for the pain to fade to a dull ache before speaking. "How long until midwinter?"

"Three weeks," Charlotte answered as a strange look passed over her face. She narrowed her eyes, all eight of them unblinking. "Your fingers are broken too."

"I know."

"Two ribs." The Spider's elongated fingers prodded over my stomach, claws scraping along the bruising on my left side. I winced and she stilled. "You must learn to keep your smart mouth shut."

I snorted, earning a scowl. "Because they'll leave me alone if I keep nice and quiet?"

She flashed her fangs at me. One set of her hands busied themselves strapping my fingers together while the other held up an empty bottle. "This is not helping."

"I don't need a lecture, Charlotte."

"Oh, you are getting one, boy," she answered, teeth clicking. "Who is giving this filth to you?"

"Goblins come down here sometimes," I answered, and Charlotte's gaze snapped back to me. Her head tilted, hair as fine as cobweb slipping over her bare shoulders.

"To give you bottles of dirty liquor?" She drew closer, claws tightening over my wrist. "Pray tell, why would they do that?"

It would have been foolish to pretend I no longer feared her, that my heart didn't jolt every time she emerged from the shadows, quiet as a ghost. Tales far older than I was were told about the Unseelie Spider, stories told upon hushed whispers, far away from the silken webs spun from nightmares.

Yet she was also my friend, the only one I had within the Unseelie labyrinth.

"I tell them things."

"What things?" A snarl rumbled up her throat. "What could you possibly hear?"

"There is a pipe in the corner." I tried to back away, to put space between myself and the fangs grazing my cheek. The Spider crawled closer, stretching lithe, jointed legs so she hovered above me. One clawed hand reached for my throat, black nails digging in. "Sometimes voices travel down. I am guessing from the laundry room above here… the laundresses gossip."

Her mouth stretched wide, as if she would swallow me whole. "You sell court secrets for a bottle of slurry?"

Her breath was cold upon my cheek.

"Idle gossip," I corrected, leaning further away from her. "Nothing of consequence."

"Nothing of consequence," Charlotte echoed, and pinned me against the cold stone. "The King is nailing his fey to the castle walls for acts of little consequence." The words hissed through her fangs. "Imagine how he would delight in pinning pieces of you up there. Little bits of you for your beloved wife to find."

"He would have your head," I threw back, "if he knew you crept down here to help me."

A sharp laugh burst past her lips. "You think he does not know? Who else patches you up? Who else makes sure you do not die in the night and deny him the fun of tormenting you further?"

With a snarl of frustration, she shoved herself off me, head twisting around to survey the cell with a look of disgust.

I took a breath, waiting until she was far enough away from my neck before I spoke. The words came out in a rush, a quick confession I could no longer keep to myself: "I hear other things too."

Her head snapped back around to me. "What things?"

I paused for a moment. "Whispers."

"From the pipe?" She pointed to the corner.

"No…in my head."

The torn fragments of her gown swirled around her as she paced the cell, the pale silk blackened at the edges. "What sort of whispers?"

"I don't know," I answered, wondering if I was already going mad. "I can't hear what they're saying. It's little more than noise."

"Are they constant?"

I shook my head.

"And you are certain you are awake?"

"I think so." I sighed, raking my good hand through my hair. I pulled pieces of matted straw away and crumbled them with a curled lip. "I'm not sure. I'm never really sure."

Charlotte ceased her pacing. "You are to tell me the moment it happens again, do you understand?"

"Am I losing my mind?"

She paused for a beat too long. "I doubt it."

"Then what is it?" I pressed.

"Most likely a dormant spirit." She ran a claw down the stone, scraping off the moss growing between the cracks. They lingered upon the scratch marks I had made. "It may have latched on to you when you crossed through the veil between the living and the dead."

I blinked. "You think I'm being haunted?"

"It is likely only an echo," she answered. "You can hear it now because the veil is thinner in the Unseelie lands. It is why we have the most wonderful creatures lurking within our forests."

"Can you make it stop?"

A nod. "I will certainly try."

It was a relief to know I wasn't going mad. "How long until midwinter?"

A claw tilted my head up, black eyes narrowing. "How long have you been here, angel?"

I attempted to look at my markings, each long scratch a count of the long days spent in the dark. The Spider's grip tightened. I thought back to when I had seen Teya last, but everything had become muddled with my dreams of her. It could have been days ago, longer perhaps…

"Angel?"

"I don't…I don't know." Panic hit me like a physical blow. I broke away from Charlotte's grip and rushed to the far wall where lines were gouged into the stone. I counted them with The Spider's watchful eyes upon me, my fingers fumbling in my haste to make it all mean something.

"A month," I gasped. "I've been here a month."

Charlotte waited, saying nothing at all.

"But I've seen Teya, haven't I?" I turned back to the marks and counted again. "I'm sure I did."

Charlotte inched closer. "It's been nearly two years, Angel."

I will come for you.

I will bring you home.

"Two years," I echoed with a bitter laugh. "There's not going to be much left to bring home if she waits much longer."

"Do not speak such things!" Charlotte hissed.

With my back against the cold wall, I slid down until I was sitting upon the flagstones, and stretched my legs out in front of me. "Allow me a little self-pity." I looked up. "Unless you want to talk about what is bothering you?"

"And what makes you think something is bothering me?"

"One of your left eyes twitches when you're angry."

She lifted a talon to her face. "Truthfully?"

"No."

Her lip curled. "Lying is a nasty little habit."

"It is a poor consolation for my Glamour, I will admit to that."

"You miss it." It wasn't a question.

I shifted on the stones, fiddling with a piece of straw. "I didn't when I was with Teya. I could sense it within her, even when she couldn't reach it. It being torn from me hurt in a way I have no words for, the strange emptiness it left behind is something I am learning to live with. But I don't miss it because I would miss her more."

Charlotte watched from the shadows, lifting a vial of glittering blue up to the faint light, she frowned at the rainbow it cast upon the stone.

"Do you ever wonder why I never gobbled you up?" she asked, flicking a glance my way, black eyes glowing beneath the candlelight.

I never made any pretence of how terrified I had been of her, how certain I was that I would never see daylight again after Teya dragged me down into her lair. "I didn't dare ask you."

She smiled, showing fangs. "I could smell your blood from way beneath the castle. It was rotten and foul. Even now I do not know how you found the strength to fight that Raven Knight and win."

Charlotte drew closer and, with a gentle shove, she had me lie down. She lifted another vial to the candlelight, this one black as coal dust, and nodded to herself.

"What is that?" I asked, but she ignored me. Claws curled around my left hand, fingers brushing over the silver glow of the band on my third finger. Charlotte had gifted them to us, a pair of rare Dragonstone rings that were worth a king's ransom.

"These were meant to bind us forever," she whispered, almost to herself. "These rings were to symbolise a forever that echoed on into the ether. Unbreakable." Her claw moved back and forth across the stone without leaving a mark. "I was born to the shadow, surrounded by beautiful darkness that was so unlike the vulgar wisps the king plays with. I breathed in the nightmares, learned with the others of my kind to weave them into my webs."

She pulled her hand away, moving it to my cheek. Her voice was soft when she spoke next, faraway. "Long, long before I came to court, I was wed. It had been arranged since we were spiderlings. I grew up loving him with a need like drawing breath. I suffocated without him."

She stopped; her hand dropped into her lap.

"I'm listening," I said, wanting her to know that, because there was little else I could offer her.

"I bore him twelve children," Charlotte continued, words brittle. "All boys save for the youngest, a girl with hair as fine as silk and the colour of flame. My Aralia, my little one." She closed her eyes for a moment as if savouring the memory. "I heard your wife scream for help that night in the castle, caring not for the bruises and blood upon her own battered body. My Aralia screamed like that, for her father and brothers, her body broken beyond saving as she begged me to save them."

I took her hand. "What happened?"

"A coven of witches in the far north covet spider-silk. I was not home. I was out gathering nightmares and the songs of the dying to use in my weaving." She looked up, eyes too bright. "I was not home."

I could not imagine the horror of losing all you held dear in one fell swoop, to come home to the broken pieces of those you loved.

"You helped us because Teya reminded you of your daughter?"

"Because she hovered over you as if she alone could protect you from me."

I smiled at that. Even without my Glamour coursing through her veins, Teya had been far stronger than I had first thought her to be. She radiated with a tenaciousness that I had initially fought against. My instincts wanted to dampen it down into something I could control, keep hold of. Break.

It had been too easy to manipulate her, to make her forget why she was wandering the dark woods. To make her think she loved me.

And then she had run, of course she did.

And drowned.

Blue-lipped and face down.

Not breathing.

"Stop that!" Charlotte hissed, snapping her fangs so close to my face, they grazed my skin. She thrust the vial of black dust into my hands. "Swallow that down."

I jerked back. My breathing rasped through my teeth, my chest tight as if someone were standing upon it. My heartbeat thudded in my ears. The tiny room felt so much smaller. Too small.

I tipped the contents of the vial into my mouth, forcing myself to swallow and not choke. It tasted of smoke and ash and dirt.

"Do you know what I would like to do?" the Spider said, claws making slow circles over my back. I shook my head, sucking in breaths through my teeth. "One day, I will lay waste to this castle and those who reside within it."

"Why stay at all?" My voice cracked, but I could breathe again. "What keeps you here?"

The slow circles on my back continued. Not so long ago, I would have flinched away.

"I stay for you, Angel," she said in the soft darkness. "For as long as you are held here, I will stay."

CHAPTER SIX

TEYA

*M*usic engulfed the room, coaxing even the candlelight burning bright above us to dance to the frantic beat. The fires raged in their grates, flames high and wild, banishing the winter chill and darkness so that for just one night, we could forget about them.

Faeries bent and swayed to the feral song. Teeth grazed along naked shoulders and bare breasts. Lithe bodies spun and whirled and danced and danced and danced. They gorged themselves on wine and forgetfulness, to dull the memory of seeing their brethren hang.

The ball was Guelder's idea, her wise council stating how my court was starved of merriment, debauchery, and a chance to fuck each other senseless. I had been reluctant to agree, unwilling to host parties without Laphaniel by my side.

Looking out at the mass of writhing faeries, I understood how much they needed it. They were not tame creatures. They were not human. They did not grieve or love or feel as humans did—if anything, they felt everything so much more.

With Glamour flowing in my veins, I could sense it. Taste it. The wickedness, the wildness, the hate, and the passion. It was a constant whirlwind of emotion set free beneath the erratic pounding of drums.

"Luthien would hold revelries nearly every night," Guelder said beside me, smoothing the folds of her skirts. Threads of frozen dew glittered at her touch, matching the tiny beads at her dark throat. "Your court needs this, even if you do not want it."

"It feels wrong," I answered, catching sight of Oonagh in the middle of the fray. "It's just another thing I don't understand."

The glow of flickering light caught the edges of the golden leaves making up Guelder's hair. She turned her head, lips forming a gentle smile.

"You may have Glamour now, your Majesty, but it does not make you fey."

No unkindness tainted her words, just stark truth that she excelled at.

"I am willing to learn," I said as I adjusted the golden silk of my gown so I could sit upon one of the twin thrones. Scarlet fur lined the billowing sleeves, the fine silk held at my fingers by jewelled rings. The neckline was also rimmed with fur and plunged low to show off the jewels dripping at my throat.

"We are honoured to teach you." The leaves of Guelder's hair crackled as she dipped her head. She looked like an autumn sunrise, warm and beautiful.

I nodded in the direction of the revel. "Are you not dancing?"

"Are you?" she answered, following my gaze to the empty seat beside me. "Dance with your fey, Teya. That throne will remain empty whether or not you dance."

"Go ahead without me. I'll join in a moment."

Guelder dipped into a deep curtsy, her skirts sighing around her. "By your leave, your Majesty."

Sat upon the Seelie throne, I watched over the hall and drank in the sight of my court as they should be. Wild and free.

Frigid air blew in from the open doors, snuffing out the candlelight beside them. Snow covered the sweeping gardens, new footprints led away from the ball and scattered in different directions as faeries sought more private locations to unclothe themselves. Laughter echoed up from the hedge maze, from the slumbering orchards, from the lakes where the selkies slept.

"Dance with me?"

Gabriel outstretched his hand, amber eyes alight. His unruly curls were more dishevelled than I had ever seen, his horns only just peeking out from the mess. The buttons on his black jacket were left undone, revealing golden skin.

"Should I at least be thankful you are somewhat clothed?" I asked, not fighting the smile that tugged at my lips as I took his hand.

"I thought it for the best." His words slurred together. "Though I must confess, I have lost my shoes."

I glanced down at his bare feet, filthy from twirling around the dancefloor. He tugged me close, hand sneaking too low upon my hips. I snatched it back up to my waist and he chuckled.

"You're drunk," I said with a smile. I could smell the wine on his breath, rich and decadent. It glimmered from the corners of his lips.

"As should you be."

Without looking away, he plucked a goblet from the tray of a passing faerie, then handed it to me. Steam coiled up from the bubbling gold liquid, filling my senses with winter spice. He took one for himself and drank deeply.

"As much as you would like to, you cannot lose yourself," Gabriel began, leading me in a dance that didn't quite match the pulsing music. "Your court is counting on your strength. We respond to the Glamour sparking through you, as much as you respond to ours…and this." He gestured to the hall with his goblet, spilling his wine. "This is what we need. What you need. You are allowed to be angry, Little Red, but it makes us angry too. Angry fey without anyone to tear to shreds are dangerous creatures indeed."

I drained my drink, allowing the warmth to flow through my body. I took another, wanting to numb everything.

"I feel as though there is a constant storm inside me," I said, following Gabriel's footsteps without thought. "It rages on and it's getting stronger. I want to burn the world to the ground, just to be able to breathe again."

Gabriel spun me, steps flawless despite the amount of alcohol he had consumed. Others waltzed around us, a constant whirl of silk and wing and naked flesh. They caught my hand, tugging me into their arms, twirling and dancing to the music that wouldn't cease until dawn broke.

"I know you wanted war," Gabriel murmured in my ear when I found myself once again in his arms. "I know you wanted to tear the Unseelie to pieces, and perhaps one day you will get your wish. Though not now, not yet. Yield to them today, scatter their bones over the battlefield when you have Laphaniel back at your side."

Thunder thrummed in the distance at his words, the heavy skies crackling with sparks of lightning. I often thought about what I could do, what destruction I could cause, if given the chance.

Another drink materialised in my hand, the contents as clear as water. I gulped it back and accepted the other Oonagh held out to me. With a cackle she slipped into Gabriel's embrace, spinning once before dragging me away.

Gabriel's wicked laughter echoed behind me, bronze eyes flashing before he found a new partner and disappeared into the chaos where he belonged.

"Come dance with me!" Oonagh called out, fingers entwining in mine, lifting our arms high above our heads.

The sleeve of her gown had ripped, the sheer fabric as thin as smoke. I could see the white of her skin beneath, the curve of her hips, the swell of her breasts. She may as well have worn nothing at all. Studs of blood-red dotted her ears, all the way up the slender points. She looked like a ghost, beautiful and untouchable.

I danced with her until I could scarcely draw breath. At some point I lost my shoes, but never the goblet in my hand that overflowed with spiced wine no matter how much I drank from it.

Nefina lost herself in the arms of a dark-haired faerie with wings of moonlit gossamer. She danced with abandon, her fair hair wild around her, the skirts of her starlight dress splaying out with every twist and turn. Her eyes were closed, her tears glittering over her cheeks like crystals. She didn't look up. Didn't see me. Didn't wish to see.

Oonagh pressed another glass between my fingers—a tiny, jewelled cup filled with something electric blue. The surrounding faeries raised their matching glasses, shouting a salute before they swallowed it all in one gulp. I followed, slamming the empty glass onto the table a fraction before Oonagh.

It tasted of starshine.

Absently, I lifted my hand to my neck, fingers lingering over the star resting along my breastbone. Oonagh noticed and took my hands once more, allowing me no time to think as she dragged me dancing again.

We swirled to the beating of drums and the melody of strings, our bare feet moving to the music my heart knew too well. Oonagh would not allow me to stop, to rest...to catch my breath. I danced until sweat dripped from me, my hair sticking limp to my flushed cheeks.

Oonagh looked little better, her usually pale face high with colour, her almost silver hair floating as a static web around her. She sunk to the floor, cackling to herself, and I joined her.

Bubbles of laughter slipped with a wonderful ease past my lips. The room continued its chaotic waltz, and I closed my eyes to make it stop for a moment. Only a moment.

A warm hand squeezed mine. "A few more days, Teya."

I sucked in a breath, feeling it heavy in my chest. "I can't believe I'm here drunk and laughing, while he's locked away."

Oonagh rested her head upon my shoulder, her fingers still folded over mine. "Why would you being miserable make it easier for him?" she said. "Tell him tales of home when next you see him. How he is missed, of course, but how in the pits of despair, you managed to keep the light...the hope." She sighed, her words soft, running tighter in a way I had never heard from her before. "Before Laphaniel left...before he went to live in the woods alone, he was always in the middle of all this." She waved a lazy hand towards the circling chaos. "He was my friend, Teya. For many, many years, he was my friend. Even after Luthien got her claws into him, even after the war that ripped our lovely court to pieces. Laphaniel was this wild, wicked creature and he loved so quickly…so deeply—" she paused, shifting so she was looking at me. "He loved Luthien, but those years of stealing away girls to imprison in this castle changed him. He no longer danced, or laughed, or cared. And then he left. I was there when he begged Luthien to go with him—she laughed in his face. I was there when Nefina begged to go with him and he shoved her into the dirt."

My throat ached. "Why are you telling me this?"

"Because when he brought you back to court with him, I saw a glimpse of my dear friend once again, because of you."

I took a breath. "What if I don't get him back, Oonagh?"

"You will—"

"No, you don't know that," I said, voicing a fear that wanted to splinter me from the inside out. "What if he never comes home?"

Oonagh rose in one fluid motion, her hand still clasped in mine, and pulled me to my feet. Her pale silvery eyes burned like hoarfrost. "Then I will lead your armies beside you, and there will be no mercy. No kindness. No respite until the shadows themselves are nothing more than a terrible memory and all else is but ash and bone."

The candlelight died in an instant at her words, plunging the ballroom into an inky darkness touched only by the slivers of moonlight that pierced through the tall windows. The music roared, turning into something so utterly primal it called to every aching need within my body.

I gasped at the sudden shift, noting how the bodies around us had stopped dancing…ceased pretending there was no other ending to the chaos than the frantic joining of bodies.

Fragments of clothes floated to the floor, discarded with no thought, no shame. Someone bumped into us, flittering wings almost tangling with my gown as they fell to the floor. A ragged gasp slipped from their lips, ending in a low sigh as another faerie toppled over them.

I stepped away, lifting my skirts so they wouldn't get caught by grappling claws or frantic wings. With a last smile at my court and untangling my hand from Oonagh, I walked away from the ballroom.

"I will come with you." She pulled away from the young faun whose tan hands were deep beneath my friend's torn corset.

The faun met my gaze, and I heard her heartbeat flutter. She tilted her head but didn't drop her hands.

"Stay, Oonagh," I insisted with a smile. "Have fun."

She grinned back at me with wine-stained teeth, turning to press a wicked kiss against the faun's mouth. Her free hand tangled in her wild curls and dragged her close. She spun with a wild laugh, gripping me tighter as she skipped from the room.

"You should have stayed," I called, skipping behind her, my skirts in one hand, her fingers in the other. "She was beautiful."

"We are all beautiful," Oonagh replied, as if that were answer enough.

I trailed my gaze over the ballroom one last time. "Where the hell is Nefina?"

Oonagh pointed to a dark corner where she sat, alone. She looked up, as if sensing us, lost and sad. She tilted her glass in my direction before downing the contents. With Oonagh's hand in mine, we walked over to Laphaniel's sister and pulled her to her feet. She stared down at my fingers clasped around hers and lifted an eyebrow. She said nothing at all as she swiped a bottle of wine from a table before following us.

We wove through the corridors on unsteady feet, taking it in turns to drink deeply from the glittering honey wine. We stumbled up the winding stairs, into my chambers, the bottle slipping from my fingers to land upon one of the thick rugs. Fizzing gold oozed over the floor. I tried to catch it, but my hands were too slow.

Everything was a little too slow.

I hauled myself onto the bed and flopped back into the pillows with a sigh, Oonagh crashing beside me, her snigger at my ear.

"A few more days," Oonagh breathed. "Then you get to kiss Laphaniel hello from me."

"I may give him more than a kiss."

Her answering laugh was soft and lovely.

"Get up here, Nefina," I said, my words a jumble. "Or do you plan to sleep on the floor?"

She moved with a groan, curling up at the bottom of the bed like a cat. She stretched, pressing her filthy, freezing feet against me.

"Would you move over," she huffed and kicked out.

I kicked her back and she hissed, swatting my legs with the back of her hand.

Then there was silence, a soft quiet broken only by the gentle sounds of deep breathing. I slipped into a sleep unplagued by nightmares or dreams, just a soothing blackness, surrounded by my family.

GABRIEL and I set out to a heavy sky, our cloaks buckled tight against the chill. We left before dawn, the light of the winter-pale suns still slumbering below the hilltops. There was no fanfare, no goodbyes, just the two of us and our horses facing the long road ahead to the Unseelie.

The weather closed in on us, the winter skies flurrying with white. Thin, watery sunlight pooled over the treetops, catching the soft snowfall like grains of salt. We shared a look, both sending up a wordless plea for the weather to hold. To let us through. To show mercy.

But the snow continued to fall hard and without forgiveness. The roads soon lay hidden beneath the onslaught of white. It piled up high around the legs of our mounts, slowing our pace to an agonising crawl. Faerie cared little for mercy.

Four days and nights slipped by, our journey halting too frequently to wait out the snowstorms, to rest our exhausted horses, to huddle close to thaw the chill from our bones.

We were not going to make it for the first day of midwinter.

Gabriel sat with his back against the rock, legs outstretched, gaze to the thick white sky visible from the cave mouth. He had found shelter, demanding we seek refuge from the storm before it claimed us.

He had snatched at my reins, raised voice almost lost to the howl of the wind. A voice of reason sounding out against the tide of emotion spurring me on.

"Pacing the ground will not stop the storm," he said, eyes flicking back to me. "Sit down."

"Is that an order?"

He sighed. "It is a request from a friend."

I didn't sit, but I stopped my pacing to check the horses. Clouds of breath panted from their noses, but they were warm and dry and fed.

"If the storm clears, we will make it before nightfall on the first day of Midwinter." Gabriel's voice was soft in the darkness. I pressed my face against the neck of my horse, breathing in the smell of straw and sweat.

"And if it doesn't clear?"

A pause. "Then it would be wise to turn back, and not ride deeper into the storm wanting to swallow us."

I said nothing.

"I know you won't turn back," Gabriel continued. "And you did not choose me to be by your side because you value my wisdom."

A smile lifted the corners of my lips. "Why did I choose you then if not for your counsel?"

"For my beauty, I have no doubts." His grin was bewitching. "And because I waltz far better than your husband."

I laughed, the sound startling me.

"You're not denying it."

"It has been a while since I danced with him—" My breath caught.

"You seldom laugh like that, Little Red." Gabriel stood, all long legs and graceful body. In two strides he was in front of me, his hands closing over my own.

We danced to the sound of the snowfall. Our steps glided over the rough stone, watched over by the two dozing horses. I spun in Gabriel's arms, my gown and cloak whirling around me in a fan of soft velvet.

We danced until the sun rose above the white clouds, revealing a stretch of perfect blue. The echoes of the storm ebbed out and died.

Gabriel's tired eyes met mine, pointed teeth glinting as he smiled. "I will dance away the storms with you, Little Red, until the time comes when I am no longer the dance partner you seek."

I pressed a kiss to his cheek. "I will always save a dance for you."

"Of course you will, when you are tired of your husband stepping on your toes."

I swatted his arm. "He has never stepped on my toes."

"Oh, my dearest queen, it has been so long that your memory fails you." He held his hands to his chest in mock concern. "Come, let us ride out before more memories dribble from your ears."

He began to pack our things and ready the horses, as eager to start moving as I was. If the storm lay off, we would make it by nightfall. A few hours late, but we would make it.

I needed to make it.

I needed him.

"Gabriel?" He swung onto his horse with ease and turned to me. "Thank you."

He nodded. The thick cloak he wore was fastened tight, the hood already up to shield him from the frigid wind. I pulled mine over my head and gripped the reins of my horse.

"We don't stop until we reach the Unseelie," he said, grim determination replacing the last of the humour in his voice. He snapped his reins and tore back out into the storm blown morning.

"We don't stop." My own voice carried after him. Bold and strong and unwavering. "We don't stop."

CHAPTER SEVEN

NIVEN

*M*idwinter arrived swift and brutal, so deathly cold that the Unseelie King stopped bothering to light the pyres outside the castle. He chose instead to let the bodies freeze, to become carrion for the circling crows.

Niven reclined upon her twisted throne, fur-lined cloak fastened tight around her throat. The fire burned high and hungry, yet the chill crept in still, seeping into her bones. The warmth of summer was an old memory, the long days spent in the castle while Phabian took out his hounds near forgotten.

The baying of dogs had echoed through the forest. So had the screams. A cacophony of noise and fear that only became louder as the light of the twin suns slipped behind the hills.

Midwinter again. Another year.

Niven cupped her goblet in her hands, savouring the warmth, enjoying the heavy dullness the liquor spread through her. Leaning against the cold glass branches of her throne, Niven turned her gaze to the window, at the double sunset that was slowly bleeding over the treetops. The hour was getting late.

"Perhaps my sister has fallen into an icy lake and drowned," she said, inciting a rare smile from Phabian.

"Can you imagine?" he replied with a sneer. "The Seelie without a queen once more."

"It would put a stop to this ridiculous tradition." Niven gestured to the hall, to the swarm of Unseelie just waiting to snap at her sister's ankles.

Phabian rested his head upon steepled fingers. "I do enjoy having her at my mercy though."

"Then you may want to ease off the torment of a certain someone," Niven said, and took another long, slow sip. "Else Teya will have nothing left to visit."

The Unseelie King's laughter rebounded off the black walls, sending the shadows into discord. They swallowed up the candlelight, teased the hungry flames within the grates. The Unseelie lapped it all up, contorting with the frantic dark, bending with it, seduced by it.

"Fear not, my love: he is not so easily broken."

Niven inspected her perfect fingernails, painted a red as dark as old blood. "If you say so."

The monstrous carved doors opened with a screech, and without moving, the Unseelie King called back his shadows. The candles flared to life, flames hissing from their wicks. The swirling mist coiled at his fingertips and flocked to him before transforming into huge hounds that flanked either side of the knotted thrones.

"You are late." Niven's voice carried across the cavernous room. A hush fell, soft and deadly. The Unseelie crept back into the darkness, eyes shining, lips pulled back from their oh, so sharp teeth.

The Seelie Queen, in her tattered white cloak, lifted her chin. Her eyes were like flint. "It took us much longer to journey through your forests. The roads are impassable."

Phabian tilted his head, waiting. Niven fought the delighted smile itching against her mouth at the power he was allowing her. A thrill ran down her body, a caress of Glamour.

Niven's eyes roamed over her sister, taking in the tattered cloak dripping over the floor. She met those bright emerald eyes that still flared with hope and life, and felt nothing.

"That is no excuse."

Her sister dared a step closer, ragged skirts sweeping over the marble. "You knew we would not be able to get through."

"Did I now?"

"My Queen could have perished in your forsaken woods."

Niven turned her head to the golden-haired knight, lifting a brow at the accusation in his voice. He did not shy away from her gaze, meeting it with his own, lips set in a firm line. Oh, she could taste his anger, his revulsion. His fear. She licked her lips, and he looked away.

"Does it not snow in the Seelie Court then?" Niven returned. "It is not my fault you are so woefully unprepared."

Her sister stepped ever closer, waves of red hair swirling around her shoulders and down over the white fur cloak she wore. "Let me see him."

A demand. The entire room stilled.

"No."

"Niven—" Her name hissed through gritted teeth. "*Please.*"

The Unseelie stood lethally calm, savouring every moment. Even Phabian waited, the shadows around him unmoving.

"You are almost a day late," she began. "We were all waiting for you, and you arrive here filthy and with poor excuses. It is poor manners, Teya, ill-fitting a Queen of Faerie." She paused to drink, the wine sweet where her words were not. "Let this be a lesson to you. Return home and be on time next year."

"Don't do this."

Niven stood, stepping from dais. Her gown of midnight blue spilled around her legs, made of woven nightmares and winter dew.

"Beg."

She heard the sharp intake of breath. "What?"

"Beg, little sister."

With a triumphant smirk, Niven watched the Seelie Queen sink to her knees, her spoilt gown swamping around her like melting snow.

Her knight stood by, eyes wide, hissing something inaudible as she bowed her head.

The Seelie Queen's voice faltered, fear coating her words. Not fear for herself, but of the creature holed up so very far underground. "Please, Niven."

Niven took another step so her heeled slippers brushed the outstretched hands of her sister. She contemplated stamping on them.

"We did not think you were coming." Niven smiled, once again catching the eye of the golden-eyed faerie. He glowered back at her, tips of his pointed teeth flashing. "Your husband—" she spat the word, "thought you were not coming. It really is a pity, but I don't think he will be in any state to enjoy your delightful company."

The Seelie Queen rose to her feet. "What have you done to him?"

"Whatever I wanted to."

"Why?" A desperate plea.

Niven scowled, disappointed she wouldn't be getting the fight she had been burning for. She lifted a shoulder, bored with the dramatics. "Go clean him up, little sister."

She was unmoved by the tears that trailed over the other Queen's cheeks, feeling nothing but a brief wondering that, perhaps...she should have felt something. Anything.

"I will give you everything I have, Niven," the Seelie Queen breathed as she snatched at her hand.

"I have all I want," Niven hissed, pulling away.

Her sister tore from the room to the manic screeches of the Unseelie Court, muddied skirts flying behind her. Claws raked at her as she fled, teeth snapped at her feet and a few followed her beyond the carved doors, screeching into the darkness.

Niven left the hall soon after, Phabian's deep, approving chuckle echoing behind her. She sought a moment of solace lost within the winding pathways of the Garden of Thorns, a sprawling maze of twisting brambles. It was a place to lose yourself, all curving smooth paths and grotesque statues that watched from the shadows. The thorns were deadly sharp too, one prick, one drop of spilled blood, and the maze would never forget you.

Snow coated her shoes, soaked against her legs as she breathed the icy air deep into her lungs. She pulled a cigarette from thin air and lit it with a flick of her fingers. She breathed in that smoke too.

Within the centre of the maze stood a stone platform. A strange, almost out of place veranda crawling with vines and blooms of ink-drop black. At the very top, Niven could see as far as the mountains in the deep north, their peaks jutting up to slice the skies. From where she stood, the world seemed to go on forever, a vast wilderness of wicked, cunning creatures.

None of them quite as wicked and cunning as she.

"Standing here, one could mistake your demeanour as remorseful, though I doubt you have the capacity for it."

Niven spun with a hiss on her lips, barely concealing the shock of being caught unaware. Shadows instantly formed at her fingertips, and the golden-haired knight took a wise step back.

"I could order the flesh peeled from your bones, and not a soul would question it."

His lip curled. "Did I startle you, your Majesty?"

"If you had, my hounds would have torn you apart."

The Seelie knight lifted a finger to one of the needle-sharp thorns, not quite touching it. His eyes flicked to her roving shadows.

"Can you transform them into anything, or does it have to be mongrels?"

"Do they remind you of your King?" she sneered, noting the way his amber eyes darkened to pitch.

"Do you also speak of your own?"

"How dare you." Niven allowed the anger to seep into her voice, twisting it into something her fey cowered at. The knight simply glowered back, anger radiating from him. The Glamour surrounding him turned as black as his eyes.

"I came out here for some fresh air, to escape your cackling demons," he said, giving her a curt bow. "I'll leave you to your thoughts, your Majesty."

He turned to leave, but he had piqued her curiosity. No one in her Court ever dared speak to her like that, and it amused her. Of course,

Niven could always count on Laphaniel to bite at her, to push and fight back, but the poor love had managed to bribe someone for a casket of mud-whiskey—and wouldn't be speaking to anyone for a long, long while.

"Wait." A command. The knight stilled. "I find you interesting. Come, join me for a drink."

The Seelie faerie hesitated, glancing back at the winding path that had brought him to her. Niven followed his gaze, taking in the nightmare that was her Unseelie home. The shining obsidian walls of the castle were not so far away. It sucked in the moonlight, swallowing it, drawing it in like a void. The spiralling towers stretched up and up and up, like sword tips. No light burned from the windows; the glass was as dark as the walls.

"Your Queen will be busy attending her lover." Niven smirked, materialising a goblet of wine from the shadows cavorting around her. She had never seen someone in such a mess, she almost pitied her sister. "Come, sit."

Niven sat upon the low stone wall, mindful of the thorns, mindful of the ivy that began to creep around her legs. The wind snatched at her hair and rippled through her gown. With a black-gloved hand, she tapped the space beside her.

The Seelie knight obliged her, possibly only because he had nowhere else to go. She wondered if he deemed her less dangerous than the faeries haunting her corridors.

No. He didn't look that foolish.

"Does the Seelie suffer without its King?" Niven asked, bringing the goblet to her lips. Another cup appeared from the whirling black, and she offered it to him. He sniffed it before taking a tentative sip.

"I wouldn't have thought you would stoop to spying."

"My shadows are everywhere."

"I have no doubts," he answered, taking another, deeper drink. "Our court is faring as well as can be expected with a new ruler. You underestimate your sister, Niven."

She lifted her head at the sound of her name on his lips, at the stark, undeserved familiarity of it. It should have infuriated her; even her shadows coiled in anticipation of her biting rage.

But…

She was impressed.

"You spit my name out, but I don't know yours," she said, willing her shadows to calm. "What is your name, knight?"

"Gabriel."

"Angelic."

He tilted his head, eyes aflame. "Your sister said the exact same thing when first we met. Perhaps you are more alike than you would have thought."

"Do you really believe that?"

Gabriel stared at her for a long while, draining the last of his wine. "I think you are a poison, Queen of Unseelie, to which there is no respite, no cure. Only death."

He placed the goblet down beside her and stood. Without another word he turned on his heel and walked towards the darkness of the castle.

Niven stared after him, refilling her cup to the brim before draining it. She expected fury to flood her, to bring out the desire to destroy something…someone…anything.

Something else stirred in her gut that was not rage, or hate, or spite.

And she did not like it.

CHAPTER EIGHT

TEYA

*T*he memory played like a broken recording, an echo of pain and hopelessness.

"I'm sorry..." His words had been slurred, falling thickly from his mouth. *"They said you weren't coming...I'm sorry...I'm sorry..."*

I squeezed my eyes shut at the memory, forced away the tears pressing against my eyes. After all, frozen tears were worthless in winter.

We journeyed home in near silence. The cold bit through the layers of furs we wore with a viciousness I had never encountered. The horses struggled on, breath freezing in front of them to form icicles that hung from their mouths like fangs.

I would never forgive Niven for leaving Laphaniel in the state I found him. My fury pulsed through my entire body with so much force, I could hardly breathe around it. With a scream, I lashed out at the air, tearing up trees from their roots before I hurtled them across the barren, hateful land.

"Teya." My name was a warning on Gabriel's lips, the single word shuddering past his frozen mouth. "Don't waste your energy."

I would never forget the sight of Laphaniel in that filthy hovel. Never forget having to prop him up so he could vomit into a bucket and not over himself. The empty bottles lay around him, the vile liquid splattered over his shirt, over the damp straw, and into the bucket as I shoved his hair back.

He had barely known I was there, not lucid enough to speak before finally…mercifully, passing out. I had cradled his head in my lap and sobbed.

I had left before he woke.

Dragged away by Raven Knights I did not recognise.

Above us, the indigo skies crackled, loosening heaps of snow that rested upon the naked boughs so it thumped to the ground. Thunder rolled; my Glamour roared back.

"Stop it."

I drew in a stinging breath. "We need to get out of this damned cold before nightfall."

"As soon as we are home, we can meet with the witches," Gabriel offered, placing a gloved hand upon my shoulder. The storm raging within me calmed. "I will make the arrangements the moment we are in Seelie."

I squeezed his hand and scanned the snow-covered land for any signs of shelter. I didn't let go of his hand. "You know you'll have to stay behind, don't you? I can't take you."

He nodded, the hood of his cloak slipping. "I know, Little Red. As handsome and charming as I may be, the witches do prefer the company of females."

"You forgot modest," I said with a small smile.

He gave me a wink. "We both know that word could not pass my lips."

We were lucky to stumble over a shallow cave just as dusk began to settle, painting the strange Unseelie sky with mottled purples and deep blue. The setting suns set the horizon alight and transformed the moody sky, for a few moments, into a breathtaking canvas.

Lighting a fire proved near impossible with the damp and rotten wood we had salvaged. My fingers were too raw, Gabriel's were too raw. The best we managed was a few pathetic embers that coughed up great clouds of smoke.

Working together in comfortable silence, we rolled out the furs we had onto the hard ground. I hadn't realised how exhausted I was until my head hit my makeshift pillow. The weight of blankets kept some of the chill at bay, but I still trembled. Sleep dragged me under before I could ask Gabriel if he would take first watch. It was a heavy sleep, a thick cloak of darkness that held no promises of a restful night.

Nightmares came swift and cruel. Relentless. Flashes of sun-soaked glades sprung up from some distant memory, taunting me. Music played. Laughter sounded before breaking off into screams.

Then...spoken upon a whisper were the few soft words that haunted me, echoing over and over and over again.

Stay with me,
Stay with me,
Stay with me,
Stay...

No matter how hard I tried, the single word I wanted to scream back at him died at my lips, twisting into the same refusal I now regretted with every bit of my soul.

Dust and bone and spiderwebs. Nothing else remained.

I WOKE WITH A GASP, instinctively reaching for the comfort that should have been beside me. My fingers curled at the empty space. Gabriel watched from the entrance, face pale and exhausted, a mirror to my own.

"Get some rest," I said, rubbing a hand across my face. "I'll take over."

He didn't protest but staggered over to his bundle of furs and lay down. It looked like sleep gobbled him up before his head touched his pillow. With care, I pulled more blankets over him, making sure he was warm enough. Snoring sharply, he hauled them over his head. I rolled my eyes at the sound and went to keep watch.

Nothing moved outside. Nothing screamed or bayed or howled. The trees kept their secrets to themselves and the wind stopped singing. The only sounds came from the lump of furs by the fire. Gabriel's snores set my teeth on edge and I had to fight the urge not to kick him.

I hadn't asked him how he fared at the Unseelie, if he dared wander the halls or stayed within the room he was given. Knowing Gabriel, I guessed he managed some sort of mischief: he couldn't help himself.

He shifted on the ground, furs slipping from his head. The meagre firelight danced over the gold of his hair and caught the tips of his horns, just visible beneath his wild curls. He snored again and I winced.

The deep rumbling sounds coming from Gabriel were so different from the soft, occasional snores Laphaniel made while he slept. Gabriel also didn't talk in his sleep, whereas Laphaniel always mumbled incoherently in my ear while he slumbered against me, babbling away as he dreamed.

It was a little comfort that the few nights I shared with Gabriel were not silent. I could no longer fall asleep to the sound of nothing.

The sudden tang of frost and blood coated my tongue, over-whelming my senses. I saw nothing lurking in the shadows, but I didn't hesitate in dousing the fire.

Gabriel was awake and alert the moment I tensed, snatching up the sword that never left his side. I pulled a knife from our supplies and kept it close.

A low hiss escaped Gabriel's lips, revealing sharp incisors. Nothing remained of the carefree faerie with the wicked laugh. His copper eyes flashed red in the moonlight before giving way to a bottomless black.

"Stay here." The word was a snarl, an unveiled command as he pushed past me and into the night.

I called upon my Glamour, weaving it into tangible threads. I allowed it to feed off the torrent of emotions flooding through me. It caught hold on a flash of fear, igniting so it pulsed at my fingertips, ready.

Gabriel lifted a hand for me to stop. We both listened, seeing nothing in the night. The smell was still there, though, sharp like death.

"What is it?" I mouthed the words, searching the shadows for any signs of danger.

"I'm not sure," he whispered. "Perhaps it is something simply passing through—"

It lunged without warning from the still, bated darkness. In one swift blow, it took Gabriel down. His head struck rock, the sound of bone crunching echoed against the night. Blood bloomed instantly in deep streaks across his chest, splattering the virgin snow.

I screamed his name. The beast looked up, towering above me. Blood splattered its snow-white fur. A Nanok: a creature of winter, of frozen hearts and brittle deaths.

It took a step closer, massive paws barely making a footprint in the soft snow. Up it stood, stretching high onto its powerful back legs, twisted horns reaching for the snow clouds above. Its maw opened, revealing teeth longer than my forearm.

I struck out with my hand, Glamour surging up to pound against its thick hide. I sent wave after wave crashing down upon it, until even the skies screamed back.

It didn't flinch.

The Nanok lunged at me, and I jumped back. Claws raked a breath away from my face, shattering a nearby tree instead. I rolled, slicing deep into the beast's belly with my knife. It roared in anger and pain, twisting around with unnatural grace before slamming me with its colossal paw. It tore me from my feet. My Glamour sputtered and died at my hands.

My vision wavered as I struggled to get to my feet. My head felt like it would explode; warmth slipped down my cheek, sticky and red.

The Nanok charged again, horns slamming into my head. Stars burst before my eyes, darkness wavering at the edges of my vision. Claws and teeth shredded my thick clothing and tore at the skin beneath. I gasped at the sudden hotness, fighting to drag back the Glamour that ebbed at my fingertips. I was too tired...

Too cold...

So cold.

The beast howled as Gabriel leapt onto its back and plunged his sword deep into its hide. It bucked, snapping its jaws with a twist of its head, and sunk its teeth into Gabriel's shoulder. It tore through skin, muscle...bone. Crimson sprayed. Gabriel began screaming.

I willed my Glamour back, begged for it. I shoved through the numbness that slowly flooded my body and fought to reach it. Weak wisps trickled over my fingers, nothing more than whispers. An echo.

With a gasp, I urged it forward, searching...fumbling for the chill feel of Gabriel's sword still embedded in the beast. I tightened my grip, Glamour curling around the hilt. My head spun. The sounds falling from my mouth, wet and bloody. I shoved down hard, Glamour slipping. Something cracked, and the Nanok stilled.

It fell to the stained ground with a thump, maw stretched wide. Fragments of Gabriel's clothing clung to its dripping fangs.

Gabriel crawled to me, leaving behind a streak of red. "Can you get up?"

His voice sounded so far away. I closed my eyes to relieve the heaviness in my head, breathing out a rasping sigh. He was alive.

"Stay awake," he hissed. I forced my eyes open, pain splintered through my skull.

"I'm so cold," I murmured. Sleep began to settle over me like a blanket. Warm and final.

"Get up!" Slick, red hands shook me. "This is not where we die, Teya...not here. Get up...please...get—"

He slumped to the floor like someone had cut his strings. He didn't move again. I tried to reach for him, but my limbs refused to obey. I called his name, the word barely making it past my lips before darkness smothered me.

Blackness.

Never

Ending

Black.

A voice slipped through the dark, soft and gentle and lovely. It whispered my name over and over again. A cold hand pressed against my face, stroking back my hair. I tried to open my eyes, tried to move, but I was told to stay still…to sleep.

Blackness dragged me down.

Down,

down,

down…

A GENTLE ROCKING pulled me back, the movement jarring my wounds and sending shocks of pain through my body. It ripped at me until I longed to slip back into nothing.

I was on a sled; my foggy brain could understand that much. Furs bound me tight, keeping most of the chill away, but I was still so cold. With gritted teeth I attempted to lift my head and failed.

Gabriel lay beside me, deathly pale and unresponsive. His lips were blue, the furs wrapped around him soaked red. I barely managed to curl my fingers around his before I lost my brittle grip on consciousness.

Sleep sucked me down swiftly, deep and unforgiving. It plunged me into a swirl of nightmares I could not claw my way out of.

From somewhere far, far away, I heard the cawing of crows.

CHAPTER NINE

TEYA

rantic voices pierced the heavy fog swirling in my head. It dragged me up and away from the black, even though I wasn't ready to wake. I prised my eyes open and blinked in the dim light, awakening upon a bed of matted furs. Everything reeked of damp.

"Quick, girl!" hissed a voice in the darkness.

"Is he breathing?" another voice replied, the same soft and gentle voice that had whispered over me as I lay bleeding.

"Not at the moment. Haste, child."

I shoved the rotting furs off me and stood, my legs shaking. I gripped a rotting branch for support, the bough curling down from the earthen ceiling. My head ached and my vision swam. There were bandages wrapped around my wounds, packed with what looked like moss. My surroundings were familiar, I knew where I was.

A black form hovered over the still body of Gabriel. Inky black feathers shook while clawed hands shoved down upon his chest.

Again,

and again,

and again.

A smaller figure leant over him, dirty blonde hair tied back in a messy knot. She placed her mouth over Gabriel's and blew. Once, twice, three times...

Nothing.

Twice more and she pressed a finger to his neck.

"There is nothing, mistress," the little girl whispered, breathing ragged. She wiped a quick hand over her face, streaking it with red. The four fingers on her left hand were nothing but scarred stumps.

Alice. The child Laphaniel and I had rescued from a harpies' nest. It had been too late for her brother, and she was too sick and weak for us to bring her home. So, we had left her in the care of an Unseelie tree spirit—the Scara, who was trying desperately to get Gabriel's heart pumping again.

"Please don't stop," I begged, my grip tightening on the branch to stop myself from falling. "Please."

The Scara turned her head to me and clicked her long black beak. "There will be nothing left to bring back soon."

Her hands never left Gabriel's chest, and with a high screech she began to press down again. Beneath her claws, something snapped. She did not stop.

Neither did Alice, who leant over and breathed for him. She touched his neck and her eyes met mine. "A pulse."

I sank to the floor.

"It is weak, but we got him back."

I could barely breathe. "Thank you."

"Well done, my little darling," the Scara murmured, wiping the blood from Alice's face with an ebony talon. The beam on the girl's face made something deep within my chest ache. The Unseelie spirit had kept her promise.

"Will he live?" I asked, not yet trusting my legs to hold me.

"The Nanok got him good," the Scara explained. "He has lost a lot of blood, Queen of Seelie—death still may call for him, and I do not believe he is strong enough to resist."

I didn't take my eyes away from Gabriel, or from the flash of white bone exposed along his chest. "What is your price for saving him?"

The Scara cocked her head, the long ebony feathers rippled over her shoulders. Black eyes stared unblinking at me, lighting up with a touch of amusement. "I am sure we can come to an agreement."

I forced myself to stand. "I have no little girls to give you this time."

The Scara huffed a laugh and turned back towards Gabriel.

"Where is your friend?" Alice asked, earning a reproachful look from her mistress. She ignored it without a hint of fear. "He was really sick too, wasn't he? When you brought me here? Mistress said the rotten blood in his veins likely killed him."

I sucked in a breath. "You knew Laphaniel was dying and you let us leave here? I nearly lost him."

The Scara lifted a shoulder, feathers rustling. "I did not have enough herbs to save the child and your pretty lover." She met my furious gaze. "I made a choice I could live with."

"You are the Queen of Seelie now, aren't you?" Alice began again, dark eyes wide with a child-like wonder. "Is he at your castle? Did you get married? That's so romantic. Is that your wedding ring? It's so pretty!"

"Child!" the Scara snapped, clicking her beak. "To work with you, now. Send the crows for more herbs, stoke up the fire and attend to the knight's wounds. Pull the skin taut and pack it good, I wish to see neat stitches."

Alice bowed her head, though her smile remained. "Yes, mistress."

"How does the King of Seelie fare?" the Scara asked. She threw Alice a warning glance as she hovered nearby.

"You know where he is, I am guessing?"

A nod. "I keep my distance from that cursed place, but my crows tell me everything."

"Do they tell you he suffers?"

She kept my gaze, unblinking. "Yes."

"Then you know as much as I do," I said.

She turned her raven head, beak clacking as she gazed over the body lying beneath the mouldering covers. Alice sat beside him, cleaning the gaping wound at his neck before setting aside the bundles of tools she needed to stitch him back up.

Red soaked the little girl. There was so much red. It dripped onto the floor, the dark earth swallowing it up.

"If your knight lives, his recovery will not be swift," the Scara said. "I have meagre supplies and that blow nearly took his head off."

"I could get you more—"

She laughed, a sharp caw echoed by the crows outside her desolate home. "Not a soul in these lands would serve you, Queen of Seelie."

"Then what do I do?"

"You leave him here." Her black eyes glinted in the miserable candlelight.

"No."

The Scara smoothed the ragged folds of her ebony gown, the ruined silk clinging to the soft curves of her body. "Are you to wait here for him to wake? If he is to ever wake again." She smiled a very Unseelie smile. "Or do you journey north, Queen of Seelie, to my sisters in the mountains?"

I froze, and her terrible smile widened.

"My crows tell me everything."

My breath caught. "Does my sister know?"

She shook her head, feathers shifting across her bare shoulders. "Secrets amongst witches remain a secret."

My head throbbed, my limbs still heavy. I wanted to sit, but there was only the bed where Gabriel lay and a stool that was occupied by Alice. No light filtered in through the cracks in the wooden walls; the old tree that housed the Scara and her ward was cold and dark and awful.

"Laphaniel once told me you were a tree spirit," I said, leaning against the rough wall.

"Did he now?" She paused, tilting her head to Alice. "Tighter, child, else everything will fall out again."

"You're a witch?" I asked.

"Can I not be both?"

"Then where do your loyalties lie?"

"To Faerie," the Scara breathed.

Talk of witches brought back memories of Arabelle. Of the chilling visions she foretold after Laphaniel and I had sought her out to gain passage to the Unseelie lands.

"Do you hear whispers of a war?"

The Scara ruffled her feathers, glancing towards the crows gathering around her dwelling. "I only get the murmurings of things close to pass."

"And?" I pressed.

"I cannot sense a war," she began. "But there is a restlessness to the wind. Something is coming, Queen of Seelie."

I swallowed. "Coming for who?"

The Scara lifted a talon tipped hand. "All of us."

"Meaning what?" I said, so very tired of the vague warnings of witches.

"This witch," the Scara said, ignoring my question, "what did she demand of you, what price did she ask for the boon she bestowed on you?"

"Arabelle didn't demand a price," I answered, unable to conceal my shudder at the memory of the witch clutching Laphaniel's hand, foaming at the mouth as she saw visions she refused to reveal to us. "She only asked for mercy when the time comes."

The Scara turned her head, body remaining still as she slowly looked to me. Alice stilled over Gabriel, glancing up too.

"You have found yourself tied up in something far bigger than you know, little Queen."

Dread curdled in my stomach. "But you don't know what?"

"The crows do not know, so I do not know," was all she would say.

She moved to assist Alice, grinding foul smelling herbs into powders, adding drops of sticky black liquid to make a sort of paste. Gabriel didn't move as she smeared it over his chest, over his bruises, his lips. He was breathing. He was breathing, at least.

My wounds were healing slowly. Warmth seeped back into my bones and my legs no longer shook. The threads of Glamour flew over my skin, healing me. I splayed out my hand, trying to see the strands of magic upon my skin so I could, for just a moment, feel closer to Laphaniel.

"You will find your horse safe and well outside, Queen of Seelie," the Scara said without looking up. "Best you leave before dark."

I hovered over Gabriel. Guilt gnawed at my stomach at the thought of leaving him behind. Black stitches trailed over his neck, down his stomach, beneath the rough blanket covering him. Some of the blood had been wiped away, but he was still covered in it, the skin underneath, pale. He breathed so slowly, staggered breaths escaping his lips in wet rasps.

"I have to go," I whispered, catching Alice's eye as she watched me from the stool beside the bed. Tears slipped over my cheeks. "I'm so sorry."

His hand moved, fingers curling weakly around mine. "Don't..." he gasped the word. An agonised sound.

More tears fell, a sob slipped over my lips. "Gabriel—"

"No." He forced his eyes open, steadying himself against the moss-covered bed. "I—"

"Don't sit up!" Alice snapped, pressing a hand to his unbandaged shoulder. "You stupid creature."

Gabriel gritted his teeth, incisors glinting despite the gloom. Sweat beaded at his temple, his eyes unfocused. I wondered what Alice had given him.

"Don't," he breathed, the words thick. "Don't go shouting your mouth off. I know you...you do not always think. The witches...will bow to no one, Little Red. Not to you...not...not to anyone, understand?"

"I understand," I replied, then turned to the Scara. "I want your word you will send for me when he is well enough to travel home."

She steepled her fingers, talons tapping against each other while she contemplated me. "I will send word, Queen of Seelie, along with my price."

It was the best I could hope for, no matter how I hated not knowing what she would ask of me when the time came. Everything came with a price in Faerie.

"Lie back down," Alice ordered, guiding Gabriel's head onto the pillow with a firm hand. He blinked up at her.

"You are a child."

Black swallowed up the soft brown of Alice's eyes. "I am the apprentice of the Scara, spirit of the Undying and Keeper of Crows. You will do as I say, or I shall feed you to my birds."

I whirled to the Scara in shock. The Unseelie faerie met my stare and grinned.

"I love her, Queen of Seelie," she sang. "With every part of my blackened soul, I love her."

A sense of unease settled over me at the obvious loss of a childhood that was no longer in reach for Alice. We had given her to the shadows, Laphaniel and I, and it mattered not that we had no choice. It was still on us.

I would never forget her screams when we left her behind, or the way she had clung to Laphaniel while I prised her off him and shoved her into the arms of the Scara.

Alice looked up from Gabriel, as if reading my thoughts, eyes once again a human brown. "You saved my life," she said with a lovely smile. "One day I will repay that debt."

"There is nothing to pay," I replied, bending low to kiss Gabriel's brow. "Just look after him."

She nodded, eyes focused on a stone bowl in her lap where she ground up purple flowers into a fine dust.

"Say goodbye to your friend, Teya." Alice tipped the fine herbs into a cup of steaming water. "Your friend needs to sleep."

"I'll see you again soon," I whispered, giving Gabriel's hand a squeeze. "Try to behave yourself."

"Same to you..." he rasped, sipping the muddy brew Alice held to his lips without question. "Bring him home."

I waited until he had finished, dribbles of murky water slipping from his mouth. He slumped back with a soft moan, eyes fluttering closed. Alice shifted in her chair, and with her good hand she took

Gabriel's arm and placed it upon her lap, two fingers resting over his pulse.

"My crows will find you if he dies," the Scara said as a farewell. "I suppose you would have him buried?"

The Unseelie burned their dead. I stared at the bed of damp leaves and moss, at my friend lying unmoving beneath a moth eaten fur. "Not in Unseelie soil. I would have him brought home."

The Scara tilted her head, a mocking caw slipped from her beak. "You do not want two of your own rotting away here?"

I refused to bite, though a retort clamoured up my throat. "Thank you for looking after Alice."

"Thank you for bringing her to me, Queen of Seelie."

With a curt nod, I secured my cloak tight around my shoulders and ventured back out into the unforgiving cold. I mounted my horse and slapped the reins hard, leaving my friend behind as I tore through the Unseelie lands and made my way home.

CHAPTER TEN

NIVEN

From the shadows, the Unseelie Queen watched her sister ride away, hidden beneath the long limbs of whispering trees. They had sung her the tale of the Nanok's attack, spinning their story upon the sounds of dying leaves. Their voices had carried on the winds, seeking her out.

And, ever curious, the Queen of Shadows went looking.

She had left Phabian slumbering beneath silken sheets; even his shadows rested. Quieted. She had to wonder why men couldn't handle their drink. Niven was restless, agitated. Her own shadows coiled in manic swirls around her, ensuring any inquisitive faeries scurried back into the darkness.

Niven knew of the unrest within her sister's court, the rebels banding against her, numbers unknown. She was not naïve to believe her own court was not as fragile. It would not take much to fracture it completely.

Rage and madness could only fuel a reign for so long before it burnt itself out. Faerie was splintering—she could sense it within the darkness, in the shadows, in the whispers on the wind. The shards would likely destroy them all.

When the echoes of Teya's horse had faded away, Niven stepped from the shadows, head tilted, listening. In the surrounding trees, the crows began to cry out, silencing only when she held a slender finger to her lips.

She stopped before the gnarled old tree where the old tree spirit dwelled. Treacle-like ooze seeped from the decaying trunk, staining the earth around it. Masses of thorned fungi sprouted from the mess, the grey, fat bodies nourished by the gunk. Smoke curled up and up through a gap in the wood, black and sooty.

Sending out a tendril of dark mist into the rotten oak, Niven sought out the heartbeats within it. She counted three. Two sang strong and steady...the other...well, it thumped, at least.

It took a moment for Niven to recognise the feeling in her chest. Relief.

A peculiar feeling.

With another thread, she willed the two strong hearts to slow, to sleep so she could slip into the dank, cold hovel unnoticed. The silks of her gown were ruined instantly, the edges heavy with the oily goo coating the ground. She didn't overly care for the dress but knew she would have to change before Phabian awoke.

She had no excuses for seeking out the crow witch.

The rotten door creaked as she entered, and Niven ducked low to avoid the dripping roots overhead. She barely glanced at the Scara who slept upon a bed of moss with a filthy looking brat in her arms. Neither stirred.

Niven passed them to stand at the foot of a crude looking bed, wrinkling her nose at the damp smell of the blankets, at the foulness that crept over the faerie slumbering beneath them.

Slowly, she lifted the covers back, an eyebrow rising at the impressive wounds marring his skin.

It looked as though they had stitched his head back on before closing the gaping hole down his chest. Niven wondered if they had to poke his guts back in. Niven looked again; they most likely had.

Blood painted his skin, black bruises snaked over his body like a tattoo.

"I must be dying…if you are haunting my nightmares."

She blinked, the only sign of unease she would show, noting how it was the second time he had taken her by surprise.

"Does it hurt much?" Niven asked, more out of curiosity than concern. Sweat beaded over his skin, dripping down into his strange bronze eyes. He nodded and gasped as the movement pulled his stitches.

"Teya is gone," he gritted out, eyes closing.

"Oh, I saw." Niven watched the staggered rise and fall of his chest, half expecting it to cease all together. "Where could she possibly be going in such a rush?"

"Ah," he murmured. "Is that…is that why you are here? I will tell you nothing, Queen of Demons."

"You Seelie bastards are all rather unhelpful, aren't you?"

The knight writhed on his bed, kicking off the sweat soaked furs. He moaned, low and pained.

"Stop wriggling, you fool!" Niven snapped. "You'll split yourself open."

His hand found hers, slick and hot. His fingernails dug into her skin. "Help me…"

"Let go," she hissed, ready to prise him from her hand. He gripped her tighter.

"Help me."

"Stop!"

"Niven…please…"

"Hush." She wanted to get away, it had been a mistake to come.

The knight was panting, eyes glazed. "It hurts…I can't…"

"What do you expect me to do?"

"Make it stop."

Her eyes widened at what he was suggesting. She could hear his heart beating, fighting. It would be too easy to stop it, would take little more than a thought.

Instead, she picked up the cup beside his head and lifted it to her nose. Her head swam with the heady scent of the herbs swirling within. Nightshade, feverfew, perhaps a dash of Wintersbreath, but not enough. A rare herb and expensive, the Scara wouldn't waste such a herb on a Seelie knight. The tonic was good though, and if his heart didn't give out, he had a chance.

A slim one, but a chance nonetheless.

"Drink this."

Niven tilted his head up and placed the cup to his lips. Her own curled as he dribbled most of it down himself. She forced him to drink it all, her hand gripping his damp curls. He sighed, breath hitching before he went limp against her. His eyes rolled back, the grip on her hand went slack.

Niven lingered a moment, sweeping a curl from his forehead. "What a wasteful way to die, Seelie knight."

NIVEN RODE HOME WITHOUT SADDLE, without reins or stirrups, nothing but her and the beast she sat upon. Its black mane whipped back in a wild tangle, foam dripped from its mouth as she urged it on and on and on. Ghostly hounds charged at her sides, their howls baying across the twilight forest.

Arriving at the castle, she tossed the reins at a stable boy. She didn't grace him with her attention before weaving her way through the labyrinthine hallways of her home. Her muddied shoes echoed sharply on the black marble, her cloak sighed behind her.

With wide fingers, she trailed her hands over the glass on the walls and followed the orbs captured within. With a painted nail, she tapped the mirror and the souls darted away, their iridescent lights dimming.

There were hundreds trapped inside, maybe thousands. Some were bought and bargained for, others taken as payment. There were some that lingered in the shadows, black and twisted and old, that had been gleaned by force.

Niven entered the great hall to the sound of manic laughter and music, but it all fell silent the moment she walked in. The dogs at her side drifted away, consumed by the shadows surging up the walls.

The Unseelie dropped to their knees, eyes cast down. The shadows cavorting over the walls crept closer, wrapping around her legs like cats.

"I was beginning to think you had lost your way in the woods," Phabian drawled from his throne. He picked at the food before him, tearing a chunk of bloodied meat from a bone before placing it to his lips. "I do trust you had a good ride."

She hadn't changed. Niven straightened her back.

"It was exhilarating," she answered, taking the throne beside him. The surrounding fey did not rise until she was seated. She cast an eye over the Unseelie King, no traces of the intoxicated, sated creature remained. "You could almost make me believe you were worried."

Phabian smiled, showing teeth. "The darkness favours you, my dear."

"Indeed." Niven returned the smile and nodded down at his full plate. "I see you started without me."

She grabbed an apple, taking a bite into the firm, red skin. The King's eyes followed the juice that ran over her lip.

"I was ravenous, my love," he murmured, leaning close to take her lip between his teeth. "I still am."

Swirls of shadows danced in his eyes. Niven leant closer and whispered, "Surprising, given how much you drank this morning."

"If I bent you over this table," Phabian began so only she could hear, "what would you do?"

Her heart quickened. "Try it and find out."

Phabian grinned and leant back, having heard the skipping beat. No doubt he could scent the tang of unease on her skin.

The Unseelie resumed their feast, unknowing and uncaring at the exchange between their king and queen.

"There are those in my court that conspire against me." Phabian took a sip of his dark wine. "What more do they want of me?"

Niven picked at the selection of rich meats in front of her, popping a piece of rare venison into her mouth. She chewed and swallowed before answering. "Maybe you could kill less of them, my love."

Phabian's booming laugh echoed around the hall. The feasting faeries looked up, wary. Many cowered into the shadows. "Do you think that would work?"

There was madness in his eyes. Niven could see little else. "Do you?"

"No." He gave a slow smile. "I want the ground itself to run red with the blood of traitors. For the crows to feast upon ungrateful flesh. I want them to scream."

"Who?"

"All of them."

The twisted, cruel creature sitting beside her was all that was left of Phabian, anything else he once was…long gone.

Niven doubted it had ever been love between them, more a shared need for power, and for her, at least, vengeance and spite. Phabian never once looked at her like Laphaniel did Teya, as if he would burn worlds for her. As if there was nothing he would not give up for her.

Their relationship was a hollow thing, slowly filling up with twisted games and darkness and madness. It had happened without her realising, the cruelty toward her, and she had been wholly unprepared for it.

"You will have nothing left, my love," Niven said, plucking a fat grape from its stem. It burst between her teeth, its juice sweet.

"Oh, I will still have you."

With a tight smile, Niven lifted her glass of wine and drained it. "Indeed you shall."

"Go change, my sweet," he said, flicking pieces of mud from the silk of her gown. "I will not have you beside me looking like a pig."

The Unseelie paused; none dared to breathe.

Niven lifted her chin. "Would you have me strip here?"

The shadows stilled.

"I think that would be unnecessary." Phabian turned away from her. "Go make yourself decent."

Niven rose, inclining her head towards the Unseelie King. All eyes followed her as she glided from the room. Not a soul made a sound.

Shame tingled at the base of her spine, hateful and poisonous. Threads of glittering dark wove over her hands. With the slightest gesture, the ruined silk vanished, replaced with a sheer gown made from mist and nightmares.

She could have gone back to Phabian, but she was angry, and anger always made her so very petty.

Down she went instead. Down and down and down, until the darkness thickened and became suffocating. The walls grew damp and slick, the steps wet with moss.

Niven stopped at the thick wooden door, fingers lingering at the lock. She wanted to hurt something...someone. With a roll of her shoulders, she dampened some of the rage that flooded her body. Some of the hurt and shame, until only a few flickering embers remained. With a nasty smile, she flicked the lock.

And recoiled.

"My Gods, you look wretched." She stepped into the woeful little cell, nose wrinkling. "You smell worse."

"Kindly fuck off, Niven."

Laphaniel shifted upon the filthy straw, pale and miserable. He took a breath and swallowed quickly.

Niven stepped back. "Are you going to be sick?"

He shook his head, but Niven waited a moment before moving closer.

"Teya had to be dragged from here," she said, leaning against the cold wall. "Kicking and screaming like a banshee. She had vomit on her dress."

He winced.

Niven picked up one of the empty bottles he had drained and sniffed it. She fought not to gag. "How on earth are you not dead?"

"What do you want?"

She smashed the bottle against the wall. Remains of thick, brown sludge trailed over the stone, leaving an oily stain behind. Niven picked her nails with a jagged piece of glass.

"Your beloved wife was attacked by a Nanok earlier today," Niven began. "Your knight, the pretty one, may not live."

Niven didn't know someone could go so, so pale.

Laphaniel shoved himself to his feet, a hand pressed to the wall to steady himself. "Is she okay? Is Teya okay?"

Niven grinned. Gods, she could taste his fear.

"Niven...please."

"There was blood and bits everywhere, splatters all over the snow." She chewed a tough piece of fingernail and spat it at Laphaniel's feet. "Bone too, I think."

His words hissed through his teeth, "She's your gods-damned sister!"

She met his strange blue eyes and shrugged. "She was."

The sudden rush of grief was intoxicating. Niven drank it in, along with his terror. It left her breathless. Her laughter shook the shadows, stirring the lone candle.

"A joke," she laughed. "She rode off into the darkness, I'm sure she's fine—"

He lunged at her, hands at her throat to shove her hard against the wall. "What the hell is wrong with you?"

"I'm bored."

He jerked away from her and retched. Nothing came up but spittle. "Why are you really down here?"

Niven took a breath to compose herself. "A little birdy told me of the whispers you hear. Of the secrets you trade for a bottle of forget-fulness."

Laphaniel swiped the back of his hand across his mouth. "And?"

"And I would like to know what they say to you."

"Something must be worrying you, Niven, if you wish for me to spy for you."

"Cautious," Niven answered, waiting while Laphaniel brought a cup of muddy-looking water to his lips and drank. "You warned me to be wary, and I listened."

"You wish for me to spy from my little room I cannot leave?" he asked, lip curling. "I doubt I will be of much use to you."

"Do you truly hear whispers?"

He nodded and looked away. "Sometimes it is the imps and the goblins, and I trade secrets, perhaps in hope that one day I will watch you burn. Sometimes it is not."

He had her attention. "You hear voices?"

A pause. "Not all the time."

She stepped closer, intrigued. "What do they tell you?"

"They tell me nothing and everything at the same time." Laphaniel watched her carefully. "I am not always sure what is real and what is not."

Niven stared at him, wondering if they had finally broken him.

He glared back. "I'm not mad."

"Not yet, perhaps," she answered, voice cold. "Have you always been able to hear these voices?"

"No," he hissed. "Only since being down here."

Niven sucked her lip. "I think your grip on reality is slipping."

"Just like the grip on your crown."

"Perhaps the ramblings of a madman will not be so helpful after all," Niven replied, dusting off her gown as she turned to leave. Laphaniel snatched her hand.

"Do you drink nightrose mead after dinner?"

She yanked her hand back, fighting the urge to slap him. "I do."

"I wouldn't tonight."

Without another word, without a backward glance to the faerie rotting in the darkness, the Queen of Seelie made her way back to her Court and to her king.

CHAPTER ELEVEN

LAPHANIEL

*N*o matter how hard I fought, I could not drag myself out of the nightmare. It tethered itself to me as if it had claws, raking against my subconscious in a relentless wash of blood and horror and pain.

The crack of a whip.

The snap of bones.

The scrape of claws along bloodied flesh.

I had long since ceased dreaming of her.

Shadows curled around the far edges of my nightmare, skittering along the floor. They made noises that shadows had no business making. A clawed hand loomed over head, shrouded in mist. It was ageless…ancient.

Angry.

From its ghostly fingers dangled something so bright, it hurt to look at it. There was not a mark upon it…no black stains…no darkness. If it were not for the deep ache within my chest, I wouldn't have believed it was mine.

"I am coming for you."

The voice came from everywhere.

"Not yet, but I see you."

I turned, shadows snaking around my legs, my body...my neck. "What do you want?"

Laughter boomed through the darkness.

"I want to split this beautiful world in two."

"What are—"

Pain lanced up my arm, ripping me from sleep. My breath shuddered from my mouth as I bolted upright. I scrabbled upon the damp straw in the pitch black to press against the cold wall.

I braced myself for the kick, the slash of talons. The frigid stone bit into my skin, ice forming in the cracks. Nothing moved. There was no sound save for my own ragged breathing.

"How the fuck did you know about the wine?"

Niven.

My breath hissed through my teeth. I was too relieved I wasn't about to be torn apart to feel any shame about cowering in the darkness.

"I told you."

"Who told you?" Niven snarled. "Goblins or the crazy voices in your head?"

I took a breath and held it, fighting to regain some sort of composure. "The latter."

It had been little more than noise, a mess of voices. Laughter. I would have brushed it off as meaningless whispers, perhaps accepting that my sanity was finally slipping, if not for the repeated words. Words that, all the way down in my cell, meant nothing to me at all. Nightrose, nightrose, nightrose, nightrose, nightrose, nightrose, nightrose...

An acquired taste, sweet and strange and disgustingly thick, I detected it enough on Niven's breath. It was too fine and expensive for the servants. I wouldn't have thought Phabian would touch it.

"I had a serving girl taste it tonight, with the entire court watching," Niven began. She lit the single candle I had, which only highlighted the gloom. "Her guts bubbled out of her mouth and ruined my dessert."

I rolled my eyes at her utter lack of empathy. "Did you come all the way down here to thank me?"

"I want to know why," she hissed, creeping closer. "Why do they speak to you at all?"

"I have no idea, Niven," I answered and shoved myself up so she no longer hovered over me. "Perhaps someone doesn't want you dead?"

Light bloomed at her fingertips as she summoned another flame, using it to light the cigarette in her mouth.

"I thought it was Phabian at first," she said, scraping a boot along the edge of the dirty straw. Her lip curled.

"He would want a spectacle." I caught her looking at the marks on my skin, visible through the holes in my shirt. The welts trailed down my shoulder, thick and white. Not a flicker of emotion passed over her face. "I suggest you find someone to taste your food."

She smirked. "Are you offering?"

"Would it get me out of this cell for a few hours?"

Niven cocked her head, lifting a slender eyebrow before she huffed a laugh. "Are you truly that desperate?"

I glanced at my markings in the stone. "It's been...a while."

"You have no idea how long you've been here, do you?"

I met her mocking stare. "No."

"I have a proposition for you," she began, blowing a perfect circle of sweet smoke into my face.

"I'm listening."

I noticed her wrists then, noting the bruises forming over her pale skin, unhidden by the smoke and mist she wore. She didn't try to hide them but lifted her chin, daring me to comment. I said nothing—I didn't want to know.

Inhaling another breath of perfumed smoke, she stalked closer and whispered, "You will tell me everything you hear. Every scrap of nonsense that pops up in that crazy little head of yours. I want every rumour, every piece of goblin gossip. Every single word you overhear, I want. Understand?"

"And what do I get out of it?" I asked, unable to mask my surprise when she offered me her cigarette.

"I will grant you one hour out of this cell every week," she answered. A nasty smile lifted the corners of her mouth as I stared at her. "Would you like that?"

I blew out a mouthful of smoke before taking another lungful. Whatever herbs inside it were doing a fair job at dulling the constant ache in my head. The world lost its sharpness, and for a moment it felt like I could breathe again.

"An hour outside to do what?"

Gods, that smile was awful.

"My, aren't we clever?" Niven purred, holding out her hand for the rest of her cigarette. I took one last long drag on it before passing to her. "It wouldn't be a fun hour if you were to spend it tied up to a whipping post again, would it?" She flicked ash at my feet. "You can do as you please. Run, skip, build a snowman or fuck the scullery maid for all I care."

"Guarded?"

"Obviously."

"And if I refuse?"

Quick as an asp, she stubbed the end of the cigarette into my hand, gripping tight as I hissed in pain.

"You think you're miserable now?" she snarled, shadows skittering around her. "I will make your life unbearable." Her hand twisted on mine, fingernails digging in. "Well? Do we have a deal?"

"Do I have a choice?"

She let go. The burn on the back of my hand was raw, the edges coated in black ash. "You have had a choice in everything, Laphaniel," she said, her voice soft. "Stealing me away, abandoning me, fucking my sister."

"Do you know what?" I breathed, flexing my fingers. "I don't think you hate me for taking you, not really. You hate me for the unforgivable crime of making Teya happy."

Niven moved with inhuman grace, almost melting into the shadows to run a finger over my cheek. Despite myself, I flinched, and her eyes lit up.

"You're going to die here. Don't you ever forget that."

She drifted away, leaving behind a darkness so heavy it was like a physical presence. The latch clicked, but not the lock.

She didn't lock the door.

I tensed and waited.

Claws scraped along the stone, followed by a cackle. Something crept down the steps, something with too many teeth and a taste for my blood.

Then there was silence, save for the creak of the door.

CHAPTER TWELVE

TEYA

I rode home as if ravenous wolves were on my tail, never stopping. My horse flew over the snow laden paths, sweat slicking over her body. Her breaths gasped in white puffs, her eyes white. On and on and on.

I stopped only when the poor beast could run no further. We found shelter amongst the ragged rocks and deep crevices, away from the howling wind and relentless snowfall. Sleep came in short bursts, my mind too wary of all the creatures lurking within the shadows to rest easy.

Oonagh greeted me when finally, I reached the gates of the Seelie castle, cloak snapping in the wind. My exhausted horse was led away to be cared for by a green-skinned stable hand; more servants swept out to help me. I dismissed them all without a word.

Questions spilled from Oonagh's mouth, her hands tight on mine. My Glamour sparked, frantic. I just wanted to get my things ready and seek out the witches in the north.

"What happened? Where is Gabriel?"

I could barely imagine what I looked like, filthy and bloodstained and half-crazed. "I need to leave as soon as possible, if the witches can help…if they can do anything, I need to go now."

"Tell me more," she demanded, her fingers digging into my skin. "When do we leave?"

"Oonagh—"

"You look as though you need to rest," she continued, heedless. "I shall send for hot water…a bath and food. Then we go. We will make these witches help us, Teya. I swear it."

She walked beside me, matching my pace. Her silver eyes took in the bruises on my skin, the way I dragged my feet, how my breath caught. She took my elbow, and I leaned into her.

"I left Gabriel there," I murmured, words slipping past my lips like a confession. "I'm not sure if he will live."

"I want you to tell me everything, Teya." She whirled around, skirts spinning around her. The movement made me dizzy. "I need to know everything—"

"I'm taking Nefina."

She recoiled like I had struck her. "Why?"

"Because I need you here, Oonagh," I began, grasping at her hands. She wrenched them free, her face stricken. "I need you to watch over this Court, because there is no one I trust more."

"Yet you do not trust me to be by your side."

"That is not—"

"To replace me with Nefina." Disgust dripped from her words, her lip curling. "You think she would have your back if the time came?"

I straightened my spine. "I do."

"Why?"

"She would protect me, to protect her brother."

"That's not a good enough reason, Teya!" Snowflakes settled upon her eyelashes, slipping down her cheeks like frozen tears. "I would lay my life down for you, because you are my Queen and my friend."

"I need you here," I said, moving closer. Oonagh stepped away, eyes cold. "I don't know how long I will be gone and I trust no one else with keeping this Court safe."

"I belong at your side."

I kept her gaze, her strange silver eyes lined with tears. "No."

She walked away and I let her go.

"SHE KNOWS YOU ARE RIGHT," Nefina said. She sat on the edge of my bed, glowering at the maids while they folded her dresses into cases. "Her pride at being left behind is hurt. In truth, she should be at your side."

I sighed, folding up a spare cloak for my own pack. I had dismissed my maids, wishing to keep myself busy. "I was meant to have Laphaniel by my side. Then I would have no need for ancient and cunning witches."

My words were bitter, and I didn't care.

Nefina swatted a hand at one of her unfortunate maids as she failed to close the latch on her bulging trunk. The maid—Rose—gritted her teeth, her wings buzzing behind her. Somehow Nefina's other two maids had managed to escape.

"I really don't think fancy gowns are going to be useful in the mountains," I said, shooing Rose away when Nefina wasn't looking. She bobbed a quick curtsy before vanishing.

"Do you think the witches will help us?" Nefina asked. She lifted her head, eyes narrowed. "Where has that useless girl gone?"

I rubbed my temples, a headache forming behind my eyes. "I sent her away. I don't know about the witches, Nefina. I really don't know."

Her bright blue eyes hardened with determination, the coldness of her features changing into something I couldn't quite place. "If there is a loophole...a way to break your bargain, we will not leave without it." She paused and smoothed out her skirts. They shimmered scarlet, the golden threads woven throughout catching the candlelight. "We are lucky Gabriel was brazen enough to seek them out."

"Then let's hope he didn't break too many hearts while he was with them," I said with a grin. "Get your cloak, we are leaving as soon as the horses are ready."

Nefina stood, glancing over her shoulder. "Do you think he will live?"

I closed my eyes at the memory of Gabriel lying motionless on a bed of moss, covered in blood and gore. His ribs snapping as the Scara forced his heart to keep beating.

"She said she would send word... either way."

My simple gown rustled as I rose, the green adorned with little jewels or enchantments. I clasped a cloak around my throat, trailed a finger over the soft fur lining.

Nefina followed beside me as we walked along the corridors and down the sweeping staircases that led to the grand entrance of the castle. It had once filled me with awe and wonder. Had once over-whelmed me with its glorious splendour and sheer endlessness. There was a time, not so long ago, when I couldn't wait to spend forever within its walls. At the new hope it had once meant to us.

A numbness had settled where the wonder had lingered. Any delight once found in my kingdom, long since replaced with an apathy that smothered me.

"Wait!"

I spun, my fingers resting within the gloved hand of a footman with long spiralling horns.

"Teya, wait!"

Oonagh raced along the gravel path, the folds of her silver gown billowing around her like wisps. The force of her embrace nearly toppled me. I gripped her back as if she alone were tethering me to the earth.

"Forgive me," she breathed. "It is an honour to stay in your stead."

Her beautiful voice broke, and I squeezed her tighter. Tears began to slip down my cheeks.

"Any hint of trouble," I began, "send word. I will move heaven and earth to get back to you."

Oonagh pulled away, ghostly eyes shining. "Go do what needs to be done, Teya."

Nefina leaned out of the carriage, impatient. "Are we going to leave, or must we embrace some more?"

"The Queen is on your watch," Oonagh said, voice sharp. "Make sure you understand that. Protect her."

I expected some snippy comment, a dismissive remark. Nefina straightened and met Oonagh's scrutinising gaze.

"With my last breath," she answered without hesitation, earning a raised brow from both of us.

I accepted the footman's outstretched hand once again and climbed into the carriage opposite Nefina. Oonagh blew a kiss as we pulled apart, her silhouette remaining on the gravel path until the horses took us far away, and the castle vanished from view.

The carriage itself was ridiculously luxurious. Red velvet covered the inside, all inlaid with gold, matching my gown. Nefina noticed and barely hid her smirk. The lanterns swinging from gilded hooks were black and ornate, the fat candles inside flickered with the gentle movement of the horses. It was cosy and peaceful.

"What do you think the witches will be like?" Nefina asked as she peered out of the window. The landscape rushed by, becoming more wooded and wilder as we left the manicured lands of the castle grounds.

"If they are anything like the witches I've met before, then cunning, deceptive and hungry."

She shifted in her seat. "Wonderful."

I allowed a smile onto my lips. "You sound so like your brother."

"Do I really?"

She sounded so surprised. "You're more alike than you would ever admit. For one, you're both pretty unlikable on the first meeting."

Nefina laughed, a quick and musical sound no one heard enough. That laughter was rarer still since losing Sage. I missed the sharp, wicked sound he enticed from her: there was a freedom to it, delight.

"My brother and I learned very young to put up a shield," she began, keeping her eyes fixed on the outside. "To not allow anyone to know you could be hurt. Laphaniel taught me how to hide my emotions from my father, and later how to force everything away so I felt nothing at all."

"I'm sorry, Nefina. For what happened to you."

Her head snapped around. "He told you?"

I could still see the vibrant silks of the countless tents, hear the soft moans that rose up from within them. I could smell the sweet, sweet smoke that fuelled it all. I shook my head. Laphaniel hadn't told me anything, not voluntarily.

"He won't talk about it." I tried to shake the tinkling sounds of the carousel that spun and spun and spun in my head. "I saw flashes of his memories when he gave up his Glamour for me."

Nefina said nothing for a long moment. From the hamper of food between us, she pulled out a handful of grapes and popped one into her mouth.

"I do not blame him, not anymore." She plucked more grapes from their stalks. "We were so young. Laphaniel could barely look after himself. We were starving when we came across that garish tent. He had carried me for miles, staying awake at night to ward off anything that wanted to eat us." She paused with a small smile, looking down into her lap. "He had this little, useless knife, and he tried to hunt for food. He just wasn't fast enough. That beautiful harlot in that awful tent fed us, sheltered us…but the first night when Laphaniel staggered back to me, I knew we wouldn't be leaving again."

She gestured to the bottle of golden honey wine nestled amongst the meat and cheeses. I nodded and she popped the cork, taking a long swallow before she passed it to me.

"I lost myself in that circus of whores," Nefina continued, voice soft as if she were not talking to me at all. "It did not take long to stop caring…to stop dreaming of something other than sex and the welcoming numbness of Ember. Why look for more? There was nothing else out there for us."

Laphaniel had never opened up about the past that haunted him and his sister. "How long were you there?"

I dreaded the answer.

"A decade," she said simply. "Time blended together after a while."

So many years lost.

"I had no idea…"

Nefina gave a dismissive shrug. She brought the bottle to her mouth again, taking a long drink.

"The Madame ensured we could never leave," Nefina said. "We had endless...patrons so we could always pay for the forgetfulness she offered, the never-ending supply of Ember in all its terrible, glittering glory. Oh, but she would always demand more than we could afford, so we were always in her debt."

I tried to keep the pity from my voice, knowing she would sneer at it. "And if you said no?"

Nefina's laugh was devastating. "Then she charged extra for us."

The wine I had consumed churned in my stomach.

"Why would it stop if we were not willing, Teya?" she said, her fingers running over the neck of the bottle. "It was easier to give in. Give up."

I took her hands in mine, surprised when she didn't pull away. I fought for words. "You're free now, Nefina."

My words didn't register until she squeezed back. "I am."

Because her brother wasn't.

I rested my head against the window and watched the thick snow fall from the blinding white skies. It gave no hint that spring would ever return. The horses cantered on and on, before after what seemed like hours, they stopped.

"We will need to stop and rest here, Your Majesty," the footman said, opening the door to the carriage. The wind picked up his chestnut hair, his curling horns as black as the night. He fidgeted, uneasy.

"What is it?"

He bowed his head. "The horses will not go through the mountain, Your Majesty."

I tugged my cloak against the sudden chill. "I know."

"You have no guards with you." He looked up at the driver, a faerie with bright yellow eyes and thick black fur.

I was grateful for his concern. "The witches wouldn't accept a visit if I had an entourage."

"It does not feel right to leave you at the foot of the mountain, My Queen," the driver said, pointed teeth flashing.

I smiled up at him. "If it will stop you worrying for me, you can wait at the mountain edge."

"Aye, it would, My Queen." His gruff voice rasped over his teeth, rich and warm.

"I don't know how long we will be."

The footman beside me shrugged, cloak snapping behind him. "We will not leave the mountain until you and the Princess return."

I reached for his gloved hand, feeling the nudge of claws within. "Then I will insist you both stay in the carriage to rest when we are gone. It is too cold to stay long out here."

"We have tents—"

"An order," I said, firm. "From your Queen."

He bowed low, his thanks slipping easy from his lips.

We stopped to rest in a small clearing, sheltered from the relentless cold and snow by towering oaks that loomed over us. Branches knotted together overhead to create a natural canopy.

Nefina and I slept within the carriage, huddled beneath bundles of thick furs while the horses were tended to. I ensured both the driver and footman were given extra blankets and that their fire roared hot.

The night passed, cold and dark and dreamless. I slept fitfully, waiting in the darkness for the sun to rise so we could be on our way again.

An unbroken sky greeted us at dawn. No more snow fell, but the air outside was merciless, so cold it had turned the roads to ice. The horses, with their massive, feathered hooves still skidded. It was down to the skill of our driver and sheer luck that we didn't roll.

"I have decided against the heeled slippers," Nefina mused, and burrowed deeper into her furs. She had already rammed her hands into a soft muff.

"I think that's wise."

"How far do you think we will have to walk?"

I smiled at the tentative worry in her voice. Nefina was no lover of physical exercise. "Honestly? I have no idea. I hope they send a guide."

"Or at least a broomstick."

"Don't get your hopes up," I said with a chuckle.

"I know you would rather be with anyone but me." Nefina twisted her long golden hair into a tight braid. "But for what my words are worth to you, I will fight until my last breath. Know this: if those hags refuse you aid, I will burn their entire coven to the ground."

The carriage rolled to a stop beneath the shadow of a mountain, the path up winding and rough. Nefina took my hand as we stepped out into the snow.

"If we get him back," she began, her words almost lost to the wind, "what do you think will be left of the faerie you love?"

I followed Nefina's gaze over the mountain, craning my neck to peer up at the mist that circled above. It was an honest, raw question, said without her usual malice.

My breath caught. "He was struggling before."

Her head whipped to me. "With what?"

I closed my eyes, feeling snowflakes settle on my lashes. "After the curse was broken, he had these nightmares, and they were awful. He thinks that some part of him was left behind, kept as punishment for coming back."

"Because he wanted to come back?" Nefina's eyes were wide.

I shook my head, blinked away tears before they froze on my face. "I think...I think whatever place he found when he died was peaceful. He didn't want to come back, Nefina. He now thinks he is destined for some sort of hell."

I couldn't bear to tell Nefina of the creatures I had encountered down in the Unseelie caves, of the soulless ghouls that had hinted at Laphaniel's fate with a gleeful malice. Eternal hunger, the loss of everything he once was.

"They keep him in a tiny cell," I continued, speaking around the lump in my throat. "He hates feeling like he can't breathe, and they have locked him deep in the dark. There is no light, no air."

Nefina curled her fists at her sides, the Glamour around her crackling with fury. "The Unseelie are well known to torture their prisoners into madness."

My heart stilled. "Don't—"

"If they break him—"

"Don't you dare finish that sentence," I hissed, my Glamour rising to meet hers. "I want to believe I can reach him in time. I have to. But if I'm too late…" I squeezed my eyes shut against the image of him broken beyond repair, of his wonderful mind shattered so completely there was nothing left of the faerie who held my heart. "If you think I would abandon him, Nefina, you can leave right now."

She stiffened, taking a step onto the mountain path ahead of me. "An eternity caring for a babbling, weeping mess is not to be taken lightly."

I caught her wrist, my other hand striking her hard across the face. "If that is all that is left, I will still love him with every inch of my soul."

Nefina placed a hand to her reddened cheek, eyes blazing. "I will hold you to that promise, Teya."

I gritted my teeth. "I would walk through hell itself to get him back."

A cackle sounded from the mist, high and wicked. "You may just have to yet."

CHAPTER THIRTEEN

Teya

The witch descended through the mist, soundless. Her blue lips lifted in a lazy smile as she stopped in front of us. With a sweep of her pale hand, she pushed down the white hood of her cloak, revealing ice-blue eyes.

"Welcome to the Coven of Bones, Mortal Queen," the witch greeted, running an amused eye down the both of us. "Follow me."

She beckoned us to follow with a flick of a talon-tipped finger, then turned to melt back into the thick, swirling fog.

With Nefina's hand clasped in mine and my pack across my shoulder, I bolted after her. My feet slipped on the icy ground, the freezing earth biting through the thick soles of my boots.

I had never felt cold like it.

The witch seemed to glide over the treacherous path, every part of her blended in with the blinding snow. I followed her cackle, the sharp sound of laughter that echoed down from the mountain pass. Even her hair behaved like snowfall, a cascade of perfect white that trailed down her back. The wind lifted it up around her, turning her into a walking snowstorm.

Up and up and up we walked, until the air grew so cold it hurt to breathe. By the time we reached the top, I could no longer feel my feet, and my entire face felt raw. The blood on my chapped lips had frozen.

"You will meet the High Witch soon enough," our guide said, leading us through a warren of circular tents. The fabric was all bleached as white as the surroundings. The witch stopped in front of a tent identical to all the others. "You will find provisions inside. I suggest you change into something warmer before you perish."

She shoved the flap back and gestured for us to enter. Inside was bare and functional. Two small cots stood at one end, laden with brown, mottled furs, the only hint of colour. A wood burner stood in the middle, blazing hot. There was a worn table, two stools and nothing else.

"You will find no luxuries here, Mortal Queen," the witch said, lumping a bundle of heavy clothes into my hands.

"I don't need any," I replied. The witch blinked before giving me a quick nod of approval.

"I am Magnhild," she said, shoving clothes at Nefina. "I would advise against dying in this place: fresh meat is so very hard to come by way up here."

She exchanged no other pleasantries before she left, moving in silence into the unforgiving snow.

"How did Gabriel escape these witches alive?" Nefina asked, sliding closer to the fire.

"Perhaps they're short on the company of men," I said with a slow grin. I shoved on the thick clothing: a rough wool dress, gloves and a cloak made up of folds of speckled fur. The hood was the carved-out head of a giant white fox. "He didn't come back completely unscathed. One of their serpents bit him."

Nefina's eyes lit up. "Oh, I would love to see one."

Bundled in scratchy wool and the hollowed shells of woodland animals, we ventured outside. The vicious wind was persistent, biting hard at any exposed skin.

Witches moved everywhere. They blended in against the stark landscape with their snow-white skin and hair, too-bright eyes flashing against the deep shadows of the skeletal trees that surrounded the camp.

Fire pits blazed hot, roasting carcasses that spat fat into the flames. There seemed to be meat cooking on each of the many roaring fires...though what kind, I didn't dare ask. I really didn't want to know.

Then we looked up.

And there they were.

Countless lithe, long bodies soared across the white skies, colossal wings spreading wide to catch the air currents. Whip-like, winding tails stretched out behind them, acting like rudders to glide them through the air as if they were swimming.

They were sapphire blue against the perfect white sky, scales glittering despite the lack of sunlight.

"Like what you see, girl?" Another witch sidled up to us, nostrils flaring as she stood close. Thin silk covered her body, the colour of snow, the colour of everything on the damned mountain. She wore the pelt of a grey wolf around her shoulders, and its lifeless, dead eyes seemed to watch my every move. The witch pointed to the sky with a sharp, silver nail. "That one is mine, her name is Eira."

"She is breathtaking," I breathed, not looking away from the serpents floating above us, their bodies more like winged snakes than dragons.

"Oh, that she is," answered the witch. "She has split a man's belly in two more times than I can count. Have you ever heard the sound of hot blood on fresh snow?"

I met her odd blue gaze. "I can't say that I have."

"By the time you leave, you will," she said, tilting her head up.

I couldn't tell if it was a promise of a threat, but Nefina pressed closer to me. I wondered if either of us would make it back down the mountain.

"When will I get to see the High Witch?"

A slender, pale brow lifted on the witch's face. "Are you in a hurry?"

"Time is important to me," I answered honestly.

"Your pretty knight told us of your little problem. We all liked him." Those wintery eyes glinted. "We all liked him a lot."

It seemed Gabriel had a wonderful time indeed. "Enough to help me?"

"Enough to meet with you, at least," she replied. "Enough that our wings grew jealous." A smile, showing teeth. "Did he get to keep that leg?"

"His leg healed fine."

She must have caught my tone, because she stepped closer until her nose was almost touching mine. "But?"

"I left him dying in a rotting hole to come here."

She pulled away with a hiss, catching the eye of some of the other witches nearby. "A pity."

"Do you think I'll receive any help here?"

The witch shrugged, already turning away from me. "How should I know, Mortal Queen?"

Remaining close to Nefina, we carried on across the frozen home of the Coven of Bones, wary of the curious looks we earned and mindful of the cruel beasts circling high overhead.

We passed racks of herbs drying beneath stretched leather canopies, tended to by younger witches with quick hands and cunning smiles. Huge pots bubbled with oily liquid beneath a cluster of naked trees, smog coiling up with the rise of cackles around it. We held our hands over our mouths when we passed, the smoke burning our throats...the pungent smell making our heads spin.

A few serpents lay coiled upon the icy ground, wings outstretched while their scales were cleaned and polished. Bones lay around their mouths, massive carcasses that had been utterly picked clean. They eyed us as we passed, intelligent and cruel. I had no doubts they had tasted human flesh.

"Wiling away the time before Her Greatness deems you worth seeing?" a voice called from the shadows. "Be careful where you wander."

I spun, and to her credit, Nefina stepped in front of me.

"Show yourself," she demanded, chin held high. She showed not even a glimmer of fear.

Laughter bubbled up from the darkness, amused and cold. A witch stepped out of the shadows and dipped into a mocking bow.

"Did I startle you, little queen?" the witch asked, her accent soft and haunting, nothing like the high cackles of the others. She bent low to pick up one of the bones littering the ground, ignoring the sharp hiss of the nearby serpent. The young witch cleaning its scales curled her lip.

"I am Datura," she continued, adjusting the furs over her deep brown skin. She gave the witch-groom a biting smile before stripping a piece of flesh from the bone and slipping it into her mouth. "I am the Priestess of the Coven of Ashes. You two look as fucking cold as I am."

A cluster of silk-clad witches shoved by us, calling out to the serpents that swirled above us. They cackled as they passed, barrelling into Datura. They knocked the witch to the snow, her cloak sprawled out behind her, her black hair wild and unbound by her hood.

"Always in the way, witch of dirt," spat one. "While you are at this Coven you will know your—"

Quick as lightning, Datura flew to her feet. She grabbed the other witch from behind, her lips at her ear.

No, her throat.

I couldn't look away fast enough before she tore through her neck and spat it against the snow.

"Does any other wish to call me names?" Datura began, red dripping from her lips. "No? More is the pity. Go tell your High Witch why she has one less acolyte in her fold. I am sure she will be more merciful than I."

The young witches fled, at least one of them weeping. The witch-groom carried on her grooming nearby, a wide smile on her pale lips. The serpent at her side minded not that the fallen witch once belonged to its Coven. Blood was blood, and meat was meat.

"Follow me, little queen." Datura scooped a silver necklace from the remains of the dead witch with a quick hand. She dangled it from her fingers before slipping the folds of her cloak. "I may have something for you."

She turned when we didn't follow. She wiped her chin with her sleeve, streaking it and her face in red.

"I will not offer again, little queen," Datura said with a shrug. "Perhaps you do not wish to see your husband."

She made to disappear into the shadows.

"Wait!"

The witch didn't look back, but her pace slowed enough so we didn't lose her in the darkness. Nefina's grip on my wrist was firm. I didn't have to look at her to know she disapproved, but if there was a chance to see him…any at all, then damn the consequences.

Through the warren of tattered, bleached tents we walked. The glacial wind howled around us, beating at the fabric until I feared they would all rip from the ground. Snow fell in a frenzied flurry, wiping out our footsteps. Nefina's nail dug into my skin, through my gloves.

"This is foolish, Teya—"

"In here," Datura interrupted with a red-lipped smile, gesturing to a larger tent on the outskirts of the camp. "Or you can wander back into the cold and see if those bone hags will eat your fingers."

I chose to follow, giving Nefina little choice but to do the same. We ducked under the tent flaps, and Nefina dropped my hand.

Candlelight danced upon every surface, lighting up the space so brightly it hurt my eyes. Furs and velvet throws lay draped over huge scatter cushions, and thick rugs lay across every inch of the ground. A four-poster bed stood proud in the middle, its posts carved with what appeared to be the faces of screaming children.

Fire burners raged all around the tent, puffing the smoke up high through the vent. In comparison to outside, it was smothering.

"I am an emissary sent to keep peace between the Covens," Datura explained, moving close to one of the burners. "We change at every Solstice, moving from Coven to Coven. I cannot abide the damn cold, but it is some condolence to know one of those icy harlots is freezing their tits off at the Coven of Ashes."

The witch sighed and slipped off her cloak, pulling a blanket from the bed to wrap around her shoulders. She gestured for us to sit, watching us both with dark eyes. Her black hair slid over her bare skin when she leant towards me.

"You followed me." Blood still stained her smile.

I unlatched my cloak, uncomfortably warm. "You said I could see Laphaniel."

"And yet you did not ask a price."

I rose, my heart sinking fast. Nefina was already on her feet. "We are leaving."

Around us, the flames flared, hissing and spitting behind their grates. Sweat trickled down my spine.

"Calm yourself, little queenling," Datura said, a cackle rising from her throat. "I will not take anything you want."

I hated witches. More than any creature I had stumbled across in Faerie, I hated the witches most of all.

"How could you possibly allow me to see Laphaniel?"

Datura smiled, long and slow, black eyes alive with wildfire. "I am a Night Hag."

Even Nefina sat up straighter.

"What exactly are you offering me?"

Datura sank back into her cushions, reaching to fling yet another log into the fire. "I haven't wandered the slumbering realms in months. My bones ache from the lack of dreams, my lips have forgotten the taste of nightmares. We could help each other, little queen."

"I don't understand." It was so hot in the tent. The flames roared, giving off a strange scent that had my mind whirling.

"I will allow you to walk with me," Datura whispered, so close her mouth brushed over my ear. "I will find him for you."

My breath caught; Nefina caught my hand in hers, squeezing gently.

"You'll find Laphaniel?" I asked.

The witch of Ashes gave a lazy nod. "You dream and he dreams, for a brief time you can be together."

"What if he's not sleeping?"

Those eyes sharpened. "I can pull a room of souls under with barely a thought. One miserable little faerie will be no trouble at all."

Hope coursed through me as feverous as the flames in the grate. The thought of being with Laphaniel again nearly overwhelmed me, even if we wouldn't be together physically. I thought of him in his cell, and the need to be beside him became unbearable, followed by a sudden bloom of fear.

"If he's asleep and they come for him…"

Datura rolled her eyes. "I will notice if he is not alone."

"I do not trust her," Nefina hissed. "She will feed off his nightmares."

"Is that true?" I asked the witch, and she lifted a shoulder.

"A taste, nothing more."

I would see him…

Talk to him.

Touch him.

Datura uncurled herself from the cushions, her black eyes alight with something I couldn't understand. Her own longing radiated from her as she outstretched her hand to me.

With her slender fingers wrapped around mine, she led me to her bed, clicking to Nefina to take a seat near the edge.

"I'll ready the fires," Datura said, her voice strangely hushed.

"Are you mad?" Nefina cried. "I can barely breathe in here."

Datura ignored her to pile logs into the burner, filling the small space with more cloying smoke. Sweat trickled down Nefina's face, her pale hair sticking to her skin as she shrugged out of some of the layers she wore.

My head spun, the tent a whirl of colours that moved even as I squeezed my eyes shut. Still more logs were thrown upon the fire.

I tried to sit up. "I feel strange…"

"Hush," the witch hissed from above me. "Stay still and keep hold of my hand. I would hate for you to get lost."

Her hand gripped mine tight, sharp nails digging into my skin. The spinning colours dimmed until there was nothing left but blackness and the sound of gleeful laughter.

CHAPTER FOURTEEN

TEYA

*T*he vice-like grip on my hand remained even when the darkness lifted, revealing a world of swirling fog. I could see nothing but clouds of white and grey. It pressed against my mouth, thick and smothering.

"Do not let go until I say," Datura warned. Her sharp nails broke the skin on my hand. I could barely see her through the fog, her form ghost-like. She tilted her head back as if scenting something.

"How will you find Laphaniel?"

Her long fingers brushed against my wedding ring, her face still turned towards the thick smog above us.

"I already have." Her hand tightened. "Can you not feel that? Ah—"

She stumbled back, eyes wide and alert.

A wall of sudden, undiluted terror barrelled into us. It sent me to my knees, my breaths gasping past my lips. Tears began to stream down my face, unbidden. Whatever lingered in the fog crept closer. My heart hammered against my chest, and I tried to yank my hand back.

Datura held me firm, beads of blood welling up from where her nails sliced my skin.

The witch dragged me up. Her lips moved, but I heard nothing…

I was screaming too loudly.

I battled against her and reached for the comforting weight of my Glamour. There was nothing. Nothing but panic…

Fear…

Loss…

and endless, endless pain…

"Go…back…go back!" The words tumbled from my mouth in sobs, but the witch kept her hand locked on mine. "Please…"

The fog coiled closer and closer and closer. I couldn't breathe, my heart screamed in my chest and I couldn't breathe.

Datura snarled in my ear, "I can't get past his nightmares without your help!"

A low whimper escaped my lips. I had never felt anything like it… an utter absence of hope. A void.

Endless.

"Stupid girl!" she hissed, blood trickling down her nose. "I'm keeping him asleep while his body is struggling to wake. If you do not move, I will break him!"

I took a step, the fog engulfing me. Suffocating. Another step.

Another,

another,

and another.

Datura dragged me forwards, her tongue lashing out to taste the nightmares that surrounded us.

The fog finally began to thin, lifting to leave behind only the tang of despair. My breath shuddered.

"I will come find you when it is time to go, little queenling." The witch released me. Her dark eyes flicked to the blood on my wrist. "Cherish what time you have."

I nodded, unable to form words.

"I have not tasted dreams this dark for an age," Datura mused, her eyes heavy-lidded. "They are exquisite."

I backed away, sickened by the thought of anyone finding delight in Laphaniel's torment. Leaving the grinning witch behind me, I walked on through the ever-thinning fog until I felt the dampness of grass beneath my feet. A subtle chill brushed against my skin and a sharp breeze lifted my hair.

The crashing of waves roared in the distance, white foam rearing up to rush against a sandy shore. I could smell the salt in the air, taste it. Storm clouds hung heavy in the sky, the colour of old bruises, fat with rain, alive with electricity.

Everything stilled when I spotted him. He had his back to me, staring out into the chaotic sea. He turned at the crunch of grass beneath my foot. His lovely eyes widened before he took a step away, then one more.

"Wait!" I called, my voice instantly snatched up by the wind.

"Leave me alone," Laphaniel murmured, the words resigned. "Please, just leave me alone."

I slowly closed the gap between us, palms up while he eyed me warily. "It's me. It's really me."

He shook his head. I felt him pull away, fighting to wake up.

"I'm really here," I said before I lost him. "I know things about you that no one else could." I spoke quickly, my words coming out jumbled. "I know you won't eat the crusts of your bread unless they're dipped in jam, but only strawberry...you hate raspberry." Tears coursed down my cheeks at the uncertainty on his face. "You think prairie dogs and meerkats are the same thing, even after I made you re-watch both shows to prove they're not. You're ticklish, though you'll never admit it. You mumble constantly in your sleep, and you make this...this adorable snorting noise when you dream. I know you, Laphaniel, because it's me. I know you as much as you know every part of me."

He didn't move. "How?"

I took another cautious step, fighting against the need to just run to him, to fling my arms around his neck and never let go. "Someone was willing to help..."

Hesitantly, he lifted a hand to trail his fingers down my arm. He brushed them over my hands before touching his forehead to mine, pulling me close. I fit perfectly against his chest, my head resting over his heart. It sang for me, a chorus to mine.

"You shouldn't be doing this," he breathed against my neck, but made no move to release me. "How are you doing this?"

"We found a witch and—"

He pulled back, eyes flashing. "Have you learned nothing, Teya?" he hissed. "You have your life in the hands of this witch, and she could just leave you here." Fear and anger flooded his voice in a wave of emotion I could taste. "How long have you known this witch?"

I winced. "About half an hour."

"Go back," Laphaniel urged. "It's not safe here… Who the hell are you with?"

Laphaniel's hands remained tight around me, his face just inches away from mine.

"Would you believe I was with Nefina?"

He closed his eyes, a sigh escaping his lips. "Where the hell are you, Teya?"

"I'm right here," I whispered. "At this moment, I'm right here, with you."

With a shuddering breath, he dragged me close again and buried his face deep against my neck. "Gods, I have missed you so much."

I couldn't speak past the ache in my throat. His moss and spice scent overwhelmed me, still there beneath the sweat and blood I could detect on him…even in his dreams. Something else lingered beneath the scent of fear, something sharp, dark…cold.

My hands roamed through his hair, down his neck and over the thick, brutal scarring on his back.

He dragged my hands away, bringing them instead to his lips. "Do you recognise where we are?"

I looked out at the roll of the waves, at the swirl of indigo clouds racing across the darkening sky. Static filled the air, a storm just waiting over the horizon.

"Cornwall."

Laphaniel led me closer to the cliff edge and sat down upon the damp grass. Thunder purred in the distance, joining the roar of waves below us.

"You loved watching the storms," I said as he pulled me closer, his arms looping around my waist.

"I loved watching them with you." His words ghosted over my neck. "You tense up when you see the lightning, then startle when the thunder rolls in."

A laugh slipped from my mouth, real and wonderful. "They still make me jump, even when I'm creating them."

"I want to see you create a storm," Laphaniel said, fingers entwining through mine, his thumb rolling over my wedding band. "With that wonderful temper of yours, I bet they are magnificent."

I laughed again. "They are better than the tantrum I threw when you goaded me. All because I couldn't even light a candle."

"That was a spectacular storm." Laphaniel's own laugh huffed over my neck. "You even managed to throw Phabian off his horse…"

He stopped, breath hitching.

"It's okay." I tightened my grip on his hand, feeling him tense. "It's just us here."

He was silent for a few heartbeats, and when he spoke again, the laughter was gone. "I'm sorry about midwinter."

Lightning forked itself across the sky, followed by a boom of thunder. The clouds awoke, lashing down rain in a torrent that left us soaked.

"That wasn't your fault," I began, not bothering to move out of the onslaught of rain.

"No one forced me to drink," Laphaniel said. "I thought you weren't coming. They said you weren't coming, that you'd forgotten me."

I twisted to face him and pushed back the soaked strands of inky hair from his face. "And you believed them?"

"Yes."

I kissed the raindrops from his cheek, tasting them upon his lips. "I will never forget about you. I will never give up on you." I kissed him, long and slow. "I will bring you home."

"Tell me about it," Laphaniel said, mouth still so close to mine.

"Of home?" I asked, and he nodded. "We held a ball, and it was…it was wonderful, Laphaniel. I drank far too much and lost my shoes…Gabriel lost his too. We danced and drank all night long, and then I couldn't bear to be alone in our bed, so I dragged Oonagh and Nefina up with me."

"I was a little worried where that was leading," Laphaniel said, mouth curving into a smile.

I smiled back, my head touching his. "There are so many meetings, and stacks and stacks of paperwork I don't really understand. The Seelie expect so much from me, but I don't always know what I'm doing. I'm trying. I don't think it's enough."

"I heard you were attacked," he began, pulling back. He ran a finger over my arms, searching for bruises that were no longer there. "Are you okay? Gabriel?"

"I was incredibly lucky," I said. "I had to leave Gabriel with the Scara. Alice was there too; she is a clever little healer. Gabriel…he didn't look good." I narrowed my eyes. "Who told you?"

"Niven."

My blood froze at the name. "Why?"

"To bring misery, Teya," he said, words soft. "There is no other reason."

More lightning streaked over the angry clouds, shaking the earth with the booms of thunder. Waves rose against the cliff, dragging rocks back into the sea with every swell. The rain slammed down around us, drenching us to the bone.

"You couldn't dream of the Caribbean?" I said, blinking against the storm.

"Where's the fun in that?"

I gripped his hand tighter, ignoring the tears running down my face, mixing with the raindrops. "I need you."

"When this is done," Laphaniel said, blue eyes shining, "I'm taking you away from the castle for a while, away from the Seelie Court, away from everything. We're going to go deep into the woods, to a cabin and forget everyone else. I'll wake you at dawn, and you'll hate it because it's too early, but you'll follow me, and I'll show you unicorns again and mermaids and the way the suns dip over the trees at dusk. I'll show you everything I once promised to show you." His voice broke, tears trailing down his cheeks. "And for just a little while, we'll live the life I once promised you."

I never wanted to let him go. "You once promised me summer, too. One with wine-soaked fruit and just each other."

"I remember."

Lightning sliced open the mottled skies, the waves rearing up as if in greeting. More thunder followed, resonant and angry. Rocks tumbled into the sea, great chunks of earth crashing into the livid waters below.

"Queenling!"

We jumped, turning our heads at the shout that echoed across the dream.

"Queenling!" Datura bellowed again. Her wild hair snapped against the winds as she grabbed hold of me. "His dream is beginning to collapse, move!"

Laphaniel gripped my hand, panic flooding his eyes. I shoved the witch off me. "I'm not going back yet. I'm not leaving him."

"Move, girl!"

"Teya!"

He screamed my name. Datura forced me away, nails raking over my arms. She hauled me back, her voice a snarl in my ear.

"I will leave you here."

"I don't care...please let me go..."

"He is waking up!"

"Just a little longer," I called back, tearing my arm from her grasp as I fought to get to Laphaniel. "Please, just let me say goodbye...I just want to say goodbye."

"I will snap your arm, girl," the witch snarled, and sank her claws into my hand to drag me away.

I turned just in time to see the storm swallow everything up. The waves rushed against the cliff edge, erasing what was left. The skies erupted in a crash of colour, the lightning slashing through it and ripping it to pieces until nothing remained.

I could no longer see Laphaniel.

The world around us spun as it crumbled away, the chill of the sea breeze changing to the stifling heat of Datura's tent. The darkness lifted, storm clouds dissipating until nothing was left but the gentle flickering of hundreds of candles.

Datura released my hand and licked my blood off her fingers as she slowly shook her head at me.

"I can smell a wrongness on that boy," she said while I panted with my head on my knees. "Something black."

For a moment, so had I.

CHAPTER FIFTEEN

LAPHANIEL

I woke with a gasp, struggling to swallow the sob clawing its way up my throat. Charlotte loomed over me, claws curling over my shoulder.

"You would not wake," she hissed in the darkness.

Anger, quick and fierce, rose inside me, and before I could think, I lashed out. I struck her hard, sending her sprawling away from me.

"I don't want you here!" I screamed, hearing the scratch of claws as she scuttled up over the walls. "I want to go back!"

Sharp talons scraped over my neck from above; fangs brushed over my throat. "Anyone else, Angel, and they would be naught but dust and bone." Her words sang against my skin, ghostly soft. "Don't you ever strike me again."

Charlotte tightened her grip, her long, long fingers cold. Her breath breezed against me, carrying with it the scent of dew and blood.

My heart quickened against my ribs, my mind unable to recognise the monster overhead as a friend. I couldn't move, cringing as she pressed closer still, fangs at my ear.

"Have I made myself clear?"

I tried to call flame to my fingertips, the movement instinctive. I needed to banish the darkness for just a moment. Nothing happened. There was nothing but a hollow emptiness where once my Glamour had been.

"Angel?"

The claws lifted from my neck, and I fumbled away into a corner, the straw scratching at my arms as I moved. Bones scattered beneath my fingertips, all long picked clean.

Light bloomed from the lone candle, courtesy of the Spider still dangling from the ceiling. I looked up and met her eyes, all eight of them watched me, unblinking.

"Did I frighten you?"

A startled laugh burst from my mouth at her wide-eyed innocence. "You are terrifying, Charlotte."

Slowly, she slid down from the ceiling, claws clicking against the stone. With a satisfied smile she settled beside me on the filthy straw, smoothing out the gossamer folds of her tattered gown. Her sleeves lifted slightly as she moved, revealing black marks that spread up over pale arms.

"Did I do that?" I went to grab her, but she snatched my hand with a hiss and pushed me back. "Charlotte?"

"You did not."

"Then who?" I paused as cold realisation washed over me. "Phabian is hurting you because you're helping me."

The Spider said nothing.

"You said he knew." I pushed myself to my feet so for once I was looming over her. "How long has he been hurting you? How long before he adds you to that damned wall? Say something—"

"Since that first night," the Spider snarled, rising to face me with soundless grace. "When I stitched the remains of your back together while you screamed." She paused. "I have no untruths upon my tongue, boy. I will leave that little trick to you. The king knows everything, and you will be wise to remember that, you and the devil that comes here under a blanket of shadow."

Candlelight glimmered over her black eyes, all eight shining with fury. Her lips pulled back to reveal her fangs, cruel and wicked and huge.

"I don't ask for Niven to come down here."

"Do not trust her."

"I haven't yet completely lost my senses, Charlotte," I said, taking a breath before leaning against the cold wall. "What do you want me to do? Ask her nicely to leave me alone?"

"I want you to be careful," the Spider warned, pressing an icy hand against my cheek. Despite myself, I leaned into her.

"You should stay away," I said. The thought of her on that wall…

"I will not leave you to this darkness alone."

I closed my eyes, feeling the chill of the stone biting against my back. Beneath my feet, the straw was damp and dirty. The rats had found the bones too.

"I don't think," I began, my voice quiet, hesitant. "I don't think I can do this forever, Charlotte."

"You cannot give up hope, Angel," the Spider whispered, another set of hands coming up to cradle my face. "She will find a way."

I met her gaze. "What if she doesn't?"

She withdrew back into the shadow. "Do you still hear the voices in your head?"

The change of subject did not go unnoticed. "Yes."

"Did they tell you someone was going to poison the Queen?" Her voice was as soft as cobwebs. Her head tilted, eyes flashing.

My heart went cold. "Was it you?"

Her answering laugh was terrible. "Do you think it could have been?"

"Don't play games with me, Charlotte," I snapped, suddenly feeling very tired. "Just don't. Was it you?"

She bared her fangs. "No."

"Who was it?"

"Why? So you can tell Niven, like a good spy?"

My head ached, from hunger, from exhaustion…from being yanked from a dream I wasn't ready to leave. Mercifully, the thoughts whirring in my mind were my own, not the whispers that sprang from the darkness, telling me things I had no place hearing.

"You will end up pinned to that fucking wall, Charlotte."

"Tell me more of the voices you hear." The Spider ignored my warning, her eyes following a skinny rat as it scurried across the stone. "Is it only the one?"

I slid down the wall, drawing my knees up to rest my chin upon them. "It sounds like it's coming from everywhere."

"And it talks to you directly?"

I shook my head. "It's like I am eavesdropping on someone else's thoughts. Most of the time it's just noise."

Charlotte circled the room, claws scraping along the walls, making my teeth ache. Her gown lifted around her, the fabric not caring for the absence of breeze.

"You will barter these secrets you hear to help Niven?"

"For an hour out of this damp hell."

The Spider scoffed. "How little you sell yourself—"

"Get out."

She ceased her pacing, claws raised over the etchings I had made in the wall. "You are playing a very dangerous game."

"As are you," I hissed back.

"Yet I will not whore myself to that raven-haired devil."

"I have whored for worse, Charlotte," I said, not caring for the wide-eyed look she gave me. "If you have just come here to bitch at me, you can go."

"Answer me one question first," Charlotte began, claws taking up their tapping again. "And listen when I say I can taste the little lies you utter."

I gritted my teeth at the tap, tap, tap. "Ask away."

"If I had slipped poison into Niven's wine, would you have told her?"

Despite the curled lip, the flash of indignation in her eyes, I saw it: a flash of fear I doubted anyone else would have noticed. For the taste of freedom, an hour with the sun on my face after so long in the darkness, Charlotte truly thought I would sell her out.

"How can you ask me that?"

"Would you?" her words rasped through her fangs.

"No," I answered, with less anger than I wanted to direct at her. "Never in a thousand years. Now please just go away and leave me alone."

She hesitated, the air between us heavy and uncomfortable. "You wish for me to go?"

I scrubbed a hand over my face before piling the straw up to create a poor imitation of a pillow. I sighed and lay back, turning away from her. I wasn't up for a sparring match with words. I just thanked the gods it wasn't Niven.

"Well?" she pressed, and I swallowed hard.

"Yes, go." My voice cracked.

"Because you are angry at me?" Gods, she was persistent. "Or because you are ashamed of the tears you are trying to hide?"

"Goodnight, Charlotte."

I waited for her to retreat, for her to call back the feeble candlelight and leave me in peace. Instead, the scratch of her claws grew closer, the straw around me shifting as she settled beside me.

So, the monster that haunted the nightmares of even the bravest fey stayed close, her cold hand once again finding mine in the darkness.

CHAPTER SIXTEEN

NIVEN

*N*iven walked past the unlit pyres that stood tall under the shadows of the Unseelie labyrinth. The wood and straw were all hidden under mounds of pure white snow that, even to her, made a mockery of the bloodshed it disguised.

Faeries were left upon the frigid earth, wings snapped, claws removed, heads gone. All to be displayed upon the great obsidian wall surrounding the castle. The bodies would be left to thaw with spring, then set alight. If the wolves hadn't got to them.

The tang of fear was constant, only overridden by the stench of madness Phabian gave off as he butchered his way through his Court.

Beneath the terror and the chaos, Niven relished the tendrils of shadows that coiled around her, a heady Glamour that spilled out from the dark Court, making her long for more.

Despite the madness.

Despite the killing.

Despite the fear creeping over her. The shadows...*her* shadows, held onto her, and she was not yet ready to let them go.

Snow crunched underfoot while she walked, seeping up to her

calves and soaking through the fur-lined boots she wore. Her cloak billowed with the breeze, its blackness was made from the fragments of broken dreams, Glamoured to keep her warm.

Niven halted a little way from the rotting oak, waiting until the witch and the strange little girl left to do whatever witches did in the woods. Niven watched them go, both heavily cloaked and armed with large baskets, hinting they would be gone a while.

"Keep lurking in the shadows, and people will think you are up to something."

Niven snapped her head to the side, gaze falling upon the Seelie knight peering at her from a bench beside the ancient oak. He was upright at least, she noticed, bundled in matted furs and ragged blankets.

"Did they leave you out here to freeze to death?" Niven stepped forward, arms crossed as she silently surveyed the knight. He still looked pale and sickly, but not as though he hovered between the living and the dead.

"The child thought it good for me to get some fresh air," he answered, shifting slightly to make room on the decaying bench. "Sit down, I don't want you looming over me."

Bristling at the order, she obliged only because she was in no mood to argue. The furious words exchanged with the Unseelie King that morning had left her with a pounding headache and a stinging cheek.

The king had snarled at the shadows rising around her, dismissing her appeal for him to cease his killing. Bruises slowly coloured her pale throat, hidden beneath the high neck of her gown. Niven had hinted at the threat of an uprising, rebel groups like the Seelie were dealing with.

Phabian had taken one look at the shadows dancing at his Queen's feet and accused her of treason.

She shoved the memory far, far down. "When will you be fit to go home?"

The Seelie knight snorted, the stitched wounds around his neck bright against his pallid skin. "Why? Do you tire of my company, Demon Queen?"

Niven pulled down the furs covering him, eyeing the hideous marks slicing down his neck and chest. "They are healing well."

Gabriel leant away, wincing at the movement. "Do you even have any fey alive? Or is it only ghosts and screaming shadows that haunt your corridors?"

"What concern is that of yours?" she asked, picking at the pieces of brittle bench. The wood splintered in her hands, damp and moss ridden like everything within the Scara's dwelling.

"The little girl...Alice, talks to the crows," Gabriel began, eyes dark, "Your Court is destroying itself from within and you hold my king prisoner. It is of great concern of mine."

She made a dismissive gesture. "Laphaniel is fine."

"Then you are not torturing him?"

Her smile was a wicked thing. "It's a relative term."

"Why are you here?" He took a breath, closing his eyes as he shifted on the bench. He tilted his head back, staring up through the canopy of skeletal trees. "Do you enjoy seeing me like this? Disappointed I haven't died yet?"

"I don't know why I came," Niven answered truthfully.

"Well, I will admit you are better conversation than the crow witch." His words were soft. "The girl doesn't talk much."

"Do you think the witch ate her fingers?" Niven asked with a delighted curiosity. "I'd keep an eye on yours."

To both of their surprise he laughed, the sound as wicked as her own. "I never asked. I doubt it though, the crow witch adores that child."

He fell silent, eyes still closed, looking like the short conversation had utterly drained him. Sweat trickled down the side of his face, colour stained high on his cheeks.

"I think I'm going to die here," he murmured. "On a damp bed with a little girl and feathered hag for company."

Niven rolled her eyes. "Would you rather go out in battle like a good knight?"

"I want to go surrounded by beautiful naked women."

She snorted. "Don't we all?"

He moaned softly, his body giving a violent shake before he vomited in her lap.

"You—"

"I...don't—" He barely managed the two words before he retched again.

"Are you quite finished?" Niven snapped, forcing his head to his knees. She swept the sticky curls from his face with a curled lip.

He nodded.

With a scowl, Niven stood to fetch a cup of water from the nearby well. "Drink this."

He sipped the water, his hands shaking around the wooden cup. "They have gone to the market," he breathed, "deep beyond the Weeping Boughs. They said they would be back before dark...but I do not feel good...can you help me lie back down?"

Something stirred deep, deep within Niven, something long forgotten, thought long lost. She shoved it away with a low hiss.

"Please, Niven?" he murmured, lifting his head up before he pitched forwards and collapsed face first into the snow.

Niven stood, and stared down in disgust at the Seelie knight. She did nothing for a few breaths, every instinct urging her to turn away and walk back to the castle. Only her shadows loitered, curling around him in a caress so soft-hearted, she snarled at them.

Instead, Niven turned to the flock of crows perched high within the withered tree, their fathomless eyes regarding her in the silence. She sneered back at them.

"Tell your mistress the Seelie knight has need of her," she began, sending up her shadows to whip at their feathers. "Tell her if she leaves him again, I'll eat her heart."

They clicked their beaks at her before taking to the air in a frenzied whirl, a cloud of black against the too white sky. Turning to the prone knight, she gave him a sharp nudge with her boot, and he groaned.

"Good, you're still alive."

With a slow wave of her hand, she cocooned him tight within her shadows, lifting him from the frozen ground to place him down upon the bed of moss and rotten furs. Niven ignited the candles stuffed within the alcoves, the light catching the frozen dew tangled up in the thick cobwebs spread over the boughs. Grimacing at the damp, she dragged a blanket over him and sat down upon a nearby stool.

"You... do not have to stay," he murmured, his amber eyes blinking against the soft candlelight.

Niven crossed her legs and leant back against the wall. "It's a shitty place to die on your own."

His lips quirked into a tired smile. "I guess one beautiful woman will be enough for me."

"I'm keeping my clothes on, knight," Niven countered, but amusement flashed in her eyes.

"Shame, I would like to see what lies beneath those shadows, Queen of Demons."

His eyes fluttered shut; Niven waited a moment before peeling back his shirt, to take a closer look at the wounds she couldn't see.

To her surprise, they were clean, dressed in dry bandages that snaked around his muscled chest. She peeked beneath them, curious to see the gouges that had split him nearly in two.

She let out a low whistle, fingernails trailing down the ragged flesh that was slowly...so slowly knitting back together. A sheen of sweat beaded against his skin, his skin feverish beneath her touch.

"Do I get to run my hands over your chest?"

She snatched her fingers back. "I thought you were asleep?"

"Your hands are so wonderfully cold," he answered, words soft, eyes still closed. "Just like your heart."

"I could have easily left you in the snow to die."

His eyes flickered open. "Then why didn't you?"

Niven stood, the shadows of her cloak folding around her like a shroud of night. "Maybe next time I will."

The words hissed from her mouth, as cold as her supposed heart, but the Seelie knight only chuckled, the sound ending on a dry cough.

"Next time?"

Niven stormed towards the doorway, turning once to see him huddle beneath the blankets. He yawned deeply. "Goodbye, knight."

"Goodbye, Demon."

Niven took three steps away from the rotten tree before she flung her arms out in a surge of rage, sending her shadows sprawling through the thick woods. They clamoured over everything, thick and brutal and angry, snuffing out the heartbeats they swallowed up.

With fists clenched at her sides, she contemplated wrapping her shadows around the neck of the pretty knight and ending him.

Ending it…

Niven sucked in a breath, calling the darkness back to her. With a flick of her fingers her vomit-soaked clothes melted away, to be replaced with shimmering black conjured up by the little souls harvested from the woodland. She allowed her bruises to stand out, wearing the ring of purple like a necklace.

Her body thrummed with a chaotic energy that made her blood scream, not dulled by the destruction she had sent out through the trees. Oh, she knew what flooded through her, what ignited in her veins fuelling something long extinguished. Long forgotten.

With great, snarling hounds coiling at her feet, Niven glided back into the Unseelie castle, not bothering to notice if more tokens were dripping from the walls. She wanted to go to Phabian. The need to quell the roaring in her blood overwhelmed her, making it near impossible for her to think of anything else but the shedding of her clothes.

But something else nagged at her. The slow shift in her fey was blindingly obvious, their Glamour pulsing with too much fear…and hatred. She could taste the discord and the threat of bloodshed like spoiled wine.

Niven was not foolish to believe there wouldn't be another attempt on her life. She had fey tasting her food and drink, more guards at her chambers lest someone sneak in and slit her throat in the night.

She trusted no one.

It was a damned inconvenience the Queen of Unseelie could have lived without. She hungered for answers, hated the feeling of weakness of not knowing whom in her Court conspired against her. Perhaps they all did.

Though there was someone within the castle who held answers, who despite everything and for reasons unknown to her, had chosen to save her life.

Passing through the kitchens, she made her way down deep into the labyrinth, down the cold, twisting staircase, to the lonely little room buried way beneath.

CHAPTER SEVENTEEN

LAPHANIEL

*N*iven barely glanced at me before dumping a bowl of something hot at my feet. She paced, silent. I was thankful at least she had not seen Charlotte leave.

I had not felt the Spider slip away, not realised I had fallen asleep on her until I woke free of nightmares to the Unseelie Queen at my door.

At last she looked at me, eyes bright, lip curling into her usual sneer to disguise the brief flash of vulnerability on her face. "Have you been crying?"

I fought the urge to wipe at my face. "No."

She sniggered.

"I have nothing new to tell you, Niven," I groaned. My empty stomach ached at the sight of the food she had bought. "Or have you come down here simply to annoy me?"

She crouched, mist and darkness swirling around her ankles. "I want to find those conspiring against me."

"Oh, I would wager that would be everyone."

"Aren't you funny." She pointed to the food with a dark tipped finger. "It's not poisoned. You are of no use to me if you faint from hunger."

I eyed the thin broth. "Have you spat in it?"

She grinned. "Maybe."

Gristly pieces of meat floated beside what I guessed was some sort of vegetable. I didn't care what she had done with it. I didn't care that she watched me. I was too damned hungry.

Her eyes narrowed. "When did you last eat?"

She tossed me a piece of stale bread she had concealed in her cloak. I snapped it in half and set one piece away for another time. I ate everything, mopping the remaining slop up with the hard bread. It warmed my stomach, driving back the ache that had been plaguing me for too long.

"I lost track of when," I finally answered, wishing for more. "Charlotte brings food when she can…"

Niven tilted her head, ebony hair slipping over her bare shoulders. "Does she now?"

I tensed, not liking the way her eyes glinted. "Leave her alone."

"That Spider scuttles on dangerous ground," she said, standing. "She would do well to observe her King now and again."

"Would that be the same king that throttles you?"

Her hand went to her throat. "A small price."

"Until he decides your pretty head will look better nailed to the wall."

Niven said nothing for a moment, folding her arms against her chest. Her next words came unsure, as though she did not want to speak them at all. "Phabian is paranoid that I may be plotting to overthrow him."

I rolled my eyes. "You were nearly assassinated."

She shrugged and the mist wavered around her. "All logic and reason appear to have fled him. I no longer know who is more dangerous, him or whoever tried to poison me."

I chewed on a piece of bone, cracking it for the marrow inside. "If only someone had warned you of the dangers of the Unseelie Court."

"I want to know who it is," she hissed.

"I bet you do." I waited for her to lash out, but she just stood over me. "I have nothing new to tell you, Niven. Though if it is advice you are after, find whoever tried to kill you and do it quick. They come after you because you sit beside that monster. Find them and wipe them out with those shadows of yours."

Surprise flashed across her face before she could hide it. "You want me to side with Phabian?"

I broke off a chunk of the bread I was saving, not caring for the black colouring the edges. "You cannot win against him. If you die, it is very likely I would follow soon after."

She thought for a moment. "Prove I belong at his side?"

The tendrils of shadows curled around her legs like cats. "Don't pretend you don't enjoy it."

Her bright eyes flicked to me, something wicked danced behind the cold blue, so unlike the dazzling green of her sister's, full of life and love and hope. Niven was a void.

"Do you want to go out and play?"

I snapped my head up. "Now?"

She laughed at the eagerness I couldn't keep from my voice. "One hour, Laphaniel."

"Today?" The pathetic word slipped from my mouth. Despite the shame flooding me, I just knew I was close to begging her to let me out of my cell.

"I'll send someone for you now," Niven purred. She crouched low again, curling her fingers to grip my face. "But you keep your promise, understand? Get those crazy voices of yours talking, else I will not just forget to feed you, I will nail that insect to the wall myself."

She shoved me away and, without another word, turned to leave.

"Niven."

She waited, her back to me, black hair writhing around her like smoke.

"If I help you, I want my freedom."

The shadows stilled. "I have given you an hour."

"I'll find out who is conspiring to take your crown if you guarantee my complete freedom. Send me home."

"Fine," she spun on her heel, slow and graceful. "Help me keep my head and the crown upon it and I'll see to it that you run free."

I stood, a hollow laugh escaping my lips. "Just like that?"

She skipped closer, her words a breath against my ear. "But I'll also want that Spider's heart in a jar."

"You deserve every awful thing coming for you, you know that, right?" I hissed back. "I hope it is all worth it in the end."

"You won't even mull it over?" She trailed a finger over my cheek, tracing my jaw. "The contract is unbreakable, you lovesick fool. Take your hour and be grateful for it." Her fingers tightened, bruising. "Do not ever barter with me again."

"No matter how much you try to hide it, Niven," I began, and her nails dug in, "I can still smell it on you."

She bared her teeth. "And what is that?"

"Fear."

Her fingers slackened for a split second before she struck me, nails raking across my cheek. Without hissing another word, she left.

I didn't think anyone would come, that Niven had raised my hopes only to crush them for her own amusement. Especially after goading her, which even with a stinging cheek, I didn't regret.

Time would tell if I ever would.

THE SHARP BANG of a fist upon the door had me scrambling to my feet. The lock clicked and candlelight slipped into the darkness. A curse filled the quiet.

"You look like hell."

I blinked, shielding my eyes as the light came closer. I recognised that voice.

"Fell?"

The Raven Knight lifted the candle, holding it up to take a closer look at the tiny cell. Out of the six Unseelie knights that had accompanied us to overthrow Luthien, only two had made it home, Fell and Faolan. Fell's twin, Ferdia, hadn't been so fortunate.

"Look at the state of you." He held the candle higher, not bothering to hide the disgust on his face. Black eyes peered down at me, almost hidden beneath his black curls.

I wasn't in the mood to be mocked. "Why don't you hole yourself up in the dark and see how you fare."

"We didn't know," he said. "About the contract."

I shrugged. "Would you have done anything if you did?"

He didn't meet my eye, and it was all the answer I needed. "So where do you want to go for your hour of freedom?"

"Outside."

Fell barked a laugh. "When you can barely stand the candlelight? No. Next time maybe, we can go after nightfall."

With an extravagant bow he gestured to the open doorway, waiting while I peered up at the narrow winding staircase. More candlelight flickered in sconces along the wall, barely banishing the shadows dancing along the stone.

"Where then?" I asked. I just wanted the breeze on my face…an open space.

Fell beckoned me on. "Just follow me."

I took a hesitant step up, then another. Something in my chest turned leaden. Fell waited, saying nothing.

There were hundreds of steps. I could not remember there being so many steps when I was forced down them. My legs barked in pain, sweat ran in rivulets down my back. I stopped again and again to catch my breath, Fell waited, saying nothing.

After what seemed like a lifetime of climbing steps, I stumbled into a wide corridor. The black walls stretched high, the ceilings arched above. Stone dragons lined the walls, gaping mouths each holding a flickering candle. There were no windows.

Fell grabbed my elbow and hauled me along. His boots echoed along the dark marble, my bare feet made no sound. He dragged me through a set of ornate doors, the handles gaping maws complete with jagged fangs.

"Oh wonderful," I said, looking around. "The library? Am I to choose some books to help pass the time?"

The library spanned further than I could see, lit only by glowing orbs that bobbed along the shelves. Ladders gilded in gold rested against towering black cases. Gargoyles crouched from the shelves, carved from the same obsidian stone as everything else in the damned castle. The ceiling above reached high, domed and made of glittering dark glass. The beams surrounding it were carved with vines, the wood looping around itself. Jagged glass thorns pierced out from the carvings, catching the light.

"Touch anything here," Fell said, "and the librarian will eat you. Keep quiet, this is the quickest way."

"To where?" I pressed, but the Raven Knight just grinned.

We passed through the library without being devoured. Fell led us through a small, indiscreet door that opened into another corridor. A much narrower corridor. I realised where we were going.

"Fell…"

"Hurry up, you haven't got long."

More steps. Going down and down and down. The black walls gave way to wet stone, water tricked down over the cracks.

I sucked in a breath, hearing it catch. Fell continued walking.

The steps led down into a passageway barely wide enough to walk down. It stretched on and on. My head grazed the rough stone above, my shoulders grazed the walls. My chest tightened, as if a fist were wrapped around my heart.

The tunnel split into somewhere I faintly recognised, opening up to my immense relief. Great doors greeted us and Fell shoved them open before he turned to me with a smile.

"Here we are." He slapped me on the shoulder. "Enjoy."

Stone serpents wound their way around the vast columns, reaching far up into the rock above. Stalactites dripped from the darkness, like teeth. I had no idea how far underground we were…the thought of all the weight of all that earth piled on top of us…

Dark water rippled in the massive pools, catching the light pouring from glowing orbs floating just below the carved stone ceiling. Behind us, the doors slammed shut, trapping me inside. The noise boomed across the cavern, disturbing the deep, deep waters.

I remembered those waters.

I forced my feet to move, fists curling at my side. The pools were empty of life...huge and dark and empty.

My Glamour had been torn away within those pools.

I couldn't see the bottom...couldn't see through the black waters... how deep it went.

"I will shove you in the water in a minute."

"No!" I staggered back from the edge, fighting to catch my breath. "Don't."

"Pull yourself together!" Fell snapped, grabbing my shoulder to haul me closer to the water. "You are filthy, and you stink worse than a pig pen in summer."

He dragged me closer and steam hit my face. Water lapped over the edge. I needed to get away...get out...get up...up...up.

Blood sprayed when my fist collided with Fell's face, and he dropped my arm with a snarl. He swore, red streaming down his nose. I slipped to my knees. My hand throbbed, a few fingers likely broken from the punch I landed on him.

Fell stared down at me as my breaths barked from my mouth. My hands slid against the smooth, wet stone as I thought to get them in.

Up...up...up...up...I needed to get up.

To get out.

"What the hell have they done to you?" He spat blood at my feet but made no other move to touch me. "What is it?" he demanded. "Underground? The tight, dark spaces? The water?"

I could barely hear him over the roaring in my head, my vision blinkered. I squeezed my eyes shut to block it all out.

If I just could get a breath in...

"I wouldn't stand up if I were you—"

I shoved myself to my feet then hit the stone hard, barely registering the pain before blacking out completely.

My head pounded when I blinked my eyes open. Fell nudged me with the toe of his boot, looking a little concerned. I swallowed the sharp, metallic taste in my mouth, unable to stop myself from trembling.

Fell sat beside me. "I can't believe you fainted."

I rested my head on my knees, fighting not to vomit. "Can we just go back?"

"I was trying to help."

My entire body was drenched in a cold sweat; my damned hands wouldn't stop shaking. "Then I would really hate to see what you do when you're not trying to help."

Fell gave my shoulder an awkward pat. "I owe you my life, Luthien's blade would have cut through me like butter if not for you. I will never forget that it was you who dragged Ferdia from that swamp, either. You refused to let him go, when no one in our group would have lifted a finger to help you. I wanted to repay a debt."

I had bitten my lip. "By drowning me?"

The memory of facing Luthien was still too clear in my mind. The flash in her eyes as she flung the sword embedded in her stomach towards the Raven Knight. That manic glee turned to fury when I slammed against him, rolling us both so the blade whistled over us. It had caught my shoulder, a thin slice I had barely noticed. Too damned close for the life of an Unseelie.

Guilt flashed over his face. "I was going for tough love."

"What the hell am I going to do?" I asked, my voice still not quite holding steady. Blood dripped from Fell's nose; I wasn't sorry I hit him. "Niven can't see me like this."

"After we didn't all make it back, I wasn't in the best place…head-wise," Fell began, swiping a hand across his nose. Blood smeared across his cheek. "Losing Ferdia was…is like losing a limb. His absence is always there. A part of me still expects them all to walk into the hall, for Cole to bark orders. It hits me in the gut every time they don't come back."

I stared at the dark waters before tilting my head to gaze up at the cavernous ceiling, at the stone serpents that coiled around the columns holding the tons and tons of rock up. My chest tightened again, and I looked away.

"So, what did you do?" I asked.

His eyes flashed. "I killed things."

I waited.

"I picked up my sword and turned the air red with bloodshed," Fell said with a grin. "After a while, I realised it wasn't the killing I was needing, but the act of swinging my blade like it meant something. I needed it to mean something again."

"I don't think murder is permitted within my hour of freedom," I said dryly.

Fell tipped his head back and laughed. "I doubt you could pick up a sword, let alone swing it." He found a loose pebble and launched it into the pool, disturbing the waters. "You need to focus that fear into something useful before it's turned against you. Learn to wield a sword again, batter something, fight someone."

"I have one hour a week."

"For the rest of eternity." Fell shrugged, as if it were that easy. "What do you say?"

I turned to him, genuinely curious. "Why?"

"Because I don't like what they're doing to you," Fell said after a moment, eyes darkening. "A lot of us don't."

His words settled over me, heavy with everything he wouldn't dare admit. Not with the shadows always listening.

Another pebble appeared in his hand, and he skimmed it over the water. It bounced three times before sinking. I watched him do it again and again, content for just a moment, to sit with someone who I might call a friend.

If it happened to be Niven's attempted killer, so be it.

CHAPTER EIGHTEEN

TEYA

*T*he screams of the serpents carried on the freezing air, echoing alongside the whoops of sheer joy that came from the witches mounted upon them. Even in the failing light, their bright blue scales glimmered as they wove through the mist.

The cold on my face felt good after the smothering heat of Datura's tent. Visiting Laphaniel's dream had left me strangely exhausted, and after exchanging only a handful of words with Nefina, I passed out cold on top of the fat pillows.

I had woken with a dry mouth and a throbbing headache.

Datura remained in her stifling tent, her dark eyes heavy-lidded, a lazy smile stretched upon her mouth. She had barely moved since dragging me back, spread languid and useless on her velvet cushions. Nefina had compared it to an Ember high, her lips curled in a disgusted sneer.

The High Witch of the Coven of Bones had finally summoned me as the twin sunset began to bleed down the mountain. Darkness would follow soon enough, and I knew all too well how nightfall stirred up witches.

"Remember to keep your temper," Nefina warned, head tilted back to watch the serpents high above us. "The witches will delight in tormenting you."

I took a breath, the cold air burning my throat. I didn't know how the witches could stand it. The chill was relentless, the wind a brutal force of ice and misery.

"I'll do my best," I replied, keeping hold of my furred hood to shield my eyes from the damned weather.

I spotted Magnhild striding through the camp towards us, flanked by another witch whose snow-white hair had been cropped to her scalp. Neither witch wore cloaks, their skin as pale as the landscape around them, eyes both burning the same cruel blue.

"Follow me, Mortal Queen," Magnhild said, her words as sharp as the wind. "Time to see if you are deemed worthy of our help."

"And if I'm not?"

The other witch snapped her sharp teeth at me, the meaning perfectly clear.

"This is Solvi, our Silent One," Magnhild began,."She will have the honour of skinning you alive if you displease our High Witch."

Solvi opened her mouth to reveal bone white teeth, all filed down to points, then she waggled the blackened stump that was all that remained of her tongue.

"Solvi is our secret keeper, our listener of whispers." Magnhild reached across the gap to entwine her hand with the witch's. "You should hear those whispers, Mortal Queen."

"I've had my fill of the musings of witches, thank you," I replied, not taking my eyes off Solvi.

With a low laugh, Magnhild gestured for us to follow. I gave Nefina a quick nod before stepping after the two witches, the latter making no sound upon the fresh fallen snow.

We wound through the campsite, the tents all in shadow, the firepits burning low. Overhead, even the serpents had quietened.

They led us between dying trees with leaves of black, down a narrow pathway of sheer ice, their cackles echoing like banshees as we fought to keep our footing.

Up we went, up steps carved from shining black rock, through more emaciated trees, their trunks bleached white. Everything looked dead and bleak, nothing lived. There was no sound but our ragged breathing and the sniggers of the witches.

Just as I thought we were coming to the apex of the mountain we turned a corner, and the heavy scent of fresh pine hit me in the face.

A forest.

Beside me, Nefina gasped as we stared out at the utterly impossible expanse of trees stretching far out into the distance. Pristine snow weighed heavily upon the evergreen boughs, the lush green beneath, barely visible.

"But…we're at the top of the mountain…" I spluttered, fighting to see the end of the woodland.

Solvi snorted, shaking her head as she stepped into the shadows of the giant trees. Magnhild stared at me for a moment, taking in my wonder with a proud smile on her face.

"Faerie has no end, Teya. You will do well to remember that."

I looked at Nefina, but her eyes were as filled with wonder as my own. "I never once thought I would walk through a Witch Wood."

Magnhild's smile was not friendly as she said, "Let us hope you get to walk out again."

We followed down a pathway cut through the deep snow. Pine needles were ground into the frozen earth where constant footsteps had trod upon it, filling the air with their rich scent. Torches blazed from the sides, knotted branches that dripped with black tar.

Drums began a slow beat in the distance, the sound all too familiar. My heart sped up, pumping fear around my already fraught body. The last time I had heard witch drums, I was bleeding and being hunted by ravenous hags.

We had escaped the Eerie that night by sheer luck. Laphaniel had managed to barter safe passage, but it had cost him three pints of blood.

I would never forget the desperate ride through the witches' camp. How we rode upon the back of a blood-drinking faerie horse with the screeches of witches bellowing behind. I remembered the feel of

Laphaniel's hands tight around me, one pressed to my bleeding side, urging me to stay awake.

The wound had scarred, despite the neat row of stitches Laphaniel had administered within the shelter of a dark cave. I smiled to myself at the memory...not because it was a pleasant one...because Laphaniel had no problems sewing me back together but couldn't bear Charlotte's glass tipped needles.

"What are you grinning at?" Nefina hissed beside me, her face pale and troubled.

I shook my head, the memory fading. "Your brother has a needle phobia."

"You are a strange girl, Teya," she said, though her lips quirked up.

Magnhild led us to a circular wooden hut, its thatched roof barely visible beneath all the snow. Smoke billowed from the chimney, green and thick. Two skulls protruded from pikes in the ground either side of the door, mouths stretched wide to accommodate the dripping candle stubs.

Solvi pulled back the hide covering the doorway, the leather stretched smooth with age, and gestured for us to enter with a nod of her head. I caught a glimpse of a faded tattoo on the corner of the old leather, the colours bleeding together. Solvi noted my horror and grinned.

Ducking under the archway, I passed the smirking witch to stand in the centre of the hut, Nefina coming up to stand close by. Her hand brushed against mine in silent reassurance.

It didn't surprise me to see the High Witch sitting upon a throne of bones, some undoubtedly picked clean by the countless ravens perched on the beams above, some still clinging to fragments of flesh.

The High Witch was not dressed in silks like the others, or in the skinned furs of wolves. She wore bone.

Her corset was made from a ribcage, the skin beneath bare, her breasts covered only by a stretch of black paint. Her skirts flared out around her, almost like shadows. But shadows they were not, for if you listened carefully, you could hear them wail.

Around her milk-white throat sat a necklace of teeth.

She smiled at me, the greenish firelight catching the points of her sharp, sharp teeth. As instructed by Magnhild, I sank to my knees, ducking low enough to scrape my head along the floor.

"Many queens and kings have bowed before me, girl," the High Witch began, drumming her curling talons upon the bones. "Some went holding their heart's desire and left without their souls. Many never left at all."

She patted her throne with an odd tenderness, reaching down to pluck a scrap of meat from the bone of her armrest. The birds overhead shrieked in outrage as she popped it into her mouth.

"What will you have me pay?" I asked, swallowing down my fear before I stood. The High Witch leant forward, fingers steepled while she sized me up. Her dress of bone clattered.

"What are you willing to lose, little Queen of Seelie?"

Nefina tensed beside me. The High Witch stood, the haunting souls of her skirts rippling around her legs. Deep emerald eyes peered at us through knots of unruly hair, the white streaked through with faded red. As if she had continuously run blooded fingers through it.

"I understand you know why we are here?" Nefina's voice held steady, even when the witch turned her focus on her with a bend of her neck.

"You want your Kingling back," she breathed, closing her eyes as the birds began to caw and click their beaks.

From the corner of my eye, I spotted Magnhild and Solvi share a look before leaving the hut, giving the inky birds a wary glance.

"I do," I said over the piercing caws.

The High Witch stretched out her clawed hand to me, her fingers hovering a hair's breadth away from my face. "Your husband?"

I nodded as her bright eyes opened. Her fingers brushed over my wedding band, tongue flicking over the points of her teeth.

"Shadows and screaming," she breathed, eyes fluttering closed. "Spiders and dust."

"I don't understand…"

"Be quiet!" she screamed, throwing out a hand in a burst of ice.

The cawing stopped instantly; solid bodies thumped to the ground in a spray of feathers. "I would leave him to die, Queen of Seelie."

She turned in a whirl of black while I stood frozen. It was Nefina who grabbed her arm and forced her back.

"Wait!"

Something cracked as Nefina was sent sprawling to the ground. Blood leaked from her nose, her mouth. The High Witch stood over her and in an instant she was at her throat, needle-like teeth sinking deep. Nefina screamed.

Glamour flooded down my arms, to my fingertips, livid and terrified. The candle stubs blazed and died out before exploding into furious flames. The wind picked up, answering the command that was tearing at my throat...thundering in my head, my heart...everything.

The High Witch turned to me, my storm whipping at her hair, and she laughed. With the barest lift of her hand, everything went still and silent. Only her cackling filled the void. The sound of nightmares.

She snuffed out my Glamour as easily as the candlelight around me, until I felt nothing of it...nothing of Laphaniel.

Struggling and panicked, I fought against her. Ice crept up around my throat, a caress and a warning before it pushed me down to my knees.

"You have no power here, Queen of Seelie," a whisper in the darkness. "Remember that."

The hold on my throat lifted, the candles all burst to life around me with a hiss. The familiar pulse of my Glamour didn't return.

Dragging myself from the floor, I hurried to Nefina and pressed my hand against the raw wound on the side of her neck.

"Is that it then?" I hissed while the High Witch licked the blood from her fingers. "You won't do anything?"

She cocked her head, red gleaming on her lips. "It is for the best."

Nefina whimpered beside me, her hand coming up to cover mine. I met the High Witch's cold stare. "I'll do anything."

She scowled. "Oh, I bet you would."

"Name your price."

A step towards us, then another, until the toes of her pointed boots scraped along Nefina's side. With a splayed hand she rested her clawed fingers just below her navel, pressing hard enough for Nefina to gasp out.

My body went cold. "No."

"Yes," Nefina breathed, closing her eyes.

The witch pressed harder; a delighted grin slashed upon her face. "I want what will one day bloom inside here."

"My firstborn," Nefina breathed while I shook my head in mute horror.

With a quick swipe, the witch held Nefina's chin in her clawed hands and shook her. "You will only ever have the one child. A bastard for the life of a bastard."

"Don't, Nefina," I pleaded, but she wouldn't look at me. "We'll think of something else…anything else…"

"This is the price of your help?"

"It is."

I gripped her hand, my fingers already coated in enough blood. "No, Nefina!"

"I will pay it."

"Then it is done."

"No!" I screamed the word as the High Witch drew a fingernail across Nefina's belly. Marking her, branding her.

The High Witch stood, tilting her head as a flock of crows swooped in through the open windows, their cawing soft and lilting. They circled the hut once before they started to feast upon the slowly thawing bodies of the birds littering the floor.

"Death would have been a mercy, Queen of Seelie," the witch mused, eyes narrowing as the last of the clicking of beaks died down. "Remember your part in all this."

"I don't need your warnings," I spat. "You have your payment, tell me how we can save Laphaniel."

I stayed close to Nefina, her hand resting on her stomach, her eyes fixed upon the witch. The bleeding to her neck slowed, little more than a slow trickle that soaked the fur of her cloak.

The High Witch slipped back into her throne, the bones creaking as she made herself comfortable.

"The Seelie line passes down through a matriarch line—since you have no heir that line ends with you."

"I know this," I pushed the words through gritted teeth, terrified Nefina had given everything up for nothing.

"What happens upon your death, Queen of Seelie?"

"The contract ends, but..."

The High witch held up a finger to silence me, even the surrounding birds went quiet. "There are many, many spells to bring upon death. There are only a few that can bring you back again."

I didn't dare hope it could be that simple.

"None of those spells will break your contract with the Unseelie."

I held tight to that hope, not allowing it yet to slip from my fingers. "But?"

"A true death will suffice, soul cleaved and your body cold." The High Witch tapped a claw against her lip. "I have heard whispers of souls called back, even after time has passed. A spell like that should be enough."

"Should?" Nefina sat up, eyes sharp.

"When can you do it?" It was my turn to ignore Nefina's horrified glare. The High Witch just shook her head, delight dancing in her eyes.

"Oh, I have the powers to kill you outright, girl." The witch laughed. "I would not have the first clue how to drag you back again."

The world stopped turning, my heart became thunder in my ears. "So, you can't help me?"

"No," The witch began, reaching out to run her long fingers down a crow perching nearby. "But I know of someone who can."

I didn't like the smile she gave me.

"And they know of this spell?"

The High Witch nodded, madness dancing behind her dark eyes. "Oh yes, Mortal Queen of Seelie. But it is an ancient piece of magic and is temperamental at best. Death never likes to be trifled with. You, of all people, should know that by now."

Laphaniel didn't want to come back, I would never forget that. He was dragged back from whatever place his soul had found peace and had returned without it.

"I hope he is worth it," the witch sneered.

"He is." Nothing would stop me getting to him. "Where can I find this spell caster?"

A laugh, low and wicked and heartless. "How would I know, Queen of Seelie? You were the one to banish her."

CHAPTER NINETEEN

TEYA

*L*uthien.

The fragment of hope I clung to turned to ash, leaving behind a gaping hole I didn't know if I could live around.

Nefina's face echoed my disbelief. She closed her eyes, tears slowly making their way down her lovely, white cheeks. She still lay sprawled upon the floor.

Her sacrifice, all for nothing.

"You cheated us," I finally said, pushing the words through the rawness of my throat. "You know Luthien would never help me."

"Oh?" The High Witch crossed her legs, waves of trapped souls slipping over her skin. "Perhaps not for your lover, no. Maybe for something else she covets so deeply."

"Your crown." Nefina's eyes widened. "Upon your death, the crown will automatically fall back to her."

Her beautiful blue eyes shone with something other than tears. I turned away.

"Luthien is a monster, Nefina."

"She is also the rightful Queen of Seelie," the High Witch said. "Perhaps it is time to restore the balance before…"

She stopped and the birds around her began screeching.

"Before what?"

The witch stood, her eyes wholly black. A phantom wind lifted the tendrils of her white hair, so it floated around her in a ghostly halo. She pointed a finger at me, teeth flashing.

"You cannot feel it, Mortal Queen, because you are not tethered to Faerie. You do not listen hard enough." She fixed her dark gaze on Nefina. "But you, deep within your heart, you know something is wrong. Something is stirring."

"What is it?" Nefina demanded, and pushed herself to her feet at last.

The witch took a breath, a euphoric smile stretching onto her face. "Everything."

Arabelle's words echoed in my mind, words of death and war and bloodshed. Her plea for mercy when the time came.

"What has it got to do with Laphaniel?" I asked. "Or is it just half-truths and nightmares? Words to sow fear and nothing more."

"Are you afraid, Mortal Queen?" The High Witch pressed a hand to her chest, over the bone she wore. "It feels as though something is crushing me here. The birds whisper. The shadows, too, as do the trees. I cannot see. It is not time for me to see. But you should be afraid."

"Is it something terrible?" I asked, needing to know more than the fragments of prophecy that were getting me nowhere.

Her grin was pure madness. "It is awful, Mortal Queen."

Laphaniel once warned me not to listen to the words of witches. "Can it be stopped?"

The High Witch shook her head, her smile unfaltering. "Not anymore, it would seem."

Nefina reached for my arm, forcing me to look at her. "We need to find Luthien, now is not the time to dwell upon the whispers of crows."

The High Witch turned her back on us, flinging something into the green flames. They burst upwards with a hiss, burning emerald for only a moment before turning black. From the embers she plucked a shining ebony feather and passed it, still smouldering, to Nefina.

"Do not forget our bargain, little whore," she began, teeth glinting. "When this becomes naught but dust, your son belongs to me."

"And if I never bear a child?" Nefina asked, back straight. Fearless.

"Then there will be nothing for me to take," was the witch's reply before she dismissed us with a wave of her hand.

Darkness had truly fallen when we wound our way back through the maze of tents. The firepits crackled low. Above, the night sky held only stars.

Someone called for Solvi over the darkness; the silent witch gave us a mocking bow before disappearing into the shadows.

"It would be wise to remain in your bunks tonight. The darkness calls to us witches in ways you could not fathom." Magnhild prised open the flaps to our tent, her cold eyes fixed elsewhere. "Sleep well, Mortal Queen."

I settled on my cot, making no move to take off my boots or the layers I wore. Nefina hovered by the wood burner, arms crossed.

"It is something," she murmured, stoking the flames until they filled the tent with warmth. "It is more than we have ever had before."

I looked up, hating the glimmer of hope in her eyes. "Who is to stop Luthien from simply slitting my throat and leaving me for dead? What will happen then, Nefina? Do you think Phabian will allow Laphaniel to walk out if I'm gone?"

She met my stare, standing cold and unforgiving. "Then let him go."

The words hit like a physical blow. "Abandon him?"

"Either seek out Luthien or—"

"Or what?" The words were a snarl on my lips.

Tears brimmed in her eyes. "Or you stop this. Just stop."

I was the one to turn away. "I can't."

The cot dipped slightly as Nefina sat beside me. "You promised us better than this, Teya. You cannot keep this up…only being half there for us all."

"He needs me…"

Her voice cracked, a soft sob escaping her mouth. "We need you."

I squeezed my eyes shut, guilt washing over me at the knowledge I was failing my court…my fey. I was the reason the rebels were gathering, the reason behind the fracturing of the Seelie. I promised to make their court strong again.

I couldn't do it alone.

"We find Luthien," I breathed, hating her name on my lips. "I don't know what else to do."

Nefina folded her hand over mine. "Neither do I."

I lay awake after Nefina slipped into a restless sleep upon the other cot, tossing and turning beneath her mound of blankets. I stared up at the thin beams holding the tent up, watching the shadows creep over the furs lining the fabric walls. Outside, cackles and screams echoed in the night. The thump of wings tore through the laughter, the screeches of serpents drowning out all other noise until there was nothing else.

Sleep didn't come for me, but I didn't want it to. I was too wary of what nightmares it would bring if I dared to close my eyes. Instead, the warnings of the High Witch swam in my mind, joined by those of Arabelle and the Scara. The whisperings of crows and trees and witches.

Of Laphaniel.

The night he died in that cursed tower came rushing to my mind, unbidden and unwanted. I could see him…feel him in my arms. Cold. He had gone cold.

Dead.

I remembered those shadowy hands, the anger…the disgust that poured from them in waves of utter, utter fury.

Because Laphaniel was never meant to come back…

Hadn't wanted to.

But something had dragged him back from wherever his soul had gone. Something bigger than Sorcha's curse. Something far bigger than all of us.

Dawn came quietly, the screams of the night silencing as the suns began to rise. Nefina slept on, still at last. I lay on my cot and swiped a hand over my gritty eyes before throwing another log into the fire.

We had to find Luthien, but I had no idea where to start. I needed to go home and organise my court, do something about the rebels. Unite my fey. Be queen. I needed to do both, and I felt as if I were failing completely at everything.

All I had wanted in the end was a life with Laphaniel away from everything else. Only us, in a house made of stone and blossoming trees.

Perhaps I could hope we would be allowed that. To live away from the Court. We could re-build the house, re-build everything we lost and just be together as we had once hoped we could be.

Just us.

A little broken, a little bruised, maybe…

But just us.

Maybe if I gave Luthien her crown back, restored everything back to how it should have been from the start, we could be happy again.

Nefina's soft curtain of hair splayed across her face while she slept, her breathing peaceful. I couldn't forget how she suffered at Luthien's hands. Couldn't forget the bruises that covered every inch of her body, the wounds on her stomach and legs so deep she couldn't walk for days.

Oonagh's hands had been broken, fingers dislocated. Gabriel only had fleeting memories of his time spent in those awful cages thanks to the fractured skull he'd suffered because he chose to side against her.

The other Seelie fared little better, some wounds running so deep they didn't heal, and I had to watch as they slowly slipped away.

Could I truly abandon them to Luthien again?

"It is too early in the morning to be that deep in thought, Teya," Nefina murmured from her cot, stretching her arms high above her head with a deep yawn. "I know what you are thinking."

"I doubt it."

She sat up, shoving the hair from her eyes. "I am not afraid of Luthien."

"She is a monster, Nefina," I began, and paused. "You could come with us, if you wanted to…and Oonagh, and anyone who wanted to come."

Nefina laughed, a quick snort of amused disbelief. "Gods, no! Imagine that, Teya. A house of lost souls. A little court of rejects. Absolutely not."

"But…"

"No." Her voice remained firm. "If you do this, go far away with my brother and just be happy somewhere. We will find our own way."

"You could just come," I said softly. "I think Laphaniel would like you close by, to know you're safe."

She smiled. "I will find my own way, Teya. I am a big girl."

I wanted to say more, to find a way everyone could be happy and safe and far away from Luthien. It was naïve and foolish, and I knew it.

I couldn't simply give everyone a happy ending, not if I were selfish enough to try and grasp at my own.

We left the tent to seek out some breakfast, the mountain wind as unforgiving as the day before, whipping against any exposed skin with its icy teeth. Datura spotted us while we made for one of the fires, dressed in golden furs, not for one moment trying to blend in.

"I have nothing to say to you," I snapped at her, still disgusted at the delight she'd found in Laphaniel's nightmares.

The witch lifted an elegant brow, eyes flashing. "I gave you what you wanted. I simply enjoyed the ride."

"You fed off his fear."

"And you got to see your lover again." Datura shrugged, the furs she wore shifting with the movement. "To which I received no thanks."

She ladled a spoonful of thin porridge into a bowl, shoving a young witch out of the way to get closer to the fire. It did not go unnoticed that she wore the necklace of the witch she had slaughtered.

"I sensed a blackness to those nightmares that sent my heart racing," she whispered. "Voices in the darkness echoing the caws of the crows nesting here."

My appetite vanished. "What did they say?"

Datura helped herself to more porridge, ignoring the lingering gazes from the other witches gathered by the fire.

"They kept repeating a name, whispering it over and over."

"What name?"

"Niven."

I didn't think it was possible to feel colder, yet a chill like one I had never known seeped deep within me. "Why her?"

The Ash Witch tossed down her empty bowl before burying her hands in the folds of her cloak. "I do not know, Mortal Queen. That name echoed within the darkness, a beacon in a swarm of black."

"What does it mean?"

"It means your sister and your husband are tied up in something none of us truly understand, and we do not like it."

Datura made to walk away, but I grabbed at her arm and dragged her back. "Go back and listen!"

The witch stared down at my hand, then slowly back at me. "No."

"You enjoyed every last minute of his nightmares, why wouldn't you do it again?"

Despite the cold, Datura began to unbutton her cloak, lifting her thick tunic to reveal a mess of bruising over her stomach. "I do not think I would make it back alive next time."

I stared at the sprawling welts on her skin, the marks trailing across her belly and up over her chest, the rest hidden by her clothing. "Laphaniel's nightmares did that?"

"No," Datura said, the words hissing past her teeth. "Whatever is coming for us did."

"It shadows over us all, Mortal Queen," Magnhild said, appearing from the mists to settle near the fire, her hands tucked behind her back. She shot Datura a quick look, dipping her head slightly before turning back to me. "We can do nothing but listen."

"The covens will all meet," Datura said to Magnhild. "And soon, I sense it in my marrow."

"Hmmm," was all the Bone Witch said, tilting her head towards the skies.

"Your own High Witch flies at the month's end," Datura stated, a grin spreading across her face at the other witch's surprise. "Oh, did you not know?"

"I would have been told."

A shrug, that grin widening, showing teeth. "And yet, you were not."

"Will you tell me what you find out?" I dared to ask, wary of Magnhild's bared teeth.

"Perhaps I will, Mortal Queen. Perhaps I will," Datura answered. "I feel we shall meet again, you and I. Not within this frozen waste, and I fear not for a long while. But, oh, I want to see how this all ends, Seelie Queen who is not."

With a deep chuckle rising from her throat, she walked away. The Bone Witch glowered at her back.

"I came here to give you a message," Magnhild said, not tearing her eyes away from the Witch of Ashes. "Would you like it?"

She held her hands in front of her, finally meeting my eyes as a horrible, wicked smile spread over her lips. If it were not for Nefina's sudden grip on my arm, I would have fallen to the ground.

Long ago, hope had taken root deep within me. A hope buried so deep, it seemed nothing could tear it out. At times it faltered…too battered and lost to make itself known, but it was always there. It wound itself around my very soul, a comfort I clung to, for when there was nothing else…I could have hope that despite the darkness, every-thing would be okay in the end.

It was stupid and childish.

I took the frozen bird from Magnhild's hands, her nails scraping over its solid body. From its bloodied, bent beak I tugged at the parch-ment it carried, breaking the seal with trembling fingers.

I didn't need to read the words. The blood splattered over the pages said all I needed to know. But I recognised Oonagh's handwriting, hurried and frantic…

Come back!

CHAPTER TWENTY

NIVEN

*T*he Unseelie king slept, red hair splayed out over the soft pillow, mouth parted as he breathed deeply. Content. His shadows slumbered too, wavering sleepily over the walls, trailing over her own, as if still fighting to claim them.

Niven stared at the ceiling, at the blackened branches trailing down to coil over the floor. The dead wood splayed out over the walls, dried blossom still clung in places, the petals curled tight. Candle stubs dripped wax from knots in the bark. She stretched out her hands, loosening the tightness in her wrists, not needing any light to know there would be bruises.

"Contemplating slitting my throat, my love?" Phabian said, not moving from where he lay, eyes still closed.

The shadows stirred, guttering out the last of the candlelight until there was nothing left but darkness. "I would have done it already."

His laughter tore through the black, eyes flashing in the pitch as he sat up. "Do you think you could?"

"Do you?"

She rose from the bed, the silk covers slipping from her body. The slight movement pulled at her aching limbs, but she said nothing while she clothed herself in mist and magic.

A hand reached for her in the black, almost gentle, a ghost of what he once was. "Stay mine, Niven, and I will never hurt you."

"Where else would I ever go, my love?" Niven breathed, her hand curling over his fingers. They tightened over hers. Possessive.

"You seem to visit that mongrel often enough, all the way down in the dark," the Unseelie King drawled. "If you thought for a moment I hadn't noticed."

Niven snorted. "I'm not sleeping with Laphaniel."

"Conspiring then?" Warning crept into his tone, those fingers gripping harder. "You let him out of his cell."

"A bribe and nothing else," Niven said. "He is helping me discover who may be leading the discord in this court."

"And how does he do that from his foul little room?"

She contemplated what to tell him...how much truth to divulge. "He has a keen ear for gossip, you would be surprised at what whispers carry all the way down there."

"And what whispers have you been told?" The pressure on her fingers lessened, his hand moved to cradle her face.

"Nothing yet, my love," Niven began. "But I will find those who plot against you."

The Unseelie King trailed his fingers over her cheek, down to her neck, then lower. "I don't want you to disappoint me." He nipped at her throat. "Do not disappoint me, Niven."

Niven arched into him, exposing more of her neck before moving her mouth to his. Her fingers snagged in his hair, clawing down and down until they raked against his back. She swallowed his groan and shifted so she hovered above him, the mist she wore trailing over them both.

She moved until he writhed beneath her, his shadows screeching over the walls and over the bed in a frenzy. Her name clawed from his throat, a curse and a promise, before he shuddered and stilled.

Again

And again

And again.

Until at last the shadows slowed and stayed away and he slept deeply.

Sometimes, only sometimes, Niven glimpsed the man beneath the madness...a fleeting glance and nothing more. She knew she would not be getting him back. The king she once wanted to tear apart the world for, now long gone.

It had never been love. A part of her wondered if perhaps it could have been if the shadows hadn't taken over.

Maybe she was more suited to madness.

Had once liked it...

The chaos and darkness and discord called to her in a way nothing else did. Niven doubted she had room for anything different.

Oh, but something different did stir, deep within her chest where her shadows lingered. There was something. It flickered almost undetected, a warming thrill that ignited cold and hardened nerves. Niven had no name for such feelings.

Sleep wouldn't find her, though her body was spent. Her mind lingered somewhere else...to someone else. Not so far away.

Restlessness coiled up her spine and would not leave her alone. With a last look at the sleeping Unseelie King, Niven threw back the covers and stormed from the room, her feet silent on the cold marble.

Niven moved without a sound through the woods, her shadows close behind her. Moonlight slithered down from the black skies, casting the trees with dancing light. Did they slumber too, she wondered, or were they silent and watching? Ready to take their whispers back to the king?

The weeping husk of a tree stood as quiet as the skeletal trees around it. No light shone from the cracks in the rotten wood, no smoke curled from the slit above.

With a brief wave of her hand, Niven sent her shadows into the decaying husk. They sought out the old crow and the little witchling and rested heavily above them, sending them into a deep slumber.

Niven followed and stood above the cot where the Seelie knight slept. The disquiet within her seemed to sigh in relief. With a soft nudge of her bare foot, he blinked his eyes open.

"What are you doing here?" he hissed into the darkness, swiping a hand over his eyes.

She could just leave…turn and leave and say nothing at all. "I don't know."

Gabriel stared up at her, bronze eyes wandering over the almost transparent mist curling around her, the only thing she wore. He shifted, his breath catching.

"Did you come to talk, demon?"

She could hear his heart thunder, scent the sudden and unexpected desire on him. "No."

The mist surrounding her vanished into nothing as she settled onto the narrow bed, pushing aside the furs to run a hand over his chest.

Gabriel swallowed hard as she traced the scarring on his skin, her shadows creeping from the corners of the room to trail over him. "That's twice you have done that now."

"I'm checking you won't split apart."

"Presumptuous of you," he muttered, eyes shuttering when she lowered her hand. She brushed lower and a gasp slipped from his lips.

"Is it now?"

She hovered over him, propping herself on her elbows and grinned as black swallowed up the bronze in his eyes. His hand came up to trace her skin, his fingers warm and rough.

"Tell me to go, and I'll never come back," she whispered, ducking her head to brush a kiss to his mouth. "You won't see me again, knight."

His fingers continued their slow stroking, patient and gentle. "This is high treason."

"Yes."

"You have bruises all over your body," he murmured, tracing them with his fingertip.

"So?"

A snarl rumbled from her throat at the pity in his eyes, her finger-nails snagging in his hair to force his gaze back to hers and away from the swirl of purple on her skin. Niven bit at his lip in warning, his answering moan set her nerves alight.

Her lips moved to the hollow of his neck, close to the row of stitches holding him together. Another low moan slipped from his lips, his hands tightening against her hips, breaking through the shadows gliding over her skin.

Whispers brushed over the shell of her ear, the points of sharp teeth grazing the soft skin. The words were not soft or gentle or lovely. Niven had no use for such words.

They were wicked things, spoken upon a hushed tongue and they set something deep within her on fire.

Niven claimed him upon the moss and old blankets, while the hitching snores of the crow witch echoed around them. Niven didn't care. She didn't give a damn about the damp bed or the damp walls or the damp mouldering floor. She lost herself in a way she never had before…not in Phabian's arms or the boys who had come before.

They were bodies and frantic kisses. Moans in the darkness. Voices lost and found within each other. Everything else was chaos and nothingness, and they lay, anchored together, as if the world outside did not hold them.

Niven found her release moments before Gabriel found his. The knight's hands dragged her closer, mouth on hers, sharing breath.

Wetness crept against her bare skin, warm and sticky and red. Niven pressed her fingers to the hard plains of Gabriel's stomach, more blood blooming beneath his bandages.

"Whatever will you tell the witch?" Niven tsked, lifting herself from his body.

Gabriel grinned, despite the pain clouding his eyes. "That it was worth it."

Clothing herself once again in shadow, Niven untangled herself from the Seelie knight and stood. Blood stained her fingertips, dribbled over her stomach, soaked through the mist she wore. Gabriel said nothing about the streaks of red on her. She moved her hands to peek at the wrappings around his torso.

"They haven't torn," Niven said. "You'll live."

"Good to know."

She wiped her hands over the blanket. "Tell the girl to adjust your pain relief, you'll be sore later."

He lifted a brow. "That's it?"

"Were you after a declaration of love, knight?" Niven smirked. "I had a need and you saw to it, to which I'm thankful."

Gabriel sat up, hissing through his teeth. "So, I won't be seeing you again, demon queen?"

"I wouldn't say that."

"I will be going home eventually."

"Maybe." Niven leant forwards and brushed her lips over his in a soft, teasing kiss. She pulled away as he made to deepen it again, her shadows skimming over his barely closing wounds. "You should sleep now."

"Don't..."

The blackness lingered, shadows creeping over him as Niven tugged them from the walls. She wove them easily into a blanket of night, draping it around the knight to keep the damp away. It was a wonder how he hadn't succumbed to some awful disease in the appalling conditions he lay in.

"Wait...wait a moment..." Gabriel breathed, sinking back into the pillow as her shadows began to drag him under.

"What?"

"Be careful."

Niven bristled and yanked the threads of her shadows tight. A deep and black sleep slammed into the knight, silencing his unwanted warnings. "I can look after myself."

Niven cleaned her hands in a stream nearby, savouring the biting cold against her skin. The blood washed away, the feelings that lingered did not.

Every part of her body ached and thrummed. The echoes of Gabriel's hands over her skin sang to her...called to her.

They didn't bruise,

Or break,

But they had not been soft and gentle either. Gabriel had moved with her as an equal, had matched every kiss and bite and moan and gasp with his own. Beneath the filthy blankets, on the damp moss, within a rotting oak she hadn't felt dirty.

Or used.

The feeling was as wonderful as it was horrifying.

Niven wrapped herself in a cloak thick enough to keep the chill away, layering her shadows until she could no longer feel the wind…or anything against her skin. They snaked around her fingers, black mist trailing like snakes as she walked back through the woods, back home.

They called to her, had done so even when she had roamed the halls of the abandoned castle of Seelie.

And yet she did not know why.

That castle still haunted her. The empty hallways and decaying bodies of things long forgotten and left behind, haunted her. They always would. Niven wondered if perhaps it was why the shadows liked her, because she had kept them company when all else had forsaken them. Kindred souls in a world of monsters.

Niven remembered the feel of a blade slipping through flesh, how it pushed through so easily and so deeply. She had struck bone. She could still hear the gasp as clearly as the day she'd done it…such a small noise. Oh, she did love that noise.

And perhaps that made her a monster too.

"It is a little late to be walking alone in the woods, Majesty."

Niven spun, too late to avoid the harsh blow to the back of her head. Her shadows scattered as another blow sent her to her knees, and another, to the ground.

Stupid, she had been so, so stupid…so preoccupied she hadn't heard anyone. A wet rasp slipped from her mouth as something slammed against her back, again and again. Her shadows fled, the mists she wore slipping into nothing as a different kind of darkness crept up around her.

CHAPTER TWENTY-ONE

TEYA

*B*lood ran over the marble, splattered across the walls and the ruined tapestries wavering in the breeze. The windows were shattered, coloured glass catching the sunlight to bounce rainbows off the destruction.

Fires still smouldered, licking at the grounds, having burnt through the gardens until nothing remained but ash. It fell like snow, tumbling to the ground in a jagged sea of grey.

My chambers were destroyed. The bed I had yet to sleep in with my husband, reduced to kindling.

My Court had rebelled against me.

All tired,

All angry.

And frustrated that I wasn't the queen they needed me to be. They still didn't have the king they had followed, either.

A part of me couldn't blame them.

I had failed.

I stood in the ruined splendour of the throne room, the throne itself burnt away upon one of the pyres in the courtyard. More glass glinted upon the marble. The vines and flowers that once bloomed around the stone pillars had been torn away and left to wither at our feet. Smoke filled the space, wafting in from the bonfires outside. There was nothing left unspoilt.

Nothing untouched.

Nefina stood at my left, fists clenched and deathly quiet. Oonagh stood at my right, blood-soaked and lost.

It would have been easy to conjure up a storm and put an end to the madness, to seize the traitorous hearts beating in the breasts of the faeries glaring back at me. I could still crush them all into nothing, and they knew I could.

They just didn't care anymore.

And I would have no court left if I ended them all.

"You slaughtered your brethren, for what purpose?" My voice rang out clear, despite the aching sorrow in the pit of my stomach. "To what end?"

A tall man with stick-like arms and legs stepped from the crowd, wings shaped like dead leaves flickered behind him. "Yours, Majesty."

Oonagh tensed beside me, her words hissing through her teeth. "Traitorous bastards."

"With respect, Majesty." Another fey stepped forward, blood still trickling over deep green skin. "We would rather rule ourselves and face whatever is to come than have you."

"The Unseelie will sniff you out in a heartbeat," Nefina snarled. "Would you all truly rather have war than Teya as Queen?"

"We have not had war in a long, long time," the bloodied faerie sang, her glittering eyes closing. "Perhaps it is what we all deserve."

I glanced at Nefina, who met my stare with wide eyes.

"Perhaps," the faerie continued, as all others turned to face her. "It is coming for us anyway."

"Then it will destroy you," I countered, noting the unease settling over the rest.

"What if it does not?" The faerie took a step forward, leaving red footprints on the marble. "What if it remakes us into something else? Something better?"

"Without a queen?" Someone shouted from the back. I could taste the rising panic…the drawing fear.

"Solitary?" Another voice, more fear.

"Can it be worse than a human queen and a mongrel king?"

"Enough!" The words tore from me with such force, such fury, it sent every soul in that damned room to their knees. The resounding crack of bone on marble told me I had shattered a few.

Glamour crackled at my fingertips, desperate and livid and hateful. The skies darkened, the tang of my impending storm raged against me, tasting of death and hate. Nefina hissed beside me, blood sliding from her nose. Her words charged through my Glamour, igniting it further.

"Do it."

A barely conceivable shake of Oonagh's head was all that stopped me from turning my court to ash and nothingness.

"I gave everything up for you," I hissed. "I should have just run and left you to rot."

"Are you any closer to getting our king back?" A fair question, as barbed as it was. "Or did you leave your court vulnerable for nothing? The Unseelie could have swarmed in."

I tensed, fighting to keep control. "It wasn't Unseelie that made my halls run red though, was it? Not Unseelie who cut down my knights… my friends, your friends. This chaos is your doing. Not Unseelie, and not mine."

"The witches proved useful," Nefina cut in, and I shot her a warning glare. "We may have a way out of this mess."

"We are listening," the stick man called out.

I stepped forward, gaze rolling over the faeries still crouched on the marble and wondered if there were any I would miss. Their faces were so familiar now. I had laughed with them, danced and dreamt of a life so beyond what we were living with them. I thought I had found my family.

But the faces I sought out didn't stare back. Luca, Guelder, Jacobina. My trusted council, loyal to the end, were gone. Even Nefina's lovely, skittish handmaidens lay amongst the dead in the courtyard. I didn't know if I would ever see Gabriel alive again.

Whatever I had felt for the Seelie court lay broken, irrevocably. They all deserved Luthien. Perhaps she would be the queen they so desperately needed.

"If this works," I began, keeping my head high, fighting the desire to just end them all. "You won't see me again—actually, if it doesn't work you won't see me either. I hope it does, because I have tried so hard, I have given so much up and I am exhausted. I just want a tiny piece of happiness for myself and Laphaniel before I utterly give up hope."

A faerie with tall, furred ears curled her lip from where she knelt on the marble. "So, what do you expect us to do while you swan off again?"

I laughed, the sound joined by the rolling echoes of thunder. "You can all burn in hell."

I would have just left them to the chaos they had created but I couldn't leave the bodies of the fallen for the crows circling overhead.

Turning my back on the Seelie Court for the last time, I wandered out into the burning gardens. The melting slush seeped through my boots, the white stained with vivid red. With Glamour screaming at my fingertips, I cleaved open the frozen earth, and the three of us gently laid our friends down, side by side.

I was so, so tired of burying friends.

Nefina knelt beside the mounds, pulling the soft, silver threads of her Glamour to create a bunch of winter blooms. She laid them down gently, a stem for each fallen friend. She didn't look my way as she made another bundle, the petals red and velvet soft. With the greatest care she placed them upon the smooth flat earth where her love lay.

"I tried." The words slipped from Oonagh as if she hadn't meant to say them. The first words she had uttered in hours. "I really tried, Teya."

"This isn't your fault." I caught her as she fell to her knees with a broken sob. "This is not your doing. None of it."

She shook her head. Her usually silken hair hung in knotted clumps, dirty and bloodstained. "You left your court for me to protect..."

I pulled her tight, her strong, lithe body collapsing into me. "Oonagh…"

Tears rolled down her cheeks. "You have come home to ruins."

Nefina placed a hand on Oonagh's shoulder, her fingers trembling. "We could have come back to bury you."

I closed my eyes, letting the tears fall. "We have to find Luthien."

Oonagh went rigid, her breath a sharp hiss. She sprang to her feet with a snarl so vicious I flinched. "Have you completely lost your mind?"

I stood, noting the new bloodstains on my cloak. "We need to move away from here, find somewhere to think and talk."

Oonagh cast her silvery eyes to the skies, watching the birds overhead. The simmering rage in her eyes dimmed. "Everything is going so very wrong."

"You feel it too?" Nefina asked, following Oonagh's gaze as she gave a slow nod. They both watched the flock of black as it meant something.

"Perhaps restoring Luthien to the throne will bring back some order," I said, weary of it all. Of faeries and curses and witches and the screeching of crows. "As it should have been all along."

Oonagh ran her hands over her ruined gown, trying to smooth out the wrinkles in silver silk. "It was meant to be Sorcha, if we want to nit-pick."

Sorcha, Luthien's elder sister and the rightful heir to the throne of Seelie had been killed centuries before in a war Laphaniel refused to talk about. It had been Sorcha's curse we had broken, dooming a mortal girl to rule over Seelie, a spiteful revenge against the sister who wanted her throne.

"Sorcha was not fit to rule."

I rolled my eyes at Nefina. "It seems you don't particularly care for the queens that rule you," I said, unable to keep the bite from my tone. "Just an observation. Come on, let's get moving. There's little use standing out here in the cold."

"Where do we go?"

I shrugged, beginning the walk away from the Seelie castle. "I don't know, Oonagh, but if anyone suggests a witch, I will smack them."

WE MOVED AWAY from the castle, and I didn't look back. I caught Nefina sneaking glances over her shoulder, longing pooling in her eyes as the towering stone faded from view. She had held her dreams in her hands for the smallest of times, and there was nothing I could say that would be of any comfort to her.

As we walked, Oonagh spread her hands over the trunks of the looming oak trees, her lips mouthing words I couldn't hear. She skipped ahead of us, long fingers brushing over branches and coiling vines, her footsteps light and sure. She made no prints in the snow.

"What are the trees telling you?" I asked, no longer finding it strange to hear the way the woods whispered. "Do they know where Luthien is?"

"Oh, if only it were that easy," Oonagh replied. "I am finding us shelter, Teya. A place to rest safely and think what in the darkest hell we do next."

I knew what she was trying to find, and I smiled.

We followed the songs of the woodland, making our way down winding pathways that twisted and turned and seemed to lead nowhere. Eyes watched from the shadows, hungry, but they left us alone. Howls rose from the shadows, focused elsewhere...on something other than us.

With aching feet and weary souls, we finally spotted smoke curling from a collection of stumps lying on the frozen ground. The log pile stood as high as my shoulder, with the little chimney coming up just above my head. Moss crept over the knotted wood, toadstools sprouting up from the damp, plump and red with little white dots. Straight out of a fairytale.

Something twisted inside me, a memory of a cosy burrow, steaming tea, and a too small bed.

Oonagh rapped her knuckles on what had to be the door, though it was only discernible from the rest of the log pile by the polished brass letterbox. I elbowed Nefina, who looked down at the log pile with her lip curled. She instantly forced a smile on her face when the door creaked open.

"Good afternoon." Bright green eyes peeked up at us beneath a mass of wild brown hair. "And what an afternoon it is to be roaming the woods."

"We seek shelter and food, hob. If you will have us?" Oonagh said. The hobgoblin stared up at us before hastily wiping floured hands over a pretty apron.

"Yes, yes!" she squeaked, opening the door wider. Her long, pointed ears twitched. "Most welcome of course, though you'll have to forgive my humble provisions, my husband has not yet returned. Come in! Come in!"

We ducked into the hobgoblin's home, following her underground where the burrow stretched high enough for us to stand upright. Roots dangled from the earthy ceiling, all threaded with beads and ribbons that trailed over our shoulders as we moved. A plump ginger cat sat curled upon a rocking chair made of twisted wood.

Oonagh and Nefina settled down upon a wooden bench covered in crochet scatter cushions, leaving me to perch beside the cat.

"Tea won't be long, and I have an apple cake baking in the oven if you are happy to wait for it." The hobgoblin ran a self-conscious hand over her hair, streaking it with flour. "My name is Branwen, I hope you find yourselves comfortable here."

"It is a little snug," Nefina sniffed, glancing around. I elbowed her again, and she scowled at me. "What? It is."

"Go sleep outside then," I snapped. "Find your manners, Nefina. I know you have some somewhere."

"You are from the castle, then I take it? Three fine faeries as you are?"

"You don't know who we are?" I asked, surprised when Branwen shook her head, sending up a cloud of flour.

"Don't have much dealings with outside folk if I don't need to," she said, patting down her apron again. "It's not safe out there."

The whistle from the kettle interrupted her and she walked off to fetch it, filling teacups with a sweet tea that smelled like cut grass.

"I will drink to that." Oonagh said, clinking her dainty cup against mine.

"You are welcome to bathe here, lady," the hobgoblin began, taking in Oonagh's clothes with a concerned eye. "And if you give me a little time, I am certain I can rustle up a new set of clothes to wear. Won't be as fine as the silk covering you, mind."

"You have my thanks." Oonagh nodded, her fingers wrapped tightly around her cup.

I took a sip of my tea, reaching over to gently spin the globe that sat beside me on a little table. The cat reached out a lazy paw, flicking at the globe so it spun and spun and spun.

"You be careful with that, Bert," Branwen said, scooping the cat into her arms to give me more space to sit back. "You'll all have to camp on the floor I'm afraid to say, but I'm sure I can make you comfortable."

"We have all slept on worse," Nefina replied, reaching out to take the cat from the hobgoblin. Her fingers moved over its fur, enticing a deep purr from the creature that echoed around the burrow.

For a few wonderful moments we just sat and enjoyed the sound of the contented cat and the warming scent of the apple cake slowly baking on the wood-burner.

A wonderful smile ignited on Branwen's face at the sound of the door clicking, her brown weathered face transforming into something breath-taking when her husband walked in. I hated myself for the stab of jealousy that struck me.

The hobgoblin didn't know which way to go...to the oven where her cake was needing to be removed from the oven, or to the doorway to greet her husband.

"I'll grab the cake," I said, standing up. A joyous squeak slipped from her mouth before she skipped from the burrow and back up the slope.

Pulling on oven gloves that were at least three sizes too small, I grabbed the cake and set it aside to cool. It smelled divine, oozing with syrup. Apple slices, lovingly carved into rose petals circled the outside, glistening with sugar.

"Guests!" came a voice from behind me. "What have we got here then, my dears?"

I spun around. I knew that voice.

"I know your face." Large ears twitched beneath wild white hair, black eyes glinting against the low candlelight. "Yet how different you look, girl."

Aurelius walked towards me, head cocked to one side while he stretched out a hand. His wrinkled fingers trailed gently over my face, dark eyes gazing deep into mine.

He glanced at Nefina and Oonagh, then quickly around the burrow as if seeking someone else.

I shook my head, knowing who he sought. He squeezed my hand, fingers lingering on my wedding band.

Laphaniel and I had stumbled across Aurelius' home while being chased by hungry trolls. It seemed so long ago that I had dragged a semi-conscious Laphaniel through the woods, drugged on poison to make him slow and helpless. We had reached Aurelius by the skin of our teeth. It was within his cosy burrow that Laphaniel first told me he loved me, the little words slurring over his lips as he slumbered beneath a pile of patchwork quilts.

A gentle smile lifted the corners of the hobgoblin's mouth. "Not lovers, eh?"

I swallowed the lump in my throat. "Maybe just a bit."

The new burrow was just as cosy as the old one, but I noted the absence of glittering hourglasses and compasses that could supposedly track the end of the world.

"What are you doing here?" I asked Aurelius, having left him all that time ago in a different burrow.

Aurelius accepted the tea Branwen handed him with a grateful smile, taking a few sips before he answered. "The trolls came back after you left, no doubt following your lover's scent. They destroyed my burrow, I made it out by sheer dumb luck—"

My heart froze. "I'm so sorry…"

"I lost my home, girl," Aurelius continued, one hand still clutching mine. "But I found my Branwen."

Tears trickled over my cheeks, and he instantly handed me his handkerchief. I offered it back but he shook his head.

"Human tears no longer, girl," he sighed, beckoning me to sit while Branwen sliced up the apple cake. "Shall we eat, then perhaps you can tell me what's happened. See if we can make it even a little better?"

I nodded, unable to say anything. Not for the first time, Aurelius held me close as I sobbed onto his shoulder.

CHAPTER TWENTY-TWO

TEYA

*A*urelius had been a little light in the darkness when everything else seemed bleak and pointless. Seeing him again made the grief crushing against my chest a little lighter, his kind eyes and wise words grounding me in a way I so desperately needed.

"Where is he?" Aurelius asked, taking a plate from Branwen with a bright smile. She passed one to me, the golden cake still steaming hot. "That tall handsome faerie who looked at you with such longing."

"The Unseelie have him," I said, noting how the hob's shoulders drooped and Branwen's weathered hands shot to her mouth.

I told my story to near silence. Told it all from the moment we had left Aurelius' burrow all that time ago. How Laphaniel had taken his last breath in my arms and how the broken curse had dragged him back again. With tears trailing down my face, I spoke of our too-short time in Cornwall, our journey to the Unseelie and of the wonderful Spider that dwelled beneath its Labyrinth. I told them how we had defeated Luthien and how he was torn away from me. I told them everything until Branwen was weeping and Aurelius had gone the colour of old milk.

"So now we've abandoned the Seelie castle," I said, tears choking my voice. " I don't really know what to do next."

I shoved a chunk of cake into my face.

"Gods above, girl," the old hob muttered, pouring himself a large cup of yellow tea. "We don't deal much with the Courts do we, Brannie?"

"We don't at that," replied Branwen, dabbing her eyes on her apron. "I have the Queen of Seelie in my sitting room!" She gave a startled squeak and dropped into a clumsy curtsy.

"No, please don't do that," I urged her. "I'm hoping not to be queen for much longer."

Aurelius pinched the bridge of his nose. "I remember you giving me an aching head the last time, girl. Both of you did."

I smiled. "I was so angry at him back then."

The old hob gave me a wry smile. "He deserved it."

"He really did." I laughed. "I forgave him."

Aurelius took my hand, finger running over my wedding band again. "I can see that. He made it right by you?"

My hand went to the silver star at my throat. "Every day."

"We are going to get him back," Nefina said, accepting another huge slice of cake.

"Well, no one is going anywhere until you're all fed and rested and clean," Branwen cut in, pouring more tea for everyone.

We ate in comfortable silence. Aurelius flicked his black eyes to Nefina, chewing carefully. Cake crumbs settled in his long white beard.

She caught him staring. "What?"

"You're Nefina." Not a question. Nefina tensed and we all stopped eating.

"How do…"

The hobgoblin smiled to himself. "I remember him murmuring your name in his sleep."

Nefina placed her cup down and crossed her legs. "Laphaniel was poisoned by those trolls before he brought Teya to Luthien," she said, voice cold. "My brother and I had not spoken in years at that point."

"Perhaps not, dear," Aurelius said, taking a sip of tea, "but he hadn't forgotten about you."

Nefina stood up, placing her plate and teacup onto the little table. "May I be the first to bathe?"

I sighed; she was as comfortable with sharing her feelings as Laphaniel was.

"Come with me, my lovely." Branwen hopped down from her chair, outstretching her hand to Nefina. She leapt back with a hiss the moment her fingers brushed against Nefina's. "Goodness me!"

Oonagh sat upright. "What is it?"

Nefina slapped Branwen's hand away, earning a sharp snarl from Aurelius. "It is nothing."

"Oh, my poppet!" Branwen squeaked. "Oh, you silly girl, what have you done?" Branwen wrung her hands, black eyes wide.

"What have you done?" Oonagh demanded, before rounding on me. "What happened with the witches, Teya? You tell me right now."

"We…"

"I did what needed to be done and that is the end of it," Nefina snapped. "We can't have Teya making all the stupid choices, now can we?"

"That's hardly fair," I snapped back. "It's not like I've wandered here with the intention of screwing everything up."

Oonagh scoffed. "Well, you have been doing an excellent job in any case, Teya."

"What would you have me do, Oonagh?" I demanded. "What would you have done differently?"

The candlelight flickered, and Oonagh hissed at the flames, stirring up her own Glamour to spark them to life again. "I would never have signed a contract I did not understand."

I stepped back as if physically struck. Anger threatened to swamp me, but it fled as quickly as it had come. It left me wrung out and exhausted.

"Then Laphaniel would be dead," I breathed the words, knowing without a doubt he wouldn't have lasted a night with the infection swarming his body.

"You underestimate the healing abilities of faeries," Oonagh said, her words clipped.

"The eight-inch scar across his stomach tells me otherwise."

Oonagh said nothing, looking away from me. Branwen took Nefina's hand again and began to lead her to the bathing room, giving Aurelius a small smile before disappearing.

"What did she do?" Oonagh demanded, voice low. Seething. "Do not keep secrets from me, girl."

"I notice I am no longer 'Your Majesty,'" I bit back. "That didn't take long."

Oonagh's eyes blazed, matching my temper. "I have a right to know. Was it a blood debt? Goodness, Teya, a life debt—"

"Her first born."

All colour left Oonagh's face. "Mother of gods."

"I said no," I stated, as if that made any difference at all.

"Faeries birth rarely," Oonagh said, ghost soft. "To give a child away…"

"What…" I could barely get the question out. "What would they want one for?"

"Do you really need me to answer that, Teya?"

What would Laphaniel think of his sister sacrificing her child for him? The thought made me sick. Cold.

"Branwen is a midwife," Aurelius began softly, shaking his head at us all. "When the time comes, call for her."

I heard Oonagh swear under her breath, the word hissing between her teeth. Without another word she pushed past us and stormed out.

"So, what are you seeking this time, girl?"

I sank back into the chair, not daring to meet his eyes. "Luthien."

He looked like he wanted to smack me. "Because that quest ended so well the last time?"

"I have a few things to set right."

Aurelius patted my knee. "It is not your place to set this world to rights, girl."

"I feel as if I've played a part in mucking it up."

"Hmm." The hobgoblin poured two more cups of tea, slipping a dash of something amber into both. He caught my eye and lifted a finger to his lips. "Hush, Branwen doesn't approve of strong liquor. I don't know where to find Luthien, girl. Honestly, I do not think it is wise to seek her out again."

"I don't have a choice."

He sighed. "Don't you?"

"No."

I drank my tea, wishing it had more whiskey.

"It's not safe here anymore."

I glanced up. "It's never been safe here."

"You know what I mean."

I swirled the last of my drink, savouring the burn it left behind. "Would you leave Branwen behind?"

His black eyes shot to the door leading to the bathing room. "No."

I sighed, tired and empty. "Have you any idea where we should start looking?"

Aurelius rubbed a hand over his face, shaking the crumbs from his beard before sneaking another sip of whiskey. With a wink he hid the flask in his pocket. "There are rumours of mortal boys wandering the Blue Meadows, far west from here. Half-starved and fully mad, they won't eat or drink or sleep or talk."

"And you think Luthien is behind it?"

The hobgoblin gave a small shrug. "Perhaps. I don't know for certain. Exiled fey are strange creatures indeed: loneliness doesn't suit them. Seems fitting she might find someone to torment and enjoy."

The same way Laphaniel had used Lily as company, and then the women who had come before.

The way he had once used me.

"I do hope you know what you are doing," Aurelius continued, looking as if he wished we hadn't descended upon him.

"Not really, no."

"Indeed."

"I never really got the chance to thank you properly for helping us."

"To see you alive, girl, is all the thanks I need," Aurelius replied, giving me a sad smile. "Even if you are to embark into yet more foolishness."

I met his gaze. "To bring my husband home."

The hobgoblin nodded, his gaze seemingly far away. His black eyes glinted, lost within some distant memory. "Oh, the way that boy looked at you. Like you were the last sunset and the first dawn all rolled into one. Like he would give up his soul for you."

My breath caught. I forced my own smile before turning away, grateful when at last Nefina walked out of the bathing room. She nodded at me, all scrubbed clean and wearing a fresh nightgown. She settled by the fire and watched the flames.

"Your turn, my lovely." Branwen smiled. "Do you have any wounds that need dressing?"

"No, I'm fine." I flicked my eyes at the doorway. "I think Oonagh may, though."

Branwen nodded and scuttled up the slope, clutching a tin of supplies in her wrinkled brown hands.

I took my time washing off the dirt and grime in the little copper tub, scrubbing at my skin with a rough bar of soap until it felt raw. I ran my hand over the fading scars on my shoulders, courtesy of the trolls who had chased Laphaniel and me without mercy.

I touched the small mark above my hip where Laphaniel had so gently sewed me back together. I thought of the thick, coiling mess of scars on his own back that would never fade, never go away.

One day, I would flay the skin from Phabian myself.

When at last Oonagh had bathed and cleaned the blood from her body, we all sat in clean nightgowns that Branwen kept tucked away for wayward guests, and ate the last of the cake. There was more tea, a darker mix of herbs, to help us all relax, so Branwen had said.

With the soothing tea drunk down to the dregs we settled down to sleep.

Branwen made a nest on the floor with cushions and knitted blankets, wringing her hands as she apologised once again that the bed wouldn't fit the three of us. That it wasn't fit for a Queen of Seelie.

"It's perfect," I said for what felt like the hundredth time. "This feels more like home than that castle ever did."

I would never forget how small Aurelius' bed had been in his burrow. How Laphaniel's feet had stuck out the bottom of the quilt, how I had slept nose to nose with him, barely a breath between us.

My body longed for that again. An ache that had not faded or dulled or eased.

"We will never forget your kindness," I said, settling beneath a worn throw and giving Nefina's cold feet a sharp kick. "Thank you."

"Well, goodnight then, my lovelies," Branwen said, dabbing her eyes. She gave us one last wonderful smile before taking Aurelius' hand and disappeared into another nook.

Nefina curled up tight and closed her eyes, dragging the covers over her head to avoid speaking to any of us. Bert the cat padded over and promptly snuggled close to her, purring loudly.

Oonagh sat with her back resting against a chair, her fingers dancing over the candlelight, making it waltz for her.

"I did not mean what I said." She still didn't look at me. "I honestly do not know what I would have done in your place, Teya. I can only imagine how it feels to be separated for so long, knowing how he…" she paused, clearing her throat. "I am here until the end. You will always be my Queen."

I took her hand, her fingertips still warm from the flames. "You know what, Oonagh? I would rather just be your friend."

Her laugh was lovely. A brightness in the dark.

"You are a strange girl, Teya Jenkins. It is so very easy to love you."

I smiled at her words, shifting on the cushions as she lay her head against me. I fell asleep without a dreadful ache in my stomach, and it was wonderful.

CHAPTER TWENTY-THREE

LAPHANIEL

I braced my hands on my knees, sucking in breaths while Fell yelled at me. The sword he had given me lay at my feet in the muddied snow. I lacked the strength to pick it back up again. My side throbbed where he had whacked me with the flat edge of his own weapon, the blade bouncing off ribs that had not long been broken and were still healing. I hadn't so much as nicked him.

"Come at me, you weak bastard!" Fell called out with a nasty smirk. He danced forwards, scooping up my sword with his foot to kick it at me. His cloak whipped behind him in a whirl of feathers.

I didn't catch the sword, my hands moved too damned slow.

"I need a moment," I panted, slipping to the floor, sweat slicked every part of my clothing to my skin. The world spun; stars danced in front of my eyes.

"Are you going to vomit again?"

"I will if you don't leave me the fuck alone!"

"Temper, temper." Fell grinned, flipping his sword over in his hand effortlessly. "You got in some decent swings there, I'm impressed."

"I didn't touch you," I said, dragging down another deep breath. I savoured the biting chill of the night air. We were outside.

I didn't feel as if my chest was going to cave in.

"You managed to lift it above your head," Fell continued, kicking at the frozen ground. "I thought your heart was going to give out just walking out here."

"Funny."

His stupid grin just widened. "I do try."

"Please stop."

I ground my fingers into the snow, wishing I could see spring instead of the endless, brutal cold. Everything was bleak and dead, the thin limbs of the branches hung heavy with snow. The sky was black and starless, the moon hidden. Winter would not let go. It would be a long, long time before it thawed out and swept back in again. Another year before I saw Teya.

The only light came from the few torches Fell had plunged into the ground, flames burning over black tar. It was a crude fighting ring, but it didn't seem to deter my opponent.

"Pick your sword back up," Fell ordered a split second before he lunged at me.

His blade came down, striking me hard on the shoulder. I rolled with a curse, grabbing for the hilt of my weapon to bring it up to meet his. The metal screeched and my feet slipped.

Fell spun, quick and graceful, sword slicing towards me. I swung my sword, gasping at its weight, and crashed it down with every last bit of strength I had left.

Blood splattered the snow.

And it wasn't mine.

"You hit me!" Fell laughed, deep and low, one hand clamped to his arm. He didn't point out that any of his blows would have killed me if he wanted them to. "Do you want to go again?"

I stared at my shaking hands. "I think I'm done for today."

"How did it feel spraying Unseelie blood?" Fell asked, a glint to his eye.

"Like I want to do it again," I answered, wiping sweat from my eyes.

"I bet I'm not who you want to tear to pieces though," Fell whispered and something dangerous passed over his face. He glanced towards the sleeping trees, as if perhaps they still listened.

The quick joy I had found in sparring faded. "You are stepping on dangerous ground, Fell. You know that, don't you?"

He twirled his sword, the blade singing through the air. "What could you possibly know?"

I shifted, wary, never knowing what was listening. "Don't play stupid with me. I know."

The wind rustled the feathers of his cloak, black on black. The Unseelie was a void of colour. He gave a careless shrug and shoved the dark hair from his eyes.

"Are you going to tattle to Niven?"

I had contemplated it. The moment I had guessed what he and the other Raven Knights were up to, I had thought about telling her. Bargaining with her. I nearly confided in Charlotte, but didn't dare, not after Niven's threat.

"Why haven't you told her?" Fell asked, my silence answer enough to the previous question.

"I hoped it would be some faceless rebels—"

"That you wouldn't mind hanging from the walls?" Fell finished, and I winced.

I gritted my teeth. The snow had seeped through my clothes... through the old boots Fell had leant me. "Would you listen if I told you to stop?"

He barked a laugh. "Without Phabian, you can go home. You could have your freedom, has that not occurred to you?"

Even the thought of freedom, hopeless as it was, stirred something deep inside. An ache that constantly ate away at me, the thought of being anywhere but beneath the shadows of the Unseelie Court. It was a dream and nothing more.

"Then why haven't you killed him yet?" I said, lifting my chin. Meeting his dark gaze.

Fell stilled, eyes widening. A low snarl ripped from his throat. His eyes tore away from mine to scan the trees...the shadows.

I lowered my voice to a bare whisper. "You can't get close enough, can you? His shadows won't let you."

"Watch your damn mouth," he hissed back, black eyes flashing.

"You couldn't even poison Niven," I continued, hating the way my teeth began to chatter, the cold seeping into my bones. "Which is probably for the best, since if you get rid of her, Phabian will massacre the lot of you."

"You tipped off the Queen, didn't you?"

"Yes." I spat the word at the idiot.

The blow knocked me backward, my head smacking against a buried log. Fell raised his fist again, and I flinched as he struck me a second time.

"You're going to end up on that wall, Fell," I said through the blood in my mouth. "You and Faolan and any other damned fool stupid enough to help." I spat red at his feet, flecking the snow.

"At least I'm doing something," he replied, fists curled at his side as if he would strike me a third time.

I stared up at him. "What have you done?"

His eyes blazed, but he said nothing.

"What the fuck did you do?"

Fell curled a lip. "What would your wife think, knowing how you feed her sister secrets?"

"But she doesn't know." I ran hand over my mouth, blood dripped over my chin. "You can't take on Phabian. He will butcher you."

"I would rather die dangling from that wall than become what you are," Fell hissed, gripping my wrist to haul me to my feet. The bones clicked. "Your hour is up, you piece of shit. Time to go back and cry in the dark."

I yanked my hand from his grip, slipping on my ass when he released me. "Something didn't want Niven dead, think on that," I hissed. "It is not Phabian's shadows whispering to me. What it is, I have no idea...but you might want to wonder why. This ends one way, Fell, and it's with your stupid head leaving your shoulders."

"Get up!"

I stood, not wishing to be dragged.

"Keep your unwanted advice to yourself," Fell began, snatching up the two swords from the ground before he walked ahead. "Or I'll just have the guards drag you down into the baths and hold you under. Understand?"

I said nothing, fear coiled in my stomach. Fell turned, snapping his fingers at me.

"Well, do you want that, mongrel?"

I stared at the Unseelie knight, blood cooling on my skin. "No."

I was tired of warning people they were going to end up dead. But then, at least he was doing something...

Fell led me back into the castle in silence, the Unseelie knight stayed in front of me without once looking back. A part of me screamed to run, to tear into the woods and see how far I got before I was taken down. I had no doubts Phabian would rip apart Teya and the entire Seelie if I dared.

I followed him down the winding stairs, ignoring the whispers and sneers of the Unseelie we passed. Some lashed out as I walked by, teeth grazing my skin. Others leered from the dark, a warning of things to come.

Down and down and down and down and down...

The door clicked shut.

Not a word.

I had no idea if I would see the outside again.

ICE CLUNG to the walls of the cell; the water that usually trickled down hung frozen above me. Some of the damp straw had frozen too. I settled down anyway, shifting it around to find some of the warmer clumps beneath.

I had been lucky so far, or so Charlotte had informed me. Lucky not to have died of influenza or pneumonia or any of the other human sicknesses that had plagued me since losing my Glamour. I was still a faerie…or so I thought…just a much weaker one.

I didn't know how Teya had endured it. To be human and face what she did, chin held high as death came after her again and again and again.

Something moved in the darkness, skittering over the slick walls with barely a whisper. It wasn't rats. I had not heard the door open.

I sighed; I wasn't in the mood.

"You really do love my company more than that madman's, don't you, Niven?"

"She does seem to, yes," a different voice answered in the dark.

I scrambled to my feet just as a burst of candlelight illuminated the form of the Unseelie King.

"I thought you'd forgotten where I lived," I said, fighting the dread tightening my chest. "To what do I owe this honour?"

"I would so like to have you whipped again," Phabian drawled, every part of him shrouded in shadow. "Just to hear what your skin sounds like as it's ripped apart."

"I'm guessing the same sound as last time."

"Delectable, wasn't it?" He smiled, utterly insane.

I took a step back, for all the good it did. Phabian moved closer, head tilting as if listening to something.

"I can't hear them."

"Hear what?"

I wasn't going to live through another sixty lashes, I had barely managed the first time. Phabian lifted a hand, coming closer, tendrils of shadows slipped from his fingers to float around me.

"The voices. Your voices. These…" He gestured to the shadows and they writhed at his hands. "These just scream at me."

"What voices?"

His eyes snapped to mine, wholly black and filled with whirling shadows. "The ones that speak to you."

Ghostly fingers curled around my throat, squeezing hard. He lifted, and my neck clicked. My toes scraped over the floor.

I couldn't breathe…couldn't breathe…

"I want you to find my Queen."

My boots slipped on the ice, fingers clawing at nothing while he continued to squeeze.

"Find her."

Everything blinkered. I couldn't breathe…

"He will be able to tell you nothing if you strangle him." Charlotte's voice rang out against the dark, and the shadows retreated. The Unseelie King released his hold.

I slammed to my knees, dragging in air as I fought to get control over the sheer panic threatening to swamp me. I sucked down another breath and another, my throat raw.

Charlotte crouched to place a hand on my shoulder, claws digging in. She caught my eye and mouthed, "Are you okay?"

Her eyes narrowed when I nodded, those extra eyes black and angry. She hovered over me, clawed feet clicking on the stone. She turned to Phabian, her words hissing through her fangs. "He will need to come to my chambers."

I glanced between the Spider and the King. Dread coiled in my stomach. "Why?"

"I need to see what's in your pretty head," Phabian answered, a manic delight dancing on his face. "See if we can coax those funny voices of yours to talk."

"I don't think it works likes that—"

"You better hope it does," Phabian cut me off, gesturing to the doorway. "Either you assist in finding my Queen, or I will reduce your mind to nothing."

"Niven came to visit yesterday," I began, then paused when Charlotte gave a slight shake of her head. Her eyes narrowed. "The day before then? It was no longer than three days ago."

Wasn't it?

Phabian shook his head. "I do hope you will be of more use to me downstairs."

The Unseelie king disappeared in a swirl of mist and shadow, leaving Charlotte to pull me to my feet. Her claws curled around my hand before she snatched it back again.

"Let me see that!" I grabbed her hand, staring down at the scarred stub where her little finger should have been. "He's chopping bits off you now? When? When did he do this, Charlotte?"

She hissed at me, snapping her teeth in my face as she yanked her hand away. "It is not your concern."

"Of course it is," I snapped back, wondering what other wounds she was hiding. "What's next, Charlotte? A leg because you have some to spare? An arm? A damned eye? Get out of here while you still can."

"Who else will ensure you don't drink yourself to death?"

The words came out before I could stop them: "There are worse ways to go."

The palm of her hand struck my face hard, claws scraped against my cheek, over the bruises already made by Fell. "Don't you ever say that to me again."

Blood trickled down my face, but I made no attempt to wipe it away. Without a word to the Spider, and hating myself for it, I stormed past and made my way to her underground lair. Charlotte followed close behind, the click of her claws and the swish of her gown the only sounds she made. I knew they were for me. Knew well how she could move utterly silent and unseen if she truly wanted to.

Down, down. Down into the fucking damned dark.

Charlotte's dwellings lay deep under the Unseelie labyrinth, dark and cold and covered in thick webbing that housed wrapped bundles of...I didn't want to know.

The fear of being dragged into her chambers had never left me. I had believed wholly that I would never see the surface again, not many entered the Spiders lair and walked out again. I still had little memory of what happened in the days I battled the fever holding me, just flashes now and again of the Spider hovering close, claws at my wrist, whispering faint snatches of song I could no longer remember.

It had been a relief to wake up and realise she hadn't eaten either Teya or myself.

Bookcases lined the wall of her chambers, ancient and bowing beneath the weight of thousands of crumbling books and jars filled with floating organs. Long shrivelled hearts lay thumping behind glass, bottles of yellowing teeth sat beside powered bone and tiny corked tubes filled with black blood.

To the side stood a bed. Worn leather straps dangled to the floor, the buckles tarnished with age. Surgical tools hung from the hooks above and swayed gently though there was no breeze. It was not the bed I had once woken in.

Charlotte gestured to the bed, pulling back the old sheets before ordering me to lie down. She wouldn't look at me, and as I made to take her hand, she pulled away.

"The King will be here soon, get yourself comfortable."

I stared at the bed then up at the sharp tools. "What are you going to do?"

She clicked her fingers when I made no move to do as she asked. "Lie down."

"Charlotte?"

A snarl slipped past her lips. "The King will use his shadows to enter your mind and pull out the information he requires."

I sat on the edge of the bed, the movement not entirely voluntary. "I don't know where Niven is."

Her claws scraped along the marble. "Truly?"

"I didn't know she was missing," I said, hoping she didn't ask if I knew who might be behind her kidnapping...but if Phabian could sift through my thoughts...

Damn it, Fell.

One pair of her hands poured something black into a vial. Charlotte wouldn't look at me. "The King believes if he digs deep enough, he may coax whatever is speaking to you, to talk to him."

"And if they don't?"

"Then I guess you get to see how mad I really am," Phabian said, stepping from the shadows as if he had always been there. "What are you conjuring, witch?"

Charlotte turned with a small hiss, teeth flashing in unwavering defiance. "This is to keep him still. If he moves while you are fiddling around in his head, the consequences could be catastrophic."

Phabian shrugged. "Not for me."

I glanced from the vial to Charlotte, feeling sick. "What consequences?"

"Paralyses at best, death at worst."

I didn't need to look at Phabian to know he was grinning. "I could make your brain dribble from your ears."

"I'd rather you didn't," I replied, taking a steading breath before I lay back onto the single pillow. Without meeting my eye, the Spider slipped the straps around my wrists, then my ankles, pulling tight.

"Why tie me down if whatever is in that potion will keep me still?"

"The Stopheart poison used is temperamental at best, it can last for hours or it can last minutes," Charlotte replied, still refusing to look at me as she buckled a strap across my chest. "I need you to drink this."

At least it wasn't a needle.

"You have tied my hands down, Charlotte."

"Oh!" To see the Spider flustered...for her to have missed such an obvious detail filled me with dread.

She held the vial to my mouth and tipped it back. Her fingers shook. It tasted of smoke and ash and coal dust, settling like grit in my mouth before I could swallow it. The effects took hold quickly, one moment I could move my toes and the next I couldn't.

Cold rushed up my legs. Up my spine to the base of my neck where it slowed and stopped. I could breathe...just. My tongue was cold too. I couldn't open my mouth to speak.

From the corner of my eye, I saw Charlotte pick up my useless hand and squeeze. I felt nothing.

"It will wear off," she breathed, sweeping the hair from my eyes. "You will be able to move again soon."

Only if Phabian didn't sever something important in my head.

"I don't think you're going to enjoy this as much as I am," Phabian drawled, stepping closer, tendrils of shadows uncoiling from his fingertips. They scraped against my temples, cold and sharp.

Closing my eyes, I braced myself while his shadows swept across my face, tentative. Probing. They lingered near my mouth, pressing against my lips before moving upwards. Phabian forced them up my nose until I choked, unable to open my mouth to take in air. They scratched against the inside of my head, clawing their way up and up until I could feel them…hear them.

Gods…

No wonder he was mad.

Something warm and sticky trickled down over my lips, the coppery taste of blood pooling in my mouth. Charlotte quickly wiped it away, but I still didn't open my eyes. I didn't want to see the delight on Phabian's face as he sifted through my thoughts.

Fingers raked inside my head. Claws digging in deep as he pushed and pushed and pushed. White agony ripped down the back of my neck, a vice, tight and unforgiving. Images flashed up between the pain, glimpses of memory and nothing more before Phabian quickly shoved them aside.

On and on and on, like flicking through the pages of a book. Endless. I still couldn't move, and I wanted nothing more than to reach up and ease the pressure building within my skull.

Phabian's laughter echoed alongside Charlotte's soft snarl, my own scream stuck somewhere deep inside.

Something popped in my ear. Moisture slipped down my neck.

"You have so many memories of your wife." Phabian's voice cut through the pain, his shadows retreating slightly. "So beautiful, a different sort of beauty than her sister, wouldn't you agree?"

I forced my eyes open, and the world spun, the light blinding.

"Do you have what you want?" Charlotte demanded, as I squeezed my eyes shut again.

"You also have a lot of memories of your time here," Phabian carried on, those shadows tightening again. I tried to arch my back and failed. "So, so many. I cannot wait until we are all that remain."

Charlotte's voice rang in my ear, "Stop!"

He squeezed, and for one merciful second the world went black and still. Everything stopped.

"I doubt you can feel it," Phabian whispered in my ear, "but you've just pissed yourself."

I couldn't bring myself to feel any shame.

"Please stop," Charlotte pleaded, voice breaking, I had no idea if she still held my hand. "Please."

"I have what I came for, witch." The shadows knotted in my head, needling and poking. "I also have something else I want."

"What?" The little word was nothing more than a breath, soft and defeated.

"You." Shadows grazed over my mind, barely there. "You bow to me, witch. Every wish, every whim of mine, you meet with blind devotion. You cease this simpering mothering or there will be nothing recognisable of the boy you love."

"The contract will not allow you to kill him."

Pressure pressed over the back of my neck, tendrils of mist snaking deeper and deeper...

Until I...

...Until...

"Who said anything about killing him?"

Nothing left in my head but mist and shadow...

I couldn't remember my name...

...anything...

...how to form words. Move...walk.

Only breathe. I knew how to breathe.

Tighter.

Tighter.

Tighter.

I knew how to breathe.

"Stop it!" Charlotte screamed, and the shadows ripped from my head.

"Consider this a final warning, witch," Phabian snarled. "Do I make myself clear?"

A low hiss shuddered through her fangs.

"Answer me!" The force of Phabian's voice brought glass smashing to the ground, the sound piercing through my skull.

"I understand." Charlotte's voice shook—the monster all other faeries feared was trembling. "Your Majesty."

"I have traitors to find," the Unseelie King said, saying nothing of Niven. "I have Raven Knights to bring to heel."

Oh, Fell...

Phabian's voice vanished along with his shadows, the echo of his threats lingering behind. My head pounded.

Charlotte's claws raked over my face, panicked. "Can you speak?" She shook me, and the room spun. "Look at me!"

I still couldn't move. I attempted to talk, but I couldn't form words.

"I am so sorry." Her claws hovered over my face, tears slipped from her black eyes, all eight glistening. I didn't want her touching me...couldn't bear anything touching my head.

It felt like it had been cleaved open.

A gurgling sound rose from my throat, and the Spider yanked me onto my side. No words came, only burning bile that splattered over Charlotte's gown.

Then nothing.

CHAPTER TWENTY-FOUR

NIVEN

*N*iven had woken to darkness and pain, the marks on her back splitting wide. Dried blood coated her skin, sticking to the chair she was strapped to. With her head spinning and pain lancing through her body, her shadows wouldn't come. She tried, of course, flexing her fingers to see if they pulled away from the walls.

They didn't come.

Time had passed slowly, though if it had been hours or days, she didn't know. Water was brought to her, though it tasted stale and strange. Thin porridge was spooned into her mouth with such force she gagged.

Why hadn't they killed her yet? The figures that lingered in the darkness, hoods pulled high. Cowards, the lot of them.

Niven missed her shadows, missed the constant feel of them upon her skin, the slide of darkness over naked flesh. Their abandonment hurt more than the King's.

"Do you intend to bore me to death?" Niven called to the darkness, scanning the wooden shack for signs of movement. She never saw anyone save for the hooded figure who forced food and water upon her. "I know who you are!"

A lie.

"I am pondering sending bits of you back to him," came a voice from behind her. "First I want to see if he misses you."

Fear, quick and sharp, lanced up her spine. "You would have done it—"

Her head snapped to the side with the blow. "Shut your gods-damned mouth, Your Majesty." Spittle landed on her cheek. "I want you to know fear. I want you to know what it feels like to sit in your own filth before we rip you to shreds."

The Raven Knight stepped closer and pulled off his hood. His auburn hair was cropped close to his scalp, feathered cloak rippling around him. Nothing but deep, burning hatred shone in his eyes. No... it was much, much more than hate.

"Tell me your name, knight." Niven's words did not falter; she would not allow that.

"You don't even remember us, do you?" he snarled. "The six knights you sent on a suicide mission to aid your sister, knowing most of us wouldn't return."

"You came back, it seems." Niven stared up at him. "You're not the one with the dead twin, are you? I think I would remember two of your pretty face."

"You are rotten, Niven," he said, voice soft...almost lovely. "Death would be a mercy for you, and believe me, you will beg for mercy in the end."

More faeries emerged from the shadows, hoods down, revealing their faces. Some were beautiful as faeries tended to be, tall and grace-ful. Others were scaled and fanged. Some had wings, taloned tipped and leathery. A few bore wings of feathers, ink black like the cloaks they wore.

"You will burn for this."

Despite herself, she shifted in her seat, legs damp with blood and... well, they were damp.

At long last she could see who had taken her.

Which meant they were not letting her go.

She called again for her shadows, bound fingers stretching wide as if to tear them from the walls. Nothing stirred, even her shadow lying in the dirt failed to draw closer.

She was too weak, had barely eaten or slept in days.

The Unseelie grinned, savouring her weakness, drinking it in like she had once drunk in their fear.

"There are only a handful of you," Niven said, voice cracking in her parched throat. "Hardly an uprising, is it?"

The twin without a twin stepped forward, the one she had ordered to babysit Laphaniel. "It's enough. Enough for those who have lost someone to that blood-soaked wall to carve out a piece of you."

"I will not beg for my life," Niven sneered.

"Perhaps not," the dark-haired faerie said. "But you will scream."

Drums began to beat in the darkness, soft and primal. Flames burst from torches, surrounding her in a circle of raging fire.

Pain lashed over her neck. Something swift leapt up at her, teeth sinking deep into her skin. Claws raked at her belly, slashing through the torn scraps of magic she wore.

Howls erupted over the pounding of drums, the beat of wings circled above her, tearing at her hair with hooked talons.

Laughter, Unseelie and insatiable, added to the manic song, and the shadows danced for them, caught up in Glamour that was not her own.

Niven did not beg, but as something pierced her side, striking bone, she did start screaming.

Then the drums stopped. Then the laughter.

The shadows stilled, waited.

Before coiling, ever so slowly, to the Unseelie King.

Black armoured guards flanked either side of him, not that they were needed. Niven lifted her head, fighting to keep her face neutral, to not for one moment show a hint of fear, of shame. Her vision wavered, shadows spinning.

"Choose one to bring back, my love," the Unseelie King said, the glee dancing with his black eyes betrayed the bored tone of his voice.

Niven allowed a sigh to slip past her lips. She nodded her head to the dark-haired faerie—the beautiful one. Pain shot up her neck with the movement. "That one."

His eyes widened.

She smiled. "I bet you'll scream, too."

The guards stepped forward, faces blank. The Raven Knight didn't struggle as they strapped manacles to his wrists.

"Take me instead!" the knight with cropped red hair screamed. "This was my doing, my plan—"

Shadows engulfed the knight, snuffing out his last words like a candle.

The other screamed his name: Faolan. Niven had no recollection of ever knowing it. The shadows retreated, leaving behind a bent and broken body.

More shadows crawled from the walls, snaking over the remaining faeries. Tendrils of black slipped down wide, silent mouths. They dropped to the dirt as one.

No one had uttered a sound.

"Take him to the dungeon." The Unseelie King waved a hand over the shackled knight. "Do what you wish with him but keep him alive."

"It is a pleasure to serve, my King," the guards said as one, bowing low.

"It is your friends upon that wall, too," the knight began, disgust tainting his words. "Fey you have fought beside, laughed with, loved—"

The pommel of a sword came quick and hard, silencing him. The last Raven Knight who had aided Niven's sister was dragged away, out of her sight.

"I thought I had lost you," Phabian said, crouching before her. "My Queen of Shadow."

"You took your time." The bindings slipped from her wrists. Cool darkness crept over her body to form a glittering gown of night. The jewels winked like starlight.

"Did you fear I would leave you?"

Niven took the outstretched hand and stood, gritting her teeth as the world tilted. "A part of me wondered if you would."

The Unseelie King swooped her into his arms, holding her close, calling more darkness to him. "For a moment, my love, I pondered it."

Niven said nothing. She allowed exhaustion and pain to drag her under and slept.

SHE DID NOT KNOW how long she had lay sleeping, splayed out in her vast bed. The silks were damp with sweat. Dried blood stained her pillow. Stitches pricked along her side, some at her neck and they itched. Her whole body ached.

There was no sign of Phabian.

She was alone save for the gaunt hag who scuttled after her with cloths dipped in foul smelling liquid. Niven ignored her, swatting her away as she checked over her wounds.

She needed someone to throttle.

The Spider's lair was not a place Niven visited often. Perhaps she was afraid...wary of the chambers way beneath the Unseelie labyrinth where many faeries went and never came back. The insect's taste for blood was well known through the court, and so her insatiable hunger.

It was wise to be afraid.

Niven ran a curious finger over the stands of webbing and called into the darkness, "Did you know who did this to me, Weaver Of Nightmares?"

Nothing answered. Niven strummed the web again like the stings of lute. It made no sounds. Nothing came.

Something akin to disappointment settled over her. With a sigh, and her bones aching, she turned to leave. The sound of a soft moan stopped her.

Niven stepped further into the darkness, past the bookshelves filled with rotten pages, her footsteps silent. She stopped at the narrow bed and sank into the chair beside it with a barely concealed wince. Her stitches pulled.

Straps dangled over the edge, buckles scratching the floor.

Laphaniel lay unmoving on the bed, and Niven took a moment to marvel at the speckles of blood that flecked around his nose, by his ears. Bruises—fingerprints marked his temples, the black slowly giving way to a dark yellow. He breathed deep and slow beneath clean sheets, damp hair curled at his neck, smelling of sweet soap.

No one had washed the filth from her hair.

Taking his wrist, Niven turned his arm to reveal the little needle mark on the inside of his elbow. She pinched until blood bloomed at her fingertips.

"Open your eyes," she snarled, and he moaned softly. "Now."

Laphaniel blinked, meeting her gaze for barely a second before his eyes drifted shut. Niven pinched harder.

"Can you hear me?"

He moaned again. "Yes."

"Did you know who tried to poison me?"

He said nothing for a long while, sucked down deep by whatever the damned Spider had given him.

"If you want…" he began, words slurring, "me to jump for joy that you're still alive…you're gonna have to wait."

"We had a deal."

"I can't warn you you're going to be kidnapped…if I don't…know you're being kidnapped." He paused, fighting to sit up. "I didn't know you were gone."

"Your voices said nothing?"

Laphaniel shook his head slowly. "They knew, though."

"What the hell does that mean?" Niven snapped her fingers as his eyes began to close.

He groaned, refusing to open his eyes. "Phabian shoved his shadows up my nose…found out where you were."

"Why?" Niven pressed. "Why didn't they tell you?"

"I don't know, Niven."

She poked one of the bruises at his temple. He didn't flinch; her bruises throbbed. "What did the Spider give you?"

He waved a lazy hand in the direction of a table laden with bottles, powders and vials of thick glittering goo. Burners stood cold on the counter, the remnants of dark dust burned on the bottom of the silver dishes.

"Something...over there." His words were thick. "Whatever it was is doing a wonderful job of making you much more bearable."

"Was it the black one?" She rummaged over the desk, wanting something stronger than the numbing salve the hag healer had given her. She wanted oblivion.

"Green."

"Hmm, can I swallow it?" She didn't like the look of the long, glistening needles. They lay in neat rows, delicate and crystal clear.

Laphaniel watched her from the bed. "Only one way to find out."

"Oh, you'd love that, wouldn't you?" Niven picked up a syringe, admiring the fine craftsmanship. It didn't escape her notice when Laphaniel turned away, his face paling. She snorted.

"Charlotte won't be happy with you pawing at her things," he said.

"You do worry about your friends here, don't you? That creepy insect and that pretty knight. Phabian left him alive, by the way, at my request." Niven leant closer, smoothing the dark hair from his face. He was beautiful, she would admit that. Something flashed behind the haze in his eyes. "When you're feeling better, you get to watch his execution."

"No..."

"I chose him so you can see him die." Niven picked up a vial and held it to the light; it gleamed a sickly green. "You didn't get to save him by not telling me."

"Niven–"

"Isn't this what you wanted?" she breathed. "For me to stay at Phabian's side so you could live too?"

The blue in his eyes was barely visible, his pupils wide and inky black. "Is that what you want?"

Niven bristled. What did she want? Whatever it was she didn't wish to discuss it with a faerie high on some gods-forsaken-concoction.

She placed a hand over his chest, fingers splayed. "Your heart is racing," she said with a nasty grin. "Are you afraid or just pleased to see me?"

Niven's hand travelled lower beneath the sheets, skimming beneath the hem of the loose trousers he wore. She lifted an impressed brow. "Pity."

He lifted a brow. "I wouldn't let Phabian hear you say that."

"Afraid he'd chop it off?" Niven sneered, before pressing a hand to her ribs.

The pain at her side was almost enough to bring tears to her eyes, the scratches and bite marks aching all over. Her jaw throbbed. She had woken alone in her bed, hadn't seen Phabian since he had scooped her into his arms and whisked her away.

He had lowered her into bed, hands soft and gentle. Pulled the sheets up high and set the candles a blaze. She had woken enough to see this...a gentleness. A game.

His shadows had wrapped around her throat as his hands caressed her. They had tightened as he whispered sweet, sweet words in her ear.

She forced a smile, showing teeth. "Do you want to hear a wicked, wicked secret?"

Laphaniel groaned. "I really don't."

Niven moved closer to whisper in his ear, her hand resting over his throat. "I'm going to kill him myself."

"Are you joking?" the words slipped slowly from his mouth. "I can't...tell if you're joking."

"I am deadly serious," Niven said, fingers tracing the bruises along his forehead. "And you're going to help me."

"Can you come back in a few hours?" Laphaniel murmured, pushing her away with a clumsy hand. "I need a clear head to process the nonsense coming from your mouth."

"He was going to let them kill me."

"But you're so likable..."

Laphaniel's head lolled back against the pillow, his chuckle slipping from his mouth. Niven curled her lip.

"I need your help." She nearly choked on the words. "Well, what do you say?"

He was still laughing at her. "Sure, why not. You can save me Fell's spot on the execution stand."

"If it works," Niven said, gritting her teeth. "you can have your freedom."

The laughter stopped, and he shook his head. "I don't believe you."

She stood, one hand still clamped to her side. She pocketed the green vial and one of the glass needles. "You have my word."

Laphaniel didn't reply; his hand slipped from the bed to dangle over the edge.

Niven rolled her eyes, wondering how much he would remember when he sobered up.

She didn't like repeating herself.

CHAPTER TWENTY-FIVE

TEYA

*W*e were to leave the burrow with full bellies and heavy packs. Breakfast had been laid out on a patchwork quilt, so much food for just the four of us. Bowls of steaming porridge drizzled with honey had rested by plates of golden toast and jam. Bacon was brought out, still sizzling, and even though we were full to bursting, we all managed to fit some in.

The hobgoblins insisted we rested thoroughly, and for three long days they had fed and sheltered us. We were safe in the burrow, warm and coddled, and I could have just curled under the crochet blankets and stayed there. We were safe. The feeling was unfamiliar and strange, and I did not want to let it go.

I enjoyed talking to Aurelius, his deep voice and wise words a comfort. I enjoyed being fussed over by Branwen, her hands flittered over my clothes, smoothing out the wrinkles.

They took their time embracing us goodbye. Branwen lingered over Nefina as if she wanted her to stay.

"Don't leave it so long next time, girl," Aurelius said, his gruff voice oddly quiet. His black eyes shone. "I want to see you happy with a brood of wild faerie children."

I couldn't help but smile back. "We shall see."

A tear slipped down his brown cheek. "I know an excellent midwife."

"I will never forget your kindness," I said, blinking back tears. "Not for this time, or the time before. Wherever I end up, you will always have a seat at my hearth."

"Go with our blessings, girl." The old hob gave my hands a good squeeze. "Until we meet again."

The world needed more hobgoblins.

We left the log pile with the crooked chimney and set back out into the cold. The skies were clear, the sunlight streamed down onto the fresh snow and turned the world around us into a shimmering wonderland. Icicles dripped from the slumbering trees, and upon the sleeping boughs...buds grew. Spring was on its way.

Our new cloaks were dry and warm, the colours earthy and raw. The clothes we were given were homespun and simple. No corsets. They hung in waves of dyed green, the hems and sleeves carefully embroidered with tiny birds, leaves, and insects. Even Nefina had not sniffed at the lack of fine silk.

"I still think what you did is incredibly foolish, Nefina," Oonagh began, as we headed out west in the hopes of finding Luthien. "Do you have any idea—"

"I dislike children," Nefina cut in. "It will not be that hard to avoid bearing any."

Oonagh shook her head and said nothing. I knew the conversation was far from over, what Nefina had given up—what she had sacrificed. I couldn't comprehend it, how Laphaniel would feel knowing what she did...I didn't believe her flippant attitude for a moment.

"How far away are the Blue Meadows?" I asked over the fraught silence, keeping stride with Oonagh. My boots sunk through the soft snow.

She carried on walking. "They are wherever they want to be, Teya."

"That doesn't make any sense—" I stopped myself at the look she threw me. "Right, sometimes I forget where I am."

"The Blue Meadows were spotted west last according to Aurelius. We will keep heading that way to see if we can still get passage through."

"What kind of passage?"

Oonagh grinned, her eyes lighting up with a wicked delight. I had almost forgotten that look on her, how she radiated with it.

"You shall see."

"Do you think Luthien could really be there?"

"There is always a chance," Nefina said, brushing aside branches while we walked on. "Since you did not specifically exile her from Faerie, it is more than likely she still lingers. Fey do not thrive well in the human world."

My thoughts drifted to Briar and Grace, the exiled Unseelie knight and his human lover. Laphaniel and I had met them while in Cornwall, learning that the old Unseelie Queen had sentenced them to death for the unforgivable crime of conceiving a child when she could not. Grace had sold her immortal soul to the Queen in exchange for exile.

I remembered the little inn on the Cornish coast that housed many wayward fey and how they longed for home…how lost they looked.

I could not imagine Luthien in such a place.

No, whatever sanctuary Luthien had found, I had no doubts that she was ruling it.

"I bet you are glad you didn't execute her now," Oonagh said, her eyes dark. "Imagine how delighted she will be to slit your throat."

"I'm putting this world to rights, Oonagh," I gritted out, in no way looking forward to my death, no matter how temporary it may be.

"No, you are not."

"Can you stop?" I grabbed at her hand, forcing her to turn. "I know you're not happy, Oonagh, but I have to do this."

She snatched her hand away. "You are choosing to do this."

"Does it matter?" I said, voice raising, desperate. "This is my last shot at saving Laphaniel. If this fails…"

"You will be dead," Oonagh breathed. "And then I will have lost you both."

"I need you there to make sure Luthien brings me back," I implored her. I wanted to reach out to her, but if she pulled away again... "I need you, Oonagh."

My friend simply nodded. No words, eyes unreadable.

"Luthien will have a short reign if she betrays you," Nefina said, leaving me to wonder which of the two faeries would rip Luthien apart first if it all went wrong.

WE CARRIED ON WESTWARD, passing great frozen lakes we could walk on. Shadows passed far beneath us, huge and black, long tails sweeping the icy depths. The trees thinned out and mountains appeared in the distance, towering up into the skies, peaks lost to the clouds.

We camped in a shallow cave, huddled around a small fire beneath crochet blankets that smelled of earth and apple cake.

When dawn broke, we set out once more, our limbs cold and tired. Our spirits battered but hopeful.

Hope. I had hope. I clung to it as if I were drowning.

I heard the river before I saw it. The sound of waves slamming against rock thundered around us, drowning everything else out. I moved to the edge, watching the furious rapids crash over stones worn utterly smooth from the force of the waters. White foam surged up at us, lethal cold.

"The River of Tears," I stated, still awed by the sight of it. "I've nearly drowned in its waters before."

When Laphaniel and I had first entered Unseelie.

The river had been much further up, bordering into the Unseelie and the only way to get where we wanted was to jump from high above and hope we would resurface. The strange river had dragged us down, feeling more like mist than water. Beneath the waves, it had shown me a life I could once have had with Laphaniel. A home on the edge of the forest, one blooming with blossoms and tangled in trees. A life with the faerie I loved and a wild little girl with tangles of black hair and bright violet eyes. It had been nothing more than a dream…a way for the waters to claim me forever…but, oh, for just a moment, I held my family in my hands and had never wanted to let it go.

"If you jump in now, you will be dead before your body even realises how cold it really is," Oonagh said beside me. "I suggest waiting for passage."

"How do you know one will come?"

Oonagh bent down and plucked a blue petal from the snow. "The Blue Meadows were here last. The only way to reach them again is to wait."

I looked around, seeing nothing but the raging waters. "For what?"

"Just wait, Teya."

I scanned up the river, unsure how a boat wouldn't simply be torn to shreds against the rapids. If it was to be a boat at all.

We waited until the cold bled through my heavy cloak, seeping so deep into my bones that all memories of a warm hearth were forgotten.

"There! See?"

Nefina pointed into the distance. Something huge floated into view, paying no heed to the raging waters it floated upon. True to Oonagh's word, it slipped in against the side of the river and waited.

I gaped.

It was no boat or ship or raft. A mammoth body coiled closer to the river edge, water lapping over its silver scales. Fins that looked like wings wove in and out of the waters, sleek, smooth feathers glinting razor sharp under the winter sunlight.

It turned its wide head to us, carp-like whiskers twitching while it regarded us. It yawned, showing rows of jagged teeth.

"Have a little faith, Teya," Oonagh said, gesturing for me to climb upon the creature's back. "It is just like a boat."

"No, it's not." I recoiled as a bony hand reached for me, too busy taking in the giant beast to notice the bent figure standing upon it. A ferryman with a tattered grey cloak and cold black eyes grinned up at me, palm outstretched.

"Payment is due for the crossing, gentleladies," he rasped, words spitting over cracked lips. He handed Oonagh a knife of bone, giving her a nasty smile.

She didn't flinch. "How much?"

"Enough for a piece of rope," the ferryman said.

With one quick slash of her wrist, Oonagh dragged the blade through her lovely hair, slicing it off just above her shoulders. "For all of us."

"Too kind, my dear." The ferryman nodded, taking the bundle of silvery hair. "Too kind."

"It will grow back," Oonagh said to me as she boarded the scaled back, curling her fingers over one of the many pointed ridges.

"You had better hope so," Nefina snipped, settling beside her. "You cut it wonky."

"I don't see you cutting your hair, Nefina," I said, eyeing the jagged remains of Oonagh's silken braid.

Nefina gave a tight smile. "I think I paid my way."

Shame washed over me. "I'm sorry…I didn't mean—"

"I know," she said, waving a dismissive hand. "I know, Teya."

The creature beneath us was slick and cold, and I had to grip tight to stop myself from slipping into the icy waters.

Slowly it glided over the rapids, the waves circling its body as if not wishing to disturb it. The ferryman stood upon the creature's head, a long oar in one hand which he dipped every now and again into the churning water.

More beasts swam beneath the waves, some long and sleek, others bulbous with many limbs that snaked out of the rapids, searching for prey foolish enough to get close. I kept my hands and legs in tight, watching the waters with a keen eye while we bobbed and swayed down the river.

Nefina watched the waters beside me, pointing out some monstrous creatures. Huge whale-like beasts rocked against our ride, rows of spines sticking out from their back. As they surfaced for air, they let out the most wonderful song before exploding back under the waves, their tails narrowly missing capsizing us.

A shoal of black, glittering fish launched themselves up over the waves again and again, as if racing us. They forced themselves up the rapids like salmon, many colliding with the hidden rocks to never surface again.

Nefina tilted her head back to stare at the skies, and I followed suit, watching a flock of sleek green birds dive into the river. They surfaced with fat slug-like eels that screeched so loudly my ears popped.

"Are you okay over there?" Nefina called, wrinkling her nose while Oonagh retched into the water. I moved to rub her back while I marvelled at the life around me.

"I will be fine when we are off this infernal fish," Oonagh moaned, leaning against my shoulder. "I thought it would be smoother."

"Faeries are prone to motion sickness, aren't they?" I smiled, stroking the jagged ends of Oonagh's hair. "Laphaniel didn't travel well either."

"You shoved that boy in an iron box with wheels," she replied, sitting up with a groan.

The creature finally slowed, slipping against the riverbank with barely a jolt. Oonagh was first off, slipping to her knees in the fresh snow.

"Safe travels to you, then," The ferryman called before wrapping the length of Oonagh's hair around his skeletal arm. He grinned with a mouthful of cracked teeth.

They disappeared into the swell of the waters. The waves rushed over the white scales before swallowing it up completely. I didn't know if it would return for us.

The Blue Meadows spread out before us like an oasis, a piece of Eden surrounded by crooked thin trees that stretched up to an alien sky littered with stars. Leaves clung to the frail branches, all in shades of deep blues, indigo and black mimicking the strange night sky above. No snow littered the ground beneath the trees, only dry grass that crackled and blew with a sweet-smelling breeze.

I could taste the heady Glamour. Smell the wine and the blood.

A young man staggered across the brittle grass, his hands wavering in front of him. He stopped when he saw us, pointing a shaky hand towards the trees. He didn't have a stitch of clothing on him.

"I still think home is that way," he mumbled, words slurring. "So, I can't be lost, can I? If I know the way home, I can't be lost."

"Do you want to go home?" I asked, catching him as he pitched into my shoulder. He smelled of sweat and misery, of hunger and desire.

His eyes went wide, his pupils huge. "Why would I want to leave?"

He pushed himself off me, sinking to the ground. Twigs matted his dirty blond hair; mud streaked his skin. He lay on his back, an arm stretched toward the sky.

"Why would I leave here?" His words were awed, soft.

"Well, I think Luthien is likely around here," Nefina said, cocking her head at the boy. Her eyes roved over his body.

"Stop it," I nudged her, and she looked away with a smirk. "He's obviously heavily Glamoured."

"And drunk on gods-knows-what," Oonagh said, poking the boy with the toe of her boot. "Lovely though, is he not?"

"It's disgusting," I snapped back, but I still stepped over the boy without a backwards glance. And if that was more disgusting than lusting after him, I found I did not care.

Oonagh matched my steps, leaving Nefina to lean over and place a lingering kiss on the boy's lips. Her laugh was wicked and delightful. I didn't reprimand her again.

"Did Laphaniel ever..." Oonagh left the question hanging, her meaning clear enough.

I shook my head, remembering how it felt to be Glamoured....how magical and wonderful and utterly awful it was. "In the months that he held me under his Glamour, he barely touched me. He would kiss my cheek and hold me in his arms until I fell asleep, then he would get up and leave me alone."

Something that looked a lot like relief flickered over her face.

"It doesn't make what he did right," I began. "I thought I was in love, and I had never been in love before. I believed it was lovely and perfect. I believed that someone as broken as I was then could have no hope of holding onto a love like that. I begged him to love me. It took a lot to forgive him."

Nefina kept my gaze. "What do you make of real love?"

I thought for a moment, fingers tracing the silver star at my neck. "I know it leaves behind a void I cannot live around. Sometimes I wouldn't wish it upon anyone."

We passed through the shadows of the skeletal trees, stepping onto the vivid green mound in the middle. Lush grass soaked over the tops of my boots. Moonlight streamed down unhindered onto the gathering at the top of the hill, laughter spilling out into the night.

And there she was.

Beautiful and cruel and wild.

The rightful Queen of Seelie.

Luthien sat at the centre of a group of beautiful men, all human and without clothes. A scrap of golden silk covered her curves, the neckline so low she may as well have worn nothing. In her hand she held a silver goblet overflowing with wine, in her lap she cradled the head of a man with golden curls and vacant eyes. I walked towards her, and she smiled up at me, her lips so wine-stained it looked like blood.

I quickly scanned the company she kept—it could have been blood.

"What honour do I owe to the Queen of Seelie?" Her words drifted to me, lazy and cunning. There was no hint of fear or shame, nothing left of the broken creature who had fled my hall. "Are you checking in on me, Teya Jenkins? Seeing how my exile holds?"

"It doesn't appear you are suffering as much as I would have hoped," I replied, allowing a little of my Glamour to spark at my fingertips.

Luthien tipped her head back, her musical laughter rousing the men dozing beside her. There was no joy to the sound. "But it looks as if you are."

I fought to keep my temper, to keep hold of the storm pulsing away in my veins, all too eager to tear Luthien's little sanctuary to shreds.

"I've come to ask for your help." The words grated against me.

Luthien lifted a brow, tilting her head so her hair slid over her bare shoulders in dark waves. "You came to me once before for a favour, I believe you came to regret it."

"A mistake I will likely spend the rest of my life paying for."

Luthien turned her gaze upon Oonagh and Nefina, lip curling at both. They remained at the bottom of the hill as I requested. I wished to speak to Luthien alone.

"Your mongrel is not with you?" Luthien began, sliding those depthless eyes back to me. "And here I thought you two could not bear to be parted."

"Laphaniel couldn't be here with me—" I stopped, suddenly realising. "You don't know, do you?"

"Know what?" she hissed the words at me. "Sit down."

I bristled at the order, obliging only because it was a fight not worth getting into. I sat across from her, snatching a bottle of wine. I took a long swallow, the taste of sunshine exploding on my tongue.

"The Unseelie have him."

Shock—real and unbridled shock flashed across Luthien's haunting face before she had a chance to shutter against it. "What have you done?"

It was hard not to stiffen at the accusation, no matter the truth behind the words. "The only way I can save him, is for you to help us."

"And why would I do that?" The mask was back on, though it was too late. I had seen her.

"How much do you want to be queen, Luthien?"

She took a moment to weigh up my words, no doubt seeking out any trick or deception I might have been hiding. She emptied her goblet in one swallow before pouring another. "I am listening."

Luthien sat as still as marble, listening to every word I said without reacting. I told her everything, I had to. I told her of the contract with the Unseelie, how Phabian's court was descending into madness, how Niven revelled in it. I told her about the witches high up in the north, of the spell that only she could wield. I told her everything and waited.

"You left him there?" she breathed, the words poisonous. "In that labyrinth?"

"Phabian has most of his court nailed to his walls," I countered with gritted teeth, allowing just a trickle of my Glamour to stir up the night around us. "I could not risk having Laphaniel join them."

She rose in one elegant sweep, the sheer silk pooling around her like liquid gold. Her chest rose and fell, betraying the lethal calm surrounding her.

I stood to face her. "You still love him."

She said nothing, not to confirm or deny. In an almost gentle movement, she swept a hand over her companions, never breaking her gaze away from mine. I closed my eyes at the sound of snapping necks, at the sudden quieting of beating hearts.

The power she still clung to without her crown was otherworldly.

"I could do the same to you." She stepped closer, a hand reaching out to caress my face. "Without a thought, Teya."

"You tried once before," I said, reaching for the storm, the wind and the rain. Her hair whipped against her face. "You failed."

"Oh, but I would love nothing more than to silence you in an instant and simply take my crown back."

I didn't move. "Do you think Phabian will let him go then?"

"You said yourself, the contract ends with your life."

I tilted my chin up, allowing Luthien's fingers to slide against my throat. "They will send him to you in pieces."

She flinched.

"Then what is stopping Phabian from slaughtering him the moment he finds out you are dead?"

"I...I don't know..." I answered honestly. "I'm hoping I will get to him before that happens."

Her look was pitying. "You are relying heavily once again on hope, are you not, Teya? Hope I can bring you back, hope you reach the Unseelie in time." She paused, taking a soft breath. "Hope there will be something left of him for you to bring home."

"It will mean nothing to you if I fail," I said, her words like salt to already raw wounds. "You get to be queen, no matter what happens."

"It would mean something," Luthien countered. "I would like to believe it would mean something."

"Do this," I urged her, shoving pride away. I would beg if I had to. "If you do this, Luthien, you get to have everything. The Seelie are yours. They don't want me...they never really wanted me. I just ask that you leave us alone, please. Leave us be. After everything, do we not deserve just a piece of happiness?"

"This world does not care what you think you may deserve," Luthien said softly. "It is not fair and it is not just. Only hungry. Never forget that, Teya Jenkins."

"Is that a yes?"

She narrowed her eyes at me, looking strangely tired, as if she too were done with it all. "I will end your life at your request, cleave the soul from your body and drag you back. I will do this for you, and you will never show up at my door again."

"I think that is a fair deal," I said, not giving myself a chance to be afraid. "You truly know the spell?"

"Would I deceive you, Teya?" Her smile was terrible.

I grinned back, a flash of teeth. "When do we start?"

CHAPTER TWENTY-SIX

NIVEN

*N*iven's laughter rang out, cold and bitter. It echoed off the damp cell walls, stirring up the shadows that stretched at her feet. She had walked past the new pyre in the courtyard that morning, erected in the courtyard for all to see. Damn the snow. The flames would rise.

And the Unseelie Knight would burn.

"Are you drunk?" she asked, the last of her laughter dancing off her tongue. "I never know anymore, Laphaniel."

"If you want my help, that's my price," he answered. She noted the dark shadows beneath his eyes, the hollow look to them. He looked as drained as she felt.

She curled her lip. "You are not in a position to barter with me."

"Then kill your king yourself–"

She cut his words off with a sharp slap, her words a snarl. "Hush your fucking mouth! Who knows who is listening."

"There is barely anyone left to eavesdrop, Niven!" Laphaniel spat back, blood on his teeth. "Get Fell out, and I will aid you in taking Phabian's crown."

The very idea of it…the risk, to save a nobody. "It is impossible."

"As impossible as slaying your mad lover?"

Niven paced the tiny room, shadows coiling and roving around her. She made no attempt to calm them, to hide her unease. They had come back to her after her bruises faded, skittish and weak, almost remorseful. Pitiful things.

"Your voices have been conveniently quiet," she said, scuffing a boot over the straw covering the freezing stone. The edges were brown, rotting away. Niven did not know if they ever replaced it.

"I am not a seer." Laphaniel leant against the wall, arms folded. "I catch whispers within a mess of noise, nothing more. Be thankful they saved your life." He snorted. "Twice."

"You don't wonder why?"

Laphaniel tilted his head at her, looking more fey-like than he had in ages. "I wonder at a lot of things."

"Why not just let him burn?" she asked, honestly curious. "Why bother saving Fell at all?"

"Because I don't want to be anything like you."

She wouldn't let the words sting. She didn't know what she was anymore, wasn't sure if it even mattered.

"Have you lost count of the broken bones you've suffered?" Niven scraped a fingernail over the ice dripping down the wall. "I think I would remember each one. The sound they made, the screams they pulled from me. I don't think I would forget."

"Your monsters have broken every bone in my body." Blood gleamed at his lip, teeth red. "Some more than once. It was at your request that they snapped all my fingers."

"I'm not sorry, you know."

"I never asked you to be."

Niven took a breath, then another. They tightened in her chest like a noose. She pulled a cigarette from thin air and placed it to her lips, flicking one to Laphaniel. With a wave of her fingers, she ignited both.

"I will ensure the guards are…away," Niven said, blowing a plume of curling smoke from her lips. "I will distract Phabian. How you get that knight out is entirely on you,"

Laphaniel took in a lungful of green smoke. "That's looking away, not helping."

"It is all you are getting," Niven snapped. "You have your hour of freedom today. Use the time wisely."

He flicked ash at her feet. "Why don't you use your time to slit Phabian's throat?"

She could tell from the way he looked at her that he was joking. Oh, but if it were that simple. Each night as she lay beside her king, her body used and aching, she dreamt of pulling a blade across his neck.

If only his shadows slept too.

"Do you have a plan at least?" Laphaniel asked. He rested his head against the wall, cigarette at his mouth, filthy black hair hiding his eyes. "Or am I to do that too?"

Niven stepped closer, until they were breathing in the same cloying smoke. It numbed the edges of everything, taking away the bite of fear coiling around her shadows. It dulled everything else too...her wits, her pride.

"If Fell's escape goes without a hiccup, the aftermath will be chaos," Niven began, words soft. "Phabian will be livid, the Unseelie will be terrified. He will make sure someone ends up on that pyre, and afterwards the halls will run with blood and revelry as they always do after he butchers someone. He will be on his guard, his food and his wine will be tasted, mine too...but with a slip of my hand, I will tip poison into my wine when no one is looking." She paused for breath, waiting for Laphaniel to react. "It will have to be real to fool him, just enough to make it look real. And when he is distracted by my convulsing body, you'll slit his throat."

She waited.

"That's it?" he said finally, tone strangely calm. "Your grand plan is for me to blindly stab at him?"

It was all she had. "Unless you have something better?"

Laphaniel took a shaky drag of the cigarette. "It's hardly fool proof."

Niven knew how messy it was, how desperate...but perhaps it was crazy enough to work. She had nothing left to say to him. She could wish him luck with Fell, but she didn't want to. She made to leave instead.

"Niven?"

She stiffened. "What now?"

Laphaniel hesitated, closing his eyes before outstretching his hand. "Can you send this to Teya?"

Niven took the crumpled, stained parchment, unrolling it to reveal messy black scrawl. She didn't want to know where he got it from. What he had traded for it.

"Your handwriting is appalling," Niven said. "Mind if I read it first?"

"I assumed you would."

She scanned the letter, noting the blobs of ink soaked into the paper as if he had written in a hurry, perhaps before he had a chance to change his mind.

"Were you drunk when you wrote this?" she asked, unable to conceal the hint of surprise in her voice.

"No."

"Really?"

"Are you going to send it or not?"

Niven nodded, outstretching her hand for the ring he slipped from his finger. He took a long breath before dropping it into her palm. It was strangely cold and heavy, seeming to glow despite the lack of light. A beacon against the dark.

Niven tried to hide her surprise. "You won't see her again, you understand that, don't you?"

"I know."

"It won't change the contract."

"I know, Niven!" Laphaniel snapped. "I should have done it a long time ago. I won't have Teya involved in this madness any longer. I want her to stay far, far away from this cursed labyrinth."

"You think we're going to fail."

He huffed a laugh. "Oh, I think it wise to take precautions."

Niven rolled the parchment up with Laphaniel's wedding ring

inside. She pulled the shadows from the walls, conjuring an ink black bird from the darkness.

"You shouldn't be able to do that," Laphaniel breathed. Niven gave a shrug.

"They seem to like me." With quick fingers she tied the letter to the bird's leg. "These shadows, this darkness. I believe I have you to thank for that."

"I have to wonder what sort of queen you will be without Phabian."

The thought of it. The freedom. "And if I am worse?"

"Then perhaps I will have to slit your throat," he said, blue eyes flashing.

Niven's hand tightened on the bird. "Teya will never be welcome back here."

"Then you won't be able to hurt her."

She gave the struggling bird a tight squeeze, causing it to screech. "Perhaps not."

Without looking away she flung the bird at the stone wall, where it burst into pieces of shadow and ghostly feathers.

Laphaniel had flicked his gaze to hers long before the bird had vanished from view. His fingers curled at his sides, the only hint of emotion he would show her.

"Do you want a hug?" She couldn't keep the smirk from her voice and didn't bother to try.

"I want you to go occupy that monster of yours, go fuck him into a coma."

"Don't you dare talk to me like that."

"You'll find, Niven," he said, voice low and deep and uncaring, "that we seem to have found ourselves on equal footing. We are both pretty close to losing our heads, and you need me to ensure Phabian loses his. I think I'll speak to you however the hell I like."

"Get Fell to the western gates," Niven hissed. "It leads down through the sewers, someone will meet you there."

Unease flashed over his face. "Who?"

Niven shrugged, tugging the shadows from the walls to form a gown that barely even hinted at clothing. Star-flecked mist glided over her breasts, trailing over her stomach to flow to the floor in tendrils of black.

"What do you think?" she asked, spinning so the shadows spun too. "Am I a good enough whore for a monster?"

"Niven…"

"If that is pity I hear, you can choke on it."

Laphaniel raked a hand through his hair, a sigh at his lips. "You are a creature far beyond being worthy of pity, Niven."

She was.

There was no denying that.

THE CORRIDORS WERE EMPTY, her sharp heels clicking against the black stone the only sound. Niven pushed open the great doors to the throne room herself, the steely-eyed guards backing off at the look she threw them.

Phabian sat sprawled on his throne, red cloak spilling down over the dais like too much blood. Courtiers stood in the shadows, forced laughter barely hiding the stink of fear wafting from them.

Where once the room had been crowded with faeries, all wicked and cunning and hungry…only a few remained. They bowed low for her, knees on the filthy marble, eyes down. They wouldn't look, wouldn't rise until she wanted them to.

"Look what I have," Phabian called out. He tugged on a length of chain gathered at his feet. A faerie jerked forward, her hands bound tight in front of her. "It's a solitary, she is all alone."

Niven gave a glance to the girl, noting the rags covering her, the torn wings hanging limp, the vacant eyes.

"Are you planning on rebuilding our court with solitaries, my love?" Niven said. "Our hallways are running empty. Our balls are not what they once were."

The Unseelie King's laughter boomed manic and wild, stirring up the shadows so they whipped around the room. The faerie girl flinched as they raced over her, tangling in her hair, at her torn wings.

"Not quite, my love." Phabian stood and lifted the chains so the girl was forced upon her tiptoes. "We will start with one girl for now. These faeries…how many can they have?"

Niven swallowed the bile rising in her throat. "How many what?"

"Pups."

"She's not a dog."

Phabian tilted his head, red hair spilling over his shoulder. "Is she not?"

"You're planning on breeding with solitary fey?" Her disgust rasped at her words, unconcealed.

"No." Phabian dropped the chains and the girl slammed to her knees. He took three strides to where she stood, his hand coming up to frame her face. "I would share my bed with only you."

Niven looked down at the cowering faerie, noting the hate burning behind the terror on her sweet face. "Then what do you have planned?"

"I will have a kennel built for waifs and strays. I will offer shelter, and in return I will fill this castle with Unseelie again. They will love me as you love me."

"That will take years." The words ghosted from her lips.

"What is time to faeries?" Phabian smiled, hand still resting upon her cheek.

Niven rocked slightly on her feet when he pulled away. The Unseelie king surveyed what was left of his court, while she stood and did nothing.

"You!" He pointed to a faerie with skin as green as the darkest swamps "What is your name?"

"Tihomir, Your Majesty." The faerie made a sweeping bow, ink-like hair sliding over his face. His words rasped over pointed teeth, and they trembled.

"Do you think he will do?" Phabian clicked his fingers. Niven didn't turn to watch the Spider slink from the shadows, her ragged gown of spider silk gliding across the black marble.

"Faeries do not conceive easily," Charlotte began, spitting out the words as if they were poison. "Birthing is not without great risk."

Phabian nodded. "I will need more girls sooner than I thought."

"Your Majesty." The Spider stalked closer, looking to Niven, ignoring the sharp shake of her head. "I beg you to reconsider this—"

"That's enough from you, witch," Phabian snapped. His shadows coiled around the Spider's throat, lifting her up until her claws scraped the marble. "They will be all under your care. Every loss will be taken out of your miserable hide, understand?"

Phabian strode back to his throne, snatching up the chains from the floor. With a quick yank he hauled the solitary to her feet, then tossed the chains to Tihomir. He didn't reach for them but cast a desperate look at Niven.

"Pick up the chain," she hissed, "as your King commands."

She hadn't missed the look in Phabian's eye at that panicked look. They had all looked to her...even the damned Spider. To see if she would put a stop to it all.

They were going to get her flayed alive.

Tihomir took up the chains with a shaking green hand, pulling the solitary to him. She held her head high, even as the Spider took one of her manacled hands and began to lead her away.

"It is better than the gallows, is it not?" Phabian called after them, a satisfied grin on his face.

Niven thought death may have been preferable.

Silence, thick and ugly descended over the court. For the first time in a long while, Niven wished she wore more than mist and shadows. She wanted something that would keep away the chill slithering over her.

"One day this court will be strong enough to tear down the Seelie, I promise you that," Phabian said, hand outstretched to her.

"You can't go to war," Niven replied, sitting beside him on her twisted throne.

"But I hunger for it." The petulance in his words rattled her. "I hunger for chaos, Niven. I can taste it in the air...in the distance. I hear it upon the screeching of the birds and the shifting of the earth beneath my feet. I saw a glimpse in the far reaches of that mongrel's troubled mind."

She feigned disinterest. "Laphaniel's?"

Phabian nodded absently, his hand lifting in the air. "It wouldn't let me see. I nearly broke his head apart for a closer look."

"I know, I saw him afterwards."

Phabian summoned goblets of dark wine with the click of his fingers before conjuring up music from the shadows. A haunting waltz played, one to stir up the gathering fey into a lilting and lustful dance. It called to them, the music. A Glamour of its own.

"He brought you to me," the Unseelie King breathed, draining his cup. "Why?"

Niven took a small sip, determined to keep what was left of her wits. "I found you, my love. Laphaniel stole me away to become the Seelie Queen replacement."

"Why you?"

She met his eyes, her reflection staring back against the black. "Why not?"

"You were never meant for the Seelie court, my love. The shadows love you too much."

I always thought the Unseelie would tear you apart, or you would end up ruling them.

Laphaniel's words came to Niven in a rush of dread and wonder. Which parts of her life had really been freely chosen by her?

"I would like to know why he thieved you for one throne, for you to end up sitting beside me in this one."

"This isn't a game, Phabian."

He swallowed down another cup of wine. "Oh, but it is, my love. We are merely pawns. Who are we to know the rules?"

Niven finished her wine before entwining her fingers through the Unseelie King's. She kept her shadows calm, holding them back while they strained to move to the music. "You feel fate has brought us together?"

He smiled back with wine-stained lips, looking in that instant like the man he once was. His hand came up to pull her close, his breath sweetened by the wine brushed over her face. The kiss was soft and strangely lovely, so different that she didn't notice his hand against her neck until she choked.

"Fate is playing a strange game with me, my love," the Unseelie King murmured, the words only for her. "I want to know what it is doing with the two of you."

Because...perhaps fate had not pushed her towards Phabian at all... but towards someone who might survive him.

"You grow paranoid, my love," Niven gasped, a hand coming up to prise the fingers from her neck.

"I have murdered most of my Court." Phabian grinned, not moving his hand. "Paranoia is common sense at this point."

"I am your Queen...my loyalty is to you."

He withdrew his fingers, and Niven sucked in a pained breath. "Is it really?"

"I bow to no one else."

She flinched when he raised his hands again, cupping her face with a gentleness that angered her. Disgusted her. She wanted nothing more than to strike him down.

She smiled instead.

"I will fill this court with faeries again, Niven," Phabian began. "Loyal soldiers with a desire for mayhem and blood, and a fearlessness none have seen before." He pressed a kiss to her brow. "But I want more than the bastards born from lesser creatures. I want heirs born from shadow, sons that will stand at my side as you do. Bear me children, Niven, and I will love you until the world ends."

Niven pushed back at the fear nestling in her stomach, shoving it down deep to rest with the scraps of her pride...the scraps of anything of her left. "I will bear you an army of sons, my love, if you promise to never question my loyalties again."

The Unseelie King stood, a grin slashed over his lips. The music drifting around the room turned manic. Niven moved with him, her hand already locked in his.

Around she spun, the shadows splayed out around her like silk.

"The Queen of the Unseelie!" Phabian screamed, twirling with her. "Bow to your Queen!"

Faeries slammed to their knees and they stayed there. Niven turned and spun and danced at Phabian's command. She kept the smile on her face even as her feet began to bleed.

Even as he ripped the mist covering her body.

And as he led her from the great hall.

She kept smiling through it all because she didn't trust her body enough to stop. What would the Unseelie King do if, gods forbid...she started weeping.

No, that wouldn't do at all.

CHAPTER TWENTY-SEVEN

LAPHANIEL

*T*he corridors were eerily quiet, empty of knights or guards, of anyone. If Niven had kept them all away, or if it was sheer dumb luck, I didn't know. Perhaps there were so few faeries left still alive.

I kept to the shadows anyway.

A bone numbing chill settled over the castle, as if the fires had not been lit in a long while. Ice formed upon the marble, over the glass in the windows. Darkness bled down from the walls, the candles remained unlit. The castle held no light...no sound. It was bleak and heavy and dead.

My breath fogged in front of me, and more than once I had to catch my footing when I slipped on the slick floor.

The lack of a plan was foolish, insane, though it seemed Phabian had massacred enough of his Court to not afford watchmen. It was a small mercy.

Perhaps no one would be watching his back when I slit his throat.

Down and down and down I climbed, clinging to the ancient

handrail as I descended deep beneath the Unseelie Labyrinth. I stopped countless times, leaning against the slimy wall to draw breath. It rasped past my lips, my knees buckling on the steps.

I swore then that if I made it alive, I would never again venture underground.

The dungeons were carved far, far beneath the earth, away from my own damp cell. Carvings were gouged into the rock, crude etchings of things that had once been held beneath the castle. Scratch marks cracked across the stone and across the ground.

The crushing sensation in my chest was enough to bring stars to my eyes. I gripped the wall, my head against the stone. The stone was all around me...above me...

Maybe Niven was right...

The thought of it had me pulling my head back from the rock. I took another step, another and another. I was getting Fell out.

Two prison guards lay slumped against the open gates, a bottle of mud whiskey lay beside them, leaking thick brown sludge onto the slabs. My stomach turned at the smell of it. Drool pooled from their black lips, frothy and bloodstained. Dampness spread through their trousers and nausea bubbled up my throat.

I didn't want to know what poison Niven had used, or if she had been discreet. I just needed to move.

The sewers were nearby. I could smell them, hear the sluggish rush of thick water as it churned through the tunnels and out into the river. I tried to breathe through my mouth, but it made little difference.

A lone torch flickered on the wall, the only source of light so far underground. I yanked it from its bone holder, ignoring the way everything was closing in on me. Holding the flame to the bars of each cell, I peered in, wondering if I would find Fell alive at all.

The first cell held only bones and mouldering rags. The second, a body recently dead, its skin still moving from the maggots feasting on it.

I called Fell's name, holding the torch up to illuminate the rows of cells. My voice was swallowed by the dark.

"Let me chew those pretty hands off you!" Something grabbed at me though the bars as I passed, broken nails snagging at my tattered sleeve. "Let me suck the marrow from them."

"Get off!"

The withered creature sank its teeth into my hand before I could yank it away, ripping out a good chunk of flesh. I slammed the torch against the bars, sending sparks flying into its face. It screeched at me, teeth red, grey skin hanging from thin bones. It sprang away, scratching at its face to cower in a corner away from the light.

"Fell!"

I didn't like the way my voice echoed.

"Fell!"

Or the way it stirred up those that death had yet to claim.

"Fell, you bastard! I'll leave you here!"

Bars rattled and claws reached out in the dark to snatch at me. Howls and jeers and snarls joined the echo of me calling Fell's name until I had no hope of hearing him. Something was going to hear the chaos eventually though…or come to check the guards.

Shining the torch through the bars of a strangely quiet cell, I saw him. He lay in a heap, not moving. The feathers on his cloak looked oily with blood, his cell reeked of it.

"Fell?" I hissed his name, resting the torch against the wall to grab the lever locking his cell. It didn't budge.

I tried again, bracing my leg against the wall to heave it down. The chains clunked slowly, each rung grating against the cogs as I pulled. It clicked open with a groan and I paused for breath before I moved.

I leapt back as the door slammed closed.

I waited for the echo to die out, cringing in the dark as I listened for anything that may have heard me.

Nothing came.

I grabbed the lever again, hauling it back until sweat trickled down my back. It thudded in place and I counted when I released the handle.

I made it to ten before it slammed shut again.

"Fell? Can you haul yourself closer to the door?" I hissed into the dark. "When the latch opens, I have ten seconds to get you out, or we'll both be trapped inside."

He didn't move. I couldn't even see if he still lived.

"If I get in there, and you're dead..." I blew out a breath, wiping the sweat from my hands on the rags I wore before taking the lever again.

I moved without thinking the moment I heard the click. Skidding into the cell, I grabbed at Fell and hauled him out, rolling over him just as the door smashed down. I seized his hand a fraction before he lost all of his fingers.

The Raven Knight blinked his eyes open, gaze roving over me as I straddled him, then to his hand in mine.

"People will start talking," he breathed, blood shining on his teeth.

"I thought you were dead."

"That doesn't make this less weird."

I shoved myself to my feet, taking a minute to catch my breath. Fell remained where he was, breathing heavily.

"Can you walk?"

Fell coughed, red trickled over his mouth. "No."

I grabbed him under the arms, forcing him up. "I'm getting you out."

"Anyone else would have just left me," he murmured before his eyes rolled back.

"Stay awake!" I snapped, giving him a rough shake. "I can't carry you all the way, you're going to have to walk. Someone is meeting us at the riverbank."

"Who?"

"I don't know, Niven said—" I stopped, wondering if I had been very, very stupid. "Someone is waiting for you."

Any colour left in Fell's face drained completely at the mention of Niven's name. "He killed them all. Everyone, and she watched. She just watched."

"I told you not—"

"Don't." He shook his head. "Please don't."

Fell clutched at his side, I could see the white of bone through his ripped shirt. Taking his elbow, I heaved him upright, bracing him while he howled in pain.

For a moment he just stood there leaning into me, his body shuddering as he sobbed.

"Fuck it," he murmured, pushing away to spit red onto the stone. "I hope you know what you're doing."

"I don't really," I answered honestly, shifting so I took most of his weight. "But surely it's better than rotting down here until they execute you?"

Fell grunted with each step, feet dragging along the ground in painfully slow movements. "I guess we shall see."

He passed out twice before we reached the sewer tunnels, and it took every bit of my strength not to drop him in the filthy water lapping at my legs.

"Is that..." He stirred and gagged.

"It is and adding to it won't help." I caught him around the waist, one hand reaching to grab at the crumbling stone. If I went under that water...

I hated to think what the putrid sludge was doing to Fell's wounds.

"I don't know if I'm going to puke or pass out again," Fell moaned, his head lolling forwards.

"I would really appreciate it if you didn't do either," I said, hoisting him up. "Just keep moving."

The tunnel turned, the water speeding up around us. At long last I spotted light ahead. I waded as quick as I could, one hand running along the cold wall, the other tight around Fell. He barely moved his legs, his entire body limp and heavy.

I fought for the embankment the moment I saw it. My feet slipped in the sludge, the muck around me running into the river water. Water...clean water. I threw Fell's body onto the snow and scrambled up beside him. My stomach heaved and I retched, not having much to bring up.

"You made it!"

I jumped to my feet, wishing I had some sort of weapon on me. "Who are you?"

Someone stepped from the shadows, hands raised in submission. Dark eyes peered up from a wild mess of dirty blonde hair, black feathers threaded through the tangles. The trees rustled overhead; crows littered the branches.

I stepped closer. "Alice."

She smiled, shoving back the knots of her hair. She pointed a ruined hand towards Fell. "I will need to clean him before I can move him. I have clean clothes."

I fought not to shudder, the cold soaking through my wet clothes. I searched the trees for any sign of her mistress. "You're alone?"

"I am." She stepped forward, little feet skidding on the bank. With a quick tug, she had Fell on his back. Her nose wrinkled.

"You're just a child." The words came out before I could stop them.

Alice looked up sharply; the crows nestled in the trees above us went quiet, heads snapping down at me.

"That is true," she said softly, black eyes peering up at me, unblinking. "But you are a prisoner here and look what you are doing."

"Point taken."

She peeled the filthy clothes from Fell with little help from me, using water from a nearby hot spring to clean him. His body was a mess of open wounds and broken bones. The Unseelie Knight didn't move while she worked, efficient and quick. The wet, hitching sounds of his breathing were the only signs he still lived.

"You should clean yourself up, too. There's another set of clothes on the sled," Alice said, not glancing up from Fell.

I wasn't used to taking orders from children. "I can help if you need it."

"You are more likely to infect his wounds in that state, but I will need a hand to haul him up on my sled in a moment." She looked up, eyes softening. "If you don't get dry you'll get sick and be no use to anyone."

I took the hint and made my way behind the hill to the hot spring. I found the spare clothes and a bar of gritty soap amongst Alice's supplies, and stripped off the sopping filthy rags that covered me.

The first bath in...I couldn't remember. The hot water bubbling around me felt too good and I scrubbed my skin raw. The dirt flaked off, the old blood, too, yet I didn't feel clean. I couldn't scrub it all away no matter how hard I tried.

The clothes I had found were warm and dry. The rough grey shirt and black trousers were worn, threadbare in places with a few buttons missing, I tightened the moth-eaten cloak around my shoulders, grateful for the warmth it offered.

It had all been a little too easy.

Alice waited for me beside the sled, her head cocked to the side. Fell lay beside her, clean and bundled in furs, waiting to be hauled onto the sled.

"How is he—" I rocked back on my heels as Alice leapt at me, arms tight around my neck.

Her voice was muffled against my chest. "I never had the chance to thank you for saving me."

I hugged her back, her fingers bunched in my cloak. "I hear I should be thanking you. You saved Teya and Gabriel."

My heart went cold at the thought of Teya receiving the letter...of never seeing her again. I held the little girl in my arms tighter before setting her down.

Alice swiped a ragged sleeve across her face. "Your wife left some time ago...to see some witches. Gabriel sustained more serious injuries but is healing. He should be well enough to travel home soon."

Alice turned to Fell, slipping her hand in mine. I noted the stumps on the other, the scars shining white.

"The Scara taught me to heal and mend, to sew and dig out rot," she said, following my gaze. "But only with this hand." She turned it over, giving me a closer look at the eaten down stumps. I remembered them. "Only when I perfected my skills would she allow me to use the other."

Guilt bubbled up inside me. We hadn't even tried to take her home.

We moved Fell onto the sled together, careful not to jolt him further, but he still moaned in pain. Six hounds waited patiently, white coats thick and heavy, blending perfectly with the surrounding snow. "Will he live?"

"Broken and bruised," Alice answered. "He's lost quite a bit of blood, but there's no fever at the moment. Once we get away, I believe he'll recover."

"Where will you go?"

Alice glanced up into the treetops, at the birds waiting above. "Very far from here."

The hounds sniffed at me while I stroked their heads, my fingers scratching between the black curling horns on their heads, their tongues lolled, fat tails thumping the snow.

"Come with us," Alice said, and the crows overhead screeched at her. "Please?"

It was so very tempting.

"Phabian will cut this world down," I said at last. "You are in enough danger with Fell, why did the Scara send you?"

She folded her arms in front of her, dark eyes flashing. "I am small, and I am quick…"

"Or she wants you out of Faerie."

She hissed at me. "Come with us."

"There is something I need to do first." I turned to the trees seemingly asleep around us. "I need to finish this."

"It is not your battle." She gestured to the snow drenched woods. "Let it burn."

"Phabian would rage war on the Seelie…on Teya."

"He has no court left," Alice said, black eyes brimming with tears. "He is alone!"

I reached to wipe her cheek, but she slapped me away. "I want this to end, Alice. I will not run. There is nowhere left I can go."

"You can't just give up."

I bristled. "I'm not giving up."

Tears slipped over her cheeks. She snatched at my left hand quicker than I could react. "Then where is your wedding ring?"

"You couldn't possibly understand…"

"Because I am a child?"

"Yes!" I snapped, and she flinched. "What could you possibly know—"

"I know more than you would believe," she replied, baring her own teeth. "I know what the crows know and there is darkness and shadow and screaming. Do not tell me I don't understand."

"I need to get Phabian off that throne." I didn't care in the slightest that I was arguing with a little girl. "Otherwise, whatever darkness you think is coming will get here a hell of a lot faster."

The crows shot from the branches in a flurry of black, screeching around Alice until she was swallowed up by wing and feather. I grabbed her, yanking my hand back when they lunged for me, drawing blood.

"Come with me," she repeated, calming the manic birds with a lift of her ruined hand. "There's nothing for you here but blood and death."

"I can't," I answered. "You need to get going, they'll realise Fell is missing soon."

She shook her head, sending feathers swirling to the floor. "Do you really believe he doesn't know?"

Dread knotted in my stomach. "Perhaps Niven is just very good at distracting her king."

"Among others," she muttered, reaching over to tuck the furs tighter around Fell. The knight stirred, a low moan slipping from his lips.

"What is that supposed to mean?" I asked, but she just curled her lip.

"Ask the Queen yourself."

On the sled, Fell shifted beneath the bundles covering him. "Are you coming too?"

"He is not," Alice said before I could speak. She pressed Fell back down with a firm hand. "Now lie still, we have a long ride ahead."

"There's plenty of room," Fell continued. "It will be a little cosy, but I'm happy to snuggle."

"Do as you are told, and be quiet," I said.

"Have you completely lost your mind?" Fell snarled. "You have the chance to escape!"

"I can't, Fell." I wanted to…Gods, I wanted to. "Phabian won't stop. He would hunt me down…hunt Teya down. I won't give him any cause to nail her to that…that damned wall…I can't…"

"You realise this is likely to be a game he is playing, don't you?" Fell sat up, ignoring the scathing look Alice was throwing him.

"I'm starting to think it could be," I replied. "All the more reason for you two to get out of here, fast."

"Lie down," Alice said through gritted teeth. "I am getting tired of faeries who think they know better than I do."

I did not miss the glance she threw at me.

"Yes, little miss," Fell sighed, placing his head back against the furs.

"I guess this is goodbye, then," Alice said, turning to me.

"Goodbye, Alice."

She didn't move away but slipped her hand in mine. "Please."

I wanted to go with her.

I wanted what she was offering me more than I dared admit.

And I wanted to make sure she stayed safe, that she arrived wherever she was going, alive and well.

I remembered the sounds of her screaming when we left her with the Scara, how they echoed long after we had walked away. Guilt, dread and something else had set its teeth in me, refusing to let go. It had buried down deep, and I had almost forgotten the feeling.

"Don't travel after nightfall," I said, and she pulled her hand away. "Don't light fires if you can do without. Stay off the paths if you can."

She lifted a brow, defiant. "Anything else, King of Seelie?"

"Are you going to listen to anything I tell you?"

She snorted a laugh, lifting her hood over her head. "I promise to not do anything reckless if you do the same."

She climbed upon the sleigh and snapped at the reins. The hounds lurched forwards with a howl, their horns slicing the rising mist, I stepped aside and watched them disappear through the trees, the sled cutting through the snow in silence.

I returned to the castle through the main gates, keeping my gaze ahead and not at the bodies swaying with the breeze. I recognised one of them, his raven cloak flapping like tattered flags.

I just hoped Niven had kept her word. I hoped it was sheer luck that I managed to get Fell out. I hoped.

I knew it was hell of a lot to hope for.

CHAPTER TWENTY-EIGHT

TEYA

*T*he spell took three days to prepare and was to take place beneath the fat full moon shining above us.

Luthien had us gathering herbs, collecting strange plants that only bloomed beneath the moonglow. The petals were whisper soft, uncurling with the gentle light. With one touch of our fingers, they withered and died. The barbed stalks were the only way to gather them.

We collected the blood of a white stag as instructed and roasted the meat over a blazing spit. We feasted under the stars together, though Luthien sat away, her fingers dripping red as she carved up the bones of some small creature.

Oonagh bottled up the sigh of the wind and the frozen dewdrops from a rowan branch while Nefina distilled the glow of thirteen shooting stars in sparkling water. They did as instructed, harvesting all that was needed to bring about my death.

We needed the mortal hearts of men, and with a sweep of her slender hand, Luthien gestured to the broken bodies surrounding her. If I wanted the spell, I was to retrieve the hearts myself.

Camping together in the Blue Meadows was as strange and

awkward as I had thought it would be. Luthien kept apart from us, busying herself with grinding down the herbs in silence. Occasionally she flicked her dark eyes to me, lips upturned. Hunger burned behind her gaze and malice behind her smile, delighting in the power she once again held over me.

The six mortal hearts she held up to the moonlight, one after the other before adding them to a black pot. She made me watch, reminding me of what I had done to bring Laphaniel home.

As if I would ever forget.

"What is that?" Nefina said, pointing into the night.

An ebony bird swooped down close to me, its feathers swirling like shadows. It alighted upon my outstretched hand, and I noticed the letter tied to its leg. The moment I untied the parchment the bird turned to mist and nothingness.

> I cannot undo our wedding vows under the laws of Faerie you will remain my wife until the end of days perhaps beyond that. But I no longer recognise you as such and renounce the token binding us.
> Do not come.
> You are no longer welcome here.

No one said a word as I tipped the ring into my palm, rereading the familiar handwriting again and again as if I could somehow change the words just by wishing it. Unclasping the star at my neck, I slipped Laphaniel's wedding ring onto the chain.

He had given up.

I had taken far too long to get him home.

"Do I still get to kill you?" Luthien broke the silence settling over us, her eyes flicking to Laphaniel's wedding ring nestled by my star.

"Nothing has changed, Luthien, don't you worry about that."

"Teya, you won't be allowed anywhere near the castle," Oonagh pointed out, eyes scanning the letter I passed to her. "The agreement was for you to visit your husband every midwinter—"

"He still is my husband," I snapped. "Once I am no longer the Seelie Queen, I am going to get him. My death will unbind me from that damned contract, and I will bring him home, Oonagh."

"You do not have a home," Luthien said. "You will not be welcome on my lands, Teya."

I took in the Blue Meadows around me, the lush grass, the soft sigh of the wind. "I won't be anywhere near you, Luthien, have no fear of that. We will find a tiny piece of Faerie tucked away somewhere for just us."

The gentle wind swept up Luthien's dark hair, the light casting the strands in various shades of deep gold and bitter brown. With the full moon shining upon her and the bodies that lay upon the grass, she looked more like a goddess than a queen. She turned to me, piercing eyes seeming to bore into my soul.

"That sounds awfully dull, Teya Jenkins."

"Winteroak," I murmured, clinging to the word. "Teya Winteroak."

I took the letter back from Oonagh and tucked it away safely. I wanted to show it to Laphaniel one day, to show him that when all hope had left him, I still fought for him. That I came for him, as I promised.

"It would sound dull to you," I said. "I don't want a crown or a castle, I never did…Laphaniel never did. I want to be still, Luthien. To remember what it felt to just sit and breathe and dream. I want to feel bored and lazy again."

Luthien curled her lip, as if the thought of such a mundane life disgusted her. "What of the two of you?"

Oonagh glanced at Nefina before answering. "I will not return to court: too much of my friends' blood has been spilled out in those halls.

There is so much of these lands I have yet to walk, I would like to see more of it."

"Would you take me back?" Nefina began, head held high and eyes bright. "Would you ever trust me enough to welcome me back to your side?"

"I would not." Luthien said, unmoved. Unimpressed.

Nefina smiled. "Then I will go with Oonagh. To wherever those uncharted paths may take us."

Luthien took a breath as if she were tired of us all. "I am guessing I have a lot of work to restore my Court to its former glory?"

"You hung your fey from the ceiling, Luthien!" I began before shaking my head. It was an argument I wouldn't win. "I'm sure you will relish in bringing them all to heel."

She smiled, a terrible, wicked smile. "You have no idea."

The fat moon shone bright, a beacon. "Thank you for agreeing to help me, Luthien."

She lifted a pale shoulder, leading me to a stone circle she had prepared. Bones lay in strange patterns upon the ground, little skulls dotted between whole rib cages, gleaming finger bones all pointing to the centre. So many bones.

"You know I am not doing this for your happiness, Teya."

"I know." I knelt in the dirt, between two rabbit skulls, mouths wide open, buck teeth on show. Luthien knelt beside me, grounding the remaining ingredients with the hilt of her knife. "I also think you will be the better Queen."

She stopped. "We will find out soon enough."

Blood went into the bowl, thick and hot. Luthien mixed it with her fingers, stirring it quick enough to slop over the edges. Then she painted it over my cheeks, down my nose and lips, tracing it down over my collar bones to the swell of my breasts.

"Is this an Unseelie spell?" I dared ask, as Luthien cracked open a human-looking bone, adding the marrow to her bowl.

"No," she answered, scooping up a handful of dirt before dumping it into the mixture. "It is neither Seelie nor Unseelie. It is from before."

"Before the Courts?"

A nod.

An ancient, ancient spell.

"How do you know of it?"

"My sister and I were always enthralled with the magic of old. The curse she used to bind the Seelie was one such spell. To know how easily it could have been broken irks me, I will admit to that, Teya Jenkins—" A smile lifted her lips. "Winteroak. I enjoy dabbling in old magic, but it is temperamental—even the witches dislike it."

I gestured to the blood and bones. "This doesn't look like dabbling."

Luthien lifted an elegant shoulder before handing me the bowl of blood and dirt. "Drink this."

"I have to drink it?"

Luthien waited. Of course, I did.

"Blood from those once living, dirt from the earth you stand upon," Luthien said, sucking some of the blood from her fingertips.

"And the rest?"

"Not for you to know," she said, nodding to the bowl. "Now drink before it spoils."

Glancing back at Oonagh and Nefina, I was not at all comforted by the twin looks of dread on their faces. Without another thought, I tipped the vile concoction back, fighting the urge to gag.

I sat forward with my head against the ground, sucking in deep breaths to stop the gritty, warm mix from coming back up. Someone rubbed my back. I very much doubted it was Luthien.

"I don't feel any different," I said, taking a deep breath before sitting back up. "Except nauseated."

Luthien flipped the knife in her hands, dark eyes glittering in the moonlight. She looked ecstatic.

With one slick movement she pulled the blade across my throat.

I COULDN'T SCREAM.

But someone was screaming.

Then nothing.

Darkness,

and emptiness. A void.

Nothing at all…

Nothing…

Nothing…

Nothing…

I WAS SO COLD…

"You are early."

So, so cold

"…or so very late. I find I cannot remember with you, Teya Jenkins."

A laugh.

"Or is it Teya Winteroak?"

The darkness didn't lift but shifted all around me. A constant swirl of freezing black. Nothing but black above me, nothing but black below my feet.

"Who are you?" My voice came from everywhere.

Laughter, deep and ancient, echoed around me. Something ran down the edge of my cheek, cold as ice and talon sharp.

"Oh, I think you know."

Fear curdled in my stomach, real and final.

"Am I dead?"

I pressed a hand to my neck, feeling nothing at all beneath my fingertips.

"I'm dead, aren't I?"

The answer brushed over my ear, soft and cold. "Yes."

I let that word settle over me, the finality of it if everything went wrong. I pressed a shaking hand to my heart, knowing how it should race beneath my ribcage, how the blood should roar in my ears. There was no sound, no thump. The song it once played was gone. I snatched my hand away, unable to bear the emptiness.

"May I see who I am talking to?"

My heart may have been dead and unmoving, but my emotions were certainly not. Dread coiled through me, my body…my spirit trembling with it.

There was a sigh, a rustle in the dark. "If you must."

The black retreated, sweeping back to a single spot. Everything around me remained grey, like hewn rock, ragged and sharp. A tall man stood in front of me, a cloak of night whipping behind him. The jagged ends spilled into shadow, leaking back into the world around him. He smiled down at me, pale skin shifting to reveal the skull beneath.

"Oh, God…" I spluttered, backing away.

"No," Death said with a smile. "Not quite."

With a quick wave of his skeletal hand, he conjured up two armchairs from nothing. They were made from stone, the backs reaching up far taller than him. Creatures were carved over the arms, over the legs and those tall, tall backs ended in faces that loomed over us, watching.

"Would you care to sit?"

I obeyed only because I doubted my legs would hold me up much longer. The stone was freezing, the face above me turned. It was indeed watching me. Death took the chair opposite me. The face above him did not move.

"I can't stay," I said, unable to keep the tremor from my voice. I didn't try.

Death steepled his long fingers, flesh turning to bone when the light hit it. "They all say that."

"There is a spell—"

"I know," Death cut in, leaning closer to trail a finger over the blood marks on my skin. "I have not seen these runes in an age, girl. You hope to trick me once again."

I remembered the monstrous shadows that had loomed over Laphaniel's body, the anger in them…the ancient fury. I remembered how they had fallen over me, and hesitated.

Not yet.

I shifted beneath his shrewd gaze, as if he could see all of me…

perhaps he could. "If it means anything at all, Laphaniel never wanted to come back."

Death closed his eyes, a slow smile crept over his lips. "That boy screamed when I dragged him back through. I was not gentle, nor kind." He shrugged, his cloak rippled around him, blackness ripped from it to scramble into the gloom. "Yet who am I to argue with powers greater than myself?"

"Are you speaking of the Seelie Curse?"

"Do you think I am?"

I had no idea what forces were playing with our lives. What the meaning was behind the whispering of witches and crows.

"Why keep Laphaniel's soul?" I demanded. The world around me darkened, the chill biting in. Above me the face tilted its head, lips pulling back to reveal fangs. Death did not move. I met his stare. "Did you take it out of spite?"

He stretched, the skin over his hands and face flickered until nothing but bone stared back. "Yes."

"Then can I have it back?" I reached a shaking hand to touch his, my pale fingers on his bare bones. "Please?"

He cocked his head, bones clicking. "When you leave here?"

"Yes."

"What makes you think you get to leave?"

I pulled away, but he caught my wrist, his long fingers trapping mine.

"Luthien knows the spell..."

"Why would you want to go back?" he asked, cold fingers stroking my skin. "You are already dead, your body left to rot. Why not just remain here and wait for your beloved to come home?"

I swallowed. "The afterlife looks a little bleak."

He laughed again, the sound filling the darkness with an odd sort of joy. "Would you like to see?"

"See what?"

Death stood with a hand outstretched. He looked more like a man again, though his skin looked too thin. It barely concealed what he truly looked like. I took his hand.

"There is a reason your lover was so reluctant to leave."

"I…"

"Time is different here," Death continued. He released my hand, but I could still feel the cold from where he touched me. He pointed into the distance, past the mist, to where something was calling to me. "Your beloved knew he would not be alone for long. You would not be alone for long if you choose to stay."

"I don't want to see," I forced the words out. It would be too easy to have a quick look…but what if I wanted to stay?

It would be too easy to stay.

"As you wish."

I waited for more, for the trick but none came. "You won't make me?"

"Today, tomorrow, a hundred years from now. It matters not. You will come back."

I stepped closer to the spot in distance, feeling it tug at me. "I still get to go there? That place you mentioned, with Laphaniel?"

Another step and warmth brushed over my face. The warmth of an early morning sunrise, one that only just melts away the night-time frost. Something crunched beneath my foot, a leaf. Gold touched its edges, the rest of it burning with oranges and reds. I could smell woodsmoke, I could…

I stopped.

Laughter sounded behind me, the sound of bone rattling over bone.

"Is it real?" I asked, retreating away. "Or simply a very clever illusion?"

Death stood back, watching me with empty eye sockets. "It is real, I think you know that, deep down." He tilted his head, studying me. "To answer your earlier question, yes, it will be waiting for you, as will I."

I nodded and took another step back.

"It will hurt next time."

I whirled. "When—"

He cut me off with a barking laugh. "I will keep that knowledge to myself, I think."

"Will I get Laphaniel back?" I asked, not caring how desperate I sounded. "Have a family? Do I live long enough to enjoy life again?"

Death put a strangely comforting hand on my shoulder, finger bones stretching long over my skin. "I am not a fortune teller. I know endings, that is all."

The world behind me called out, a gentle coaxing that sang to me.

"You do not have to go back."

I looked back to what lay only a few steps away from me. "What would happen if I stayed here?"

The bone hand lifted from my shoulder, leaving behind traces of cold. "I believe you would be missed, but the world would carry on as is the way of things. Those you leave behind will carry on, until at last they reach this place."

Laphaniel...

"Will it hurt?" I asked. "Returning home?"

Those empty eyes stared into me. "I would think so, yes."

He pulled a cigarette from nothing and drew it to his lipless mouth. Smoke curled around his bones, swirling around his ribcage.

"What would you do," I asked. "If you were given the choice?"

Death said nothing for a moment, and I wondered if I had surprised him with my question.

"I think I would like to watch," he said. "See for myself how easily your world can be ripped apart. I would like to see it burn."

"You want to see everything die?"

He flicked his still burning cigarette away. "That is not what I meant at all, Teya Winteroak."

I took in the surrounding darkness, knowing I was being watched. The pull was still there, tempting.

I knew it was real.

It was nothing like drowning in the River of Tears. There was no forgetting, no illusions. I could feel it from where I stood, a hair's breadth away from never going back.

It felt like going home.

"As much as I delight in your company," Death began, appearing behind me, making me jump. "But need I remind you that your body is rotting away somewhere. There will be no choice at all soon."

"You're not angry with me?" I asked. "You were furious when Laphaniel came back. I have never known anger like that."

"I was angry with him." Death ran a bony finger over my neck, tracing the ghost of a wound. "He belonged to me. Dead as dead can be. His body grew cold and would have started leaking like bodies tend to do."

I did not need reminding.

"You, Teya Winteroak, are here only because of a spell. A foolish and dangerous spell, but you are not simply mine to take." He paused, seemingly lost in thought. "I am not angry with you."

"I'm going back."

Death stepped away from me, letting the illusion settle over him so he looked like a man again. From his pocket he pulled out a glowing ball of light, tossing it absently from one hand to the other as if it were nothing.

"I had a feeling you would."

It was so bright. Unmarred...untainted and perfect.

"Your beloved is going to need this more than I do," Death mused, rolling the ball over his knuckles and back again. "Though I wonder what it will look like when I see it again."

He threw Laphaniel's soul at me, and instinctively I held out my hands to catch it, feeling it disappear the moment it hit my incorporeal body. I sensed it on me, hidden away in some phantom pocket, like a lucky coin.

"I will be waiting for you," he said, his words not a threat but a promise. "And you will belong to me. Your beloved will belong to me, as will your children and your children's children, until the end of time. I will not allow you to leave when next we meet."

I nodded, taking what comfort I could. With a last glance behind me, I held out my hand. "Until we meet again, then."

Death lifted a brow but took my hand, bending low to place an icy kiss upon the back of it.

He vanished into the darkness without another word. The cold felt heavy around me, pressing against my chest until I thought I might crack in two.

The black ended...lightened.

But I was so cold.

And tired.

I lay on my back and through half-open eyes, I could just make out trees. All dark and bare and huge.

No blue leaves to be seen...no oasis.

I tried to call out for my friends, but no words came. Only pain. With a trembling hand I brought my hand to my neck, fingers running over the raw, sticky wound slashed across it.

I didn't know where I was.

Luthien had indeed kept her end of the bargain but had dumped my body somewhere in the woods.

Alone.

CHAPTER TWENTY-NINE

NIVEN

*T*here would be no squalling brats any time soon, Niven made sure of that. The tonic she swallowed down in secret every morning ensured she would not conceive. She knew, of course, that she could not carry on indefinitely. Phabian wasn't stupid. He would expect an heir eventually.

She just had to make sure he didn't live long enough to suspect anything.

The Unseelie Castle still reeked of bloodshed and fear, of the burnings that had taken place after Fell's escape. Two guards had taken the place of the Raven Knight, and it had not been quick.

The Unseelie King had not looked her way, not voiced another accusation while she had glared out over the courtyard, head held high, her shadows entwined with his. She allowed the smile at her lips, the glint in her eye, letting him think it was for the flames licking at the hides of the unfortunate faeries and for the screams that followed.

He did not know of the little vial of poison tucked away in her skirts, or that she had slipped a gilded dagger to Laphaniel a few days earlier.

So, the Queen of Unseelie smiled a wicked, wicked smile.

And waited just a little longer.

NIVEN WAITED DEEP in the shadows near the Scara's dwelling, scanning the treetops for the mass of pitch-black birds nested in the branches above. They stared back at her, ebony eyes glinting with a hunger she could not quite understand.

The strange little girl had long gone, taking the wounded Unseelie knight far away with her. It was easy for Niven to persuade her to go. The Crow Witch had given no protest to losing her ward, packing the girl off with a haste that unsettled Niven. She went with a full sled and a black cloud of squawking birds.

There was nothing left to do but ensure the golden-haired knight was sent on his way home. Away from Unseelie.

Away from her.

In case it all went to hell.

"Lurking in the shadows, Demon?" Gabriel walked towards her, standing straight and tall. Whole. "What are you hiding from?"

"Only my responsibilities," Niven answered, leaning back against a dying oak. "I hear you're fit to travel home."

"Does that bother you?"

She shrugged, mist and nightmares shifting around her. "Why would it?"

He closed the gap between them, one hand tangling in her hair. The other lingered at her back. He pulled her close, his mouth at her neck, her ear, her lips.

Niven let him kiss her, his teeth grazing over her skin.

Shadows wrapped around them, teasing at exposed skin. They lifted her hair, pulled it from the jewelled clasps pinning it back so it tumbled down her back. Niven lost herself within his arms, and simply forgot for a while.

"Come with me."

Niven allowed the words to settle over her. Not long ago she would have laughed at such words—they didn't seem all that funny anymore.

"I am not one to run off into the sunset, knight," she said, pressing her mouth to the hollow of his throat.

"Because you want to be Queen?"

Gabriel arched his neck, and she bit down. "Yes."

A moan slipped from his mouth before he pulled away. His hands came up to frame her face. She allowed that too.

"Then what is this?" Gabriel kissed her again, slow and lingering. "What am I to you?"

"A fucking awful distraction."

His hands skimmed lower, over her breasts, beneath the darkness she wore. Niven arched into his touch, eyes on his. The bark of the old tree scraped along her back, but she didn't care.

They moved together to the screeching of crows, beneath the trees that slumbered. They became a clash of teeth and hands and breath and gasps. Until, at last, they were one body and there was nothing else.

Niven breathed him in, needing him closer, needing more, until with a final joint cry they were but bodies on the still frozen ground.

Niven dragged the shadows to her, slipping them over her body in a gown of night. Gabriel's hand lingered over her skin, a thumb brushing against the bruises there.

"Niven—"

"Don't," she breathed, and shrugged him off. "That's enough of that."

He kissed her again, awful, slow kisses that ached.

"Come away with me, Niven," Gabriel said, hands trailing over her arms until his fingers were threaded with hers. "Bring your shadows, and we can rule over a piece of darkness together."

She would not allow those words to take root. "I thought you Seelie did not care for the dark."

"It has grown on me."

She didn't pull her hands away from his. "You would leave my sister?"

"For you, yes."

"Why?" The word slipped past her mouth, barely a sigh.

He closed his eyes. "Because I have fallen in love with you."

Niven wrenched her hands away, breath hissing through her teeth. She sucked in a breath before the back of her hand snapped Gabriel's head to the side.

"I love you," he repeated, blood shining on his teeth.

"Go home, knight!" she snarled back. "Go home to your Queen and your Court and your life. You have no place beside me."

"If I go, you won't see me again," he said, watching her closely... too closely. "I will not come back, Queen of Demons."

"A few fumbles in the dark and you lose your head." A nasty chuckle slipped past her mouth. "You are nothing to me."

With a snarl of his own, he kissed her again, fingers snagging deep into her hair to drag her head back. His teeth found her collarbone, then bit lower. She couldn't swallow her groan quick enough.

"I love you, Niven."

"I don't care." She shoved him away, her neck aching where he had bitten it...everything ached where he had touched her.

"You are lying," Gabriel said with more blood on his teeth. Her blood. "I know you are lying, Demon."

"You want for me to be lying, knight," she hissed. "I want more from this life than to be someone else's whore."

"You are more than that." He made to touch her again, but she wrapped a veil of shadows around his wrist and held him back.

"I am a poison, Gabriel. Nothing more."

"Niven—"

She called more shadows to her, looping them tight around his body, his neck. He fought against them, eyes going wide.

"Leave here and forget any notion of love you have in that pretty head of yours, else I will hang you from this tree and leave you for the crows."

He struggled, toes scraping the ground. The words were still on his lips, the ghost of them lingering to haunt her.

Niven held tight to her shadows long after she walked away. She left him behind and he didn't call after her.

She hated the craving that gnawed at her. The way it all felt like weakness. She hated the way her body fit perfectly to his, hated the words he uttered, as if they were a poison and not her.

Niven hated the way it no longer felt like hate.

NIVEN HAD BARELY MADE it through the towering gates of the castle before one of the remaining Unseelie guards came running to her. He bowed low, curling ram horns scraping the stone, his breath caught in his throat.

"Your presence is required in the Great Hall, your Majesty," he rasped, his long tail twitching behind him like a cat. "The King is waiting."

"What for?" she demanded, her voice mercifully holding steady.

The guard shook his head, gesturing Niven to follow with a heavy paw. "I have orders only to bring you to the King."

With a slight incline of her head, she followed him, painting on a smile, calling her shadows to her side. The twitchy guard bowed low, and Niven followed. Her hand went to the small vial tucked away in her skirts. She would drink it beside Phabian, and she would suffer in a way that could not be faked. The poison was not a pleasant one...but it was dramatic. A few sips and no more, the Spider had told her after she had snuck deep down into her lair.

She would foam at the mouth before convulsing. It would definitely get Phabian's attention and hopefully keep it while Laphaniel lingered in the shadows.

She was so, so close.

Niven strode into the vast obsidian hall with as much indifference as she could spare, not bothering to glance at the scant Court that dropped to their knees as she passed them. Phabian stood before his knotted throne, holding out a hand to greet her.

He grinned like a madman.

"Sit, my love," he ordered, fingers folding over her hand before hauling her up the dais. "You will want to see this."

"Another solitary to use as a prize mare?" she asked, feigning boredom.

"Do you know what was happening when you lay sprawled out in my bed, my love?" the Unseelie King said. Shadows danced in his eyes, no colour...just roving dark.

"I was not doing a lot of thinking while tangled up in silk."

Phabian chuckled, low and soft before clicking his long fingers. Two more guards entered the hall, huge beasts of fur and fang. Their hooves hammered over the black marble.

Her heart froze; she had to remember to breathe.

Niven forced her gaze to the Unseelie king, away from the guards dragging Laphaniel to the foot of the twin thrones.

"What has he done now?" she asked, willing her shadows to keep steady.

"He helped my prisoner to escape, thinking I would not notice." Phabian stood, boots echoing in the bated silence surrounding him. "He forgets I know everything."

Niven brought her shadows to heel. "Then why let him get away?"

Phabian glanced back at her before he dismissed the guards holding Laphaniel. "Because this is much more fun."

The Unseelie king circled him like a vulture. Laphaniel kept his gaze to the floor. Niven couldn't look anywhere else.

"The little maggot you bribed to steal away my knight is quick, isn't she?" Phabian began, voice a near whisper.

No mention of her, he didn't suspect her part in it all. Perhaps that should have sparked some shame, some guilt.

Niven felt nothing but relief.

Phabian stood a fraction taller than Laphaniel, getting so close Niven could barely hear the words he hissed. "My dogs are faster."

She saw the sudden shift in Laphaniel, the alarm he was too slow to hide, the fear not for his hide, but for someone else. Phabian saw it too, realising he had hit a nerve.

Laphaniel tilted his head up. "You have sunk to a new low if you're now hunting little girls."

The Unseelie King bared his teeth. "I will not tolerate thieves in my court."

"It seems you tolerate very little, Phabian."

Shadows streamed from the Unseelie King's hands, wrapping around Laphaniel to shove him hard to his knees. He hit the marble hard, the echo of bone stirring up the watching Faeries. Niven's shadows rushed forward, too tempted by the King to remain at her side.

"Do you have anything to say for yourself, mongrel?"

"What do you want me to say?" Laphaniel answered, neck bared as shadows coiled tight around it. "Your wall was looking a little cluttered, you have no room left. I did you a favour."

"You still have a mouth on you," Phabian hissed. "I thought by now you would have learnt to keep it shut."

To Niven's surprise, Laphaniel shrugged. "I blame my wife. She always had trouble keeping quiet, I guess it rubbed off."

The Unseelie backed away a few steps, a chuckle on his lips. "Your wife no longer, if I hear correctly. Is that right, my love?"

Laphaniel's head snapped towards Niven's, eyes flashing with betrayal. Niven held his stare. "I sent his letter myself. As I told you I did."

She had no idea if the bird had reached her sister, if Teya knew to stay far, far away from the rising madness destroying the Unseelie.

"Pity really," Phabian drawled, taking a knife from his belt. He flicked it over and over in his hand, catching the bone handle with ease. "I would have loved to have sent his finger with it."

"Why don't you anyway?" Niven said, relaxing slightly against her throne. Her shadows calmed. The candlelight flickering around the hall stilled. She allowed a wicked little thrill to run through her.

The knife edge glinted. "Oh, I think I might."

Only a finger.

He was so fucking lucky it was only a finger.

Chaos and dark Glamour poured over the hall, the surrounding Unseelie stirring at the promise of Seelie blood. Not their blood, it was a relief that it wouldn't be theirs.

Hungry eyes watched from the shadows, wings twitched, and teeth gleamed. Not a soul uttered a word, none dared make a noise to draw attention to themselves. They simply watched and waited.

As did Niven.

She longed for that rush, that burst of power. It called to her in a way nothing else did, thrummed though her blood until she finally believed she could belong somewhere.

It drowned out the thoughts of her belonging anywhere else.

She watched Laphaniel stiffen as Phabian forced his hand out onto the pitch-black marble, fingers splayed.

"I am going to send this to your whore," he said. "And you will remember to keep your tongue, else I will remove that from you as well."

"Are you going to gift wrap it?"

Unafraid. Niven willed him to show just an ounce of fear.

"I will break you in the end," Phabian breathed, nicking the blade ever so slightly over Laphaniel's knuckle. Blood welled up. "I will leave nothing behind but darkness and madness."

Laphaniel met his stare. "Just like you."

"Just like me."

The air shifted, almost too subtle for anyone but the Queen of Shadows to detect. A gasp...her gasp, broke the silence.

Followed by the shriek of a blade striking bone.

Another and the blade hit the marble beneath, slicing clean through Laphaniel's hand.

It felt like forever before he started screaming.

CHAPTER THIRTY

LAPHANIEL

I blacked out.

If it was from pain or blood loss, I didn't know. Likely both.

I remembered a skittering hag pressing wads of cloth to my arm to stop me bleeding to death. I remembered that she didn't laugh or cackle, that the words she whispered over me were strangely comforting.

Before passing out, I had murmured Charlotte's name and the hag only shook her head.

I remembered the sound of Phabian's laughter.

And that Niven didn't laugh at all.

I woke in my cell with a sour taste in my mouth and a spinning head. The cold pressed in in a way it never had before. It fused to my bones. Bandages covered the lower part of my left arm, tied tight, soaked through with red. I couldn't bring myself to look closer.

My hand was gone. Phabian had cut my hand off.

My hand was gone…

Sitting up proved near impossible. Dizziness forced me back down, a heavy black swept over me, and I dreamed.

She spun in the sunlight streaming through the leaves overhead, the light catching the reds and golds, so it looked like they were aflame. Her pale, slender hand reached out to me, fingers folding over mine to pull me close. So close I could smell her, the scent of thunderstorms and fury, of hope and everything in between.

We danced under a canopy of autumn leaves, the shadow of home lingering in the distance. Smoke rose from the tree-entwined stone, coiling lazily from the tall chimney reminding us that we would soon have to break apart to eat.

"I will find you," she whispered, her lips at my ear. "I will bring you home."

For a moment I believed her.

"I will bring you home."

"I will…"

Dreams and nightmares flickered between the welcoming periods of darkness and nothing. Sleep was broken only by brief moments of hazy consciousness. Time passed…at least I believed it did. It hurt to move.

To breathe.

To do anything but sleep.

I stirred to a driving ache in my arm that splintered into agony as the darkness lifted. A shadow hovered nearby, kneeling upon the filthy straw to wrap clean bindings where my hand was supposed to be.

"There was a time," I began, my words thick, "not so long ago that I would wake up and you weren't there."

Niven didn't look up but finished tying off the dressing. "I didn't know."

She sounded almost sorry.

Her hand lingered on my arm, her fingertips were red. "I thought he was going to take a finger."

I shrugged her off and pushed myself to my knees with one hand. My legs shook as I stood, my vision swimming. The lone candlelight illuminated the new bloodstains on the stone, a trail of red leading to the pallet of straw.

"What's a finger between friends?"

"I didn't know it was a trap," Niven said, rubbing her bloodied hands over her gown, smearing the sheer silk in red.

The room tilted and I leaned against the cold wall to steady myself, holding my arm tight against my chest. "I had a hunch."

"Would it be better if you lay back down?"

I had never seen Niven rattled before; in any other circumstance it would have been amusing. "It would be better if I still had my hand."

"Well, you don't," she hissed, sounding much more like herself.

"Where is Charlotte?" I dared ask.

Niven shrugged, a casual gesture that irked me. "Hopefully, she's scuttled off with that little crow brat and the Raven Knight." She paused. "I've not heard otherwise."

I caught her meaning. The thought of Charlotte on that wall…if Phabian's hounds had caught the scent of Alice…

"Gabriel is getting out too, he is—" she cut herself off. "I just thought you would want to know. What with him being your Captain and all."

The hint Alice had let slip started to make sense. "How long have you been sleeping with him?"

Niven didn't even try to deny it.

"Have you lost your damned mind?" I wanted to throttle her. "Do you really think Phabian doesn't know? That he hasn't known everything all along, Niven!"

"Gabriel left," she said, not seeming concerned for her own head. "I don't think Phabian ever suspected him…he never once hinted at it." She looked me square in the eye and finished, "Phabian thinks it's you."

Of course, the clever little bitch.

"Then I'm going to lose more than my hand." I wished I wasn't standing. "Why on earth would he think I'm sleeping with you?"

It became clear then. All the times she had visited me…sneaking down to see me in the night. Even coming down into Charlotte's lair to check Phabian hadn't ripped my head in two. She wanted me to spy for her, of course…but it didn't warrant so many meetings…so many trips to a lonely dark cell.

"You made sure he wouldn't suspect Gabriel."

"It was easier than I thought," she admitted. "I liked having that power over him, to be able to manipulate him. It made me feel like there was a chance I could end it."

"Do you love him?"

She knew I didn't mean Phabian, yet she still flinched at the word as if the thought disgusted her.

"I don't even know what it's supposed to feel like."

"Yes, you do."

She twirled shadow through her fingertips, and despite the darkness she controlled, she looked very human. I could smell the faint hint of fear on her…only slight. It wasn't fear for herself.

"He's going to kill me, isn't he?"

Tears slid down Niven's cheeks, real fucking tears. She made no attempt to wipe them away.

"High treason," she breathed.

I would be taking Fell's place.

"I failed," she said, the words dull. "I'm sorry."

"Is that why you came down here?" I hissed at her, not believing her remorse for a moment. "Just to tell me I'm going to die?"

She shook her head, glancing at the door. "He needs to believe it's real."

"What is?"

Footsteps sounded from far above us. Voices and snarls trickled down the long winding steps. They called for her, their Queen. Niven spun, panicked.

"I need to make sure Gabriel gets away," she whispered, frantic. "Please Laphaniel! If you want me to beg…I will. I will beg you."

The realisation hit me with a jolt. "Phabian is not sparing you?"

Niven laughed, the sound bitter and full of self-loathing. "Why would he?"

The crash of feet became louder, closer. Shouts rang up through the darkness, Unseelie guards doing whatever it took to stay in their King's good graces…to ensure they didn't end up in pieces on a black wall.

Niven had run out of luck.

She looked a lot younger, stood in the centre of my tiny damp cell with my blood drying on her gown. Not innocent…

Never innocent.

I was going to die anyway…

"I'm not doing this for you," I said, the words rasped through my teeth.

If it gave Gabriel more time to get away…if it meant him, Fell, Alice and Charlotte got away. It would be something at least. I could live with that.

I could go to my death knowing that.

Niven made to say something, most likely some snarky retort. I pulled her to me instead, my mouth on hers. For a moment, she froze, then with a sharp gasp she kissed me back.

It was wrong and broken and hopeless. Her fingers raked through my hair, her teeth biting against my lip. I tasted her teardrops and the tang of my blood.

"You know I'm not her, don't you?" Niven breathed, leg hitching around my waist, her body clothed in nothing but fragments of shadow.

"I don't care."

She grinned at me through her tears. "Liar."

I wouldn't have stopped; I knew that much. If the Unseelie had not crashed through the doors with their hisses and their snarls to find me wrapped around their Queen…I would not have stopped.

Niven felt wrong. Firm to Teya's soft curves…cold. Her smell was different too, nothing like the rain and fury I longed for. But at that moment, it hadn't mattered. Nothing mattered except losing myself in the arms of someone who wanted to be lost just as much as I did.

Clawed hands dragged her off me and tossed her to the ground. One of the Unseelie spat at her, leaving a trail of spittle down her cheek.

"You will burn for this," he hissed, rows of thin teeth clicked together. "Both of you."

Niven smirked, even as they yanked her hands behind her. She kept her chin up, defiant to the last. "We all will in the end."

I had no way of avoiding the blow to the back of my head, too fixed on Niven to see it coming. I crumpled forward, instinctively trying to break my fall. Pain exploded up my left arm and the world went black.

CHAPTER THIRTY-ONE

NIVEN

*S*he was going to die, Niven knew that.

She wondered when Phabian had begun to plan her death, if she could remember a time when his hands had not left bruises on her skin. A time when they had not wanted to kill each other.

For all the good it would do, Niven could. She remembered wanting to tear the world apart together, to watch their shadows wreak havoc on everyone and everything. Just because they could.

There had been a time, long before his eyes blackened, that for a moment...only a moment, she thought she could love him. At least in a way she could love someone.

Perhaps he had once loved her too.

It would have been a different sort of love with Phabian...not wild and strange and unbroken.

Not free.

The Unseelie King had not locked them deep underground to await the pyres, but upon the highest tower overlooking the stark and bleak forest that lay heavy with snow and thick with ice. The land slumbered and waited for a spring she would not see.

It may have been mercy, not to be chained deep underground like a dog. Niven believed it was simply because the King of the Unseelie wished to be dramatic.

"Look." Niven nudged Laphaniel with her foot. Her hands were bound tight above her head, the chains ice cold. "Our last sunrise."

The faerie beside her opened his eyes, sweat glistening against his skin. "I had a feeling I would die here."

The chains clunked together as he shifted, one set around his right wrist, the other around his neck. He sat a little straighter to gaze out at the twin suns sinking below the horizon. Pink tinted the indigo sky, streaks of crimson and orange bleeding down through the clouds to stain on the snow beneath. It had slowly started to thaw, green buds just visible through the bleakness of winter.

"Maybe it would have been best if you stayed dead the first time," Niven said, willing her shadows to her. Nothing came, not even a flicker. Fickle things.

Laphaniel turned to her. "Perhaps you shouldn't have stabbed me."

"Would you really have stayed in that forsaken castle with Teya?" Niven knew the answer before he replied. She just couldn't fathom the sacrifice.

"I think it would have been a more bearable hell than this place." He shifted again, sucking in a breath when he jolted his left arm. Niven noted the seeping bandage, the way he held it against his chest.

"Were you left-handed?" she asked, not turning her head away from the darkening sky.

"I was," Laphaniel replied.

"You could always learn to use your right—" She stopped with a snort, knowing they wouldn't be leaving the tower. "Never mind."

"I favoured my left hand," Laphaniel began, resting his head back against the stone, "but I can still fight with my right if needed."

"Can you fight us out of this?"

He huffed a laugh. "I don't think so, Niven."

"I think the Spider is still alive," she said after a pause, "for what it means to you."

"It means something," he murmured, gritting his teeth. "I don't suppose you have a bottle of anything tucked into your skirts?"

Niven snorted. "I would check my pockets, but my hands are tied."

Her little bottle of poison had been taken away. Niven didn't dwell on what manner of execution Phabian was plotting.

"Shame."

"You don't want to die with a clear head?"

It was his turn to laugh. "No, I really don't."

The chains rubbed against her raw skin, over the bruises caused by the rough hands of the guards, and over the older wounds yet to heal. There was an emptiness inside Niven where once her shadows dwelled. No matter how deep she reached, she couldn't sense them, reminding her once again, she was human.

"Would you have still taken me," she asked, as the last crimson streak of sunlight slipped below the distant mountain tops, "if you knew this was how it would turn out?"

"Teya once asked me that," Laphaniel replied, closing his eyes. "I told her, I would choose this path no matter what, because it led to her."

"And now?"

He shook his head, and when he opened his eyes again, Niven saw tears. It seemed pointless to mock him for them.

"I don't know," he answered. "We never had the chance to just be together. We had so little time."

"It wasn't worth it?"

"It was worth every heartbeat, every moment I had with her was worth every moment of pain since. But no...I couldn't do it again."

The cold bit deep into her bare feet, it crept beneath the veil of shadow she wore and could no longer shift. Niven's arms ached, her fingers were numb.

"Teya seems to have found some spirit," she said. "She was a pointless creature before."

"No." His chains rattled as he faced her. "You never gave your

sister enough credit. For coming for you. To bring you home."
Laphaniel took a breath, and it ghosted past his lips. "She was so angry
when I first saw her. She was a determined whirlwind, dressed in
nothing but a ripped black dress and stupid shoes. She was drunk and
lost, but she wouldn't turn back...she didn't turn back because she was
trying to get to you."

"Spurned on by guilt," Niven added. "Nothing else."

"Does it matter?" Laphaniel asked, and she struggled to keep his
gaze. "She came for you because she wanted to put everything right,
even though it was never her doing. Never her fault. None of it,
Niven."

"It took her ten years—"

"She was a child."

"So was I." The words hissed through her teeth. Pointless. After so
many years it was all so pointless.

He looked away. "Teya gave everything up to get to you and in the
end it all meant nothing."

"Do you want me to apologise?"

"Would you?" Laphaniel stared out into the dusk, the dying light
catching the specks of dried blood on his face, highlighting the odd
blue of his eyes. A reminder of what he had given up for her sister.
"Apologise?"

"I think it would lack a sort of sincerity now, don't you think?"

"Why don't you try it?" Laphaniel said, voice far away.

Niven looked toward the mountains, at the peaks circled by wisps
of fog. From where she sat upon the freezing stone, she could see the
silhouette of great wings and a long, graceful body. She could hear the
chorus of dragons on those mountains.

There were worse songs to die to.

"Phabian believes you were always meant to choose me," Niven
said.

Laphaniel scoffed. "So we could die together?"

"I thought maybe to kill him together—I don't know anymore."

Night slipped across the sky, swallowing up the last remains of day until there was nothing left of it. Niven knew there would be no more. Fear curdled in her stomach, real and human and worthless.

She heard the clatter of Laphaniel's chains before she felt the cold touch of his fingers curling around hers. Niven didn't move away, she just kept her hand in Laphaniel's, and waited.

The Unseelie King came alone, shrouded in shadow he pulled from the night sky. The moonlight glinted on his black eyes, illuminating the madness behind them.

"Get up."

The chains binding their hands turned to shadow. The tendrils looped around their bodies to force them upright. Niven's bones clicked, her limbs stiff and frozen. Niven held tight to Laphaniel's hand, forcing him to stay upright. She lifted her chin and refused to flinch.

"I have something for you," the Unseelie King began, black eyes on Laphaniel. He outstretched his hand, allowing something to dangle from his fingertips. "It was found in the mud, not too far from here."

Niven tightened her grip on Laphaniel's hand, her nails digging in. The Unseelie king waved his finger, causing the silver necklace to swing back and forth. The two Dragonstone rings clinked against each other; the star pendant was broken beyond repair. Niven could smell the blood from where she stood.

"The goblin who looted it had no idea who it belonged to," Phabian continued. "I believe the body was unrecognisable."

Niven couldn't stop Laphaniel from falling to his knees; an awful noise slipped from his mouth, no words...just an awful, strangled noise.

"It looks as though your contract has ended, for all the good it did you." Phabian pocketed the necklace with a manic grin. "She always said she would find a way, didn't she? Clever little bitch."

"Get up!" Niven hissed, but Laphaniel didn't move. "Get off your knees and stand up!"

"I have something for you too, my love."

Niven turned at the Unseelie King's tone. He tossed something at her feet.

"A gift," he continued. "Since you never wanted mine."

It landed with a quiet thud, rolling twice before it stopped.

The heart could have belonged to anyone. It could have belonged to anyone because Gabriel had got away. She had told him to leave....

Niven knew he had got away, returned home to her sister...

...who lay dead somewhere cold and alone.

Grief, foreign and heavy, replaced the emptiness where once her shadows dwelled. A noise unlike any she had ever made erupted from her throat, ripping at it like it had teeth.

Or claws.

Shadows, real and solid and hers poured from her mouth. More trickled from around her, tentative and slow. Curious.

"There's my Queen," Phabian purred, moving forwards to cup her cheek. "Come back to me. It's done now. Promise to behave, and you can come home."

His fingers on her skin were bloody. "You're mad."

"Sit beside me on my throne, Niven," he murmured, running a hand through her hair. "Rule this darkness with me."

"You have no one left," Niven said, reaching out for the rest of her shadows. They hesitated. Uncertain.

Cowards.

"I will soon, my love." He pulled her close, his mouth brushed hers. "If we are patient, soon enough the halls will be filled with life again."

Her gut tightened. "Phabian..."

"Do you think it will be loud?" He tilted his head to look at Laphaniel. "Are children noisy?"

Laphaniel said nothing, the horror on his face echoed her own.

"I asked you a question!" the Unseelie King screamed. Shadows rained down from above, skidding along the stone in a manic dance. "Answer me."

"I believe so," Laphaniel gritted out, shoving himself to his feet, face bloodless.

"That won't do at all." Phabian paced along the tower, seemingly oblivious to the shadows Niven called back to her. "Do you have children?"

Laphaniel shared a look with her before answering. "I never had the opportunity, being locked up here and all."

Mist swept over Phabian's neck, a soft caress and nothing more.

"Perhaps for the best." The Unseelie King nodded. "What with your wife dead and you soon to follow."

Niven tightened the wisps of night, aiming more around Phabian's chest. At his heart. Just a few more and she would feel it beating.

And stop it.

Crush it.

"How do you keep those voices of yours so quiet?" Phabian took a step closer to Laphaniel, polished boots making no sound upon the stone. "I tried Ember, but it only made them more manic. My shadows did not like it."

"I'm not mad."

"You think I am?" the Unseelie King breathed. He crouched low. Laphaniel's head tipped back, threads of black seeped up his nose until he choked. "I could make you wish for death. A mad man would make you beg—"

Laphaniel's head crashed down against Phabian's just before Niven yanked on her shadows, sending the Unseelie King sprawling to the ground.

Blood poured from his nose, down over his chin, thick and black. Niven dragged more and more shadows to her, revelling in the thrill of them flocking back. Tighter and tighter, she looped them around Phabian until he gasped. Gods…that sound….

Then he started laughing.

Monstrous hounds burst from the corners of the tower, springing up from mist and starlight to land solid at Phabian's feet. They lunged for Laphaniel, teeth sharp and oh, so very real. Niven barely had enough time to drag them back, her own shadows buckling under their weight.

"Do you really think you can take my crown?" the Unseelie King bellowed over the baying of dogs. "You could have stayed forever at my side! I would have given you forever."

Snarls rippled through the air as the hounds turned on her, teeth snapping down on her skin, not made from shadow at all. A howl escaped her mouth, pain lashed like lightning across her skin. Blood splattered the stone.

From the corner of her eye, she spotted Laphaniel hurling himself at Phabian, his good arm wrapped around his neck, fingers digging in tight. The dogs faltered.

Flickered...

...faded...

Hope bloomed within her chest, a quick nudge and nothing more.

She wasn't paying attention to his shadows, too focused on the sudden thudding of Phabian's heartbeat, how it jolted as Laphaniel refused to let go.

She willed him not to let go.

She could hear it slow...stutter.

And it was wonderful.

Niven screamed out as she was tossed aside. Thin loops of darkness nudged over her skin...barely there...but enough because she wasn't paying attention. Her head hit stone. Blood filled her mouth. She rolled, skidding over the icy ground, fingernails cracking as she scrambled to stop herself.

But,

she went over the edge.

Freezing rock bit into her hand as she clung on. Her legs dangled off the edge of the tower, finding no footholds on the smooth, smooth stone.

The slow thud of Phabian's heartbeat quickened...

No...

No...

No...

No...

"No!" Niven screamed as Laphaniel reached down for her.

"Take my hand, Niven!"

Darkness rose up around her, the shadows whispering...curious.

"That's how this all started," she gasped out, "With me taking your hand."

"Niven!"

More and more of her shadows rushed forward, shifting into wolves and bears to thunder over the slick, black stone.

Laphaniel's hand clasped hers, rough and strong. He fought to haul her back over the edge, cracked nails dug into her skin. Niven gripped his wrist, her shadows looping around his arm. She couldn't hold his gaze. Grief and loss and anger stared down at her.

And it was no longer amusing.

No longer worth it.

Her sister was dead. Niven didn't know where to put those feelings, unsure if they were grief, or regret or something else entirely. They didn't quite fit in the space she allowed Gabriel, as if her heart were only big enough for one.

Hounds of writhing shadow crept towards the edge, hackles rising like smoke. Phabian followed. Moonlight struck the edge of the knife he held.

He slashed it down. Not for her...

"Move!"

The word screeched from her mouth, frantic. Shadows burst forward to shove him away, ripping her hand from his. The knife hit stone, striking hard.

Laphaniel shouted for her, making another desperate grab for her hand, and she fought to reach him.

But it didn't matter,

Niven slipped,

and fell,

and continued to fall even as the Unseelie King screamed for her, his shadows charging down and down and down.

A fraction too late.

CHAPTER THIRTY-TWO

TEYA

*S*ome thieving creature had taken my necklace. Something had clambered over my cold, dead body and robbed me. The thought of it angered me more than Luthien dumping my corpse in the middle of nowhere.

It had taken me a while to find the strength to sit upright, to move. To remember how to breathe. The world around me spun and whirled, feeling strange like I could float away from it.

I stretched out my limbs until they clicked, they were stiff and sore. Heavy. I didn't know how long I had been dead.

With hesitant hands, I checked myself for any signs of decay...of anything that hinted at rot. My stomach turned, and I gagged, bringing up a mouthful of dirt and brittle leaves.

My fingers touched pale, cold skin. Ripped cloth. Tangled hair. But I was whole. My heart pumped beneath my hand, fluttering quick and frightened. But beating. I breathed.

I lived.

My fingers shook as I brought them to my neck. The slash across it was sticky and sore, barely stitching itself back together. I had no doubts it would leave a wicked scar. What was one more, if it meant I could get Laphaniel back.

Ripping off a length of my tattered dress, I tied the silk around my neck like a grotesque scarf, tying it in a bow because I still wanted to look nice.

Above me the sky was just beginning to lighten, the black giving way to a violet dawn that was all too familiar...

I had woken up in the Unseelie lands, seemingly as close as Luthien could get me. Perhaps I would thank her one day.

Maybe I wouldn't.

On unsteady legs, I wound my way through the looming trees and narrow pathways, my feet crunching over the slowly melting snow. I didn't know if I would see Oonagh or Nefina again...if they knew what had happened to me. If they knew I was alive. That it had worked.

We had done it.

The contract holding Laphaniel to that cursed court was finally broken, and there would be nothing and no one stopping me from taking Laphaniel home.

Nothing.

Hope reared its head within me, a surge so overwhelming it brought me to my knees. Tears ran unhindered down my face, sobs shaking my body so violently it hurt to breathe. I would walk out of that damned labyrinth with Laphaniel, or I wouldn't walk out at all.

His letter was still tucked away, the paper creased and ripped where I had read it over and over, my fingers smudging the ink where I had run them over his words. The closest I could get to him, until...until I walked through those gates and took him home.

I will bring you home.

I wanted him to burn the letter. Then I was going to smack him so hard for thinking I would ever abandon him. If I could ever have let him go.

Sweat pooled down my back, every muscle in my body aching with every slow step I took. I drank water from a nearby stream, gulping it back to ward off the thirst plaguing me. Swallowing hurt my throat; I had yet to try and speak.

Untying my scarf, I cupped water into my hands and rinsed off the wound on my neck, biting back a bark of pain while I scrubbed. The last thing I needed was for it to fester.

I tried to call Glamour to my hands, hands that for a fleeting moment had conjured up storms. A flicker came, nothing more. A mere echo.

A Queen of Seelie I was no longer.

Glamour lingered over my fingertips, soft and lovely. Enough for magic tricks and illusions. To create a little chaos.

Smiling, I clicked my fingers and watched a flame dance upon them. "I'm coming for you," I whispered. "I will bring you home."

I tore a new strip of silk for my neck, shoved myself to my feet, and carried on walking.

I fell twice, slumping down in the soft snow when my legs gave out. Each time, I forced my eyes open, forced myself to my feet, to get up and carry on.

The sound of cawing birds revealed where I was before I set eyes upon the rotting oak. Relief hit me hard, and I ran towards the old tree, ignoring the carrion birds as they began to screech.

I called for the Scara as I ducked inside, wincing when the smell of damp hit my senses.

Just before the tang of old blood.

So much blood and black feathers.

I willed the remains of my Glamour to my fingers, barely able to call up a weak flame in my panic to light the greasy candle stubs dotted around. The feeble light rested over the still body of the Scara, her head twisted at an impossible angle, even for her. Black eyes stared blankly back, her sharp beak frozen open in a silent howl.

"Alice?" The word rasped from my throat. "Gabriel?"

The rotten dwelling lay in ruins. Glass shards glimmered on the earthen floor, the remains of potions pooling together in the dirt. Roots had been ripped from above, the bed smashed to pieces.

I searched the space for any sign of Alice, tearing from the dark hole to look outside. She had to have escaped. I needed her to have escaped.

The sled was gone, the hounds too. Track marks were almost buried under new snowfall but recent enough that they were not covered completely. I took a breath, silently giving thanks to whatever dark gods looked over such a black and harrowing world.

Alice had escaped.

Then I saw the blood,

and the body of my friend.

My feet skidded on the snow as I ran to him, my knees hitting the ground when I called his name. No sound came from my lips. It didn't matter, he wouldn't have heard it anyway.

"Gabriel?" With a hesitant hand, I brushed his hair back, the golden curls snagging around his broken horns. His eyes were closed, and there was a hole in his chest where his heart once beat.

We had danced together, laughed together, and fought together. He had flirted and teased and told me where the witches were so they might have helped me.

Scars shone bright against his pale skin, the golden hue having ebbed away. Deep scars ran over his neck and shoulder, down his chest to his navel. They shone white and whole, fully healed. He had survived them all.

"The witches remembered you," I whispered the words, near silent. Rasping. Tears streamed down my cheeks. "One in particular seemed to like you very much." I gave him a small smile. "Though I couldn't fathom why."

I kissed his cheek. Wiping some of the dirt away.

"You were right," I continued, my throat aching. "The witches knew a way to break the contract. We did it…you did it, Gabriel."

I buried my friend in a shallow hollow beneath Unseelie soil, far away from home. For the Scara, I built a small pyre and stood to watch the flame, thanking her for keeping watch over my friend, and for loving a dying girl.

The crows high in the treetops were silent, unmoving, their cruel black eyes fixed upon the smouldering funeral pyre of their mistress.

Leaving the rotting oak behind me, I forced myself onwards. Hunger gnawed at my belly, but everything was barren and cold and empty. I had been fortunate enough to find three wrinkled apples among the rubble of the Scara's home—they were sour and near rotten, but they kept me going. That was all that mattered.

"Are you lost?" a voice called out, smooth and soft and lilting. "You look like you are to me."

Those words...

I knew those words...

...that voice.

"Laphaniel?" I spun around, seeing nothing in the shadows, no movement beyond the still trees.

"You look lost," the voice repeated, achingly familiar. "Are you lost?"

"Who are you?" I called out, willing Glamour to my fingertips. There was barely a warmth, hardly anything at all. Though, it was still a comfort to have something of Laphaniel so close to me.

"Who are you?" the voice echoed back. "I am me, and you are you."

"Show yourself."

A laugh. "I am not hiding."

I looked up, scanning the trees. Something stared back at me, green eyes shining bright. It sat hunched upon one of the branches, long furred fingers curled tight around the trunk as it leaned closer to me. Thick black hair covered its slender body, its long tail swishing back and forth while it grinned and showed off its sharp, sharp teeth. A phooka...as wild and fickle as faeries went.

"Then can you help me?" I asked.

The phooka twitched its long ears, reaching out a thin finger to touch the silk around my neck. "I do not know yet. You have not said what it is you want."

The lilting tone of its voice remained, the softness changing into something stranger, darker, so it no longer sounded like Laphaniel. I had no idea how it could even mimic him...I didn't want to know.

"Can you take me to the Unseelie castle?"

With a sharp hiss the phooka snapped its hand back, hackles rising. "Why would you wish to go there, of all the places you could go?"

I sighed. "Because I have already come such a long way."

The phooka tilted its head at me, leaning over so far it toppled forward. Its long tail coiled around the branch as it slipped, leaving its body to swing gently.

"I could take you to the Echoing Marshes instead?" the phooka began, still swinging. "There are dragon bones half sunk in the mud. Some say they still move when the moonlight hits them. Or, perhaps across the lakes to the east, where the giant's dwell? They feast for days and days and may not eat you if you sing to them."

"Maybe another day," I answered. "Can you point me in the right direction or not?"

"I can."

"Could you then?"

"I could."

It was really easy to hate faeries.

Ah, but it was all too easy to love them.

"Forget it," I muttered, too weary to deal with the riddling creature. "I'll find it on my own."

"The King is angry," the phooka said, looping around the branch to squat back on top again. "His shadows are angry too."

My head snapped up. "Why is he so angry?"

The phooka shrugged, tugging a long furry ear down to groom it. "He has broken all his toys."

"What does that mean?"

"What do you think it means?"

"You are an insufferable creature!"

It had the nerve to look wounded. "Do you think so?"

Sparks tingled at my fingertips. My Glamour stirred, sleepy and weak. "Goodbye, phooka."

It hopped down from the branch as I began to walk away, standing far taller than I imagined it would. "I thought you wanted my help. You did ask."

"Are you going to help?" I snapped, losing the last of my patience. "Or just annoy me?"

"I am very good at both."

It took a step closer, looming over me. It hadn't seemed dangerous before…and I realised how utterly stupid it was to think that.

"What is the price for helping me?"

It grinned, teeth flashing. "Would you give up the name of your first-born child?"

"No," I backed up, but it followed me, slipping down onto all fours.

"The sound of your heartbeat?"

"No!"

Its body twisted, bones crunching and snapping as they jerked and moved. The phooka's body stretched, shifting into that of a shaggy pony. Green eyes blinked back at me through a thick black mane.

"Then perhaps," it said, its teeth still so, so sharp, "you will climb upon my back and allow me to run."

"That's all?" I took in its greasy coat, the glint in its eye.

"I want to go very, very fast."

"You'll take me to the Unseelie castle?"

"If that is truly where you wish to go."

I moved closer, my fingers hesitantly touching its matted coat. It smelled of damp and moss and the forest after rainfall. "Will I be safe with you?"

"As long as you hold on tight," the phooka replied with a rumbling chuckle.

Knowing how foolish and dangerous it was, I still climbed up onto its back. I imagined Laphaniel's face, the exasperation in his voice telling me how I never learn. With a defiant smile, I curled my fingers tight into the phooka's mane.

I simply had to hold on.

"It has been a while since I have carried someone," the phooka said, rearing up. "I will try so very hard not to crush your bones."

It tore through the forest before I could scream. Earth ripped from beneath its hooves, clumps of frozen ground spraying upwards to smash against my legs. I clung to its neck, my face buried deep in its greasy mane while its laughter bellowed across the forest.

Over mounds it ran, fast enough to steal my breath away. Through twisting pathways of skeletal trees it bounded, breath fogging from its mouth. On and on.

Branches snatched at my face, ripped at my hair as we raced through the woods. My breath caught, my lungs aching.

A screech exploded from my mouth when it leapt into a swamp. Icy mud flooded over me, almost dragging me off. It covered my legs, up over my waist. My cloak became leaden with it.

Its laugh thundered from its mouth, wicked and cruel and uncaring. I clung tighter, gripping my fingers so tight into its mane that it hissed. If I was going to drown, it was coming down with me.

So cold.

It was so damn cold.

The phooka waded through the deep mud, its hooves slipping while it pulled itself up the bank. I dug in my fingers as it bolted again.

Trees whipped my face, the rocks flying up from the ground struck at my legs. I could barely draw in a breath.

The phooka never stopped laughing.

It stopped without warning, dropping its head so I was flung forward over its neck to land upon the unforgiving ground. My head struck first, the snow thankfully saving me from splitting my skull in two.

"You did not die." The Phooka beamed down at me over the sound of his bones crunching. He shifted back into his other form, his fur covered in dripping mud. "How fortunate for you."

I curled my body into a ball, not daring to move. "I think…I've broken a rib."

"Just the one?" It bent to poke me, fingers prodding my side. "My last rider impaled himself on a tree. He dangled in the woods for weeks."

Pain lanced over my ribs. "Stop touching me."

"Do I not get a thank you?"

I managed to get to my knees, grunting. "You've had your fun... now leave me alone."

"I promised to take you to the castle."

"I'd rather go on my own." I spat a mouthful of blood onto the snow, gritting my teeth hard as I forced myself to my feet.

"As you wish it." The phooka bowed low, ears flopping over its head. "It is but half a mile down that pathway."

"Thanks."

It grinned back at me, "I hope whatever is in that labyrinth is worth it."

"You have no idea," I replied, but the phooka had already disappeared. It didn't even leave behind footprints.

Half a mile didn't seem far, but with a cracked rib and bruises the size of my hand, it felt like the furthest I had ever walked.

So close. I was so close.

I will come for you.

I will bring you home.

THE STRIKING TOWERS of the Unseelie castle still took my breath away. The bridges linking the tallest towers swayed in the wind, wisps of cloud curling around them. The black stone seemed to consume all light.

It was a mournful place, as if the very stone had absorbed the horrors the King inflicted on his fey.

I expected guards to stop me at the gates, as they always had each midwinter. They had been towering great beasts, eyes hungry and wanting. Our horses were always led away, stabled beside the horned creatures favoured by the Unseelie. They had screeched as they were taken.

Yet no one came. The courtyard was empty save for the pyres that stood tall and imposing and unlit. Dried blood still gleamed upon the obsidian walls, and I looked away from what hung there.

Shadows moved and writhed over the too-black walls, sweeping across the blood-soaked snowdrifts in waves of fury. I could taste the anger...the madness. The very air was alive with it, the clouds drawing close in a blanket of black.

The monstrous doors towered before me, locked tight. The creatures carved within the wood stared back, mouths gaping wide. Etchings marked the grain, old runes faded with age. The door creaked even after I had removed my hand, making me wonder if it still listened. If the wood merely slumbered like the sleeping boughs surrounding the castle.

I had never known the doors to be locked, for the courtyards to be so very empty. With no other choice, I made my way around the overgrown creeping pathways that led behind the sprawling labyrinth.

Brambles and rotted boughs lay twisted along the disused paths, sticking up from the mounds of snow like severed limbs. Thorns snagged at my skirts, scratched at my legs, peppering the white with droplets of red.

Overhead, the sprawling towers sliced into the heavy sky. The echo of screams tore through the air, stirring up the wanting storm until it burst from the bruise-like clouds in a hail of thunder and lightning.

There was a devastating anger to it, one that screamed at every nerve, every sense in my body to stay away. To run. To get out.

I moved quicker, feet sliding over the snow and ice, my head turned towards the raging wind.

Dread and fear curdled in my stomach, instinctive. My hand went automatically to where my pendant should have rested.

I'm coming.

I'm coming.

I'm coming.

With my heart crashing within my breast, I fought to find a way into the labyrinth. I was looking everywhere but at my feet, seeing nothing until the toe of my boot caught something and I tumbled to the ground.

I turned, and something fragile shattered within me.

She lay perfect in the snow, a fallen doll. Black hair fanned around her, dusted with glittering white. There was not a mark upon her. Red spilled from beneath the snow like a velvet bloom.

Death had yet to dull the blue in Niven's eyes, and they stared upward, unflinching and unforgiving as they had been in life. Something had frozen against her cheek, and I reached to sweep it away. A teardrop.

But only the one.

Bitterness rose up to smother out the strange pangs of grief. I had nothing left to give. Maybe one day I would truly mourn for Niven, but in that moment all I could think about was the utter waste it all was. That everything— after all these years—had been for nothing.

Above me, the chaos screamed. Blackness and shadow screeching in a way I had never heard before. I turned back to my sister, seeking answers she could not give.

The old door to the tower lay ajar, and without another thought I flung myself up the steps, almost slipping upon the slick stone. Blood coated the walls and had dried against the steps in red smears. Drag marks. Someone had been dragged up.

My sister bore no marks.

An inhuman noise escaped my lips, my fingernails scraping along the walls as I hauled myself up the tower stairs. Around and around and around.

The sounds of mayhem surged down the steps, followed by tendrils of shadow that nearly knocked me back down.

Terror threatened to swamp me, not fear for myself, but for the one I knew...I knew was caught up in the madness upon that tower. I burst through the door, stumbling straight into the middle of the Unseelie King's rage.

He stood in a wave of black, shadows racing around him like hounds ready to tear Laphaniel to pieces.

The Unseelie King screamed, the sound demonic in its madness. If there had been any traces of his humanity left intact...it had all gone.

Laphaniel's name tore from the ruins of my throat, lost beneath the cacophony of madness and hate that spewed from the Unseelie King.

He didn't look up from where he lay sprawled on the floor, panting and soaked in blood.

"GIVE THEM TO ME!" the Unseelie King screamed. The force of the screech sent Laphaniel tumbling backward. One hand reached out to slam against the wall so his head didn't. The other...

Oh gods...

Filthy bandages had come loose around his lower arm, whipping around in the growing storm. From beyond the shadows, I could make out the bloodied remains of his wrist.

They had taken his hand.

I moved without thinking, lunging through shadow to slam against the Unseelie King's back. My hands went to his throat, fingernails digging in as if I could pull his hateful head from his body.

He stumbled, throwing his weight forward so I flew over the top of him and slammed hard onto the stone. The world went blinding white, my breath rattled from my lungs.

My name echoed across the tower, a question and a curse and a plea.

We were going to die. I knew we were going to die.

A hand grabbed a fistful of my hair and hauled me upwards. Blood trickled over my mouth. The Unseelie king wrenched my head back, splitting the barely healed wound at my throat. I fought for the Glamour sputtering at my fingertips, knowing there was a time when I could have called the storm to me.

"Your whore has returned," the Unseelie King hissed. Shadows coiled around my arms, around my neck. "It looks as though she has crawled from her own grave to find you."

Laphaniel stood, black mist dancing around his feet. Anguish burned bright on his face, his eyes tormented.

"What are you doing here?" His words came out strangled. There was no relief in his gaze, only stark, unbridled horror.

"My contract has ended," I whispered into the shadows, tears of pain and sorrow trailed over my cheeks. "I have come to take you home."

I was so very very foolish.

The Unseelie King did not release his grip on me, but one long finger reached down to stroke down my cheek, down to the mess of my throat.

"I will pin you to the wall together. Through your heart," he whispered in my ear, "and then through his."

The storm crackled and surged above us, alight with Glamour. More and more shadows wove around Laphaniel, swirling and twisting to every boom of thunder, every fork of lightning that slashed against the ink-spill sky.

A hiss slipped from the Unseelie King's lips, utterly inhuman. "Give them to me."

Laphaniel stood frozen. Shadow and blackness rose up and up and up, streaming from below to circle around his feet, his legs. Slow and testing.

They were not the feral, furious shadows that the Unseelie King commanded. I recognised them…quieter, cunning.

Whatever strange Glamour had attached itself to my sister was now seeping upwards, claiming Laphaniel as it had once claimed Niven.

"They belong to me." The Unseelie King stepped forward, dragging me behind. Rage twisted his voice, the blackness around him snapping back and forth as if desperate to be let loose. "GIVE THEM TO ME!"

His scream ripped through the darkness, through the storm above us, and let loose an onslaught of freezing rain.

Nails dragged along my scalp, my hair twisted tight in the Unseelie King's grasp. His shadows noosed around my neck, tighter and tighter until I could barely draw breath.

"They were hers and now they belong to me," he yelled over the lashing rain. "They were hers!"

A howl erupted from the Unseelie King, filled with madness and tinged with grief. For my sister? I didn't know.

But I could taste it in the air, feel it alive and heavy around me. An all-consuming pit of black that left nothing behind in its wake. It was a yawning void, and it was going to swallow us whole.

We were edging towards the ledge, the Unseelie King still screaming, shadows still a riot around us. His hand yanked upward and my knees left the floor.

Laphaniel's cry joined the chaos, the wisps of shadow circling him growing darker and darker.

He moved. The shadows moved quicker, colliding with the Unseelie King in a swarm of black and fury.

The hold on my hair released and I tumbled to the ground, rolling over and over until I slammed against the stone.

The screams coming from the Unseelie King were relentless, chorused by the booming of thunder until I thought my head would explode with it all.

I turned, wiping the blood from my nose, to see the tangle of black and smoke and mist and anger rip at each other. Lightning struck down upon the stone, scorching where it hit. Again and again.

It was screaming and noise, and my own cries were swallowed up and unheeded as Laphaniel lost himself within the black that had claimed him.

His sodden hair was plastered to his face, his eyes fever bright and wide. Blood trailed over his forehead…If it was his, I didn't know.

They danced in a riot of shadow, wild and feral and lost. Both of them.

I bit down a scream of my own as tendrils of black crept up over Laphaniel's shoulder, slipping down his arm to form monstrous talons where his left hand once was. He didn't seem to notice, not as they solidified and gleamed black against the constant flash of lightning. They reached out towards the Unseelie King, those talon-tipped shadows. Almost curious, so very softly.

"Laphaniel—"

They cut through flesh in a way shadow should not have been able to do. The Unseelie King's head fell from his shoulders in a spray of red, his mouth open wide in a silent scream.

It bounced and rolled to my feet.

For one split, sharp second, I met Laphaniel's gaze. The strange blue was vivid against his pale skin. Then they darkened, black bleeding in like ink.

Within a heartbeat they were pure ebony.

"No," Laphaniel breathed. "No, no, no, no."

The single word tripped over itself, a plea both hopeless and meaningless. The remaining shadow surged up, spiralling around him until the light of the sky was blotted out and there was nothing but darkness.

I forced the golden threads of my Glamour to the surface, and they danced weakly at my fingertips. Beneath that, however, I could feel something else awakening. Something darker.

"Laphaniel." I stepped closer. He didn't move, his black eyes fixed upon the spectral talons of his left hand.

His voice rasped in the darkness. "You were dead."

Another step, the shadows paused. His gaze snapped to me.

"You were dead."

There was blood on his fingertips.

"You were dead."

He was clinging to the words…a cold hard fact. More shadow slipped across his body, lifting up the drenched ends of his hair. He wouldn't acknowledge them.

I closed the gap between us; he still hadn't moved.

Talons of black mist reached forward, wavering at the scarf around my neck.

I could hardly breathe. "Only for a little bit."

A noise that was neither a sob nor a scream slipped from my mouth. Laphaniel trailed a cold, ghostly finger over my cheek, his eyes blacker than the shadows surrounding him.

"I came to take you home." The words were brittle, the last dredges of a promise I was unable to keep. "I wanted so much to bring you home."

The shadows around him tensed, then began to writhe, slow and snakelike. None remained upon the floor where Phabian lay.

They belonged to the new Unseelie King, every last one of them. And they would not let him go.

Laphaniel's hand wrapped around my wrist, cool shadow against my skin. "Please don't leave me here."

"I will never leave you." I dragged him close and breathed in the smell of him, spice and liquorice and the wild woods, noting the scent of something different beneath it all. "Whatever path we have found ourselves on, we go down it together."

I wanted to say more, so much more, but I could no longer trust my voice to hold. There was nothing to be said that could not wait, nothing more important than at last…at long last, having his arms around me.

CHAPTER THIRTY-THREE

TEYA

*T*he late winter breeze swept through the thin glass, sweeping up the gauzy curtains so they billowed out into the massive circular room. A fire burned low in its hearth and furs covered the great, carved bed we slept in. High above the Unseelie labyrinth, nestled within the tallest tower, darkness covered everything.

We had spent the first few days taking long, sweet hours getting to know one another again. To close a gap that had fractured between us, our souls screaming out for one another so fervently even the shadows fled from us.

We lay together, drinking blood-red wine long into the night. I would sleep and Laphaniel would carry on drinking.

It had not been evident then, with the two of us barely breaking apart to draw breath…to speak…to realise how not okay Laphaniel was.

Days would pass with him not uttering a single word, eyes blank. Lifeless. He was a ghost, drifting through the halls, never still, never resting. Haunting the darkness that had claimed him.

I held out a hand in the restless dark, fingers skimming over the cold space where Laphaniel should have been. Calling Glamour to my fingertips, I tried to banish some of the shadows roving over the walls. It took everything I had to get them to listen, to scurry back and allow me to light the candles. Even then the flames continued to splutter out.

I found him on the floor of our bathing room, hands tight over his head. He rocked while shadows raced in circles around the walls.

Ghostly wings stretched above us, scratching at the vaulted ceiling, absorbing every glimmer of light. The dark swallowed it down, hungry. There was no light.

Black flowed from his bare back, dark veins spreading over the thick scars, the shadows beneath his skin swirled and writhed as if his very blood were made of it.

"I'm here," I murmured, kneeling beside him. My nightgown pooled around me, the cold crept through the thin silk. "I'm right here, I'm not going anywhere."

Laphaniel lifted his head to look at the shadows hanging over us. A choked cry forced its way up his throat as he scrambled to get away. They followed, and he screamed at them.

"Look at me!" I forced him to focus those black eyes on me. Not a hint of white…just ink-drop black. "They are reacting to you. To your fear of them."

And he was afraid. I had never seen him so afraid.

I pulled him close, and he dug his hands into my arms, both of them. I could feel the chill of shadows on my skin, the nudge of ethereal claws. They pierced my nightgown, scraped along my skin.

I held him tighter.

Laphaniel heaved in a shuddering breath, then another and another…too quickly. The shadows whirled like dervishes around us, spinning…

"Get…off…me," the words panted from his mouth. He struggled, barely making it to the toilet before he heaved his guts up.

I pulled back his sweat soaked hair, willing my Glamour around him…to slow the thundering of his heartbeat. His shadows wouldn't allow it, screeching back at me in a wall of black.

Eventually his shadows tired or grew bored and curled back into the walls. And exhausted, we fell asleep on the cold bathroom floor, far above the Unseelie castle.

The days bled together. Laphaniel wouldn't enter the pools or go down into the lower levels of the labyrinth. Sometimes he barely left our rooms. He barely ate, he never slept.

Sometimes he sat beside me on the black and twisted throne and stared out at the Unseelie that now bowed before him.

In the beginning some of those faeries had questioned his right to rule, all too wary of the shifting and unravelling of the dark court they both knew and feared.

They had whispered words like *broken* and *weak* hissing their discontent to the shadows they believed kept their secrets.

Laphaniel had lifted his hand of shadow and smoke and turned them to ash and nothingness.

"CHARLOTTE WISHES TO SPEAK TO YOU," I said, sitting beside Laphaniel on my throne of cavorted glass. The shards knotted around his, forged together for all time. They were unbreakable, and even the full force of the King of Unseelie couldn't make a scratch upon it.

Because he had tried.

And they wouldn't break.

I wore a gown as green as the deepest moss, the fabric thick and heavy and beautiful. Silver thread hemmed the flared sleeves, and the edges of the billowing skirts. Flowers were embroidered into the bodice, along with delicate tiny, winged insects. The neckline dipped low, exposing the swell of my breasts. A green scarf sat knotted at my throat. As Queen, I would not be forfeiting colour for Unseelie black.

Laphaniel chose simpler clothing, a favoured white shirt tied loose. Black trousers, black boots. His wedding ring hung at his throat, dangling on the chain that had once held my star. A circlet of twisted silver sat over the wild black of his hair. Though he didn't need the crown. It was obvious by the power he exuded who he was.

The Great Hall was empty, my voice echoed across the endless black. So much black. Sunlight spilled through the huge windows, tempting the shadows to dance. The late winter light looked strange upon the inky darkness, I had never seen it look anything but desolate and bleak.

"Why?" The single word fell from his lips dull and empty.

With a fingertip I tilted his head to look at me, keeping my hand against his cheek to pull him closer. I kissed him, slow and lingering. "Because we can't keep pretending this is going to get better on its own."

"I'm trying—"

"I know," I cut him off, my forehead to his, sharing breath. "I know, but we cannot do this alone."

The massive carved doors boomed open, making me jump. Laphaniel went still beside me, eyes closed.

"This hall!" Charlotte cried, swooping into the centre before spinning around and around, arms flung out as she teased the shadows she awoke with her fingertips. "This hall was made for dancing, for revelry." She paused before curtsying low, ragged skirts pooling around her in swathes of white. She grinned up at us. "For debauchery."

"It may be too soon for that," I said with an easy smile.

The Spider rose, fangs glinting. "The stains upon this castle will fade. Never forgotten, but they will fade."

It was hard to see beyond so much darkness and bloodshed. The fear and anger and hatred that literally marked the walls would never go away.

But if we were to move forward, then we needed to hope for something better. To make it something better.

I had become the Queen of the Unseelie. I had been content with losing my crown and finding a piece of happiness with Laphaniel... more than content. But another crown had been forced upon my head, one of darkness and shadow and shrouded in the memory of madness. It had been my sister's crown.

And I did not know if I could bear the weight of it.

"I have something for you, Angel." Charlotte stepped up the dais, handing Laphaniel two vials. Scars criss-crossed over her pale, bare arms. The little finger on one of her hands was missing. "The purple bottle is for the night, the green for when you wake."

He stared down at them, rolling them in his hands so the glass clinked together. The light caught the shimmering powders inside so they cast little rainbows over the black marble.

With a sigh, Charlotte crouched in front of Laphaniel. One set of claws rested upon his knees, the others curled around both hands. He flinched but she took hold of the shadows anyway, her talons against his.

"Look," Charlotte began, "There is no malice here because there is none in you."

The ghostly claws of his left hand held onto her, gentle and careful. The same way they touched me when he wasn't looking.

"If you do not step out of this darkness, it will consume you." The Spider gripped his hands. "Take the elixirs I make, you are not expected to walk through this alone."

Laphaniel gave a small nod, saying nothing at all.

"Thank you." I took one of her hands. Her long, cold fingers squeezed mine.

The Spider inclined her head to me. "You, my darling girl, are long due a visit to my chambers. We have missed you."

"I will come down in the morning," I promised. "Tell Oonagh to keep the kettle warm for me."

Charlotte's answering smile revealed her massive fangs. "It was Oonagh's idea to use knotwhite root in the sleeping tonic, making it much easier on the stomach. She is a wonder."

Light…light in the darkness.

"She really is."

It had not been hard to find Oonagh and Nefina, for they had tracked me through the Unseelie and stumbled upon the castle in absolute turmoil. Convincing them to abandon their fears and prejudice to stay took more work.

It was only because Oonagh refused to leave Nefina's side, and Nefina would not abandon her brother that they remained.

Oonagh had quickly found a strange refuge deep beneath the

labyrinth with the Spider that dwelled there. She showed a keenness for potion making and healing that kept both her hands and her mind busy.

Nefina wouldn't touch the bottles and burners and pots of herbs, saying they reminded her too much of Luthien.

Instead, Laphaniel's cunning and resourceful sister had taken a swift and unforgiving control over his Court. Beneath her shrewd gaze, the fractures of the Unseelie slowly began to heal.

With Nefina watching over the Court, it left Laphaniel and me to focus, for a time, on each other.

I had not spoken to Laphaniel of the sacrifice his sister made for him. Nefina had demanded we never did.

"I am glad Oonagh has you to look after her," I said to Charlotte. I would never forget the sight of the Spider taking my trembling friend into her arms, calming her as she had once done for me. "I am glad I have you, Charlotte."

Charlotte kissed the tips of my fingers before stepping down from the dais. "I have much work to do, darling girl. Come by in the morning, I will find you if you do not."

"How are they?" Laphaniel asked, speaking of the solitary fey Phabian had imprisoned to fill his corridors with more faeries. There were twelve of them. All with child.

"They are doing as well as you are," Charlotte answered. "You should go visit them again."

He nodded. He would go up to them, high up in one of the ever-twisting towers of the Unseelie. He had visited before and sometimes he sat with them for hours.

Charlotte dropped into a graceful curtsy, claws clacking upon the marble. "These shadows belong to you now, Angel. You cannot change that no matter how much you wish it. But you can be better than what was left behind, you are better."

NIGHT SLIPPED OVER THE CASTLE, slowly turning the Unseelie sky from violet to deep black. Silence fell, an unnatural quiet. No laughter echoed, no music played, there were no screams of things dying in the dark.

Phabian had well and truly broken his court.

I curled up beside Laphaniel, beneath mounds of fur and soft blankets that were slowly beginning to smell like us, familiar and comforting. Vines curled around the posts of our bed, alive. Their odd, black leaves threaded over the gossamer canopy. In spring, huge purple flowers would bloom to scatter petals over the bed.

They were not my sister's old bedchambers, but ones that had been disused because they stood at the absolute peak of the Unseelie castle. They sprawled out over six rooms, and I was slowly adding more colour. Cushions of scarlet red, blue velvet throws, and tapestries embroidered with beautiful art.

I collected vases of strange flowers, their midnight blooms unravelled in the moonlight and filled the room with the scent of rain-kissed night.

If the labyrinth was to be our home, I would make it so.

Laphaniel's shadows quietened with the hush of evening, though I could still sense a tension within them, an energy that did not want to sleep. Unsettled like a restless child. It must have been exhausting.

"Are you going to drink that," I asked, slipping into my nightgown. Cobweb and starlight settled over my skin, sighing to the floor in waves. "Or just stare at it all night?"

Laphaniel lay in bed beneath one of the countless throws. The moonlight danced off his bare chest, off the pale scarring that snaked over his shoulders. I just took a moment to look at him, to let it sink in that he was there. That I could touch him.

Laphaniel's arms came around me as I slipped into his embrace. His heart thudded against my chest, its familiar song singing to mine. His soul chorused too, somewhere deep within him again, pure and whole and him. Not a mark upon it.

We kissed in the moonglow, unhurried. We had forever.

We had forever.

Laphaniel turned the bottle of purple dust over in his hand, the other still held me tight to him, his shadowy fingers cool on my skin.

"I can't take this for the rest of my life, Teya."

Because it would knock him out completely. No nightmares, no dreams. Nothing until late morning, where he would wake confused and groggy and cranky.

"It's only for tonight." I folded my hand over his. "For tomorrow. For the day after that, until you decide you don't need it anymore. You need to sleep." I took a shuddering breath. "I need to sleep, Laphaniel, and I can't while you're stalking the corridors for hours on end."

"What if you need me?"

Tears slid down my cheeks. "I do need you."

Shadows skittered across the walls, slipping over the bed to tangle around me in gentle waves. Laphaniel tensed instantly. His breathing hitched. "Please stop it."

"I'm not doing that," I whispered. "You are."

He took a deep, trembling breath, allowing it to blow through his lips before he downed the elixir. The shadows settled instantly. They calmed, coiling around us like sleepy cats. Laphaniel stared at them, and we both watched in mute horror as a large, more solid shadow drifted from the walls.

I could scent the fear coming from him, hear his pulse quicken before the elixir started to slow it down again. The shadow crept toward the bed and Laphaniel backed up, eye closing. A low moan slipped from his mouth, a sound filled with dread and pain.

"Look," I urged. He didn't move. "Laphaniel, look."

He obeyed, mouthing a curse as the giant form of a black hound padded onto our bed. Mist and darkness whirled over its body, swirling with every beat of its fat tail. It nudged past me, over the covers to settle at Laphaniel's side.

I took his hand, lifting it so it hovered over the roving shadow of the hound's head. Laphaniel kept it there, curiosity igniting in his black eyes. With another soft curse, he let his hand fall upon the spectral muzzle. The hound lifted its head, nudging closer.

I rested my head on Laphaniel's shoulder. "Okay?"

"I think so," he murmured, rubbing his free hand over his eyes. He pulled away when he realised what he had done, the shadowy fingers he had pressed to his face. "I don't know."

"We have time," I breathed, tugging him against me as he started to sway. "We have all the time in the world."

Laphaniel fell asleep with his head resting on my chest and the shadow hound curled between his legs. I watched him for a while, watched the slow rise of his breathing as he slept deeper. His hand slipped from mine, his long legs stretching out, looking more at peace than he had in far too long.

With heavy eyes, I settled against the pillows and waited for sleep to claim me.

"I love you," Laphaniel murmured, his words sleepy and jumbled. The same as they had been the first time he had mumbled them, all that time ago in Aurelius' cave.

Smiling, I nestled closer, my gaze falling onto his hand of shadows as it slowly curled around mine. I touched my nose to his, pulling the furs tighter. "Do you love me?"

I repeated the words I had whispered deep in that burrow, saying them without the fear and doubt and guilt that once plagued me. Knowing his answer— knowing it so deep within my soul that it ached.

Laphaniel answered with a soft snore. "More than anything."

The shadows at my feet shifted, the spectral head looking up. It tilted its head before turning to Laphaniel sleeping soundly beside me. It thumped its massive tail, fangs glinting as it lolled its tongue out. It drew more and more shadows from the walls, flickering the candlelight but allowing them to still burn.

It dragged the darkness closer and closer until it resembled a monstrous hellhound. Then it settled its head upon Laphaniel's chest and closed its eyes.

"Good-boy," I whispered, unafraid. "But any bigger and you're sleeping on the floor, understand?"

It didn't move, but in the gentle, soft darkness I could have sworn it grinned at me.

CHAPTER THIRTY-FOUR

TEYA

*S*pring came slowly to the Unseelie, the harsh snow reluctant to melt away and give in. To let go.

Life, however, decided to force its way through. Buds began to peek from the half-thawed ground and early blossom weighed heavily on the strange, spindly limbs of the Unseelie trees. The dawn rose earlier, banishing away the heavy night long before we were ready to rise. The frost still did not melt until long after midday, the grounds remained white.

I still missed the bright, sunlit sky of the Seelie, I believed a part of me always would. It was the first part of Faerie I had fallen in love with. It was where I had fallen in love with Laphaniel, and him with me.

It would take a long, long time to accept the dark, winding labyrinth of the Unseelie castle as my home.

Sitting beside Laphaniel on a throne made of twisted glass, my hand in his, I looked out over the dancing faeries that writhed in the centre of the hall. Music beat a wild melody that called to something deep within me, something that hadn't always been there.

Something wicked.

I could feel it thrumming through me, calling me. When I peered into the darkness, I was no longer afraid of what might look back.

No, the Unseelie was not yet my home, not quite. But I was no longer Seelie.

And neither was Laphaniel.

He stared out at his fey, head cocked, black eyes watching. Around him, his shadows moved, coiling further into the fray but he dragged them back.

Dance.

They begged him.

Dance with us.

Play with us.

Join us.

Be with us.

But he wasn't ready.

With a spark of Glamour, I sent the wayward shadows scuttling back to where Styx, the shadow-hound, waited to gobble them up, growing larger and larger by Laphaniel's side. I sat back with a smile, dancing my awakened Glamour back and forth over my fingers.

I wore black.

A backless gown of shimmering twilight. My crown sat threaded through my hair, along with buds of deep green, and winding vines that tumbled down my back. Laphaniel dressed similarly, under Oonagh's orders. Though the silver circlet sat a little wonky on his head, his mess of wild, dark tangles not needing the vines to look untamed. I didn't know if it was his shadows, or the way he raked his hand though it… but it had never been so unruly.

I did not dislike it.

"You're staring at me," he said with a rare smile.

"Only admiring how pretty you are."

"You look beautiful." He pulled me close, lips on mine. "So damn beautiful. My Queen."

I nodded to the goblet of wine resting on the arm of his throne. "Are you drunk?"

The smile bloomed brighter. "A little bit." He paused. "Don't tell Charlotte."

"And what will you give me," I whispered, smiling against his mouth. "In exchange for keeping your secret?"

"The world."

And he would. He had.

Sometimes it hurt to love him, but it was a welcoming ache, and one I never wanted to be without again.

There were still so few faeries in our court. And they were ghosts of what they once were, their steps faltered to the music, their feet hesitant. Many of them still cast glances at Laphaniel—their king, to check his temper.

As if he too would rather see them impaled upon some wall.

They no longer cowered every time he walked but there was a stiffness to their dancing I had not seen before in faeries, as if it were all an act for us. To appease us.

Phabian had fully destroyed his court, leaving us to pick up the pieces.

It was a challenging job, mixing Seelie and Unseelie under one roof. Though fraught as it was…it seemed to be working.

"Your sister is enjoying herself," I said into Laphaniel's ear over the frantic music.

He lifted an eyebrow. "So it would seem."

Wearing little more than sheer red silk, Nefina spun in the arms of a reed-thin faerie with curved talons the length of my arm. Her curtain of golden hair splayed out around her, unbounded and unadorned. From where I sat, I could see him graze her throat with pointed teeth. Her laugh was sensuous, fiendish, and utterly without shame.

I had not seen her dance like that since Sage. I couldn't remember her ever laughing the way she did then.

Perhaps we were all a little darker, more wicked. And perhaps it suited all of us.

"Where's Oonagh?" I scanned the mass of writhing faeries, finding no sign of my friend.

"With Charlotte, I believe."

"Oh?"

Laphaniel took a long drink of his rich blood-red wine. "Don't meddle, Teya."

I plucked the glass from his fingertips. "I don't meddle."

"Right." He rolled his eyes. "Then you'll have no problems leaving it alone—"

The banging of the massive doors cut him off and we were both instantly on our feet. The wine glass tumbled from my fingers to smash upon the marble. The music screeched to a stop. My hand curled tight around Laphaniel's arm, digging in hard, the scene all too familiar.

Talons of smoke brushed against me, reassuring, drawing me close. His lips murmured against my hair, a comfort. No one was taking him.

"You have visitors, Majesties," a horned guard said, breathless. He bowed low before gesturing behind him. His hands shook and he had blood on his lip. "I ordered them to wait, Your Majesty—"

"I am done waiting in the gods-damned cold!" A cloaked figure stormed past the guard, only to slam to his knees as Laphaniel's shadows flocked to him.

His voice was as dark as the shadows around him. "Move again and I will kill you."

Another figure darted forward with a cry. Laphaniel's shadows also slammed them onto the marble.

He hadn't moved an inch from my side.

"It is true then?" the figure choked out. The hood slipped from his head, revealing cropped black hair. "You never know with rumours, do you? In that case…do you think you could lift my exile? I would very much like to come home."

Briar.

Laphaniel stepped down, calling his shadows back. I followed, stepping over the marble to crouch beside the other cloaked figure. I lifted her hood. Blood matted her golden hair, her lovely face streaked with dirt. She reached for my hands, her fingers like ice.

Grace.

"Please," she breathed, gripping harder. "Please don't turn us away…"

I searched for Nefina in the crowd. "Get Charlotte."

She nodded, disappearing in a wave of red.

Laphaniel dragged Briar to his feet, grabbing his shoulder when the faerie stumbled into him. "How did you get here?"

Soren, the old Unseelie Queen, had banished Briar and Grace from her court many years ago, all for the crime of conceiving a child when she was unable to.

We had met for only a fleeting moment, in a grubby pub, in a little fishing village in Cornwall. Grace had swiftly taken me under her wing and for one night, I had someone to talk to that was as human as I was. Briar and Laphaniel, having taken an instant dislike for each other, exchanged punches instead.

"We took the long way around," Briar began, sinking to the floor as his knees buckled. Laphaniel slipped to the floor beside him. "Some of the ancient paths were still open to us, lying near lost and forgotten. You couldn't imagine the creatures we came across, beings of legend, monsters I have no name for..." He shook his head, lost in a memory we had no part in. "I ask again, your Majesty, is it okay if I come back?"

"That depends," Laphaniel replied, keeping Briar upright. "Are you going to punch me in the face again?"

Briar laughed, then coughed, blood spitting on his lips. "I can't make any promises."

"Teya," Grace's lips were bloodless. "You will have us back? Truly?"

"I once promised you I would help in any way I could," I said, and Grace gave a small sob. "Our home is yours."

"Are you able to stand, girl?" Charlotte asked, having moved silently over to us. She pressed a hand to Grace's face and tutted. To her credit, Grace did not flinch. A choked noise slipped from Briar.

"I think so..." Grace said softly, "I'm just a little dizzy, "if you could help me up—"

"Lie back," I said, noting the way she held a hand to her stomach.

"She fell sick a few days ago." Worry filled Briar's voice as he crouched beside Grace, wincing at the movement. "I don't know if it's something she ate, or if something bit her…"

Charlotte nodded. "Nothing I cannot fix, take her to a bedchamber, she needs rest." She slapped Briar's hand away. "Not you, you can barely stand."

I took Briar's hand while Laphaniel scooped Grace into his arms.

"I may puke on you," she protested, looking a little alarmed.

Laphaniel gave her a genuine smile in return. "I seem to have that effect on women."

He carried her out, following Charlotte to one of the many spare bedrooms in the castle. Grace would be able to rest and sleep and get well knowing she had a home. They both had a home with us.

We would fill the hallways of the castle again.

"Where is everyone?" Briar asked, hesitating before following after Grace. He stared out into the Unseelie, perhaps searching for any familiar faces. He would likely find none.

"This is everyone," I replied, giving a nod for the frantic dance to begin once more. "Come on, I'll explain everything on the way."

GRACE AND BRIAR swept through the Unseelie castle like an ember, a spark. Igniting those they touched to set our little world on fire. There was a lightness between them I couldn't help but envy.

I quietly mourned the loss of it between Laphaniel and myself.

It hit Laphaniel harder, though he hid it well enough behind the forced smiles and laughter. I could see it in his eyes, a flatness…a longing for something lost.

Perhaps he saw something he thought unattainable in Grace and Briar, the raw joy they shared. The easy happiness.

It was all too easy to get lost in the darkness when you were drowning in it.

EXHAUSTED after yet another feast that lasted well into the night, I wanted nothing more than my ridiculously large bed. My feet hurt from dancing with Nefina, with Oonagh and Charlotte and Grace.

Even Laphaniel danced with me, hands low on my waist, lips at my throat.

My chest hurt from laughing, my heart ached with the growing joy of it all.

I fell asleep the moment my head hit the pillows, barely managing a goodnight kiss before I curled up in Laphaniel's arms.

I woke long before dawn to an empty bed.

With a flick of my hand, I lit the candles around our room filling the space with gentle light. Down the curling flights of stairs, I walked into the winding corridors of the labyrinth.

The halls were empty, the torches hanging from the stone, all unlit. Light flickered as I ignited them all. I called strands of darkness to me, and it circled my bare feet, my body, folding over my shoulders like a cloak.

I called Laphaniel's name and it echoed back.

Down and down and down I went. Through the great library with towering stone bookcases and the carnivorous librarian. Through corridors so damp, stalactites had crept down from the ceiling like dripping fangs. I walked until I was deep beneath the ground, my footsteps finally echoing on the smooth stone of the bathing pools.

Why he chose to go down to them, I couldn't guess.

Perhaps just to see if he could.

Laphaniel sat right at the edge of one of the pools, legs in the water. From where I stood, I could see the soft rise and fall of his bare shoulders.

"You don't have to talk," I began, sitting next to him. Water lapped at my feet, rushing over the pools in gentle waves. It was warm. The stones were not. "But I'm right here, beside you."

He didn't look up. Didn't move as I ran my hand over his back, lingering on the thick scarring stretched over his skin. "I can't do this."

My breath caught, little more than a whisper. "What are you doing down here?"

He didn't answer for a long while, staring into the deep, dark waters. "I don't know."

I forced him to look at me, touching my forehead to his. "You're freezing. Come back with me. Come back."

"They won't go away," he murmured. "They're never going to go away."

"The shadows?"

He nodded before pulling away, drawing his legs from the water to rest his head on his knees.

"Talk to me."

He said nothing for a long, long time.

"There was nothing left of him," Laphaniel breathed, not looking up. "At the end. There was nothing left of him but this—this shell and it was filled with madness—there was nothing else there."

He took a breath, and it caught in his throat. He wouldn't look at me.

"I got Fell out and I should have gone with Alice...I made her go alone." The words slipped out in a rush, tumbling over each other. "Phabian sent his dogs after them, and I don't know if there's a little pile of bones out there, because I should have gone too."

My gut twisted at the thought of Alice. "We sent out riders, there has been no sign of them. Nothing to say they were caught."

He sat there, fingers curling over the edge of the pool. "Phabian tossed Niven from the tower like a doll, and then he screamed for her," he said, breaths hitching. "She hit the ground..."

I flinched.

"She hit the ground and he just kept screaming. There were shadows all around...on the ground...everywhere. They had to go somewhere so they chose me, but I didn't want them." He paused, shaking his head. "I thought you were dead. He told me you were dead. You were dead and—"

Laphaniel raked at his hair until it was a wild mess. Tears streaked down his face. His voice was thick with them.

"I keep seeing it...hearing him," he choked out. "He wouldn't stop screaming and then...and then the shadows came, these claws...and

I..." He sobbed into his knees, the words tumbling from his mouth near incoherent. I reached for his hand and squeezed. "I ripped his head off."

I gripped him tighter. "I know."

"His head hit the ground and it didn't bounce." Laphaniel looked up then, face desperate. "I just wanted to stop him screaming. I didn't want this. I don't want this."

I ran my hands over his face, over his hands, holding tight. "That's the most you've spoken in months."

Laphaniel nodded, as if he had nothing left to give. Without taking my hands away, I called down the winding trails of candlelight, having it dance across the stone in swirls and waves. They stirred up the shadows, teasing them.

"You are not like Phabian," I said, digging my fingers into his palms. "Nothing like him, Laphaniel."

"He didn't start off nailing his fey to the walls." The words came out raw and quiet. He sounded so lost and I didn't know if I could bring him back.

"But he was always cruel." Shadows swept up around me, warm and gentle. Laphaniel's eyes gleamed utterly black as he met my gaze. The colour of a starless night. "Phabian was always a monster, just as you have always been wicked." I kissed him deeply. "And cunning, and wild." Another kiss. "And wonderful."

His words whispered against my cheek, feather soft. "You didn't ask for a life of darkness."

"Neither did you when you chose to spend forever in a cursed castle with me." I kissed his tears away, not bothering to hide mine. "It seems the dark has taken a liking to us."

His breath caught, and I waited until it had calmed again, saying nothing. Just listening.

"You fear the dark, Teya."

"I am not afraid of you."

I leant forwards to kiss him again, slow and gentle. My hands reached into his dark tangles, pulling him closer. His shadows crept in to tease my hair, lifting it upon strands of swirling black. I broke away from Laphaniel when they curled around my arms and watched them. They sidled lower, to sweep over my legs, lifting the hem of my night-gown. I lifted an eyebrow while Laphaniel stared in wonder.

"You still doubt they are your shadows?"

He swallowed. "What if I hurt you?"

With a sweep of my hand, the shadows dispersed reluctantly back into the corner. Then I stirred up a storm outside, just because I could. "I am the Queen of the Unseelie, my darling. I would like to see you try."

There...there for just a moment, something wicked and lovely flickered in his eyes. An ember at last.

"I want to see what those shadows of yours can do. What they really can do," I said, willing that spark into something more.

"What if I burn the world down?"

Thunder rumbled in the distance. "Then burn it."

He was still so unsure. His head lifted at the sound of the storm I was coaxing up from Glamour and shadow and everything in between. I tilted my throat as Laphaniel ran a ghostly finger over the scar that ran all the way across my neck. A low snarl slipped from his lips.

"We owe nothing to this world," I began, closing my eyes at the sensation of ethereal claws at my neck. "If you want to burn it to the ground, burn it. I will stand beside you and watch the ashes eddy into the wind."

We both bore our marks, some seen, others not. Others were carved so, so deep I feared they would never fully heal. The world had not been kind to us. Fate had not been kind. I was ready to set it all alight if it meant getting Laphaniel back.

"But Faerie is changing," I whispered, my mouth close to his, my teeth grazing over his lip. "Change with it. Be something better than what we have inherited here. Grace and Briar came home, Nefina and Oonagh are here...with us. Open the doors for faeries like them—like you. Set this world on fire."

Laphaniel gave a small, humourless laugh. "It would be chaos, Teya."

I nudged my Glamour towards his. My storm to his shadows, spell-bound at the way they embraced one another.

Laphaniel held back, leashing the darkness while it strained to reach me. It wanted out. I knew it would never give him a moment's peace while he continued to trap it.

I didn't push but I waited, my Glamour tangling over his. The shadows relaxed, almost languid beneath the golden threads of mine. More and more of them slipped from the walls, spluttering out my candlelight. They trailed over the stone, covering everything in a wonderful velvet darkness.

Laphaniel's hands were tight on mine, the spectral talons on his left curling against my palm. A low moan rumbled from his mouth, not one of fear or horror. One I felt deep within my soul. Gods, I had missed that sound.

"Look up."

My golden threads interlaced with the coils of darkness, spinning... waltzing to a beat I knew like no other. I pressed my hand to Laphaniel's heart, tilting my head back to watch the Glamour above us. It moved through the candlelight, fractioning into tiny prisms of colour that rained down upon us.

I stirred up the storm outside, sending up flashes of light to spark against the pitch way down underground. Not to fight against Laphaniel's dark, but to illuminate it.

"This used to frighten me." I touched my forehead to his. "The dark and the monsters it hid within it. I am afraid of neither because of you."

Another flash of light raked against the stone, revealing wings of shadow and mist that stretched up over the ceiling in a roving surge. More shadows cavorted over the walls, huge and beautiful, all moving to the screaming of the storm I created.

Laphaniel watched on, mesmerized...frozen. Then his mouth met mine in a clashing of teeth, his heartbeat a manic song within his chest. The chorus to mine. His tongue swept in, the kiss desperate and needing. I needed it, wanted it...longed for the closeness. For him.

And still the shadows kept coming, as if there were no end to them, coaxing and caressing.

Loving.

"I am not afraid of you," I repeated, between breaths. Between kisses. "I am not afraid of this."

The shadows broke away from the cavern, fleeing back up the corridors like unleashed dogs. Shouts and screams and cries joined the roar of our storm, a cacophony of disarray and panic.

Then laughter...

Rapturous laughter that went on and on and on, until the castle was alive with it.

We were all alive with it.

I held tight to Laphaniel as the wall he fought so hard to keep up, crumbled away into nothing. My tears mingled with his, the full force of our storm running rampant.

Shadows contorted into hounds and bears and horned beasts, escaping from us to wreak havoc on the castle at last.

Distant howls joined the laughter, loud and manic and so very alluring. Every bone in my body strained to join the fray. It sang to my blood in a way nothing else had. It sang to my soul.

I had no doubts it sang to Laphaniel's, untainted and perfect and his once again.

His coal-black eyes met mine, no longer the strange blue or the deep violet I had come to love, but they were beautiful. The way the darkness could be beautiful if we let it.

"The Court of Chaos." I grinned. "Has an awfully good ring to it, don't you think?"

EPILOGUE

LAPHANIEL

THIRTEEN YEARS LATER

Snow fell heavily outside, a rush of frantic white against the night black sky. The storm crashed upon the windows, hardly audible over the frantic music. It screamed around the hall— a living beat without end.

For a moment, I sat still. Watching.

Shadows ran riot, unchecked, whipping the candlelight into a frenzy. They left nothing still. Everything moved, writhed, danced.

Styx, my faithful shadow hound, tore through the fray, stealing more and more wisps of black from the walls until he was the size of a bear. He charged on, upending faeries and tables as he ran heedless to anyone in his way. A swarm of shrieking children chased him from the Great Hall and into the corridors, their laughter lost within the chaos.

More children would come in the following months, they always did after the Midwinter Ball.

Nefina sat beside me, shoeless feet propped up on the table laden with food and drink and sprawling evergreens. Her ice-blue gown was ripped at her neck, the skirts in tatters. Leaning over me, she refilled her goblet with spiced wine, spilling half over my arm as she went to refill mine.

"I am sure Teya will lick that off later," she said, tipping her goblet back.

The thought of exactly what my wife's mouth could do almost had me surging into the middle of the frenzy to haul her over my shoulder and back to our chambers.

"You cannot leave the ball so early." Nefina tutted, reading where my thoughts had drifted to.

"I can do as I please."

"Indeed," she began, and leant back in her chair, unbound hair drifting around her. "I will bet you one small boon you cannot get Teya away from the dance."

"How small?"

She smiled. "The boon of a king."

I laughed. "You look lovely when you smile like that."

She brushed me off, but a blush coloured her cheeks. She turned her attention to the small boy wandering up to our table. He gave his eyes a quick rub.

"What are you snivelling for, Sebastian?" Nefina asked, eyes sharp.

The boy glanced at me, then back to his mother. "Violet bit me."

"Then bite her back." Nefina shooed the child away, then called after him. "Pick your wings off the floor, they are filthy."

"Yes, mother," he muttered, scowling as he lifted the heavy black wings. His whip-like tail still trailed along the floor, its black point covered in what looked like blue paint. Blue streaked his white hair, his little horns dripped in it. He gave me a beaming smile. "Thank you for the sword, Uncle."

I didn't need to look at my sister to know she was glaring at me. "He is six-years old."

"Marcus has one and he is five," I countered, slapping her hand away as she reached for the last bottle of wine.

"Because Grace and Briar are just as irresponsible as you are."

I glanced at the mass of dancing faeries and spotted Grace. I lifted my goblet to her, and she did the same from the other side of the room. One hand lingered on her swollen belly, her fifth child...where the others were, no one knew half the time.

"You are completely reckless."

I drained my cup and poured another, grinning at her. "Thank you."

She scoffed and turned away.

I felt something tug at me from beneath the table, scrambling up my leg to fall clumsily into my lap. It was stickly, filthy and half asleep.

"Did you bite Sebastian?" I asked, plucking twigs and dried leaves from the mess of dark tangles. "Violet?"

"Yes," she murmured back, burying her grubby little face into my neck. "Because he is stupid."

Nefina stood, bracing her hand on the table as she staggered. "Did you gift weapons to your three-year-old?"

"Oh, I think it is in everyone's best interests that I did not."

Her lips quirked, reddened with wine. "Each year you look as though you enjoy this more. As though we are no longer a burden you are forced to carry."

I looked out at the mass of writhing faeries, at the shadows that swept over the walls, across the marble. They were joined by Teya's threads of glittering gold, roving around the cavernous room in a whirl of light and dark.

In the beginning we were inseparable, following one another everywhere from the moment we woke to when we tumbled into bed. Living shadows of each other. It had taken a long, long time to bear being away from her.

Our friends had finally intervened, proving that the world would not implode if we pursued separate interests.

"I think we deserve it, do you not?" Nefina said, jolting me from the memory of being forced on a hunting trip with Briar. One I remembered very little of. "This piece of happiness in the shadows."

She sought her son in the crowd, finding him perched high on

Oonagh's shoulders, his wings unfurled. They spun, arms outstretched, laughter drifting over the music.

I tightened the hold on the child slumbering in my arms, pulling her close. She smelled like the earth, of dirt and the grass and the forest. Of the blankets she stole every night.

"I think we do."

She nodded and I followed her gaze to where her son still danced.

"No one will take him," I said. "I promise you."

"I know."

No one had deigned to tell me what my sister had given up, the bargain she had entered into. Not even Teya. They had kept it as a terrible secret between them, believing nothing would ever come of it, because Nefina loathed children.

An unplanned pregnancy later and I guessed she had done something awful and stupid, when the night she gave birth, thousands and thousands of black feathers had filled her rooms.

They had vanished by dawn, leaving behind the one she kept hidden away, waiting for it to crumble to dust and for the witches to stake their claim.

Her firstborn child. She had given up her child for a chance at my freedom.

She had glared up at me from her bed, pale and bloodied and defiant. The child had been born with crow black wings, small and wet, not yet uncurled. The father, I was told, had no such wings. Who it was, she would not say.

"They will have to drag him from my still, cold body," Nefina had said. "I will not let him go."

"They will have to pass through the hungry mouths of the Unseelie," I had replied. "Then through the waiting shadows, and find there is no kindness or mercy."

I would go to war with the witches to keep my nephew safe, to keep my family safe. To silence their constant cries of the world ending — of great shadow and death that still hadn't bothered to come for us all.

The witches had grown silent. Some of the covens had disappeared completely, taking their serpents with them.

The voices that had whispered against my skull were silent too, leaving behind a strange absence I could not explain. Charlotte had said it was a sign of healing, and I so wanted to believe her.

We never found a trace of Alice or Fell, though we looked and looked and looked. As time passed, the likelihood of finding them alive grew slim, yet we still searched. Still waited, still hoped. Our very Court was built upon the power of hoping.

The crows were quiet, though they still watched, and they waited too. We just didn't know for what.

"Do you want me to put that disgusting thing to bed?" Nefina nodded to my daughter, curling her lip as she yanked something squirming from her black hair.

"She will be your Queen one day," I reminded her.

She scooped Violet from me. "Then may the gods have mercy on all of us."

I remained where I was for a moment longer, watching the swirl of shadows in the centre of the room. Just watching.

Because I could.

Because I needed to.

Even after so many years I had to remind myself it was all real. That I wouldn't wake on the cold ground, in a cold cell. That she was real...

And had come for me.

Just as she had promised.

Blackness enveloped her like silk, clinging to the curves of her body before splaying out across the glittering floor. Her hair moved like flame, flowing down to her waist, trailing over her bare shoulders as she spun and spun and spun.

Teya noticed me looking and held her hands out, not stopping... never still. I caught her mid-twirl, stumbling slightly as I took her hands. She cackled back at me, drunk on the music and the Glamour and far too much wine.

"Dance with me!" She laughed, leaping into my arms. "Until sunrise."

I spun until she begged me to stop, her laughter more enchanting than the feverish music thundering around the hall. Lightning sliced against the night sky, thunder rolling in time to the beat of drums.

Her Glamour spurred on my shadows, never shying from them... never leaving them alone. I didn't even need to be near her to feel her coax them up, sometimes she did it just because she was bored.

And she found it amusing.

I found it incredibly distracting.

"I have misplaced the feral beast you call a daughter," she murmured against my neck, teeth grazing the hollow of my throat.

"Shame." My mouth found hers. "Do you want to go and make a replacement?"

"You are awful."

Long ago I had promised Teya a summer of wine-soaked fruit with just us and the song of the forest. We had since enjoyed many of those long and slow summers, but it was the one with too much wine and a lot less caution that had ended up with Violet.

I kissed her again, long and slow, my hands trailing through the mist she wore instead of clothes. She cackled again as I choked.

"We could sneak away?"

Those vivid green eyes flashed. "I said sunrise."

"Then perhaps you should have worn something—"

"Other than your shadows?" she finished for me. "Are they not fit for a Queen?"

I fought for words and lost. "Teya..."

She lifted an eyebrow, leaning back slightly in my arms. "How drunk are you?"

"Very, why?"

"Because I want to dance with you until the sun rises," she said, her smile the most beautiful thing I had seen. "And after that..."

"And after that?" I coaxed, ignoring everything in the room but her.

"I would like more."

I knew what she meant. "How many more?"

"One more? For luck?" For a moment, uncertainty flashed across her lovely face. "Unless you think you may regret it?"

The very thought once would have terrified me. I couldn't have imagined ever wanting a child...loving one...let alone having another. Not so long ago, the thought of feeling anything but a crippling emptiness was unimaginable.

My court existed because Teya had dreamt it possible when all I could see was endless darkness. She radiated a hope that spilled over to everyone she touched, changing the minds of those who doubted that our strange little court could be home.

"Nothing I do with you is a regret," I said. "None of it, Teya."

And I meant it.

More than I could ever say.

Within our castle of shadows and storms, away from the cold and the fear and the unknown, I dared hope. I hoped for us as we were in that moment, finally together sharing every whispered promise of our forever.

ACKNOWLEDGMENTS

I cannot believe it is that time already! Another book done.

My first thank you, again, is to my readers. Thank you for coming along on this journey with Teya and Laphaniel, for keeping by them through everything. Thank you for your kind words, your reviews and the fan art. You have made my author dream come true and I am forever grateful.

I could not have done this without the help, enthusiasm, and fiendish fiendship of Chesney Infalt. Thank you for reading the words in their earliest of drafts, for staying with me from the start. For the rewrites, the GIF wars, the laughs. You are the Unseelie Queen and I love you!

A massive thank you to the spellbinding Kate Macdonald for all her wisdom, advice, and long, long chats on all things important. Thank you for sharing my love of whump, too small beds and princes with tails.

To my wonderful, magical Beta readers: thank you for reading the early drafts, for helping iron out the later drafts, for typo spotting in the last drafts. I could never do this without you.

The gorgeous formatting is once again thanks to Nicole Scarano. Thank you for making this book look as beautiful as possible.

To my family, my husband, my children, thank you. Thank you for building me a spot to write that is not hidden away. For giving me time to write. For buying me all the books. Thank you for being everything I ever wanted and needed.

This, dear readers, is not the end of The Wicked Woods. There is much left unsaid and undone and we will return.

I am taking a little break away to write another book that has been creeping into my head, and I hope you come to love it as much as I do.

Until we meet again.
Lydia.

ABOUT THE AUTHOR

Lydia Russell grew up on a farm deep in the Dorset county-side along-side her three elder brothers, using the fields and woodland as their playground.

As an adult with two young children, she has now used the memories of the wild woods of her youth to write The Wicked Woods Chronicles.

Stories of lost sisters, whispering oaks and dark romance.

Oh, the woods are dark and wicked…

Website:
lydiarussell63.wixsite.com/intothewickedwoods

TikTok: @into_the_wicked_woods

 twitter.com/fey_girl63
instagram.com/intothewickedwoods

Printed in Great Britain
by Amazon